OATHS OF DAMNATION

More Warhammer 40,000 from Black Library

THE SUCCESSORS: A SPACE MARINES ANTHOLOGY
by various authors

• DAWN OF FIRE •

Book 1: AVENGING SON
by Guy Haley

Book 2: THE GATE OF BONES
by Andy Clark

Book 3: THE WOLFTIME
by Gav Thorpe

Book 4: THRONE OF LIGHT
by Guy Haley

Book 5: THE IRON KINGDOM
by Nick Kyme

Book 6: THE MARTYR'S TOMB
by Marc Collins

Book 7: SEA OF SOULS
by Chris Wraight

Book 8: HAND OF ABADDON
by Nick Kyme

Book 9: THE SILENT KING
by Guy Haley

LEVIATHAN
by Darius Hinks

• DARK IMPERIUM •

by Guy Haley

Book 1: DARK IMPERIUM
Book 2: PLAGUE WAR
Book 3: GODBLIGHT

OATHS OF DAMNATION
AN EXORCISTS NOVEL
ROBBIE MACNIVEN

BLACK LIBRARY

A BLACK LIBRARY PUBLICATION

First published in 2024.
This edition published in Great Britain in 2025 by
Black Library, Games Workshop Ltd., Willow Road,
Nottingham, NG7 2WS, UK.

Represented by: Games Workshop Limited – Irish branch,
Unit 3, Lower Liffey Street, Dublin 1,
D01 K199, Ireland.

10 9 8 7 6 5 4 3 2 1

Produced by Games Workshop in Nottingham.
Cover illustration by Artur Nakhodkin.

Oaths of Damnation © Copyright Games Workshop Limited 2025.
Oaths of Damnation, GW, Games Workshop, Black Library, The
Horus Heresy, The Horus Heresy Eye logo, Space Marine, 40K,
Warhammer, Warhammer 40,000, the 'Aquila' Double-headed Eagle
logo, and all associated logos, illustrations, images, names, creatures,
races, vehicles, locations, weapons, characters, and the distinctive
likenesses thereof, are either ® or TM, and/or © Games Workshop
Limited, variably registered around the world.
All Rights Reserved.

A CIP record for this book is available from the British Library.

ISBN 13: 978-1-80407-729-0

No part of this publication may be reproduced, stored in a retrieval
system, or transmitted in any form or by any means, electronic,
mechanical, photocopying, recording or otherwise, without the
prior permission of the publishers.

This is a work of fiction. All the characters and events portrayed
in this book are fictional, and any resemblance to real people or
incidents is purely coincidental.

See Black Library on the internet at

blacklibrary.com

Find out more about Games Workshop
and the worlds of Warhammer at

warhammer.com

Printed and bound in the UK.

Dedicated to Kate and Nick, with thanks.

For more than a hundred centuries the Emperor has sat immobile on the Golden Throne of Earth. He is the Master of Mankind. By the might of his inexhaustible armies a million worlds stand against the dark.

Yet, he is a rotting carcass, the Carrion Lord of the Imperium held in life by marvels from the Dark Age of Technology and the thousand souls sacrificed each day so his may continue to burn.

To be a man in such times is to be one amongst untold billions. It is to live in the cruelest and most bloody regime imaginable. It is to suffer an eternity of carnage and slaughter. It is to have cries of anguish and sorrow drowned by the thirsting laughter of dark gods.

This is a dark and terrible era where you will find little comfort or hope. Forget the power of technology and science. Forget the promise of progress and advancement. Forget any notion of common humanity or compassion.

There is no peace amongst the stars, for in the grim darkness of the far future, there is only war.

DRAMATIS PERSONAE

The Hexbreakers

Exorcists Tenth Company Vanguard Strike Force

Almoner-Lieutenant Daggan Zaidu

Reiver Squad Belloch

Lector-Sergeant Belloch

Almoner Azzael

Brother-Initiate Makru

Brother-Initiate Nabua

Brother-Initiate Shemesh

Infiltrator Squad Eitan

Lector-Sergeant Eitan

Brother-Initiate Balhamon

Almoner Hasdrubal

Brother-Initiate Hokmaz

Brother-Initiate Kleth

Brother-Initiate Nazaratus

Brother-Initiate Pazu

Brother-Initiate Urhammu

Brother-Initiate Uten

Infiltrator Squad Haad

Almoner-Sergeant Haad

Brother-Initiate Akkad

Almoner-Commsman Amilanu

Almoner-Helix Adept Gela

Brother-Initiate Kephras

Brother-Initiate Lamesh

Brother-Initiate Marduk

Brother-Initiate Nizreba

Eliminator Squad Anu

Lector-Sergeant Anu

Almoner-Marksman Dumuzid

Almoner-Marksman Lakhmu

Attached: Codicier Torrin Vey

Prominent Hexbreaker Orison Sub-Cults:

The Hermetic Brotherhood of the First Degree

The Blade and Skull

The Order of the Eagle Most High

The Fraternity of the Eleusinian Mysteries

The Inner Circle of Tranquil Enlightenment

We are living in the end times, and the doom of mankind is at hand. I know this to be true for I have witnessed the canker that eats at the bedrock of our beloved Imperium, have borne the corruption of the daemonic and know the price that must be paid to cast it out. To know Chaos is to know the folly of existence, the ruination of life and the damnation of too much knowledge. But all things serve the Emperor, and even such maddening wisdom may find its use... The daemonic can be beaten, but the sacrifice it entails will be greater than many of you will be able to sustain.

– Lord Inquisitor Marchant of the Ordo Malleus,
at the MXII Conclave of Andrastacles

PROLOGUE

NOWHERE

Containment ship C5-17 was screaming.

Inquisitor Harrow fled through its depths, unmade by her own terror. This should not have happened. It could not have. Her tarot, the visions, Lord Inquisitor Mundar's missives – how could she have been misled by all of them?

And how could she get out of this place alive?

She raced along another corridor of corroded pipes, ancient prayer scrolls and mesh decking plates, her ears aching from the shrieking of the alarms. The ship – every passageway, berth, brig and bunk room – along with all of its crew, they were all screaming, howling ahead of the damnation Harrow knew she had unleashed.

The lumens blinked over to emergency protocols, red. Red like the blood she had shed when, in a moment of madness, she had allowed herself to become infected with the rage of the thing she had come here to interrogate. That was all it had needed. Anger, and a little vital essence spilled in its presence, and its wards had started to burn.

It was all wrong. Harrow had been given assurances, ones she now realised were lies. She had been investigating rumours of warp-related discordance among the mega-smelteries of Keliso VIII's hives when she had first become aware of the portents. The work on Keliso had been dropped in favour of intercepting C5-17 as soon as she had realised just how serious the situation was. As soon as her sanctioned psyker, Heldar, had torn out her own eyeballs and eaten them.

Every tarot reading since had been the same. The cards had shown the Psyker, the Tower and the Daemon, over and over, even when Harrow had reconsecrated and reshuffled them. Mundar had confirmed the growing threat via astropathic séance. She had been authorised to do the unthinkable: to intercept an Exorcists containment ship at Nowhere, the unmanned beacon station that pointed the way to the Purgatomb.

It had all been lies.

A hatch to Harrow's left juddered open as she neared the end of the corridor, causing her to come up short and drag free her long-barrelled Lucius laspistol. Two figures tumbled through the gap, grappling furiously. They were Chapter-serfs, members of the containment ship's crew, dressed in dark robes, their scalps shaved and carved with occult symbology.

They were killing each other. One was bleeding badly from a gash in his throat. He was hauled to the deck by the other, who was wielding a bloody crowbar which she smashed over her fellow serf's head once, twice, three times, the hideous crunches audible even over the ear-aching assault of the alarms.

As the serf raised the bar for a fourth blow, she seemed to sense Harrow's presence. She turned, snarling, her lower face a mask of blood that glistened black in the hellish lighting. Harrow realised she had torn out the other serf's throat with her teeth.

The inquisitor shot her through the head and stumbled past, clutching at the porthole leading to the stairs beyond. There were bodies there, more serfs and crew, their eyes wide and white, locked into awkward death throes. Madness had gripped the entire ship the moment the binding seals had been broken, the same madness that had caused Harrow's interrogation to falter in the first place.

She should have been better prepared. The host body, the thing the Exorcists called the Broken One, contained three Neverborn, but it was only one she was interested in. The Red Marshal. She had merely wished to confirm its identity. The portents, and Mundar, had claimed that the Red Marshal had to be stopped from reaching the Purgatomb, even in a captive state. But none of them, even the Exorcists, seemed to have realised just how powerful this particular entity was.

The unthinking, unknowable rage that had gripped her in its presence was now gone from her own thoughts. It was as though the thing she had unleashed wanted her to suffer all the horror of these last moments unfiltered and uninhibited, like it was taunting her, making her bear witness to the true extent of her failure.

It was coming for her, she was sure.

She hammered down the stairs, trying desperately to remember the route she had taken up from the docking bay. She needed to get back to the Arvus. Then she could take the shuttle back to the *Share of Defiance*, send an astropathic alert, and turn the light cruiser's guns on C5-17. She could end this before it deteriorated any further.

Before the Broken One escaped these last, desperate confines.

There was a figure standing in the hatchway at the bottom of the stairs. Harrow almost shot it, before realising the red-robed man was not attempting to block her. He was a tech-priest, the twin mechadendrites rising from his hunched back inserted into a control panel beside the hatch. The doors were half shut, juddering but not closing. It seemed as though the adept had been attempting to seal them manually, but both he and the interface were now malfunctioning. He was standing rigid and shaking, sparks leaping over his mechanical components, while his remaining organic eye and ear wept blood. A garbled mess of static-chopped binharic cant was scraping from his vox-maw. He showed no sign of being aware of Harrow's presence as she forced her way with manic haste through the half-shut hatch and past him.

A refectory hall lay beyond. It was a scene of bedlam. Regular members of the crew were slaughtering each other with anything they could grasp. One was beating the head of a deck over-seer repeatedly against the floor, the man's face broken mulch, while another was strangling a cyber-cherubim with the chain of its censer ball, the sanctified incense fogging the air but doing nothing to banish the warp madness. Harrow choked as she stumbled past, tears stinging her eyes and half blinding her.

She pushed on, brandishing her laspistol, but none of the crew seemed to notice her. They were lost, lost and damned.

There were two hatches leading from the refectory, one on the left and one on the right. Harrow forced herself to pause, to not choose on impulse. She was an inquisitor, a Plutonian and a former interrogator under Lord Inquisitor Mundar. She had endured the horrors of the warp before. She would not compound the errors she had made here with further mistakes.

Right. She remembered seeing the litany above the hatchway during her journey up from the docking bay. *Damnatio pro nobis omnibus venit*, a line from the *Liber Exorcismus*. *Damnation comes for us all.* Too fitting.

She began to descend the next set of red-lit stairs beyond,

feeling sudden, renewed determination. As she went, she caught an unmistakable sound ringing down from the decks above, punching repeatedly over the noise of the alarms.

Bolter fire.

Almoner-Sergeant Hekez rallied his Intercessors in the corridor before the containment berth. He linked his vox to the bridge and gave clear, uncompromising instructions as his brethren checked their bolt rifles.

The Oblivion Protocol was to be enacted, which meant they would all soon be annihilated. Hekez accepted that, just as he accepted the knowledge that he had failed. He should have forbidden the inquisitor, denied her boarding rites and ignored all the evidence she presented that the containment ship had to be stopped from reaching the Purgatomb. All of those realisations counted for nothing – retrospection would be pointless now. All that mattered was buying a little more time.

'The Black Psalter of Primordian Primus,' Hekez said to his squad over the vox, seeking to focus them on what lay ahead. 'Brother-Initiate Hammurabi, lead us in verse.'

As the Exorcists began to chant, the almoner-sergeant received confirmation from the bridge that the Oblivion Protocol was under way. It was simple, and came in two parts. Once the order was given, the ship's chief tech-priest would overload the engine drives, resulting in a catastrophic meltdown that would rip C5-17 to pieces. Even a Neverborn would not be able to survive both the devastating blast and the ensuing vacuum of space.

The second part of the protocol involved the remote station, Nowhere, cutting its signal, temporarily removing the link between the way station and the Purgatomb and thus making the isolated prison impossible to find.

Once the protocol was initiated there was no way to stop it, and C5-17 had no salvation pods or other means of egress. It would take approximately ten minutes of overdrive before the engines began a chain-reaction meltdown.

Ten minutes to keep the Neverborn and its host contained. Hekez ensured a round was chambered and faced the blast door sealing the berth off from the remainder of the ship. It was laden with purity seals, layer upon layer of ancient, discoloured black and red wax and folds of yellowed parchment, inscribed with prayers of warding and abjuration. The only parts of the door clear of them were the locking wheel and the central plate, embossed with a horned, fleshless skull – the Calva Daemoniorum, the grim Chapter icon of the Exorcists – that was mirrored on the left pauldron of Hekez's armour.

A series of shuddering blows echoed down the corridor. At the same time, one of the purity seals adorning the door caught light. The flame leapt across the dry parchment and wax, quickly forming a blazing curtain of fire. Only the horned-skull sigil remained visible in the centre of it, slowly blistering and blackening.

The impacts continued until there was a metallic shriek. The flames burned themselves out, every last purity seal gone, revealing the scorched metal beneath.

With a dull groan, the door swung ponderously open.

The lumen strips started to go out, one by one, starting with those nearest the door and sweeping down the corridor, a rapidly advancing wall of darkness. The alarms continued, though they had changed, becoming more akin to true screams, wails of despair and roars of anger, mirroring the primordial fury that had swept through the ship and gripped so much of its crew as the monstrosity bound at its heart broke its bonds.

For his own part, Hekez's blackened soul suffered only the faintest twinge of anger. It was no match for the only other emotion he felt: cold, hard determination.

His auto-senses kicked in, preysight stripping away the darkness. He caught a slight heat blur of movement in the doorway.

The Exorcist managed one semi-automatic burst before the Broken One was on him.

It was a Primaris, or had once been. It was naked bar scraps of singed prayer cloth and broken chains, its flesh bleeding with damnable sigils that appeared to have been freshly carved in its brute, heavy musculature. Around its neck was a thick metal collar stamped with the aquila, while a visor, similarly marked, covered its eyes, ears and nose. Its jaw had been sealed shut by bolts, screwed into the bone. It had been a warrior of the Chapter. Now it was a Broken One, its sole remaining purpose to act as a vessel for damnation. But the vessel had failed and damnation was loose.

It slammed aside Hekez's bolt rifle then ripped away his gorget and the upper part of his breastplate with monstrous, unnatural strength, before flinging him against the wall. One-handed, it pinned him there, fist closing around his throat.

Hekez drew his combat knife. Even as the Broken One drove him to the wall, he was already stabbing the blade up and under the Primaris' fused ribcage, then wrenching it from left to right, disembowelling the creature.

No blood issued forth. It didn't even appear to realise it had been wounded.

Flames surged down the corridor in the Broken One's wake, the scriptures decorating the walls igniting like the ones that had guarded the blast door. Smoke, ash and burning scraps of parchment filled the air.

Hekez found himself face to face with his Chapter's darkest secret. Though the collar was still in place, it had managed to shatter half of its visor, breaking the Imperial aquila in two. One eye stared at Hekez. He had half expected it to be riven with unnatural energies, but it was still altogether too human, bloodshot and wide with horror. The soul of the host's body – Ashad, his name had been – was not yet altogether lost.

The other Intercessors opened fire, filling the corridor with wrath to accompany their dark litany, but even at point-blank range they had no effect. Instead of striking and detonating, the rounds were transmuted into molten metal mid-flight, so that only a hissing splatter struck the monster's flank.

'You will not be free,' Hekez rasped with what air he could drag through the Broken One's grip. 'Oblivion will claim us all.'

The thing should not have been able to respond, for though they glowed red-hot, the screws in its jaw were still in place. But as Hekez struggled, a horizontal slit appeared along the Broken One's sinewy neck, just above the restraining collar. It tore open, dark, vital blood flowing down its broad chest.

'Do you really believe that?' the wound slurred, offering Hekez a red-raw smile that exposed the thick, glistening tendons underneath.

'You will know nothing but banishment,' Hekez managed. He had started a timer on his retinal display as soon as he had received confirmation that the protocol had been initiated. He could already feel the vibrations of the overcharged engines thrumming through the wall at his back, threatening to shake the ship asunder.

'Oh, poor corpse-slave,' the possessed Primaris spat from its wound-maw, steaming blood spurting over Hekez. *'You think I have no means of escape? Have you forgotten all about the good inquisitor you so nobly permitted on board this ship?'*

Hekez realised his mistake. Harrow had broken the containment procedures in more ways than one. She had damned them all.

The Broken One's eye had rolled back, but the hideous wound was still grinning. With its free hand, it held something before

Hekez's visor, between two fingers. A tarot card, one belonging to the inquisitor, which she had shown him after arriving on board. It was the Daemon. As Hekez looked at it, embers running along its edge caught light and burned it away to nothing.

The Broken One let go. It was gone before Hekez had even hit the deck, blasting aside the other Intercessors, disappearing down the fiery corridor in a flash of crimson lightning.

Hekez regained his feet. For a short while, he finally knew rage – true rage, enough even to stoke what was left of his shattered soul.

Harrow's memories had betrayed her, just as everything seemed to be doing on this accursed ship. She kept going regardless. She had recovered enough from the shock and horror of the initial containment breach to work her way through C5-17's bowels until finally, blessedly, she stumbled into the primary docking bay.

Her Arvus lighter was still there, lumens gleaming from its scarred silver hull. Even better, Rumann had already fired up the engines and engaged the airlock's uncoupling protocols.

Harrow marshalled her relief into further action, determined not to falter again. The shuttle's rear disembarkation ramp was lowered, and she swept up it, holstering her laspistol and calling out as she went.

'Rumann! Seal the hatch and let's go! Get us back to the *Share of Defiance*!'

To her surprise, near silence answered her. While the numbing alarms continued to scream elsewhere in the ship, in the docking bay they cut off abruptly. The stillness sent an involuntary shiver through Harrow.

She drew her laspistol again, stepping through the shuttle's empty hold and into its cockpit blister. After the pounding adrenaline that had carried her down through the ship, she felt suddenly weightless and weak. Her limbs shook.

'Rumann,' she began to repeat, then froze.

The Broken One was inside the cockpit. The tall, pallid form of the lost Primaris was standing stooped forward, facing away from her, looking at her reflection in the darkness of the shuttle's viewing port. Rumann was slumped across the controls next to it, skull split open, blood steadily puddling beneath him.

The Broken One had ripped away the bolts and visor muzzling it, though its collar remained. Its eyes stayed on her via the reflection, but it dabbed at its face, almost tenderly. Harrow realised it was carefully marking itself with Rumann's blood and brain matter, like an actor about to take to the stage applying the last of his make-up.

'Hello again, Inquisitor Harrow,' the thing inside the Broken One said. *'Going somewhere, are we?'*

The cockpit juddered and lurched. Despite his mangled state, Rumann's limbs were moving, like a puppet's, stoking the shuttle's engines into life, angling it towards the exit bay as the blast doors began to roll open.

'I am looking forward to meeting the rest of your retinue,' the daemonhost said. *'It is always a joy to show the souls of the faithful exactly what eternity has in store for them.'*

Harrow began to scream. She would never stop.

RITE I

PROGNOSTICATION

CHAPTER ONE

THE SUMMONING

Damnation came howling out of the ether, reaching for the Hexbreakers with talons formed from hatred and hunger.

Daggan Zaidu sent the first back to where it had come from with the knife in his left fist, the straight-bladed combat dagger scything up and through the monstrosity's distended neck as it lunged with a maw filled with fangs. Stinking black ichor drenched his armour, sizzling as it evaporated off the sigil-etched surfaces.

The monstrosity came apart, already replaced by another. Claws raked at his left shoulder but failed to register as the knife in his right hand carved off the offending limb before delivering the banishing blow.

They were fast, these ones, and numerous. The abbey was almost overrun, its heart ripped out by a pulsing abomination, a rent in the very essence of reality. Above the altar, the air was buckling as more and more warp matter forced its way into the materium, feasting on the warmth of existence. Translucent flesh hardened and became scabbed with scales and blotchy hides, horns sprouted and curled, talons went from soft and brittle to firm and wicked. Amorphous beings, denied for aeons, finally found form and threw themselves at the mortals before them, desperate to consume.

The Exorcists had come to deny them that. Though it seemed like reality itself was unravelling around them, the focus of the Hexbreakers never wavered.

Zaidu cut down another skittering horror and made a split-second assessment. The formation was going to be outflanked and overrun if they didn't reduce their frontage.

'Pattern cheit,' he ordered his Reivers.

His Reivers. Simultaneously true and untrue. They were Hexbreakers, and thus under his command, but since his promotion to almoner-lieutenant just before the campaign on Demeter, he was no longer their squad leader. That honour fell to Belloch, who now snapped at Makru and Nabua to show alacrity as the exposed line cinched into a defensive circle.

It was knife-work, this – no bolters. Zaidu noticed that the abbey's vaulted roof had started to come apart, the stones shaking loose from one another. Rather than caving in, though, they remained suspended in mid-air, forming a fractured arch of drifting stone, defying the natural laws of the galaxy.

Existence itself was about to collapse. Whether they were going to be overrun or not, they had to go on the offensive. They had to reach the rift and seal it, before it widened any further.

'Accelerate tempo,' Zaidu barked to his Reivers – *his* Reivers – trying to drive their efforts with their blades to the next level ahead of an offence order. He couldn't fail now. It was unthinkable.

'Pattern lamed,' he barked. 'On me!'

The Exorcists formed into a spearhead with Zaidu at the tip, the almoner-lieutenant dealing destruction with his twin knives. He was the Sin Slayer, a hunting hound of the Chapter. He would not be denied.

The altar, caught beneath the widening warp rift, had started to fracture, foul tentacles bursting and writhing from the splitting stone, as though some nightmarish beast had been sealed within it and was now free. The rising tide of flesh and fury railed at them, trying to rip them apart, trying to break their formation and drag them down one by one, yet the long blades of the Reivers kept the daemonspawn at bay, gleaming silver in the hellish, kaleidoscopic light that was beginning to suffuse the abbey.

A few steps more. The altar split apart fully, shattered stone forming jagged teeth as it became a gaping maw frilled with squirming appendages. Zaidu drove himself on, preparing to leap it and bury his blades into the mass of flesh spilling from the rift above it.

He faltered. The madness he had been in the midst of blinked from existence, not with the mind-aching horror of a daemonic infestation, but with the instantaneousness of a slide change in a pict projector. He was no longer in the abbey, no longer fighting alongside his brethren.

This was not what had been agreed. Was Vey giving him some new test? He attempted to raise his knives but found he could not. He couldn't even turn his head.

He tried to speak but found it impossible. He fought to reach out to Vey, but the scene before him dragged at his attention, breaking his focus.

Two figures were locked in combat, fighting in the middle of a void that Zaidu's mind seemed unable to process or comprehend. One was undoubtedly Adeptus Astartes, though a golden luminescence was shining from him, hiding his features and his heraldry.

The other was a Neverborn, a blood daemon. Zaidu knew it. A rare flaring of emotions torn from him long ago – hatred, rage, revulsion – suffused his thoughts, before realisation dawned and the cold control he was more accustomed to returned.

He knew what he was about to witness. It had played out in front of him before, many times.

He found he could move again. The golden warrior was gone – now Zaidu stood in his place. The daemon remained, shrieking a name with raw fury, garbed now in a face that Zaidu knew yet could not fully recognise.

'*Demetrius,*' the daemon wailed.

With a roar, Zaidu drove the blade in his hands into the beast. Reality finally collapsed around him.

Discordance ripped through Torrin Vey's thoughts, and for a moment his psychic essence floundered like a man who could not swim being cast into a frigid, raging ocean.

He hissed a catechism of focus, fingers gripping the sides of his throne until his knuckles were white and the brass skulls that decorated the rests were threatening to buckle.

It took barely a moment, but it felt like an age. He managed to regain himself, loosening his grip and easing out a slow breath that clouded in the freezing air of the psykhanium.

Something was wrong, very wrong, and he was not yet sure what.

The drill had been proceeding as planned. Almoner-Lieutenant Zaidu, seemingly dissatisfied with his current training facilities, had requested that Vey lead him and his Reiver squad in a psychic bout. Vey had agreed, conjuring a simulation of a particularly vicious daemonic infestation for the Sin Slayer and his fellow hunters to fight their way through. Such illusions were not simple, but the amplification of the psykhanium combined with the willingness of the participating minds had ensured the experience was not more than Vey could endure.

That was until he had felt Zaidu straying. The illusion had been broken by something, something that did not belong. And then, moments later, the discordance. Vey had not had a chance to piece it together, but it had caused him to experience something he was highly unfamiliar with – a loss of control. For a second, damnation had yawned, and he had been certain he was about to lose his grip and plunge into its embrace.

Not today. He had reasserted himself in time. But he needed answers.

The psykhanium chamber crowned one of the towers of the Basilica Malifex, second only in height and gothic grandeur to the astropathic relay pinnacle. Its interior lay beneath a dome of shielded, psi-reactive crystal, centred on a vision throne that sat at the top of a control column wreathed in cables and wiring. Arrayed around the column's base were ten upright sarcophagi of brass and Banish corestone, linked back to it by more thick spools of power lines. Six of the ten slabs were currently occupied by Zaidu and his Reivers, while Vey sat upon the throne overlooking them, linked to them via the thickets of cabling plugged from the throne's high back into the base of his cortex.

He experienced a moment's pain as he broke both the physical and mental connections and rose, descending the ladder to the psykhanium's mesh-plate decking. Doing so also caused the sarcophagi to disengage, the bolts containing their purity-seal-studded fronts thudding free. Hissing steam momentarily obscured the occupants before they emerged through it – hulking, skull-faced nightmares that Vey offered a fraternal greeting to.

Zaidu was among them. Like his Reivers, he was garbed in a black bodyglove that acted as his under-vest, the synth-skin dotted with ports that would allow his Mark X battle plate to interface with the Black Carapace beneath his upper dermal layers. Besides that, he wore nothing but his twin combat knives, sheathed over one another on a mag belt, and his death mask, a leering, fanged holdover from his days serving with the Reivers.

'What happened?' he demanded of Vey, voice as sharp as one of his knives.

'I do not know,' the Librarian admitted, unused to such an admission. 'I experienced a psychic disturbance. Abrupt, and of some magnitude. I have not been able to identify its source yet.'

Zaidu began to respond, but the words faded to Vey's hind-brain as a new sensation demanded his attention. A presence entered his mind, one he recognised. It was Enlightened Brother Dornmar, the only other Exorcists Librarian currently stationed at the Basilica Malifex. He came to Vey not with words, simply imprinting the knowledge he wished to convey directly onto his consciousness, an act that spoke of urgency.

'A signal has been received,' Vey told Zaidu, straightening out the impression made on him. 'I must depart immediately to the astropathic relay. This session is over.'

'Should I initiate emergency protocols?' Zaidu asked. The other Reivers had gathered from their own sarcophagi around their leader, their skull masks grinning at Vey in the dissipating steam.

'Not… immediately,' he said as he finished ordering and interrogating Dornmar's imprint. 'I recommend you conduct purification rites. If there is pertinent news, I will inform you.'

'I saw it again,' Zaidu said, the statement catching Vey off-guard.

'Saw what?'

'My vision. Caedus. I defeated it again, but it was not like the first banishing.'

Vey knew of Zaidu's visions, or at least what the almoner-lieutenant thought of as visions. He had been experiencing them since his initiation. Vey recalled how he had felt Zaidu's mind stray moments before he had experienced the discordance. Were the two connected?

'I will seek answers for both of us,' he told the Sin Slayer. 'Hold fast until my return.'

Vey did not go to Dornmar and the astropathic relay. Instead, he journeyed down, to the heart of the Basilica Malifex, the Cloister of Scars. From there he passed the Threshold into the Chapter Librarius, undoing the wards and speaking his name so he would be known to both the spirits of the place and the combat servitors hardwired into its outer pillars.

He knew what he was doing might be a mistake. Logic dictated he go immediately to Dornmar and receive his report. But the universe did not run on logic. There was something gnawing at the back of Vey's mind, something more than the echoes of his Never-brother, Amazarak. Zaidu's vision could not be a coincidence. The nature of whatever report Dornmar held would not solidify into the truth until Vey had received it. He believed he would find certainty not with the data-raving of an astropathic choir, but in the silence of the Librarius.

The primary chamber was vast, a cavity at the core of the Exorcists' fortress-monastery, hollowed out and filled with the sum total of knowledge acquired over four thousand years spent warring with the daemonic. Arcane grimoires, cursed tomes, Ecclesiarchy doggerel and the ruminations of generations of the Chapter's own Librarians and mystics filled the shelves, stacked under, alongside and above briefing transcriptions, tactical-goetic summaries, combat divinations, gene-files and star cartography.

No other Chapter was so wedded to theomantic esotericism as the Exorcists. Knowledge was power, and they knew its value. They had made the Basilica Malifex one of the greatest repositories of occult information in the segmentum, hidden from all but the Chapter and a select few members of the Ordos.

The floor of the Librarius – cold, smooth Banish corestone – was sub-divided into hundreds of sections via the thousands of towering bookshelves that filled the place. Made from black mirewood timber and carved with strange figures and goetic inscriptions, they sagged and creaked beneath the weight of multitudes of books, scrolls, parchments, data-slates and information crystals. The stacks formed narrow rows that seemed to go on forever, dimly illuminated by cobwebbed lumen orbs suspended from brass chains overhead. The shelves carried on up past the orbs, their uppermost levels lost in the musty darkness that shrouded the vaults.

Before Vey could advance into the library proper, he was approached by a gaggle of shuffling, hunchbacked figures – mortals, but garbed in the dark blue robes of the Librarius. They were bibliognosts, a subsect of the Chapter's serfs, humans bound to live out their lives within the confines of the Librarius.

All of them had their tongues cut out at the beginning of their service. The first to reach Vey signed silently at him while keeping his gaze averted from the towering Exorcist, a ritualised greeting that put him at the Librarian's disposal.

Vey waved the mortals away. He did not need their aid to find what he sought, and besides, he wanted to tangle up as few souls as possible in the web he was beginning to sense was now surrounding him.

He strode into the Librarius. The place reeked of damp and old vellum, dusty pages and cloying incense. It seemed to swallow the sound of Vey's footsteps as he made his way in amongst the towering stacks. The only noises were the occasional soft fluttering of wings from things in the darkness above and the dry rustle and crackle of pages being turned somewhere amidst the endless shelves.

The rows loomed over Vey as he went deeper, the weight of their blasted knowledge seeking to bear him down. He muttered litanies he had learned on his first day as a Lexicanium, using their familiar beat and cadence to locate himself within the vast chamber and keep his path true.

It did not do to stray in a place such as this.

As he progressed, he passed several figures working in silence. The first was another blue-robed bibliognost, a series of brass magnification lenses lowered over her eyes as she tottered atop a ladder resting against one of the stacks. The second, a dozen rows on, was a wheezing servitor unit, bent-backed beneath a mound of books it was transporting with slow, shuffling steps.

Vey's catechisms led him true. He found the centre of the chamber, the nexus where the stacks converged. A dense circle of lecterns, cogitator units and data-nodes, dusty, their screens fuzzed with age, surrounded a statue of a robed figure, head bowed, features lost in the shadows of a graven cowl. The Emperor of Man, in His guise as the Keeper of Knowledge. At the statue's feet, in the centre of the cogitator circle, a set of black iron stairs spiralled away into darkness.

More bibliognosts stood at the lecterns and cogitators, the scratching of quills and the dull rattle of runeboards the only sounds. They were cataloguing, transcribing, translating or researching on behalf of the Chapter's Librarians or the Inquisition. None looked up from their labours as Vey passed between them to reach the stairs.

He began to descend beneath the gaze of the Emperor. Down the tightly twisting stairs led him, into the space known as the Crypt.

It lay directly beneath the main Librarius, smaller than the grand chamber but still large and vaulted. Here the most damnable works were confined, not only texts but artefacts too – all manner of trinkets and reliquiae, from skulls and withered, shrunken heads to strange crystals, blades and daggers, cups, tarot decks, looking glasses and other arcane paraphernalia. The Exorcists knew the power of such objects, as well as their danger.

Vey was target-locked by another combat servitor at the bottom of the staircase, but it allowed him to pass. The air had a sudden, bitter chill to it, and he could feel the psychic tug and pull of the warding runes carved into the stonework around him.

He moved into the Crypt, beginning to scan the shelves. The books here were bound like beasts in chains and fetters, and every stack's front was covered either with iron bars or sheer plates of armaglass. The latter was crazed and scarred by the scrapes of talons and the imprints of clawed hands. All the markings were on the inside.

Vey knew these shelves, knew the cursed weight they bore up. His hearing detected what sounded like whispers, breathed softly from between the stacks, but he ignored them. He counted himself past the Sixteenth Catechism of the Red Saint of Ophidia, the diary of Lord Commander Elgor Faust, Aktor Krell's *Lemegeton Profundis* and the first and third scrolls of the Klepas Didactics. Between the final scroll of the Didactics and *The Revelations of the Ruberics*, he found what he sought.

There was a scrape of rusting metal as a servitor approached. The bibliognosts were forbidden from entering the Crypt. Servitors alone ran this part of the Librarius. Often one or more of Vey's brethren would also be present, but currently he and Dornmar were the only Librarians in the Basilica Malifex – the weight of recent conflicts had spread the Chapter thin.

Vey used his gene ident to unlock the glass and unchain the tome he had sought out, before stepping aside to allow the servitor to properly remove it. The thing's forearms were crude metal augmetics wrapped in purity seals and litanies from the *Liber Exorcismus*. Its function was the retrieval of texts such as these.

After a few tries with its pincers, it was able to heft the book down from the shelf and transport it to the nearest reading slab. Vey watched warily as the book was set down, its covers still chained. Its name was the *Daemonarchia Claviculus*, and it was the most complete list of Neverborn in the Chapter's possession. It had been compiled over four millennia, a record not only of the common names – and sometimes even the True Names – of the warp spawn that had plagued humanity, but also a catalogue of their titles, ranks and appellations, and their standing within the damnable hierarchy of the empyrean. It was at once a vital and dangerous weapon in the Exorcists' armoury, and only desperate circumstances made its evil a necessary one.

The reading slab lay beneath another large lumen orb, its light a rancid yellow, the inside of its lower half befouled where grime had collected over the millennia. The slab itself was carved with hexagrammatic runes and the names of the Seven Planetary Talismans, along with five versions of the diagrams of the *Sigilus Dei Imperator Aemath*, the Seal of the Emperor's Truth. Vey would have preferred to employ more arcane tools – his black-and-red Rod of El and his incantation bowl. For a proper reading he would have anointed himself with sanctified acid-water from the marshlands surrounding the Basilica Malifex, or pentacle runes in ash from the Eternal Pyre that burned atop the fortress-monastery's pinnacle, but there was no time for any of that. Vey was experienced in the occult ways of what the Chapter called *goetia* – black magicks and daemonologie. He had to press on, or he would run out of time.

The servitor retreated, and Vey stood over the book. It took a moment to find his focus, briefly touching two fingers to his forehead before undoing the chains.

The response was immediate. Before he had even touched its cover, the *Daemonarchia* slammed open with a clap like thunder. At the same time, the lumen overhead stuttered and went out.

Vey's body went instinctively to combat readiness. He heard a whirring from nearby – the servitor. The whispers he had caught earlier returned, scratching at the edge of his hearing. His hands clenched into fists, and he half turned, seeking an enemy he knew was not there. He yearned to feel the hilt of his force sword, Kerubim, in his grasp.

The lumen struggled back to life. Damnation lay open before Vey – the *Daemonarchia*, darkness coiling up from the flayed skin of its pages, the physical corruption visible to Vey's witch-sight. The taint was bleeding from it, clawing at the bindings of the reading slab as it sought to reach him.

It would find no purchase in him. His soul was a fallow field where even the deepest, bitterest root of corruption would not lodge itself.

The servitor had turned and was now staring at him, its one organic eye dull but fixed on him.

Vey returned its gaze for a moment, then, slowly, turned back towards the book. Twin hearts beating, he leaned over and forced himself to read the blasphemous names and titles inked with blood onto the ancient skin, pinning each writhing word in place with a murmured catechism of command.

The Red Marshal, formally Seneschal of the Fortress of Bone and Keeper of the Blood Hounds Carnus and Slaught. Known upon Arava Prime as the Crimson Vengeance, upon Antraxus VI as the Warlord of Warlords and within the Ignatius Sector as the Butcher Baron. Since its great and grievous defeat upon Fidem IV, it has been called most commonly, in the vulgar tongue of mortals, Caedus.

The servitor lunged for him. Subconsciously, Vey had been ready for it. He caught the clumsy thrust of its forearms, twisting and grasping its head in one great hand as he put his body between it and the book. He wrenched at its skull, his positioning ensuring the blood and oils from the torn flesh and ruptured machinery did not strike the *Daemonarchia*. Blood, touching the accursed pages, would have unleashed more than Vey was prepared to deal with.

The servitor went stiff and still, dead. Vey dropped it and turned back to the book.

'It has returned,' said a voice.

There was a figure, standing in the shadows between the book stacks opposite the slab. Vey found himself looking into the face of death.

He realised Zaidu had followed him.

He did not bother to question how the almoner-lieutenant had gained access to the Crypt. Though they guarded their knowledge carefully from outsiders, any within the Chapter's complex command hierarchy – be it the Twelvefold Commandery, the Convocation of Four or the Lesser Convocation of Forty-Eight – could access the Librarius. As a newly inducted member of the lattermost body, Zaidu's presence here was not unwarranted. What irked Vey was that the Sin Slayer had followed him, and that he had done so without Vey sensing his presence.

'It has returned, yes,' the Librarian said, making himself answer Zaidu directly and speak the truth, despite his reluctance to do so.

Zaidu made no physical response to Vey's confirmation, other than to pause briefly before speaking again.

'Then it is bound for Fidem IV.'

'That is likely.'

'Have the Chapter hierarchy been informed?'

'I do not know. I have yet to visit Dornmar. I wished to test the weave of fate here before I committed to speaking to him. But if it is as we both fear, I am authorised to take immediate action.'

'And what will that action be, enlightened brother?'

Vey took a breath, fixing Zaidu with his gaze before speaking. 'You will prepare your Hexbreakers, and be ready to depart aboard the *Witch-Bane* on the eleventh bell.'

'Is there a briefing packet? Hypno-data for the voyage?'

'There will be by the time you board. I will compile it as soon as I have received the astropathic report.'

Zaidu nodded. Vey knew he needed to be as careful with the almoner-lieutenant as he was being with the *Daemonarchia*. He was like a keen, unsheathed blade – deadly when used well, but capable of wounding its owner if not wielded with control. Vey decided it was better to press him now rather than later. He needed to get a good, confident grip on him if he was going to use him correctly.

'Will the Hexbreakers be ready at such short notice?' he asked.

'Yes,' Zaidu said. Vey experienced a quickening of his senses, an unwelcome sharpness that linked back to the days of his initiation rites, long ago. It was akin to the heightening all Space Marines experienced when about to enter combat, a glanding of stimms and hormones, but this was something more, something truly predatory and instinctive. He tasted a passing sweetness in his mouth, and swallowed it. Amazarak's parting gift, and curse.

Zaidu had just told him a half-lie.

'And will you be ready, Sin Slayer?' Vey pushed on, not pausing to address the untruth.

'Yes,' the lieutenant repeated. More vicious sharpening, more sweetness, a full lie this time. Vey could hear the pulse of Zaidu's hearts – both of them active, just like his own – and see the individual beads of sweat as they ran from his bare, scarred brow. His fingers ached to grasp Kerubim.

'You are lying,' Vey told the lieutenant. 'I can taste it.'

'Your line of questioning is vague,' Zaidu replied coldly, still lingering in the shadows, his half-skull mask grinning. 'If you wish to get at the truth, hone it.'

Vey smiled coldly. That was more like the Daggan Zaidu he had known, ever since the desperate day he had dragged him through the blood and broken bones and burning meat of his own initiation rites. The unsheathed blade, cutting and quick. Sin Slayer, a champion of the Chapter, hunter of daemons, ruthless, relentless, uncompromising.

'Caedus is your Never-brother,' Vey said, attacking Zaidu head-on, just the way he liked it. 'During your initiation into the Chapter, it was Caedus who possessed you. Who shared your flesh. Who, before my own eyes, you tore out and cast back into the warp.'

'Clearly, I did not cast it far enough,' Zaidu said, voice taking on a bitter edge. 'How was it allowed to return and infest another aspirant so quickly?'

'There will be an inquest into that,' Vey assured him. 'Right now, that is not my most pressing concern.'

'Your most pressing concern is whether or not I will be an asset or a liability,' Zaidu said with customary forwardness.

'Correct. Even banished, the bond we share with our Never-brothers is potent. It affects us all in different ways. Now that Caedus is free, those effects will be even more pronounced. Tell me, why did you follow me here?'

'It felt like something was calling to me,' Zaidu said. 'In my blood. And outside too. Not just the usual echoes but...'

'Whispers,' Vey said.

'You have heard them too?' Zaidu asked sharply.

'I hear much, and see more, Sin Slayer,' Vey said, falling back on the time-honoured mysticism of the Librarius. 'Speak to me again of your vision. The one you experienced in the psykhanium. Was it the first occurrence since returning from Demeter?'

'Yes. A warrior like us, Adeptus Astartes, clad in golden-yellow light, battles a Neverborn of the Blood God amidst towering ruins. The daemon is Caedus. The warrior defeats it and banishes it to a place beyond all human understanding.'

'And you still believe this warrior is you?' Vey asked.

'It is a vision that has been shown to me and no other since my initiation,' Zaidu said. 'Sometimes I see it second-hand, but often I view the fight through the golden warrior's own eyes. I have always known my purpose is to destroy Caedus in the material realm. The fact that it has come back to the Chapter and broken free, and the fact that I now stand ready to hunt it down, only confirms it. You know as well as I, Lie-Eater, that there are no such things as coincidences when it comes to the workings of the warp.'

'True,' Vey allowed, keeping his counsel about Zaidu's vision to himself. 'But you must know too that you will be tested on this hunt. And not merely your battle skill or your art with those daggers of yours. All of our Never-brothers detest us. Caedus will seek to twist the pieces it left behind in you, and break you in every conceivable way.'

'The daemon will be the one who is broken. I will consign the Red Marshal to the warp so utterly that it can never again threaten the Emperor's domains,' Zaidu growled. 'I will give you an Oath of Damnation on it, right here and now.'

'I do not require that,' Vey said, raising a hand to placate his younger brother. He had pushed him far enough, for now. 'And in all honesty, there are none in the Chapter I would rather have at my side during an undertaking as vital as this. You have never been found wanting before, Sin Slayer, and neither have the Hexbreakers. I do not expect that will change.'

'It will not,' Zaidu agreed. 'With your permission, Brother-Librarian, I will go and ready them.'

Vey dismissed Zaidu. Only when he was gone did the Librarian slam the *Daemonarchia* shut and lash chains of psi-deadened steel about it, snarling the necessary Oath of Binding as he felt it shudder in his grip, like a living beast brought to heel.

No such thing as coincidences. He could hear the clanging of a heavy bell from somewhere high above, its clapping the only sound from outside permitted within the Librarius. The eighth toll of the day, Vey realised. *Expulsiars.*

Time was still slipping through his fingers.

He hurried to the astropathic relay.

CHAPTER TWO

PILGRIM TOWN

Jair was all out of las, and that meant she was probably going to die.

She refused to accept it. She was still telling her brother to hang on, to not give up, and she didn't want to seem like a hypocrite.

The herdsman came at her with a sharpened shovel. Jair reacted on instinct, managing to snatch his wrist before he could get a proper swing in. He did the same to her knife hand, and they wrestled, crashing against the shot-up remnants of the shack's stove. Old pans clattered and fell, and Jair managed to stamp on the herdsman's bare, dusty foot, which produced enough of a reaction for her to wrestle her weapon free.

She punched the bayonet through the raggedy kepe cloak the man was wearing, feeling its tip jar off a rib and lodge somewhere in his chest. Wild on adrenaline, she ripped it free and stabbed again, and again, snarling, spitting in his gaunt, bearded face.

Strength deserted the herdsman. He slumped down against the cooking unit, the shovel slipping from his fingers.

There was no time for her to savour her victory. She barked back at her brother, Trex, who was lying against the back wall of the half-demolished kitchen space.

'Stay with me!'

Trex's face was deathly white, a sharp contrast to the bright blood drenching his hands and lower fatigues. Jair knew that he was already dead, but still she fought to save him. She couldn't let go, not yet.

The Guardswoman knelt to check the herdsman for any spare las-packs, but before she could find any, more of the heretics began to push in through the doorway. There were two, garbed in the kepes effected by their cult, the patched-up cloaks wrapped over their shoulders, across a mismatch of scavenged fatigues and flak armour. One had also stolen a Militarum helmet, complete with the fused las-beam hole in its side that had presumably killed its previous owner. Neither were carrying firearms.

That was about the only good news. Jair lunged upwards at them with a feral snarl, trying to get at the first before he could make room for the second to follow him fully into the shack. The man was armed with nothing but a tube of metal piping, but the old blood crusted on its end showed it had been used to deadly effect.

He swiped aside Jair's attack and met her charge, grunting as she managed to plant her flak pauldron into his stomach. He didn't give way though, cracking the pipe awkwardly against her other shoulder and shoving at her in turn. He was a big, strong brute, and he stank of stale sweat and old wool and grease. His forearms were bare and covered with crude tattoos. Even only half aware of them, they made Jair feel sick.

He flung her off, his fellow herdsman getting by and going at her with an axe. It missed as she stumbled over the body of the previous cultist, the weapon clanging off the stove instead. As she struggled to regain her balance without dropping her bayonet, she realised she was probably going to die.

That was when the front wall of the shack exploded inwards. Jair went over amidst a hail of splintered pulpboard and bent corrugated iron. She sprawled beside her brother and, driven by the manic desperation of the fight, was back on her feet again almost immediately, bayonet in hand and teeth bared.

She stopped. She had assumed the shack had been hit by a grenade blast. Now, she realised it had been nothing of the sort.

In the three or so seconds it had taken Jair to scramble back up, the giant figure that had demolished the front half of the dwelling had already killed one of the herdsmen, decapitating him with such force that the cultist's cranium flew away and bounced off the wall to the right before slapping wetly down on top of the stove. As Jair watched, paralysed by shock, the giant grabbed the head of the second cultist in one massive gauntlet.

This was the one with the helmet on, but it didn't make much difference. There was a faint whirr followed by an ugly crack as the giant squeezed. The helmet deformed beneath his grip, crushed inwards like an overripe fruit. The skull went next, steel from the helmet driven into it at multiple angles. After a brief, utterly futile struggle, the herdsman went limp, blood and brain matter oozing down over the remnants of his staved-in face.

The giant let go, allowing the body to fall. Jair dropped too. Her strength, flushed out in the wake of the surging adrenaline, deserted her, and she found herself on her knees, looking up at the monstrosity, her teeth aching from the raw energy that thrummed around the giant's charged armour.

He must have stood at least eight feet tall, and wouldn't have been able to remain upright in the shack if he hadn't already demolished half of it. He was clad in deep red armour, its surface etched with row upon row of cursed arcane runes. Lengths of parchment were wrapped around his vambraces, inscribed with more of the unnatural scrawl. In one fist, held in a reverse grip, he clutched a combat knife as long as Jair's arm, still dripping with the blood of the beheaded herdsman. There was another, similar knife still attached to his hip, alongside the biggest bolter Jair had ever seen. The giant's skull was bare, the tough skin criss-crossed with scars, while his forehead seemed to have been branded with another foul rune. Worst of all was the mask covering the lower half of his face, fashioned to resemble what looked like a daemon's skeletal jaw, all wicked leer and vicious, bared fangs.

Jair knew that he was death and damnation, given form and now come to claim both her body and her soul.

Like most other Guardsmen, she had scoffed at the whispered claims that there were Heretic Space Marines operating on Fidem IV – indeed, the slightest suggestion that such a thing even existed was an immediate death sentence if any of the commissars found out. Still, the rumours persisted, of gigantic warriors in bloody red armour, etched with blasphemous markings, herding their cultist flock callously into battle and, sometimes, even leading from the front. Wherever they struck, a massacre ensued. One corporal from the 43rd Vendoland had told Jair that any survivors were then summarily executed on the orders of their own high command, to stop accounts from destroying morale.

Jair could almost understand the reasoning of that. The war on Fidem IV was already a nightmare, a bare-knuckle, broken-knife fight that eclipsed even the last campaign against the orks on Artemis. She had privately come to terms with the belief that most, perhaps all, of them were going to die here, their bodies added to the layers of battlefield detritus that had made this world sacred in the first place.

But now that the end was suddenly upon her, it was so difficult to accept. She dropped her bayonet and, unable to snatch quickly enough at the aquila token she wore on a chain under her flak, clapped her hand instead against the identical eagle stamped on the left side of her chest plate. She couldn't think of any other means of warding off this heretic, besides begging. In that moment she forgot everything else, forgot her pride and her faith and even her beloved brother, lying dead beside her.

'Please,' she managed, voice a dull croak. 'Please, don't kill me.'

The giant stared down at her, and she stared back, into those brown eyes, so dark they were almost black, their inhumanity only accentuated by that daemonic skull-grin. The pair shared a strange, brief moment of total stillness. Then, abruptly, he turned away.

He left, having not said a word, stepping out into the harsh daylight. Just like that, he was gone, leaving Jair kneeling in the blood and the dust, shaking but alive.

'Curious,' Zaidu mused as he moved off again, down the rutted track that passed for one of the shanty town's streets.

'What was?' Vey's voice clicked in his ear.

'A soldier of the Astra Militarum. She just begged me not to end her.'

'Unsurprising,' Vey said with the merest hint of humour. *'We know the spawn of Lorgar are operating on this world. To a common member of the Guard, caught up in the midst of combat, we might be confused with the enemy.'*

'Surely not,' Zaidu said incredulously, disgusted at the mere suggestion.

'Regardless, we should remain alert to the danger of being mistaken for heretics.'

Zaidu picked up the pace, the Guardswoman he had left

behind already forgotten. The street was so narrow he could barely pass down it without his flanks scraping crooked door-frames and wallboards. His boots splashed through the muck underfoot, leaving deep imprints stamped in his wake, and as he went, he ducked smoothly beneath several electrical cables that had come loose and now criss-crossed the street.

An autogun chattered nearby, followed by the battering echo of sustained heavy stubber fire. Zaidu did not slow or stray. Every street resounded with the background cacophony of war. The heretics were pushing, and the Astra Militarum were pushing back. And in the midst of it all, Zaidu was hunting, alone, when he knew he should've been leading instead.

The slum was known as Pilgrim Town, and it was a miserable warren of derelict prefab hab-units and shanty dwellings that had accumulated with all the planning and architectural flare of flotsam washed up by the tide. Built over time with layer upon layer of scrap metal, recycled pulp and whatever detritus the destitute mendicants could get their hands on, it had coalesced around the Tower of the Praetorian, the spiritual heart of the shrine world of Fidem IV. After nearly four thousand years of pilgrimage, it was a hovel that had become a sprawl-city.

According to the data briefings Zaidu had memorised pre-planetfall and the hypno-eidetic programming that had started to trigger when he came up against the relevant stimuli, much of Pilgrim Town rested upon an ancient battlefield. Really, most of the planet's inhabited surface did, for it was war that had given Fidem IV its status, war that had made it sacred. Zaidu did not pause to consider the irony.

'You are straying, Sin Slayer,' Vey observed via the vox-link.

'I know,' Zaidu said tersely. As much as he respected the Van-guard Librarian, he had no time for another of his lectures. Their prey was close. He could feel it.

'Damnation comes for us all,' he said, a popular Chapter catechism. 'But today, I will find it before it finds me.'

They had hunted Caedus here aboard the strike cruiser *Witch-Bane*. The ship the daemon had infested, the *Share of Defiance*, had been discovered adrift in Fidem IV's low orbit, its interior turned into a charnel house. There had been no survivors. The absence of one salvation pod, however, combined with reports of a recent crash landing on the surface of the planet below, had ensured that the trail had not gone cold.

The buildings around Zaidu shook as something exploded nearby, rusting metal and old boards clapping off one another. Based on the direction and the sound of the detonation, Zaidu decided it was medium artillery, Imperial, and badly off target. Heavy shelling was occurring to both the east and west, but he had specifically requested that the Guard leave a corridor running north untouched. Close artillery support would have been a boon, but there had been no time to build a sufficient connection with the Astra Militarum units in the area, at least not enough for him to be confident that they wouldn't shell the Exorcists strike force by accident. Or, if Vey's observation from earlier was to be believed, on purpose.

There had been only minimal communication between the Exorcists and the other Imperial forces already fighting on Fidem IV. It had been over a year since an Archenemy incursion that had spilled from the Cicatrix Maledictum and changed this place from shrine world to war world once more. Zaidu had not come here to turn the conflict's tide, a fact he had made clear during the short, terse holo transmission he had dispatched to Guard high command when the *Witch-Bane* had translated in-system.

He reached the end of the street, where he paused for several seconds to reassess his location. Despite the vambrace readout of his armour's auto-senses and its inbuilt auspex, navigating the tangle of alleys and lanes towards Pilgrim Town's northern edge was no easy task. That was why he had broken away from the rest of the Hexbreakers, even his old fraternal brethren in what was now Squad Belloch. They had become bogged down amidst the main thrust of the heretic advance. Before he had been given command of the strike force, Zaidu had been a Reiver sergeant. He knew the benefits of slipping away and finding his own path.

According to his vambrace, the objective – the salvation pod's crash site, pinpointed by scans run from the *Witch-Bane* – was now only a quarter of a mile further north. Frustratingly, the street he was on took him first east, then west again before turning in the correct direction. But there was an alternative.

He could feel Caedus slipping away. It frustrated him, made the frayed edges of his soul smoulder. After a short assessment of the structural integrity of the buildings directly opposite, he decided going straight through was the optimal choice.

He slammed down the plyboard wall of the first shack, leading with his left pauldron and raised forearm. This time there were no occupants – Pilgrim Town's inhabitants were long since dead, fled or taken – and he predicted he was now between the front of the heretic offensive and any reserves they had coming up. That, or Lector-Sergeant Anu was doing an even better job than usual at keeping his path clear.

Casting aside all caution and subtlety, Zaidu carried on through the next few dwellings, emerged onto another alleyway running east to west, then slammed through the next block as well. The shoddy materials crumpled before him, leaving devastation in his wake. By the time he emerged onto a street with a direct route to the crash site, he was caked in dust, and his armour was scraped but undented.

'*You should not be advancing so far alone,*' Vey reiterated in his ear, his conscience made manifest.

He did not respond. He was accustomed to acting on his own initiative, to relying on his own wits, his reflexes and his twin blades. It was what had made him suitable to be a Reiver, and what made him suitable now to hold the rank of almoner-lieutenant in the Exorcists Tenth Company, a force of Vanguard elite out of step with the Codex Astartes but in keeping with a Chapter that prided itself on hunting its foes to extinction. Zaidu was the Sin Slayer, bore the Third Mark of Admonishment upon his brow. He was a war dog, bred to hound the Emperor's foes, and he would not relent until this one in particular was brought to heel and savaged into oblivion.

He caught movement on the roof of a shack to his left. A pair of cultists, these ones armed with lasguns, moving along the tops of the slum buildings, probably hoping to get a good angle once they got to the main fight.

Zaidu had his Occulus bolt carbine unclamped and raised in one fluid motion, but before he could fire, the top half of the cultist in front simply exploded. As blood and viscera rained down, the one behind looked at the fist-sized hole that had appeared in his torso.

One shot, two kills. Both bodies fell into the street.

Zaidu lowered and re-clamped his carbine, the weapon unused.

'I'm not alone,' he told Vey.

CHAPTER THREE

SIX

There were six heretics coming to kill Anu.

He ignored them, for the time being. Perfection permitted no distractions. He couldn't remember if that was one of his own sayings or Cy'leth's, but that didn't matter right now. They were often indistinguishable anyway.

Sixty steps.

There was movement on another set of mismatched roofs, just over one and a half miles out from Anu's perch on the top of the scrap church spire. He locked his optic goggles to his rifle's occuscope again, the twin machine spirits of the devices combining to give him a full target data burst – range, wind speed and direction, projected movement, armour and potential weak points, the effects of temperature, local azimuth and barometric pressure and more, all calibrated by the advanced wargear in under a second, and all assessed by Anu just as quickly.

The targets in question were three more cultists, scurrying along the top of a series of flat corrugated-metal roofs, carrying mismatching autoguns and wrapped in their herdsmen's cloaks. If they turned right and dropped down to the lower levels of the shacks built beneath them, they would find themselves with an angle on the lieutenant's rear as he continued to push northwards.

Anu wouldn't permit that. The Sin Slayer was closing on the objective and could not be delayed. Besides, Zaidu was also part of the Fraternity of the Eleusinian Mysteries, one of Anu's Orisons. Guarding him was his duty as a fraternal brother.

He locked on to the three and took a brief pause to settle his aim. With his rifle resting on the spire's rusting parapet, he eased the breath from his lungs and locked the servos of his power armour with a blink-click, becoming as still as one of the graven statues that lined the interior of the Basilica Malifex, back on Banish.

Forty-five steps.

There was still fractional movement to contend with – not from him, but from the slight swaying of the scrap church's spire. It was not an ideal perch, but it was still the best spot in the engagement zone. He had known as soon as he had seen it that it would be his home for the rest of the afternoon, if not longer.

He compensated with a three-millimetre adjustment to the right. There was a sharp, hot wind, kicking up swirling eddies of dust from the other rooftops and tugging at the cameleoline cloak and cowl that shrouded him. He had already accounted for both.

He eased off the shots, one-two-three, a trio of beats in quick succession that translated into the familiar, dampened recoil of his bolt sniper rifle.

Three more kills. Too easy. There was no perfection to be won here. Anu felt something akin to disappointment.

The six heretics were still coming to kill him.

They were clattering up the spire's metal stairs, climbing ever higher. When Anu had mounted them earlier, on his way to setting up the perch, he had counted each one, reaching one hundred and five in total. He had since deleted much of the background discordance of the battle playing out across Pilgrim Town's suburbs, focusing instead on the noises rising from the stairwell at his back. He had detected the presence of the cultists in the main body of the church below, and had then caught the sound of their feet, hurrying up the stairs, trying to reach him. Since then, he had been counting their progress as he continued to provide Zaidu with long-range fire support.

Twenty-five steps.

He still had plenty of time. He did another scan sweep of the roofs above the Sin Slayer's push, but they were clear, for now. The northern edge of Pilgrim Town lay before him, a jumbled, stinking sprawl slowly baking beneath a cloudless sky. Anu's optics overlaid it all with a screed of data, from the marker tags of his battle-brothers to the trajectory arcs of both the Imperial and Archenemy artillery batteries that were pounding away at the neighbouring districts.

Down on the ground, he knew his brethren were experiencing a debilitatingly slow slog, the narrow, refuse-littered alleys and miserable hovels thick with heretic infantry. Up here, though, Anu ruled. He had been sweeping the rooftops since Zaidu had detached him from the rest of the Hexbreakers and assigned him to overwatch. Nothing lived here without his permission.

Still, the heretics tried. He detected a figure to the north-east who had just emerged onto the balcony of a rickety-looking prefab hab-block. He appeared to be scanning the area through a set of magnoculars. A spotter, Anu assumed, for the foe's artillery. He wouldn't permit such a presence in his engagement zone.

Ten steps.

The target was right on the edge of effective range. Effective range for most, anyway. Anu pushed himself to take the shot, to make the kill despite the intensifying time constraints.

His servos locked. His sights aligned. A fractional adjustment, then another recoil, dampened by the bolt rifle's suppressors. There was a brief moment of stillness while the round was in flight before he saw the wall at the spotter's back painted red.

Five steps.

Time up. He allowed himself the briefest moment to refocus. He could kill as easily in close as he could at range, but it always required a different kind of effort. Pinpoint accuracy gave way to something more instinctive, more primal.

Three steps.

He set aside his rifle, rose to his feet and pushed his optic goggles back onto his forehead, brushing aside the strip of long white hair that ran down the centre of his shaven scalp.

Two steps.

He snatched his bolt pistol and combat knife free from their mag clamps at his waist.

One.

The first heretic to surmount the stairs, panting with exertion, had his head detonated by a single shot. Anu prided himself on being as fast and lethal at point-blank range as he was at maximum.

There was no time to let the heretics come to him, not now that he was giving them his full attention. He charged the stairwell, hitting the ones behind while they were still climbing.

The second and third were put down by bolt-rounds fired so close that the muzzle blasts ignited their capes. The fourth tried to shout, but was too breathless, and died when Anu's knife crunched through his eye and into his skull. The fifth had his chest cavity laid open before he had even properly realised the cowled, dark red horror was bearing down the stairs onto him. The sixth managed to squeeze off a burst of hard rounds that rattled and sparked impotently off Anu's plastron.

The Eliminator kicked the burning, bloody remains of the first five back down the stairwell while snatching the sixth by the throat. He ran with him back to his perch and threw the screaming heretic over the parapet, before grabbing his rifle from where he had leaned it against the wall and crouching back into his sniping position. As he had feared, there were two more figures on the rooftops, trying to get at Zaidu. In the six seconds he had been absent, one had opened fire on the lieutenant.

Anu killed them both. His preternatural hearing, further enhanced by the razor-sharp honing effect of his stimms, caught the sound of the one he had thrown over the side striking the ground below just after he had made the second shot.

He permitted himself to ease off. Cy'leth would have taunted him for that, which gave him another reason to be thankful he had torn the howling Slaaneshi Neverborn from his soul and forced it back into the immaterium on the day he had become an Exorcist. It had spoken to him so much about seeking perfection, but it had proven itself unable to appreciate the balance necessary to find it.

'*Is there a problem?*' Zaidu asked him over the vox.

'No, fraternal brother,' Anu said, experiencing a bitter draught of disappointment. 'Overwatch continues.'

Despite his best efforts to be quick, Zaidu had still noticed the brief break in support. Anu sighed. He was still so far from perfection.

Torrin Vey stood alone, surrounded by the warriors of the Archenemy.

None of them moved to strike him, even the ones within

touching distance. Vey remained still, the cowl of his camo cloak drawn up, Kerubim and his bolt pistol deactivated and mag-clamped. He did not like the feeling of bared steel in his hand when he was questing.

He made a slow gesture towards the closest heretic, index and ring fingers extended. The man was tall and wiry, dressed in a grubby woollen smock, fatigue bottoms and cobbled-together combat webbing. His cheeks were bony, his beard unkempt and his eyes vacant. He perched on the edge of a battered metal table, running a dirty cloth over an ancient-looking autogun, not looking at Vey. His head was uncovered and bald, revealing the sigils he had daubed into his skin with ash. Vey suspected he was attempting to copy the markings he had seen on the armour of his masters, but they were painfully childish and inaccurate.

The Librarian murmured a litany of focus, softly, lest he disturb his work thus far. The street outside was loud with the cracking of lasguns and the roar of bolter fire, but in this particular shack dwelling, all was peaceful. Vey intended it to remain that way.

He fashioned his thoughts into a needle and eased it into the heretic's mind, slow and precise. He found himself up to his waist in the psychic essence of the man's soul. It was dark and frigid, with dragging undercurrents of pain and despair. There was nothing wholesome, nothing nourishing. None of it disturbed Vey. It was inconsequential compared to the horrors of his own battle-brothers' spirits.

He plunged his hands beneath the murky depths, seeking the memories he required. He tasted the raw, rancid meat and stale bread this miserable creature had eaten that morning, heard his quivering voice raised in prayer to his uncaring gods, listened as the herd leader had barked orders in what had once been the dialect of the agri worlds of Irenoth, now twisted and warped by the Dark Tongue. He experienced second-hand the panic, fear and exhilaration of combat, emotions alien to the Space Marine. And then, nothing. Just the present stillness, the calm, wholly unnatural in the midst of such fighting.

Nothing useful. Vey withdrew himself, wading his incorporeal being free from the psychic slurry, and moved on to the next heretic.

There were six in all. Using his warpcraft, Vey had shrouded himself in an illusion when he had first walked into the shack, then spread that illusion so it filled the shabby confines of the scrap building and the equally shabby confines of his victims' heads. The six servants of Chaos now believed themselves to be back in whatever passed for their own quarters after a hard day's combat. Time for them to enjoy the closest thing to relaxation their short, brutal lives would experience. And while they were uncomprehending and docile, Vey moved from one to the other, ransacking their thoughts for any evidence about the target they were hunting.

So far, they had not been able to provide what he sought. They knew nothing of the crash site. Vey did his best not to become frustrated. That would not help.

His psychic abilities were extensive, but maintaining such a powerful illusion while also questing – delving into souls in an effort to extract memories and knowledge – was a taxing combination. He could feel the familiar pain of a migraine building in his head, and knew that if he carried on for much longer, he would start to taste blood. And that was when it became truly dangerous.

He pushed on. Zaidu had one way of finding the target, and Vey had another. They would see which was more effective.

The next heretic was a herdsman, one of the cult's proper fighters, rather than just the las-chaff that constituted the flock.

His soul was not so dissimilar to the last one, though there was a little fire to it as well. Pride, determination. The vestiges of a warrior. Vey sank himself a little deeper than he had before, and found the source of a great deal of that pride.

Six days ago, the heretic had seen one of the gods he worshipped. A giant in dark red armour pinned with black scriptures and wreathed in shadow and hate. Despite the difficulty his own soul had in feeling any emotions, Vey experienced a short, sharp spike of revulsion.

The reports were true. The Word Bearers were on Fidem IV.

It was a useful confirmation, but it still wasn't what Vey was looking for.

As he withdrew from the herdsman, there was a flurry of gunfire from directly outside. Several of the heretics twitched as Vey fought to keep them invested in the shared illusion. On his vambrace display, he noted that Helix Adept Gela was about to enter in through the shack's front door. He thought about warding him away, but decided it was time to move on. These particular prisoners were useless to him.

Gela ducked inside, bolt pistol raised until he realised what Vey was doing. The Librarian stepped swiftly from one heretic to another, placing the index and middle fingers of both hands against the left and right temples of each. With a psychic tweak, he induced a series of quick, fatal brain ruptures. One by one they dropped silently to the floor, spasming before lying still. It was over in seconds.

'Enlightened brother,' Gela said by way of greeting.

'Brother-medicae,' Vey responded, feeling the pain in his own head slowly starting to recede. 'The street is clear?'

'Yes. Almoner-Sergeant Haad is moving on.'

Vey could sense Gela wished to ask how his own efforts were going, but did not want to speak out of turn, especially to one who wasn't part of either the Hexbreakers or any of the Orisons he was a member of.

'The questing has proven to be unfruitful,' Vey admitted, deciding to save him the trouble. 'Besides confirming the presence of the Excommunicate Traitoris.'

'The almoner-lieutenant is about to reach the crash site,' Gela observed.

'So it would seem,' Vey said, checking Zaidu's location on his tactical display before looking to the Helix Adept once more. 'But his advance is reckless.'

'His desire to terminate the target is understandable,' Gela said, voice slightly tense.

Time seemed to slow. Vey felt his senses quicken, his surroundings becoming hyper-focused. At the same time, he caught the barest hint of something sweet in his mouth, there and gone again.

Both were predatory echoes of the daemon that had once, briefly, inhabited his flesh. Its true name, which he had eventually hunted down and committed to memory, was beyond easy pronunciation, but he knew it commonly as Amazarak. A silver-tongued servant of Change, it had been able to sense when mortals were lying. Vey had inherited its ability, and while he doubted Gela had just outright lied to him, he had said something he only half believed.

Vey decided it would be unfair to press him. In his experience, the sweet taste of untruths quickly turned bitter.

'Squad Belloch are not far behind the lieutenant,' Gela pressed on. 'And Lector-Sergeant Anu is providing overwatch. They will not permit any harm to befall him.'

'Nor will I,' Vey said. 'Come, brother. Let us press on.'

CHAPTER FOUR

DISCORDANCE

The Hexbreakers rallied on the crash site.

Infiltrator Squads Eitan and Haad established a perimeter, overseen by the returned Anu and his other two Eliminator brethren, Lakhmu and Dumuzid. Zaidu, Vey and the Reivers of Squad Belloch swept the wreckage itself.

The crash had been caused by a salvation pod that had been fired from the bowels of the cruiser *Share of Defiance* while in low anchorage above Fidem. Part of it had broken up during entry, but the main section had carved a scar six hundred yards long through one of Pilgrim Town's suburbs, obliterating countless shacks and lean-tos. Debris had scattered over an even wider area, but it quickly became apparent that the core cylinder of the pod had remained intact and was buried now in the ploughed-up earth at the end of its blackened furrow.

As Zaidu had suspected, there were no obvious signs of the target. He clambered down into the cylinder, but found it empty, its harness restraints unused. The only evidence was the water that stood ankle-deep at its bottom.

'Meltwater, from ice,' he said as he clambered back out and dropped to the dirt beside the wreckage. 'Until recently, the interior was frozen.'

'It was opened from within,' Lector-Sergeant Belloch added from where he stood above Zaidu, on the buckled chassis of the pod's hull, looking down at the container's hatch. 'Not torn open from the outside.'

'Caedus is gone,' Zaidu said, looking to Vey. 'Do the heretics have it?'

'I do not know,' Vey admitted. He had drawn back his cowl, revealing a scalp carved with the occult markings of his Orison, the Broken Tower. 'My instinct is that they do not, but that does not help us one way or the other.'

Zaidu collected his thoughts. He briefly felt his anger flare, but it soon burned away, back into black nothingness. In truth he had always feared they would not be able to catch the Broken One as soon as it made planetfall. They were gaining on it, though.

None of this had been foretold, not until the moment his vision had beset him in the psykhanium. As part of the Exorcists Tenth Company – composed entirely of the Primaris Vanguard elite – Strike Force Hexbreaker had been recovering on Banish following the purging of Demeter, a long and fraught campaign that had cost almost twenty per cent of their strength. Most of the Exorcists had anticipated a few short weeks back at the Basilica Malifex, repairing armour, renewing ammunition stocks and putting fresh edges on their combat knives before reassignment. There was also the matter of taking on fresh recruits, working through the Halls of Testing and renewing the fraternal bonds of the Orison cults. Instead, after eight days, the message had come through about the incident at Nowhere.

In a way, he had been unsurprised to learn that Caedus had returned. The daemon's echoes did not trouble him the way some other Exorcists struggled with the remnants of their Never-brothers. He had always believed that was because Caedus was still close, still a physical threat and not a mere haunting.

Then there was the matter of the vision. He had been living with its reoccurrences since he had first been initiated into the Chapter, since he had first encountered Caedus and bested the blood daemon. He believed it was a prophecy of final victory. With the Emperor's light blazing around him, he would break the Red Marshal into uncounted shards. If ever the daemon was able to repair itself in its bloody master's citadel, it would not be for many aeons.

The crash of artillery strikes in the neighbouring streets reached a brief crescendo. It gave Zaidu a sense of renewed purpose. If the action was continuing unabated, it implied the enemy were still hunting for their prize. And that meant he would do the same.

'Brother-Initiate Amilanu,' he said, contacting Squad Haad's commsman. 'Attend me at the primary crash site.'

Amilanu arrived, his modified backpack bristling with the antenna and aerial spikes that facilitated his role as the Hex-breakers' primary communications adept.

'Update us on the current state of the heretic offensive,' Zaidu ordered him.

'Our own advance has torn the heart from it,' Amilanu said. 'But it remains strong on our flanks.'

The commsman tapped part of the array fixed over the right side of his helmet, transmitting a three-dimensional holo display to Zaidu's and Vey's gauntlet uplinks, allowing them to review a map of the engagement zone while he spoke.

'According to Astra Militarum communications, the enemy's main strength has diverted to the west. A brigade-sized force is close to overrunning the neighbouring sector there. The action further east seems to have quietened.'

'What are the Guard saying about enemy reserves?' Zaidu asked.

'They are uncertain. An aerial sweep was conducted to the north an hour ago by a squadron of Imperial Navy Lightnings. They detected some movement in the valley beyond Pilgrim Town's edge and the Sacred Ways, but struggled to calibrate numbers. As you know, the sky there is heavily contested. The Guard do not know if enemy reinforcements are still en route.'

'I will have the *Witch-Bane* scan the valley between Pilgrim and Deliverance,' Zaidu said. 'We need to build as complete a picture as possible of the enemy's movements. They may already have the target, and be extracting it towards their stronghold at Fort Deliverance.'

Amilanu made no comment, leaving the analysis of the data his arrays had picked up to his commander.

'If they are still pushing to the west, it may be the trail has led there,' Zaidu continued. 'We should follow it.'

Rather than answering Zaidu, Vey nodded to Amilanu, sensing he had more he wished to add.

'Speak,' the Sin Slayer ordered the commsman.

'I have detected an anomaly,' Amilanu said. 'The Guard have lost contact with a detachment holding a strongpoint two miles to our south-east, deeper into Pilgrim Town. It is a particularly large scrap shrine. It was occupied by a battalion of Guardsmen, the' – he paused for a second as he checked the unit roster on his display – 'Nineteenth Vendoland. There were no reports of an enemy push on their sector, and no sign of any contact. They have simply stopped responding.'

Zaidu exchanged a glance with Vey, but he remained silent.

'Unusual,' Zaidu admitted. 'Are there any forces en route to find out what has happened?'

'Only a company from another reserve regiment,' Amilanu said, again scanning the data his vox had picked up and stored from the wider Guard communications he was tapped into. 'They can spare nothing more.'

'It is an anomaly that deserves further investigation,' Vey pointed out to Zaidu.

'But it lies in the opposite direction from the renewed offensive to our west,' Zaidu said. 'Either could be evidence of the Broken One's presence.'

'I believe the disappearance of the Vendolanders is the more likely candidate.'

'Is that based on some particular insight?'

'It is based on instinct.'

'Understandable, but I do not wish to commit the hunt to such a gamble. Time is still pressing. I shall split the Hexbreakers.'

Zaidu half expected Vey to query the order, but he did not. Zaidu carried on.

'The enlightened brother will take Squads Belloch and Haad and move south-east, towards the scrap shrine. I will take Squads Eitan and Anu and meet the heretic offensive to our west. Between us, hopefully we will pick up the trail again.'

Vey waited until Amilanu had left to rejoin his squad before voicing his concerns.

'It is unwise to divide ourselves,' he told Zaidu. 'My questing has shown that the Militarum's intelligence is correct in one regard. The Word Bearers are on-world.'

'In what strength?' Zaidu asked.

'Unknown. My prognostications suggest their leader is powerful, possibly daemon-tainted.'

'Aren't they all?'

'Do not underestimate them.'

'I will not,' Zaidu said. 'But nor will I allow them to dictate strategy. Locating the Broken One is our absolute priority.'

'There was a time when you would have heeded my advice, Sin Slayer.'

'I mean no disrespect, Lie-Eater,' Zaidu responded levelly, voice scraping from behind the jagged leer of his mask. 'I merely wish to see our mission completed.'

'I know it weighs on you,' Vey said. 'I was aware that choosing you for this assignment would be a burden. But I trusted that it would also expedite a successful outcome. You have already beaten Caedus once. You share a bond with it like no other. We can use that to our advantage.'

The Librarian's perceptions were as accurate as ever. Zaidu had been preparing himself for another encounter with Caedus, but he had not expected it to still be shackled within a Broken One. The practice of binding multiple daemons within failed aspirants was, of course, a matter of utmost secrecy. If the mere existence of the initiation rites or the Purgatomb became known, it would undoubtedly lead to the Chapter's extinction. In the report she had transmitted just before intercepting the transport, the inquisitor who had unwittingly unleashed the Broken One had claimed that consistent portents had identified Caedus as being too dangerous to deliver to the Purgatomb, even ostensibly bound. In the end, she had managed to unleash the very evil she had sought to contain.

It seemed to Zaidu that Inquisitor Harrow had slipped into a self-fulfilling prophesy. He could only hope they were not still a part of it, acting it out to some despicable tune. Such things were beyond him. He knew he had to trust Vey's wisdom and ability to ensure that they did not become entangled in the warp's maddening snares. Treachery and misdirection were beloved of the forces they fought.

He was here merely as a hunter and a killer, not a prognosticator.

'It is… difficult,' he admitted, understanding that lies were no good against Vey. 'Knowing my Never-brother is almost free, knowing that it is so close. It…'

He trailed off. He was unused to discussing matters such as feelings, though in truth there were none he would do so with more willingly than Vey. He was one of the few he had known since the beginning. Since his own initiation, and the madness that had changed him forever.

'It claws at me,' he went on. 'It is like… talons beneath my armour, like a parasite in my skull. I cannot ease these thoughts. Every life Caedus claims, every step it walks in the material plane, is my fault.'

'That is not true,' Vey said firmly. 'And to believe so is foolish.'

'I was the one responsible for banishing Caedus, yet clearly I did not do so fully. If I had been able to break it, the daemon would not have had the strength to return to plague us, not this quickly.'

'Do not ascribe normal strengths or frailties to a creature of the immaterium,' Vey cautioned. 'They do not operate in such mundane ways.'

'I must find it,' Zaidu reiterated. 'And that means I must find the Broken One. I cannot stop until then.'

'But if you believe your vision to be true, you know you will triumph. Have you not foreseen it?'

'You are the one who told me the future is never certain. I cannot take my vision as a guarantee of victory, not if I do not act on it. It is up to us to make sure of it. To that end, the Hexbreakers will divide.'

Vey nodded, and Zaidu was silently thankful that the Librarian had decided to cease his protests. Though he would barely admit it even in his own mind – for it felt like adding one further weakness to the many he already saw within himself – it was difficult going against Vey's advice. The enlightened brother had been Zaidu's mentor since he had first been inducted into the Chapter. It was Vey who had been with him as he had torn out Caedus during the initiation rites, helping to collect and salve the burnt remnants of his soul in the aftermath. It was Vey too who had so often guided him through the early years of his service to the Chapter, who had helped purge as much of the lingering horror from his thoughts as possible, as he had done with so many other brethren of the Exorcists. To have the Librarian at his side during this most crucial of hunts was a boon, even if it sometimes caused frustration.

'Come, we have wasted enough time here,' Zaidu said, extending his hand to clasp Vey's forearm, briefly but firmly, hoping to dispel any lingering discord between them. 'The hunt continues, my brother.'

CHAPTER FIVE

SACRILEGE

This was where Caedus had longed to be, and now that he had arrived, it filled him with sacred fury.

What had they done? What had these pathetic, ephemeral little sparks of existence done to his places of worship? They had raised their own, mocking him with shrines made of detritus and squalid, crowded, filthy hovels. Did they have no shame? No comprehension? Did they truly wish to goad him in such a manner?

His body stumbled. Angrily, Caedus righted it and forced it onwards, through the slums. When he had first broken his chains, he had experienced a moment's triumph, piercing the veil of his frustrations. Then his wrath, smouldering for so long, had roared back into existence. He had brought, until the bulkheads had run with viscera and the hull had vibrated with screams. That had been an indulgence, one that he had even permitted the others to partake in. Who was he to deny them an opportunity to worship his master with him, to share in the shedding of so much blood?

He had recovered himself, and with it, control of his prison. He had crushed his kindred's dissent and set a course for this place, a seat of his master's former majesty, the world where the past, present and future of his own existence had tied together in a thick, tough knot. When the moment came, he would split it with his mighty war axe and reclaim his destiny.

How he had dreamed of this, sleepless dreams in a timeless place, far removed from the realm of his birth or the kingdom of his master, from blessed brass and blood and bone. How long had it been since he had last stood upon this ground? A day? A millennium? An hour? An age reckoned in the birth and burning-up of stars or in the beat of a single heart, that sacred, vital organ? He supposed it did not matter. He had returned, as he had sworn, and now the road to renewal, to triumphs afresh, had begun.

He could feel the blood-blessed soil calling to him, singing through the host, that body that was supposed to be his prison but which he had instead made into his vehicle. It was strong, as mortal forms went, enhanced well beyond the capabilities of most of Terra's spawn. And yet, it was still lacking so much. Caedus wished to twist it, to make it into a shape more befitting of his glory and the glory of his master, but still it resisted him. Caedus was weak – detestably so – and he had not the strength to warp its flesh or, more importantly, to break the collar that still bound him and his kindred within it.

The body had a name once. Names, like blood, held power. Caedus knew this one's because he still had its soul in his possession. Ashad. A dull little thing, its mentality akin to that of a child. Caedus had allowed the others to play with it for a while, though it remained imprisoned rather than destroyed. He did not have time for that, to snap every bone and scrape away every scrap of skin and rupture every organ in Ashad's spirit form, so the little soul with the strong body would remain his captive, for now.

The body stumbled again, and Caedus experienced revulsion so potent it caused his stolen flesh to shudder and wail, the nightmare sound ringing through the narrow streets. It was disgusting, utterly disgusting, to be wearing this puppet of skin and bone, and to be so confined in a place where once he had been whole. Even his thoughts were not truly his own, not unknowable and raw and raging with the majesty of the immaterium, but fettered by the soft grey meat within this unworthy skull, unable to commune fully with the warp, to be at one with purest *sensation*, the essence of the turbulent, crashing storms of emotion that comprised his master's realm. That he was forced to share this dull, limiting prison, to experience thoughts and stimuli as it experienced them, was the final insult. It was almost more than he could bear.

He began to claw at his host, ripping at its collar. He had been able to burn off, tear out and shed so many of the other bonds forced upon him, but this one he could not remove, not without destroying this body and finding himself cast adrift before he had marshalled the strength to fully materialise. It was a lodestone around his neck, bearing him down, biting into his spirit, making it ache. How he longed to replace it with the spiked, warp-forged iron that showed his master's favour.

The other two, the rot scholar and that pathetic addict, were clamouring at him, begging him not to ruin the host. He was tempted to do so just to spite them. They too were repugnant, their weakness anathema to one such as he. That they were right meant little. Still, he forced himself to abate, dragging the blood he had spilled back into the host and healing its tough body, gaping wounds becoming red welts. Now was not the time for the shedding of more vital essence. He did not deserve the honour of doing that, not until he had reached the first sacred place.

It was before him now. He was not entirely sure how he had found it, only that it had been calling to him, thrilling through the host's blood. He had wandered in a daze from the wreckage that had brought him to the surface, and now he was here, entering into a structure of battered old metal, a false shrine, built to mock him, hammered together in ungainly, ill-fitting sheets over soil made holy by battle.

There were mortals both around and within it. He was only vaguely aware of them, and only then because they had the merest spark of warrior spirit about them. They were soldiers, fighters, and that meant he shared a bond with them, albeit a bond as imbalanced as the one shared between the worm and the hawk.

At first, some tried to stop him, but that did not last long. He ignored them, passing through their midst as they turned to exulting his master instead, their little weapons put to a better use. As they sawed and hacked and stabbed and beat at one another in their sudden, raving lunacy, Caedus stepped into the shrine.

He had anticipated some resistance, his warp-being revolting against the nature of a place such as this, but there was only a passing discomfort. This was not even a true shrine of the Corpse Emperor, merely a desperate imitation made by the vermin that infested this place.

He kept going, to the shrine's end, the screams of those within bringing him some small solace. This was the place, he could feel it. One of the four sites on this accursed, blessed world where he had been humbled, a waypoint in his fall from power.

Demetrius. He made the host spit the name, using the stolen skin and sinew and muscle to taste it, to feel its shape. It stoked his fury.

The end of the shrine was dominated by a crude altar made from the turret of a long-broken battle engine. It felt like a further mockery. Warriors of titanic strength had fought here, upon this very spot, and the mortals sought to commemorate it with rusting wreckage?

He reached out and slashed the host's forearm along one edge of the ruptured metal. Almost immediately, the wound clotted. These creatures, these new, enhanced toys, did not like to be injured.

Caedus cut it, again and again, until blood was spattering the turret and pooling around the host's bared feet. Then, finally, as the fluid sank between the mismatching riveted plates beneath, he felt the change beginning.

The host's fingers ached as nails became wicked talons, slowly splitting the skin around them. Caedus turned a hand this way and that, admiring them, feeling the rush of renewal that came with the shedding of blood. The collar about the host's neck was a little lighter. This was where he was supposed to be, as his master had ordained, and none would stop him.

It was a good beginning, but he had much further to go.

The remainder of the mortals in the shrine slew each other, snarling and spitting their mindless hatred to the last, a prayer to Caedus and his liege lord made with bloodied lips. Now the shrine looked closer to a true place of worship, daubed in slaughtered remains. Still, he could not linger. Already he could feel others closing in on him. They flattered themselves with the belief that they were hunting him, especially the *one*. Demetrius. It had taken many a demeaning pact with change-spawn and lie-kin to engineer his presence, all these millennia on. How Caedus would enjoy tormenting the remnants of that one's soul. He would bring it as a gift, make its skull gibber for eternity upon his master's great throne. That would be his final, greatest triumph, and even his bitterest rivals in the realm of the Blood God would acknowledge that he had not only regained his former glory but had surpassed it.

The next old battle site was calling to him. He could hear its growling, faint, rising up from the earth beneath, from a place forgotten by even the detestable pilgrims that infested this place. He sought out a set of stairs, leading into the shrine's under-croft, and a tunnel long covered up and forgotten.

Let them believe they hunted him. It would only save him the need to find them when the time came.

CHAPTER SIX

THE CHALLENGE

This time the enemy had armour with them. It was a rickety old war engine, built on the chassis of a Leman Russ battle tank with weapons systems that appeared to have been largely scavenged from old metal pipes. Its flanks were marred with blasphemous iconography daubed in blood, while its turret had been wrapped in a mangy fleece. It clattered as it advanced down the street, its rear exhausts churning out a cloud of oily smoke, its rattling treads knocking down the shacks in its path.

The sight of it was almost enough to stir Uten into rejoicing. He was going to destroy it.

'Nazaratus, Kleth, strike pattern dālet,' he barked, not bothering to highlight the tank on the retinal display the Infiltrators of Squad Eitan shared. They would already know his intentions.

The Sin Slayer had led them from the crash site westwards, into another melee, a fact that suited Uten just fine. The foot-soldiers of the Archenemy were pushing in force through this northern suburb of Pilgrim Town, with armour and artillery in close support. The Astra Militarum, overstretched and fragmented, had started to fall back through the warren before them.

Then the Exorcists had arrived. Without waiting for the Guard to rally, they had plunged like a spear into the warp foe's guts, Zaidu again leading at the fore. Squad Eitan were driving through three parallel alleyways and lanes, the lector-sergeant himself along with Pazu and Balhamon to Uten's immediate left, while Almoner Hasdrubal, Hokmaz and Urhammu took the right. Nazaratus and Kleth, Uten's companions, were deferring to him as the longest-serving of the three, both in the squad and in the Orison cult that Kleth and Uten were members of. In truth, Uten had little interest in leadership. He merely wished to break the war machines of the Archenemy.

Nazaratus launched one of his smoke canisters down the street into the oncoming tank's path while Kleth took up position on the edge of a hovel on the opposite side and sent a burst of bolt-rounds into the heretic infantry moving up in support. The lead cultists fell, blown apart, and the rest scattered.

Uten moved left past Kleth, into the shack, scanning the detritus for a doorway. It seemed possible to pass through adjoining entrances and passages all the way down the row of dwellings without actually having to step out into the street, and Uten intended to use that to outflank the war engine.

Predictably, the tank's makeshift stubbers began to hammer away as soon as its occupants realised their vision was obscured by the smoke now billowing up from Nazaratus' canister. Kleth and Nazaratus answered it with their bolt carbines, keeping its attention as Uten began to work his way from shack to shack.

It proved more difficult than he had hoped. Where there were doors, they were too small for the Primaris to use. He was reduced to kicking and shouldering his way through, spitting a string of vicious curses as he beat down pulpwood walls and trampled over the debris. At one point he had to heave a corrugated-metal roof off his shoulders after it collapsed on him.

He almost lost track of the tank until he suddenly found its treads bearing down on him – it was having as much difficulty moving along the street as he was, and its right flank was simply ploughing through the ramshackle dwellings, unwittingly setting it on a collision course with the Exorcist.

Anyone else would have stepped aside and allowed it to pass before striking, but not Uten. The slaughter-hound's echoes had awoken. The memory of its hunter's rage became his own, and for a while he knew what it meant to feel again.

Slamming his boots down through the flooring of the half-broken shack, he braced himself and met the tank's right side. He snatched at the stubber sponson protruding from the flank, the weapon already buckled by the passage through the slum.

The steel of the war engine met the steel of Uten's genhanced body, neither willing to yield. Like all Primaris, Uten bore within himself the blessings of the sinew coils, those durametallic cables that provided power and endurance beyond even the biscopea organ that gave Space Marines their strength. His armour locked out too, his servos and actuators beginning to grind as they reinforced him in his struggle.

There was a moment of impasse, and an aching, metallic groan as the tank slowed and began to slew to one side. Uten felt a roar building in his throat, teeth clenched, eyes bulging and every vein and muscle in his mighty body straining. It was almost more than he could bear. Almost.

There was a shriek, like a damned soul bound for the warp fire, jagged and piercing. Uten felt the sponson abruptly give way, plasteel tearing, the extension crumpling. He dragged in a breath and bellowed once more, driving home his victory, punching his fists against the buckled metal and heaving back, until he had wrenched the whole sponson off.

He tore his way inside the tank. His intention had been to demolish it with a brace of krak grenades, but that was before it had challenged him. He was snarling and drooling like an animal now, but he didn't care. He wanted to get at the meat, at the flesh and blood hiding inside this pathetic engine. He wanted to see how much easier they were to break than their machine.

The interior was in disarray. A coolant pipe had ruptured, spraying scalding water across the lower crew compartment, the steam mixing with the filthy smog of the engine.

The driver was the closest to Uten. The wiry man was naked from the waist up, the markings he had daubed on his body with ash now reduced to dark streaks by the sweat drenching him. He shrieked in horror as Uten clawed his way inside and grabbed at him, dragging him away from the gear stick and directional levers.

Uten was vaguely aware of the unarmed man scrabbling impotently against his rune-etched armour. He headbutted him, the collision blasting the heretic's skull to pieces and momentarily painting Uten's visor red. He cuffed the slurry from his vision and fought to get deeper into the vehicle, struggling to fit, keening like a wild animal.

The heretic manning the prow gun mantlet had seen the fate of his kinsman and had managed to get the hatch on the opposite side of the tank open. Sunlight speared in as he made his escape. The engine commander was less fortunate. Uten was able to lunge up into the turret cupola as he fumbled with the top hatch, clamping one gauntlet around the man's ankle. He pulled and the leg came away at the knee, blood drizzling down into the lower compartment. The screaming cultist collapsed, which just brought the rest of his body within Uten's reach.

Nazaratus and Kleth were waiting for Uten when he eventually hauled himself back out. The defiled Leman Russ lay still and silent now, its engine as dead as the majority of its crew, its tortured machine spirit freed.

Uten stood for a while, towering over even his brethren, silent but for the scrape of his slow panting over their shared vox. Eventually, Kleth reached forward and slowly placed a hand on one of Uten's bloody pauldrons, leaning in so his helm was almost resting against the gorget of the taller Primaris.

'*Klesh nal, tali reth,*' Kleth said softly, in one of the Chapter's many tongues. Unlike Nazaratus, who was an outsider, both Uten and Kleth shared an Orison, the Rite of the Fifth Degree. Kleth now did his best to soothe his fraternal brother.

'Echoes,' Uten said with some difficulty, voice still an ugly growl.

'I know,' Kleth said. 'But we must push on. Lector-Sergeant Eitan demands we rally.'

For emphasis, he highlighted their squad leader's latest order icon on the display. Uten managed to nod.

'Pattern khaf,' he said, the brief moment of kinship dissipating as though it had never existed. 'Kleth, take point.'

CHAPTER SEVEN

BLACK BENEDICTION

The Blessed One was close. Artax could smell it in the air – blood and more besides, burnt metal mixed with the cloying scent-taste of the warp, alternating between sickeningly sweet and achingly bitter. He had removed his helmet to inhale it. It made him shiver with a degree of anticipation he had not known for some time.

'The rear of the shrine is clear,' Kordiron Seventh Tongue growled, stepping back into the nave of the rickety structure. Even by the standards of the corpse-slaves, this particular place of worship was an embarrassment. It had been made from old scrap, based around the hulls of several ancient Leman Russ battle tanks. The altar had once been a turret, its main cannon long sheared off. Like much of Fidem IV, it was a tribute to the war that had made this ground sacred in the eyes of the Imperium, and detestable to the followers of the True Gods.

The Blind Shepherd had come to change that. Mordun, Saviour of Irenoth, Leader of the Flock, Dark Apostle. Like Artax, he was a Word Bearer and a champion of the Long War. He now stood separate from the rest of the warband, clutching his crooked staff two-handed, head bowed. Much of his deep-red battle armour was hidden beneath the long, thick robe of the fleece he affected. His face was cracked and lined, like the cover of one of the vast library of sacred tomes maintained by the warband's bibliognost, Dalamar, on board the *Psalter of Slaughter*. His eyes – or what now passed for his eyes – were inscrutable, hidden behind the prayer parchments he wore wrapped around much of his upper head, inscribed with the Litanies of Eightfold Devotion.

He was the only other member of the band who had been fighting the Long War before Artax. At times, were it not for his armour, Artax felt like he was looking at an old man, wizened and bent. At that particular moment, the Blind Shepherd seemed to be listening to a voice none of them could hear.

Artax assumed that was indeed the case. Mordun had long borne within his flesh a daemon of Change, a sly warpling which had once tried to conquer him with talons made of lies and a razor-beak formed from betrayed hopes. They had eventually reached an uneasy accord, and now shared one body as equals. The daemon's advice was a blessing that filled Artax with envy, though privately he wondered if he too would have had the strength and guile necessary to tame such a creature.

Mordun turned slowly in a circle, his warpwood staff tapping on the drenched floor. It was slicked with a wake of blood, spilled from the ragged corpses of the Imperial Guardsmen that littered the shrine. It was not the work of Artax or his brothers. The Word Bearers had arrived to find it like this.

'The wounds were self-inflicted,' Dalamar the Bibliognost observed, rising from where he had been crouching over a body carved from shoulder to crotch by the wild, repeated hacking of a bayonet.

'They did an impressive amount of damage, considering the pathetic nature of their armaments,' Kordiron said. To emphasise his point, he stood on one of the discarded lasrifles, cracking its stock and barrel beneath his boot.

'It only shows the power of the Blessed One,' one of the younger members of the band, Ikar, said. 'I can feel its presence here.'

'We all can,' Artax said, shooting him a cold, dismissive look.

'Bring in the flock,' Mordun said abruptly. 'I need… six.'

The rest of the warband exchanged glances among themselves, before Ikar stalked to the shrine's entrance and barked at the closest cultists gathered outside.

The flock had come from Irenoth. Mordun had taken over the remnants of the warband not long before leading them there, replacing Deacon Zarhash, who had guided them for so long before his death during the void action off Klevar. It had seemed the shattered warband was close to disintegration, but Mordun had held them together with promises of a miracle.

It had happened on Irenoth. The Word Bearers found the agri system sparsely defended and swept by famine. It had not been a difficult thing to promise the wretched populations salvation, not when the True Gods were blessing Mordun so bountifully. Daemon pacts had abounded following his ascension to the rank of Dark Apostle and his alignment with Erebus' faction on the Dark Council, and even more material alliances were forthcoming once Irenoth was secure. The charnel fleet of mad Admiral Vexar had allied itself to the warband's Repulsive-class grand cruiser, the *Psalter of Slaughter*, as had a swarm of Heldrake daemon engines led by their sire, Cruexis. Following a successful raid on the forge world of Diamantus, Mordun had led them here, to this dusty, benighted junk-world. He believed that true, lasting glory would be won by claiming a vessel of holy power, the Blessed One. Beyond that, he had explained few of their objectives. It was, apparently, the will of the Eightfold Path, and for most of the warband that was sufficient. Artax almost wished he was as easily reassured.

Hounded by Ikar's snarled oaths, half a dozen of Irenoth's former agri workers scrambled into the shrine and threw themselves down amid the blood and the bodies, wisely not looking up at Mordun. Artax knew that some, like Dalamar or Syro the Lector, found the fawning of the flock endearing, but such obsequiousness disgusted him. Mordun had reprimanded him more than once for the way he treated the cult they had built, but he found it hard to maintain the charade. He and his brethren were wolves, not shepherds. These fools simply hadn't realised it yet.

'Children,' Mordun said, beginning to address the shaking cultists. 'Dear ones. My precious fellow believers! I have chosen you for a great and vital task. Rejoice!'

The stammered acclamation of the small congregation filled the shrine. Mordun moved among them, looking like a giant next to the poor, starved wretches as he reached out and lifted them up, one by one, raising their heads and permitting them to look upon his ragged, parchment-bound face.

'Rejoice,' he repeated as he did so. 'Rejoice!'

The worship of the six grew louder, more hysterical. Several of them were crying. Syro and a few of the other Word Bearers added their voices to the praise. Artax rolled his eyes.

'May I bless you, my fellow believer?' Mordun asked one of the cultists, leaning forward so he did not seem to tower so intimidatingly over the woman as he addressed her.

'Yes,' she stammered, grinning ecstatically, her tears streaking tracks of purity through the mire befouling her face. 'Yes, my shepherd, yes!'

'Bow your head, lay your hand upon the staff, and say your

prayers, my beloved sister,' Mordun said, proffering her his crook. Trembling, the woman obeyed, lightly gripping the bent black warpwood of Mordun's staff as he, with a care that belied the disparity in size, gently placed his gauntlet against her scalp.

He spoke the Dark Tongue. Artax was too long versed in it to feel much more than a stirring deep within his core, but he saw Ikar and a few of the others physically shiver in their armour. The effect on the cultists was even more pronounced. They began to wail, struggling to enunciate their own, lesser prayers while blood filled their noses and ran from their ears and mouths.

After just a few syllables the woman collapsed, shaking uncontrollably as her body went into seizure. Mordun moved on, repeating his blessing to the next in line, and then the next. By the time he had reached the fourth, the first was howling and writhing through the blood on the floor.

There was a loud crack as she arched her back so hard her spine snapped in two. Her neck followed, then both arms. Her screaming, to Artax's mind, became something akin to the squealing of a pig as she ripped at her woollen clothing, exposing flesh that had started to bubble and blister. It flowed, melting like wax, distending and swelling. New meat was added to her bones, fresh muscle and sinew packed into her body from beyond the veil of reality by cackling, insane entities. It continued to split apart and deform, her broken back swelling and bulging, becoming hunched over, her head partly subsumed into the thickening mass. One arm and one leg became similarly misshapen while the others remained unchanged, bent at unnatural angles. Bone spikes burst wetly from the newborn flesh all across her body, and the squealing became guttural, inhuman.

Despite his own desire to appear detached and disdaining before the rest of the warband, Artax found himself staring like the others, drinking in the display of the Blind Shepherd's favour. It was moments such as these that helped Artax reaffirm the sour scraps of what remained of his faith, if only for a while.

The second to have received Mordun's black benediction was on his knees, gripping his head and shaking. Abruptly, a fleshy knot burst from his skull, from eyes and nose and mouth and ears, dozens of tentacles slimy with brain matter that squirmed and writhed furiously. More ripped their way from the skin all over his body as he too began to change, finally howling in horror from a fresh mouth that gaped open, sideways, from his sternum to his stomach.

By now Mordun had reached the last member of the flock. Able to see what was happening to the others, some self-preservation instinct finally managed to claw its way, screaming, through the man's derangement. He tried to take a step back, stumbling on one of the bodies that littered the defiled shrine.

Mordun snatched him by the scalp, holding him firmly in place, blood running down the man's face as the clawed tips of the Word Bearer's gauntlet dug into his skull. The Blind Shepherd snarled the last of his blessings, his own black, rotten blood running from split lips and spattering down his fleece tabard.

The transmutation was now unstoppable. All six of the former cultists were writhing and shrieking, being torn apart and re-formed to the capricious whims of the things that had been allowed to reach them from beyond reality. Soon, none of them were even remotely recognisable as coherent, sentient beings, let alone humans.

At last, their rampant flesh began to settle into some vague sense of stability. They continued to shriek and gibber vigorously, clawing at one another and the bodies beneath them.

'Silence,' Mordun barked, snapping at the spawn as if they were a pack of overexcited bloodhounds. Immediately, their squealing became a muted pule. Mordun raised his crook, and the things pressed their writhing bodies low. Artax realised they were genuflecting, as best as they were able.

'You smell the Blessed One,' Mordun declared loudly. 'You taste him. Now you must find him. Put your new bodies to good work, my fellow worshippers.'

He cracked his staff against the floor. Immediately, the spawn began to scatter, chittering and panting excitedly, scrambling over and around each other before bolting off in different directions. Artax felt a stab of revulsion when one came dangerously close to brushing against him as it scuttled past.

'You think these pathetic things can find the Blessed One when we cannot?' he asked Mordun.

'They are closer to the warp than you, my brother,' Mordun said, his tone dismissive. 'Closer than you especially.'

Artax offered no reply to the offhand insult, watching as one of the transformed monstrosities – its lower half now resembling a giant slug, its upper a mass of eyes blinking and roving as they sought focus – dragged itself towards the entrance to the shrine's undercroft, smearing the blood on the floor in its wake. Ikar had already checked down there, and reported nothing but more Imperial detritus. As Artax watched, though, a second, then a third spawn likewise began to shift in an ungainly manner towards that same passage.

He was about to demand to know what Ikar had managed to miss when he heard a sound that was at once familiar and different. It was bolter fire, issuing from outside, though it had a metallic echo to it that set it apart from the roar of the firearms carried by the warband.

'They are here,' Mordun said. There was a clatter, ringing through the scrap shrine and making the spawn twitch, as the Word Bearers readied their weapons.

'The loyalists?' Vost, another of the younger brethren, rasped excitedly.

'Yes,' Mordun said, striding through their midst towards the door, his staff tapping the floor. 'Come. We have lingered too long. Let us be gone from this place.'

'We're not confronting them?' Ikar asked, sounding outraged. Mordun didn't deign to respond.

'You can,' Artax said with an unfriendly grin, smacking Ikar on the pauldron as he passed him on the way after Mordun. 'I'm sure the True Gods would love to see that. I know I would!'

He dragged on and clamped his helmet as he stepped out of the shrine with Mordun, giving a snarl and smacking its side as the auto-senses of the aged, corrupt armour struggled to come online and link with him. When his vision properly resolved, he found himself in the midst of a scene of absolute carnage.

The slaves of the False Emperor were already upon them.

CHAPTER EIGHT

SIN-HUNTING

Vey had picked up the scent, of that he was certain. He could sense a presence ahead, malignant and dark, bleeding corruption into the ether surrounding it. The vileness of Chaos, akin to the rancid souls of the heretics he had waded through earlier, but infinitely more ancient and potent.

'Go carefully, brethren,' he voxed Squads Haad and Belloch. 'We have more than mere cultists before us.'

Squad Haad sent back a non-verbal affirmative over his vambrace display. The Infiltrators were already clearing heretics from the structures to Vey's left and right as they advanced, the slam-crash of their bolt carbines echoing through the slum.

'I have a visual on the shrine,' Belloch responded from further ahead. *'There are heretic infantry arrayed around its doors. Company-strength. Permission to engage?'*

Vey considered denial, but he no longer had any doubt that they were on the right path. If the spawn of Lorgar had taken the shrine, then the Broken One would almost certainly be close too. The time for caution was at an end.

'Permission granted,' he voxed Belloch. 'Squad Haad moving in immediate support, strike pattern resh.'

He blink-sent a data burst to Zaidu, highlighting the shrine and the likely presence of the target. Then he broke into a run and unclamped Kerubim, beginning to waken the blade and link his psychic essence with it.

From ahead, he heard the unmistakable sound of bolter fire. Squad Belloch had engaged.

Lector-Sergeant Belloch led the way.

As the new commander of the Hexbreakers' Reivers, it was something he was still growing accustomed to. Until Demeter it had been Zaidu, always Zaidu, who was first into the fray. He was the Sin Slayer, hunter of the damned, forever hungry, ever relentless. But now he directed the entire strike force, a position Belloch suspected sat ill with him. He still wished to be first, but the requirements of his new role demanded restraint. For a while, as they had driven in on the downed salvation pod, Zaidu had slipped the shackles of command and pushed ahead of even his old Reiver brethren.

It had been an infringement on Belloch's new-found position, but one he had not questioned. He privately doubted his own suitability for the role of sergeant, to command the squad that now bore his name. He was not Zaidu. He did not bear the scrolls of the *Liber Exorcismus* wrapped around his arms or runes of abjuration on his blades.

All that was forgotten when he broke into the small, detritus-littered square that lay in front of the scrap shrine. There were heretics before him, a stinking herd who turned from gazing at the ramshackle structure to looking in shock at the giants who came charging at them from the alleys and side streets.

Belloch roared the Litany of Admonishment, his half-skull mask's amplifier turning the words into a howl that battled with the hammering of his heavy bolt pistol. The nearest cultists were cut down, the rest scrambling for their crude weapons.

The lector was in amongst them before they could raise them, his combat knife unsheathed and running red. He was partly aware of the rest of his squad following him in, but his concentration was fixed on the shrine, and on the figures that had started to duck out from within.

They were hulking creatures, clad in battle plate the colour of congealed blood, trimmed with brass and bone and scrawled with rotten catechisms and prayer scraps made from flayed flesh. Even through his mask, Belloch could smell their rancid warp stink. They were the children of Lorgar, Excommunicate Traitoris, Word Bearers.

Belloch expected them to take up defensive positions and meet the Reivers' charge. Instead, they began to withdraw, forming a protective phalanx around one of their number incongruously carrying a crooked staff. Belloch snarled and forged towards them, refusing to allow their escape. He snapped over the vox for his brethren to close on him, guarding his flanks from the cultists who now, recovered from their shock, were throwing themselves suicidally into his path.

One of the traitors was lingering, seemingly torn between instructions to withdraw and a desire to face the charge of the Exorcists. Belloch sent the last bolt-rounds in his magazine slamming into the figure, the shots cracking off his breastplate and pauldrons before detonating, perforating the abused ceramite with exploded fragments. The salvo had the desired effect, a clear challenge which the Word Bearer stopped to meet.

'*Gloria Aeterna*,' barked the heretic, before bracing himself and opening fire with his own bolter, its muzzle fashioned in the likeness of a fanged daemon's maw. Belloch had already mag-clamped his sidearm and now snatched the nearest cultist, holding him out by the throat as he closed the last dozen yards. The man's struggles lasted only a second before the Word Bearer's bolts slammed into him, triggered by the meeting of metal and flesh. The heretic was blasted to pieces in Belloch's grasp, and he threw what remained in his fist at the Word Bearer before slamming into him.

The traitor was fast, but Belloch was faster. He knew this kind, had killed them before. His dagger was up and under the joint between plackart and breastplate before the heretic could abandon his bolter for his own blade, sawing through the exposed cabling of the power armour's umbilical feeds before punching through flesh. He twisted and ripped the knife free as the heretic responded with a punch to the face that cracked off Belloch's grinning death mask.

The lector-sergeant sensed immediately that this was no Long War veteran, but a wretch only lately inducted into this tainted brotherhood. The traitor tried in vain to match him sinew for sinew for a few moments before headbutting Belloch's gorget. The lector stabbed again, once more up and into the traitor's abdomen, trying to hack his way in beneath the fused ribcage and open the vital organs there.

Then something hit him from the right, something with considerably more mass and force than the heretic he was fighting. He almost went over, servos locking out, reflexes allowing him to brace and twist to meet his new assailant.

He found himself grappling with a creature that should not have been able to exist in any sane, ordered universe. An amorphous mass of pulsing flesh, bone spikes and writhing tentacles was trying to haul him to the ground and drag parts of him into the half a dozen drooling, shrieking maw rips. Belloch roared back at the thing and plunged his knife into the nearest growth, ripping and wrenching. Stinking ichor sprayed from the wound, but it simply sprouted fresh fangs made from shorn ribs, turning the gash into a new mouth that snapped at him and dribbled black viscera.

Hatred and revulsion ignited within Belloch, more potent than his ruined soul had known for a long time. He began to punch and stab, unable to turn his attention back to the Word Bearer as the spawn continued to grapple with its twisted limbs. He hacked them off, then plunged his knife into the wriggling mass of tentacles that seemed as though it might have once been the monstrosity's head. The blow made it shudder, which gave Belloch the second he needed to abandon his knife where it was lodged and smack a fresh magazine into his pistol.

He opened fire on the creature, emptying the magazine into it. Blubbery flesh and squirming organs exploded, its steaming, stinking offal painting Belloch's front. Part of the horror ignited under the ferocious fusillade. Still, though, it came for him, claws and bone fangs scraping lines in his armour's ceramite, scarring the occult runes he had etched there.

Before Belloch could reload there was a cracking discharge, like lightning. He took a step back as an actinic bolt struck the spawn. What remained of it slipped apart, perfectly bisected, its nightmarish writhing finally reduced to mere twitches as its inner horror was laid bare.

Torrin Vey stood beside Belloch, force sword in hand, crackling psychic energy playing across its blade, causing the black ichor of the monstrosity to evaporate from the blue-tinted, psi-reactive steel.

'My thanks, enlightened brother,' Belloch growled, stooping to retrieve his combat knife from the smoking remains before looking towards where the Word Bearer he had been grappling with had been.

One of the other Heretic Space Marines had come back for his erstwhile brother, and was now dragging the one Belloch had wounded out of the melee. The other traitors were already disappearing into the alleyways on the far side of the square. There was no sign of the one he had seen with the staff.

He turned his gaze in the opposite direction. The Infiltrators of Squad Haad were dispatching the last of the cultist infantry, along with more of the loathsome spawn that seemed to have burst from the shrine in the wake of the Word Bearers.

'A distraction,' Vey observed, as the slamming of bolt carbines competed with the shrieking and squealing of the spawn. 'And an effective one.'

'Permission to pursue?' Belloch asked.

'Yes, but do not engage,' Vey said. 'Only attempt to ascertain where they are going, and whether they have the Broken One.'

Belloch didn't question the instructions. He immediately ordered his four Reivers – Makru, Azzael, Nabua and Shemesh – to close on him, leaving the Infiltrators to finish the gruesome work outside the shrine.

Belloch would show that it was not only Zaidu who could hunt down prey such as this.

'Move, you warp-smitten fool,' Artax spat furiously, dragging Ikar along with him. The youth had been wounded, but Artax didn't care about that. He was cursing himself for being idiotic enough to go back for him. If it hadn't been for the spawn, they would likely both be dead.

Briefly, while confronted by a roaring warrior in butcher-red, rune-etched battle plate and a skull half-visor, Artax had thought they were being assaulted by a berzerker of the Blood God. But the attacker was too big, and he bore the accursed aquila of the Corpse Emperor, burnished and displayed proudly upon his cuirass.

Artax almost understood Ikar's desire to stay and confront the Throne slave's challenge, but it would have been a madness deserving of the raving of the flock's cultists. Acting on impulse, Artax had broken momentarily away from the others to haul Ikar out of the embattled square. He knew he shouldn't have risked himself for the youth, but the warband had few enough remaining members as it was. Ikar hadn't yet overcome his pride enough to offer him any thanks, not that Artax cared for it.

'What in the name of the Eightfold Path was that?' he demanded of the rest of the warband as he rejoined them, pushing through the slums towards the open valley to the north of the sprawl-city. He pushed Ikar in amidst the protection of the group. 'Did you see the armour? Its markings?'

'They are the brothers of the Blessed One's host,' Mordun said from ahead. 'Dorn's get.'

'I have never seen children of the Wall-Builder who looked like that,' Artax exclaimed. 'And they are loyalists?'

'More so than most,' Mordun said. 'I knew they would come for their walking prison. Now that they have arrived, we must accelerate our own hunt. We cannot allow them to steal back the Blessed One. He is essential if we are to ascend.'

Artax wondered how Mordun knew all this, but realised the daemon hiding in his flesh had probably slid the knowledge into his skull.

'He tells me much more besides, brother,' Mordun said. Artax started, and felt a moment's shame that his thoughts had been so easily snared and eaten up by the trickster Neverborn.

'Does he know where the Blessed One has gone then?' he demanded, trying to save face.

'Yes,' Mordun said. 'Down.'

CHAPTER NINE

CULTISTS

The Exorcists regrouped on the northern edge of Pilgrim Town, amidst the Sacred Ways. Beyond was the valley that separated the sprawl from the neighbouring settlement, Deliverance Town. Originally built around a stronghold known as Fort Deliverance – the site of one of the sieges that had secured Fidem IV's glory – the two scrap cities were identical insomuch as they were both mazes of destitute, squalid slums. The ground between them had avoided being subsumed by either thanks to the fact that it was one of the Eleven Hundred and Eleventh Sacred and Most Holy Fields of Battle, to use the archaic parlance of Fidem's faithful. During what they called the War of the Faith's Founding, four thousand years before, the valley had been the sight of ferocious fighting. Now it was again, becoming the point of separation between the forces of the Imperium, holding Pilgrim Town, and the servants of the Archenemy, who had overrun Fort Deliverance and its surrounds near the start of their new invasion.

'The heretics have crossed the valley,' Belloch reported to Zaidu as the lieutenant arrived with Squads Eitan and Anu, uniting them once more with Vey, Squad Haad and the Reivers. 'We began to pursue, but they called in artillery to cover their withdrawal. The enlightened brother ordered me not to carry on beyond the lines.'

'Do they have the Broken One?' Zaidu demanded, looking between Belloch and Vey. The Librarian answered first.

'I am unsure.'

'Could you not sense him?'

'The leader of the heretics was among them. His warp presence drowned out my ability to be certain. I do not believe they were able to locate the Broken One before we drove them out, but I am unable to accurately quantify that belief.'

Zaidu glanced away momentarily. He had chosen incorrectly. Vey had been right to identify the shrine's significance. But why?

'Why would Caedus go from the crash site to a random scrap church?' he wondered aloud. 'And in the midst of Imperial defences. Was it feeding off the fighting? But if so, why not head to the area of greatest contention, further west?'

'Why come to Fidem IV at all?' Vey expanded. 'We know that Caedus has links to this world. This is where it was defeated, four thousand years ago. I summarise it has come to avenge that loss, and in doing so regain the power it has been bleeding for millennia.'

'Then perhaps the shrine had some significance to battles past? If not the structure itself, then the location? Perhaps we can use our knowledge of Caedus' campaigns here to predict its movements?'

'That knowledge is thin,' Vey warned. 'I did my best back on Banish, and here, to consult what texts I could find, but the reliable details of the war that was fought in this place can be summarised in a few paragraphs. All that remains are the stories handed down by generations of pilgrims and scrap-scavengers, and the remnants of the battlefields themselves.'

'How can details of the struggle have been forgotten when they are all about us, still under our very feet?' Zaidu demanded, gesturing around.

'Scars will remain, even after the stories of how they were won are forgotten,' Vey pointed out.

Zaidu did not question that truth. He took in the sight of the Sacred Ways, stretching off to the left and the right from where the Hexbreakers had assembled. They were trench-lines, or the relics of trench-lines. During that first, great war, they were where the defenders of Fidem had lived, fought and died in their millions, in defensive works that spanned the planet's primary continent. That sacrifice, and the Imperial victory it had bought, had transmuted hasty military necessity into ten thousand holy trails that zigzagged onwards for miles.

In the thousands of years since the War of the Faith's Founding had turned Fidem IV into a place of pilgrimage, uncounted numbers of Imperial subjects had made the journey from across the subsector and beyond. They walked the old trenches, trying to go from the clifftop defences of the Kastern Sea to the Dormuz Strait, via the Tower of the Praetorian, the site of the final victory and the Red Marshal's banishment. As Fidem IV's renown as a place of worship had grown, the trench works had steadily lost the trappings of conflict, the sandbags long decayed, the duckboards worn away by the endless shuffling of feet. Dugouts had become holy shrines, where those who could pay in either coin or a period of indentured servitude spent a few breathless, shaking moments, praying in front of the sacred relics of the holy war, items that, almost anywhere else in the galaxy, would have been considered nothing more than waste. Rusting helmets, muck-encrusted bayonets and shovels exhumed from the dirt, long-dead lasgun power packs, shell casings, scraps of fatigue cloth, an ancient boot, wizened and cracked with age – each was treated with the same fervour that Zaidu had seen worshippers display towards the bones of blessed saints and Imperial cardinals on other, more mundane shrine worlds.

Of course, now that war had once again found its way to Fidem, the Sacred Ways had rediscovered their former purpose. The Militarum had availed itself of the premade fortifications, and soon the lines were filled again with armed and armoured warriors rather than barefooted, raggedy processions of supplicants. The holy icons had been covered up with flakboard, waypoint shrines had become dugouts once more, fresh parapets had been heaped high with sandbags and new coils of razor wire had been dragged over the rusting remnants of the old. The guides of the Eleven Hundred and Eleventeenth, who had made their living taking groups of pilgrims out into no-man's-land, went there no more.

War had stormed back in, as though affronted that any believed it had ever left, eager to tear apart the faded, musty memories and bury them under horrors anew.

'This ground was anointed by the blood of millions,' Vey said, watching Zaidu carefully as he surveyed the lines. 'That was what made it sacred. Blood. Never underestimate its power.'

'I cannot,' Zaidu said, his tone sharp. 'Because Caedus never would. What is my Never-brother, if not a creature of blood?'

'You know the Chapter's tenets,' Vey replied. 'We all carry damnation within us. It is the price we pay for allowing it to take root in the first place, for welcoming it into our bodies at the beginning of our new lives. But your particular damnation, Sin Slayer, comes from your hearts. Hot and vital and quick. It is the very essence of existence, for our species and uncounted others across the galaxy. You can no more deny Caedus than you can deny what pulses through your own veins.'

'I do not wish to deny it,' Zaidu said darkly. 'I wish to find it, and to break it, forever.'

'Yet we know not where to find it,' Vey pointed out.

'Across,' Zaidu said, gesturing out over the valley. 'By your report, and Belloch's, the Word Bearers withdrew too easily. If they do not already have the Broken One, they know where to find it. We must take the fight to them, and maintain the pressure.'

'You intend to strike the heretic lines across the valley?' Vey asked. 'An assault?'

'Yes.'

'In this sector, an Astra Militarum army group of over two hundred thousand combat effectives has failed to do that with any success for almost a year.'

'Do you not think a little over two dozen Exorcists will be enough?' Zaidu asked. He caught the merest hint of humour in Vey's expression as he responded, his eyes glowing golden from beneath the cowl of his camo cape.

'More than enough, Sin Slayer.'

'We will conduct Orison rites,' Zaidu said, voice firm with conviction. 'And tonight, when darkness falls, we resume the hunt.'

The Hermetic Brotherhood of the First Degree met in what had once been an abattoir on the northern edge of Pilgrim Town. The main structure consisted of a warehouse and adjoining packing plant made from mismatching old sheets of metal and ply cobbled together amidst a particularly precarious-looking set of prefab hab-blocks. There were channels in the cracked rockcrete floor underfoot, leading to drainage grates dark with blood rust. Meat hooks still hung from a conveyor rack overhead, their wicked, curved points gleaming in the last of the light shining in through the high windows.

The coolant pipes running along the walls and ceiling, once intended to keep the produce frozen, had long since ceased to function. Outside it was growing cold as the sun set and night crept in on the sprawl-city, but within the warehouse the air was still close and stinking. It must have been months since the last grox carcasses were strung from the ceiling, yet still the reek of slaughter pervaded.

Uten considered that fitting. What were they, if not more slaughter beasts?

He pushed such thoughts aside, trying to ignore the low, hungry growls of the animal within. Echoes, that was all he was hearing. The echoes of damnation.

'Fraternal Brother Uten has offered to lead us in our rites tonight,' Hierarch Eitan said, calling the rest of the Hermetic Brotherhood to order. There were seven of them gathered in the warehouse, preparing to conduct the Orison rites peculiar to their sub-cult.

There were dozens, perhaps hundreds of Orison fraternities within the Exorcists Chapter. Some were accessible by invite only, others were open to all, though membership of one never precluded membership of another. Each Orison had its own distinct ranks, modes of address and ways of meeting. Their purpose was, at the most basic level, to pool and share the vast wealth of esoteric and occult knowledge the Chapter had accumulated over the four thousand years of its existence. Most Orisons, however, fulfilled many more secret duties.

Uten had been a member of the Hermetic Brotherhood of the First Degree since joining Squad Eitan. The lector-sergeant was a senior member, known within the Hermetic Brotherhood as a hierarch. The Exorcists operated with a number of battlefield ranks – from brother-initiates to almoners, to those who had earned First Company laurels, lectors – but when in the presence of their Orison brethren, most used other designates unique to each sub-cult, adding further layers of mysticism.

Uten was thankful Hierarch Eitan had invited him to the Hermetic Brotherhood. He could conceive of no other way to quieten the echoes, not when they came on as strong as they had since the strike force had arrived on Fidem IV.

'We shall here conduct a Rite of Reconsecration with Uten, in fraternal brotherhood,' intoned Eitan.

'In fraternal brotherhood,' the other five members of the gathering repeated, Uten alone staying silent. He bowed his head in supplication, giving thanks.

The Hermetic Brotherhood was the largest Orison within the Hexbreakers. It consisted of the seven members then gathered in a circle in the centre of the abattoir, plus Brother-Initiate Pazu, who had volunteered to forego the evening's meeting to act as a sentinel upon the Sacred Ways, and Brother-Initiate Urhammu, who was fulfilling his role as the Keeper of the Outer Door, in this case the warehouse's main entrance, which he was to ritually guard throughout the meeting with drawn combat knife.

Each of those present had removed their helmet, confirming their identity to their fraternal kin. Deformities and scars that were normally strictly hidden, especially while fighting alongside other Imperial forces, were at last displayed openly. There were Brother-Initiate Balhamon's jet-black eyes, the red lesions of Brother-Initiate Hokmaz's latest pox outbreak, and the spiny growths that protruded and distorted Brother-Ritualist Kephras' skull.

Uten's own abnormalities were on show more than any of the other brethren present, for he had shed his upper armour. All he wore from the waist up was his pentacle, the occult metal token hanging from a chain around his neck. His massive, ruddy musculature was deformed around his lower arms by spikes of bone that protruded from his radius and ulna, their sharp tips glinting in the fading light. It had been almost a year since he had last hacked them off, and in that time they had once again pushed their way up through his flesh, as they always did, marring his body in the same way the animal within marred his broken soul.

Brother-Initiate Hokmaz rang the small silver bell he was carrying. Eitan stepped forward and raised his combat knife, its blade inscribed with a litany from the *Liber Exorcismus*.

'Do you accept this night's blood rite, Fraternal Brother Uten?' the hierarch demanded.

'I do,' Uten managed. His jaw was aching, a sure sign his fangs had started to distend, making speech difficult. He could hear the beast clearly now, its growls echoing around the stinking slaughterhouse.

Two more of the Exorcists stepped before Uten, Brother-Ritualist Kephras and Brother-Deacon Marduk. They too had drawn their blades. Uten held forth his arms for them, feeling a stab of shame as vicious as the spikes that perforated his skin. He was deformed, warped, forever marked by what he had once borne within his flesh. There was no denying the damnation that awaited him.

Kephras and Marduk began to cut out the spikes. The sound of the serrated lower edges of their knives sawing at the protruding bone filled the abattoir.

It was painful. Uten welcomed it, clenching his jaw, feeling his body as it reacted to the assault. Pain-nullifiers began to turn his forearms numb, while stimulants from his glands punched through to his fingers, making sure he could still flex and use them. Pain and injury could not stop a Space Marine, either in combat or out.

The other Exorcists not working on Uten directly had started to chant, the words low and indistinct at first, but rising as they found their cadence. Hokmaz rang his bell again, the soft chime a strange contrast to the ugly sawing.

Eitan stepped up to Uten. The hierarch's one eye, dark like most Exorcists', held his gaze levelly, the cold green glare of his other – a bionic optic – making Uten feel as though he was being target-locked.

'Do you accept the reconsecration of your flesh, fraternal brother?' Eitan asked.

'I do,' Uten snarled, struggling to enunciate between his wicked canines, spittle flecking his chin.

'*Tu subicis cicatricem carnis tuae?*' Eitan went on, switching to High Gothic. Uten gave his affirmation again.

Eitan clapped a gauntlet against one of Uten's pectorals and leaned in, carving the hooked tip of his dagger into the thick, craggy flesh of his chest, above where his pentacle hung. Blood welled reluctantly, Eitan having to cut deep and hard as he continued to murmur the Orison's arcane rites.

Uten still bore the scars of his last reconsecration, but they were faded now, almost illegible, their potency withered. Eitan reinscribed them with naked steel, and Uten latched on to the fresh pain, trying to use it to drive out the echoes.

It only made the beast angry. He could feel it in his skull, no longer merely prowling in the shadows but snapping and barking, raw and untameable. He shuddered, body going rigid, fighting to stay in control as the chanting of the Orison continued to rise and quicken.

The light had almost wholly died now, darkness stretching and deepening through the warehouse. Hokmaz's bell chimed again, though the Exorcist hadn't moved. Uten realised he was growling, but couldn't stop himself as his blood ran in glistening streaks down his torso and marked his pentacle.

The last of the evening's light blinked out. There was a juddering noise, a pained shriek of rusted motors, followed by a repetitive clattering, loud enough to pierce the haze that gripped Uten's thoughts. Dimly, he realised that the overhead conveyor belt holding the meat hooks had activated, seemingly of its own accord. It was moving.

The rotation brought the implements swinging through the midst of the Orison's formation, just past the heads of Eitan, Kephras and Marduk as they continued their bloody, brutal work, refusing to be distracted. By now Eitan's knife was carving lines into Uten's abdomen, working down his stomach, the blood running across his cuisses and poleyns.

He could endure it no more. It felt as though the beast within him was a heartbeat away from tearing itself free. It was as though he was reliving his initiation rites all over again.

Unable to stop himself, Uten reached up and tore one of the passing hooks free. Then, with a howl, he plunged it into his skull.

The Order of the Eagle Most High met in a place ill suited to their nature, but borne out of necessity. Anu and his two Eliminator brethren, Lakhmu and Dumuzid, made preparations for their rites in the basement of one of the taller hab-shacks on Pilgrim Town's war-flayed edge. The height of the structure had drawn Anu – it would have made for a tolerable perch – but the upper levels were currently acting as a billet for a platoon of Militarum Guardsmen. Rousting them from their slumber would have gone against the ideals of the Order of the Eagle Most High, for they sought the least disruption possible in all things. The fear, anger and confusion created by appropriating the block's highest floors would have been an ill start to their ritual.

Better to serve in the depths of the highest place than stand upon the highest point of the lowest. That was one of the eso-teric sayings of their Orison, and it seemed to apply here in abundance. So, the three snipers had descended, silent and unannounced, into the basement.

It was a miserable place, with a low ceiling and a single, bare lumen bulb. Two of the walls were little more than timber frames and packed dirt. The stairs creaked heavily, threatening to collapse with their weight, even though they descended one at a time. Anu had to brush cobwebs from his path and clear rat filth from the centre of the room.

'It is sufficient,' he announced after the rudimentary sweep. In truth, it was no worse than many of the living cells in the Basilica Malifex.

The trio went to work. Dumuzid removed three sticks of chalk from a small leather pouch sewn to the inside of his camo cloak and handed them out. They began to inscribe the necessary sigils in a triangular shape onto the floor. Lakhmu also dared to remount the stairs and make identical markings around the frame of the doorway at the top. They did not wish to be dis-turbed. More pointedly, they did not wish for anything to get out and disturb those sleeping above.

The soft clicking of the nubs of chalk seemed loud in the otherwise silent space.

When the sigils had been written out in full, Anu murmured the opening rites and bade his fraternal brothers join him in that night's act – prognostication.

'The armaments,' he intoned.

The Eliminators had brought their weapons. With great care, they laid the Mark III Shrike-pattern bolt rifles on the floor, each muzzle touching the stock of another, so that they formed a triangle in the room's centre. They then unclamped their combat knives and laid them within the triangle, blades pointing towards the middle.

There, Anu placed a small candle he carried in a pouch of his own and lit it with a striker.

The little flame flared into life. Anu raised the cowl of his cape and nodded to Lakhmu, who switched off the lumen hanging above, leaving the candle as the only source of light.

It felt as though more than mere illumination had been stolen from the room. Anu found himself breathless, and the darkness that swept in around them seemed to coil and twist, like the slow constrictions of some great black snake.

The candle flame flickered, but held.

They sat, each in front of their own rifle. Both Dumuzid's and Lakhmu's weapons had kill tallies notched along the stock, but Anu's possessed no inscriptions, no decorations. He refused to mar it with anything he considered unworthy. The only tally he would make would be when he made the perfect kill, and that had not yet happened.

It will never happen.

Anu ignored the whispered taunt, checking that his fraternal brothers were ready. Dumuzid and Lakhmu sat cross-legged, heads slightly bowed, features lost in the shadows of their cowls. Their cloaks, wrapped around them, seemed to twitch and blur in the candlelight, the cameleoline properties trying to drag them fully into the darkness at their backs.

'Detach the prognosticators,' Anu instructed.

The three reached to the occuscopes bolted to the tops of their rifles and began to unscrew them, breaking not only their calibration but the essence of the machine spirit that inhabited each weapon. To Anu, it felt as though he was conducting a cruel torture, like he was tearing sinew from bone. He could sense the spirit's pain, but he forced himself to carry on regardless, murmuring soothing words. Tonight, they needed the scopes for a higher purpose, higher even than dealing death to the Emperor's enemies.

When it was done and the machine spirits had settled, Anu spoke again. He uttered the Seven Unutterable Names, named the Nameless Master and spoke the Unspeakable Curse. Then, feeling his teeth aching and his throat burning, he ordered his fraternal brothers to begin their divination.

As he started to raise the targeter to his eye, he realised something.

There was someone standing in the dark behind him.

The presence triggered the potent reflexes of his transhuman body. Every heartbeat, every sinew and muscle, screamed at him to turn, turn and fight. Remaining seated in a position of vulnerability, not resisting a threat once it made its presence known, was anathema to his kind. It went against every second of hyper-indoctrination, every last muscle memory born out of a hundred thousand vicious, desperate bouts of combat. It was the true unthinkable act, and yet, Anu performed it.

He didn't turn. He remained sitting and ignored the presence, instead slowly and deliberately raising his scope to his eye.

And through it, he saw betrayal, death, and the final damnation of them all.

CHAPTER TEN

THEURGY

When Uten's soul had first been opened to the raging madness of the immaterium, it was a beast that had latched its claws into him, a warp entity that did not even bother with the barest veneer of civility. It was a slaughter animal, a bloodhound, one of Khorne's war dogs, rapacious kill-lust and relentless violence made manifest. Its snarling haunted him, its primal drives entwined now with what remained of his own being, so that he had lost where his own thoughts ended and the animal's began.

Uten could feel its claws raking at the cinders of his soul as he wrenched the meat hook free from the conveyor belt and dug into his skull. He struck the point into his forehead, hissing from between distended fangs as he dragged it in a semicircle, then from left to right. He tasted blood, bitter iron and salt, raw vitality.

None of the Hermetic Brotherhood of the First Degree moved to stop him. They continued their work, the chanting rising to a crescendo as Eitan slashed the last of the warding marks into his torso.

Uten felt his clarity returning as the hierarch did so, combining with the pain of the meat hook. He could sense his animalistic Never-brother's vulnerability then, feel how the hunter was becoming the hunted.

A beast it was, but it still had a name, one that its master could use to call it to heel. Uten knew it, and now he carved that blasphemous sigil into his scalp. He was its owner, at least until it was able to tear its way from the brass shackles that had bound it to the foot of the Blood God's throne. It had been there since he had ripped it from his soul, and it would remain there for a long time yet.

Here, in the material existence, its echoes would trouble him no more.

He lowered the hook in his great, trembling paws, then, with a final grunt, sent it skittering and clattering across the floor, away into the shadows. Eitan stepped back, Kephras and Marduk likewise, the bone spurs on his arms sawn down to nubs.

Uten took a slow breath, then let it shudder back out in the near darkness that gripped the abattoir. The hook belt had come to a halt, he realised. The Orison's chanting was at an end too. All was still and silent.

'*Consummatum est*,' Uten rasped.

'*Consummatum est*,' the others echoed dolefully, accompanied by one final ringing of Hokmaz's bell. *It is finished.*

And it was, if only for the time being. Uten flexed his powerful body and clutched at his bloodied pentacle, feeling fresh scabs stretch and break. He turned his forearm over as he inspected his brethren's efforts to purge him, not of true taint, but of its after-effects, of the ever-present resonations of the infernal. He found his thoughts clear and calm, more so than they had been since setting out from Banish. The beast had withdrawn. Its malignant, snarling presence was no more.

It would come back, as it always did. And Uten would be ready for it, as he always was.

At first, Anu's scope could tell him little. Its machine spirit had not yet recalibrated, and it refused to work in the basement's confines. The data it usually provided him with was scrambled, numbers either freezing or rapidly rising and dropping on repeat. He could see nothing.

Six heretics are coming to kill you.

Again, he ignored the voice. There was nothing and no one behind him.

He could hear Lakhmu and Dumuzid murmuring, though their voices were so low it was impossible for even his hearing to detect whether they were praying, invoking or simply responding to their own echoes.

He blinked, slowly twisting the occuscope's rune-etched magnification-adjustment ring, seeking clarity. Still, nothing.

Will you continue to ignore me forever, my lover? whispered the androgynous voice right into his ear, so close he could smell that addictive, sickly-sweet warp stink, the words slipping like shards of ice down his spine.

Despite himself, he shivered. The echoes were loud tonight. Too loud.

'Leave me,' he rasped quietly, lowering the scope.

The thing behind him crooned with theatrical sorrow and slipped a slender, white-fleshed arm around his broad shoulders.

But you know how I love keeping you company. You know how I require attention.

'You are not here,' Anu said. 'I banished you, and in the pits of your prince's lair you will remain, for six hundred and sixty-six years.'

Less a decade now, but who is counting?

'You will be, certainly.'

There was a slight giggle. The arm withdrew, thick, crustacean-like claws tugging playfully at his camo cape.

See, we are starting to have fun! I missed your sense of humour.

The ceiling creaked, causing dust to cascade down onto the seated Exorcists and making the lonely candle flicker. Anu detected voices above, real ones. He had no doubt the unfortunate Guardsmen who had been slumbering before now were being disturbed by night terrors and hellish visions of their own, oblivious to the presence of the three cultists casting their magicks beneath them. He knew he could not push them too far. The prognostication was already straying into territory he had not intended to visit.

'Be gone,' he snarled softly, his patience at an end. 'You are nothing but an echo, and you will inhabit this space no longer.'

How can you say that to me, my sweet? Were we not entwined once? Did we not share our flesh? Were our souls not bound as one? Didn't we enjoy a period of perfection together?

'No,' Anu said, staying resolutely in control. 'I ripped you out, like the rotting cancer you are. I will entertain you no more. I abjure thee. I cast thee out. By the blessings of the Nine Loyal Sons and the curses of the Nine Treacherous Prodigies, I command thee, depart from me!'

The thing hissed with anger and frustration, but he kept going, hammering it with invocations and catechisms, using them to order his own thoughts and fill them with the certainty and purpose his hollow soul lacked. Eventually there were no more taunting words, no more hisses and laughter. When an echo was cowed into silence, did it really still exist at all?

He realised the presence behind him was gone. There was now nothing but the dirt wall at his back, and a darkness that no longer coiled and twisted, nor leered malignantly over him. It was simply darkness, and nothing more.

He returned his attention to his scope.

Now it had answers for him. He caught a flicker of movement. With aching care, he adjusted the dials of the device, silently mouthing the foundational litanies of the Order of the Eagle Most High.

There it was again – a flash, an image of something that most certainly wasn't in the basement, nor even in the present. This time he was able to home in on it, resolve it, if only briefly.

He saw two figures, locked in combat. Both he knew instantly. One was the almoner-lieutenant, his knives in his fists, gleaming in the ruddy red warp light that suffused the scene. The other wore the blue battle plate of the Chapter's Librarius – Vey. His force sword was ignited, his cowl drawn up, but his eyes did not have the golden glimmer they wore when his psykening was in full flow. They were foul with the same butcher-light that filled the rest of the scope, making Anu's own questing eye ache.

The two Exorcists fought one another furiously, exchanging body blows rather than yielding. Anu experienced an unexpected shock at the sight. He could sense that an evil had taken root in the enlightened brother, yet how could that be? How could the warp again make a home in the burnt husk of any of them?

Vey raised his sword to strike Zaidu down. A premonition gripped Anu. He had the shot. All that remained was to take it.

The scope's data outputs had completely frozen now, digits reading a uniform set of zeros. He didn't need them though. The reticule was intact. That was all he required for perfection.

He fired. As he did so, his head snapped back from the scope, his eye feeling raw and bloodshot. He was panting, both hearts hammering.

The candle had gone out, plunging the basement into darkness. There was a despairing, terrible wail from somewhere above. As Anu's occulobe fought to locate and drag the merest hint of light into his vision, he realised something chilling.

The snapshot he had taken hadn't been at Vey. It had been directed at Zaidu.

CHAPTER ELEVEN

BROKEN THINGS

'Will you be joining us, fraternal brother?' Belloch asked Zaidu.

'I will not,' he replied, inclining his head slightly. 'There are matters I must attend to. Shipmaster Nazmund is currently conducting scans of the new target area, and I wish to communicate with the local Militarum forces to ensure they can provide sufficient support. You will act as First Blade in my absence.'

Belloch made the Orison's sign of affirmation, index and middle fingers making a small, swift cutting motion, before he withdrew. Zaidu suspected that his excuses were transparent, but that Belloch was also secretly relieved that his absence from the evening's rites had been confirmed. He was still a fraternal brother of the Blade and Skull, the Orison cult to which almost all Reivers in the Chapter belonged, but he had not attended any of their meetings since his promotion. It did not feel like his place any longer. He intended to relinquish his membership of the sub-cult, certain that Belloch would make a good First Blade for them once he had formally departed.

Relieved of the burden of fraternisation, he stalked out to the edge of the Sacred Ways. The Militarum had reoccupied most of the trench-lines, but the local brigade had agreed to leave a hundred-yard gap between the two neighbouring regiments, the 14th and 33rd Alban Thunder Corps, and allow the Exorcists to make the space their own. Most of the Hexbreakers had withdrawn into the nearest slum buildings to the rear to conduct their rites with a degree of privacy, but three volunteers from the Infiltrator squads, Pazu, Lamesh and Akkad, had chosen to forego their own meetings to act as sentinels. They were positioned in the forward observation posts, gazing out over the valley and the setting sun.

Akkad almost missed Zaidu's approach. The Sin Slayer had deleted his location marker from the shared display, wishing for a short period of privacy, and his footsteps were so quiet even his fellow Primaris failed to detect him until he was almost on him.

Akkad turned sharply, bolt carbine coming up. Zaidu halted, suppressing the instinctive combat response that came with facing a raised firearm.

'Forgive me, lieutenant,' Akkad said, immediately lowering the weapon. Zaidu assumed his apology was not for the levelled firearm but for failing to catch his presence sooner.

'Join your fraternity, brother-initiate,' Zaidu ordered him. 'I will take the watch here.'

Akkad offered a short genuflection and withdrew. Zaidu spent a moment looking over the sandbagged parapet of the observation post, at the sun setting in bloody red hues across the far slope, darkness already pooling in the valley's depths below.

The dusty expanse was about a mile from one eminence to the other, a cratered moonscape of old wounds and new.

He wondered briefly whether someone whose entire existence hadn't been whittled and honed down into a killing tool would have found the way the light blazed in orange and crimson over the rugged landscape beautiful. How would they have shared it with a sightless bystander? He fought for a description, but gave up quickly. There was no poetry in him, no words that didn't belong in a battle-cant. Was that simply because he was Adeptus Astartes? Or was it because, in ripping out the Never-born horror that now stalked this world, his soul had been burned and torn beyond repair?

He decided it did not matter. The low grumble of distant artillery was considerably more interesting than the sunset anyway. Zaidu spent a minute analysing it. While the valley lay quiet, seemingly resigned to the evening's creeping advance, the plain that flattened out further east was underlit by the flashing of discharges, playing counterpoint to the low thunder rising up to Pilgrim Town's northern edge. Both sides were contending there, unwilling to let darkness usher in an end to their rivalry. It might have sounded fearsome to an untrained, unenhanced ear, but Zaidu could detect a languidness to it. It was not a battle tempo, not a determined effort to break the foe. For the time being, it was mere formality.

Satisfied that there was no movement in the sector directly ahead, Zaidu detached the Occulus from his bolt carbine, murmuring a request for forgiveness for dividing the conjoined machine spirits from one another. He placed the scope on the parapet, facing out into no-man's-land, and checked his vambrace to ensure that it was still functioning and linked to his armour's auto-senses. Its advanced machine spirit would alert him to any movement in the valley, allowing him to momentarily shift his attention elsewhere.

He sat down on the fire step with his back to the trench wall and plucked a short length of flakboard away from where it had come loose. Then, laying it on his knees, he began to carefully unbind the prayer scrolls from around his forearms.

They had been damaged and bloodied by the day's combat, and while it was not unusual to leave them until they came apart, Zaidu wanted to take the opportunity to replace them. It felt like it might allow him to refocus. In truth, he suspected it was merely a learned response that would be of no true help.

He finished carefully undoing the last of the scrolls, then reached into the leather pouch at his hip and drew forth a fresh sheath of parchment. He replaced them in the pouch with the old ones, then took out a stylus and unclamped his right gauntlet, laying it on the fire step beside him. He flexed his hand, looking down at it, at the pale, scarred flesh, a contrast to the dark red ceramite that clad his forearm. Then, on impulse, he reached up and unclasped his death mask.

It felt unnatural to be without it. He found he could more clearly smell the unguents of his armour, the vellum of the pages beside him, the ink of the stylus. He caught the stink of fyceline and hot metal, drifting through the valley from the bombardment further east.

He ran his fingers lightly over his jaw, feeling the scales there, rough and craggy, wondering if they had changed lately. Two unnaturally long canines too, an unsubtle reminder of how he had been marked by the one he now hunted. He had torn the fangs out once, spitting blood, but they had only grown back.

He had been twisted by the taint of the Archenemy. But more, he supposed, by the Chapter, by science and artifice as ancient, arcane and unknowable as any Dark Tongue ritual. Both sides, fashioning him as a tool in their eternal struggle. Seeing how much they could twist and change before he broke.

He supposed others might have railed against such a fate. He found he did not care. There was not enough of him left to feel any anger at the injustice.

He put the leering mask back on, welcoming its suffocating grip, and smoothed out the new, blank scrolls over the flakboard on his knee. Then, taking up his stylus in his unarmoured hand, he began to reinscribe the esoteric marks of the *Liber Exorcismus*, slowly and carefully.

It did not take as long as he had anticipated. He bound the prayer scrolls around his forearms, parchment crackling softly, and then, satisfied that they were secure, checked his occuscope.

There was still no movement in the valley. An aerial dogfight was playing out to the west, but it may as well have been happening on another planet. Darkness had fallen, but its grip was not yet absolute enough for the Exorcists' purposes.

Another thirty minutes and it would be sufficient. Zaidu settled back down again on the fire step and stared silently down the trench, his eyes seeing nothing, his thoughts as empty as his hollowed-out soul.

The sword and the bowl.

Vey laid them both down reverently on his camo cape. He had made a rudimentary altar for them on an old set of pallets, lying discarded in an unoccupied rockcrete blockhouse overlooking one of the communications trenches now held by the Exorcists.

The two objects could hardly have looked more different. Kerubim was a magnificent example of the artificer's craft, a hand-and-a-half broadsword whose blued steel bore upon it flowing, millennia-old inscriptions of expulsion and sanctification. By contrast, the incantation bowl was a humble, rugged earthenware vessel that Vey had moulded himself. Within it were seventeen circular lines of text and symbols in the goetic script of Banish, spiralling from its upper edges down into its centre, where a crude little Calva Daemoniorum had been carved. It had to be continuously turned to be read, a design that was said to speak to the ever-changing nature of the warp, and the need for continual vigilance and activity among those who would stand against it. Every household among the goetical tribes of Banish owned an incantation bowl, and with good reason. The idea that – if properly inscribed and then turned upside down – they could be used to trap unclean spirits was not without merit.

Both the sword and the bowl were redolent with Vey's psychic presence. They were the tools he needed for this particular ceremony.

He spent a while settling himself, collecting his thoughts, testing what emotions he could find and gather against the cold and unfeeling metal of his mind. There was a strangeness in the air tonight, an uncanniness that seemed to worm its way into everything whenever the Orisons conducted their rites.

Vey had no intention of joining them. He was a member of numerous sub-cults, but besides the Broken Tower – the Orison composed almost entirely of the Chapter's Librarians – he never partook in fraternal rituals. He considered them an indulgence, nothing more.

The allure was understandable. They were a means for the Chapter to share its esoteric knowledge and provide a sense of commonality, of unity, of brotherhood.

That was the lie of it. In Vey's opinion, the ultimate reason for the Chapter's dizzying tangle of cults and clandestine societies, for the endless ranks and hierarchies, the strange rites and the secret phrases and gestures, was to fill a gap that could never be filled, to slake an unslakeable hunger. It was all a game, all theatre, designed to give a veneer of meaning and purpose to the empty vessels that had once been men. They were broken things, trying in vain to put themselves back together with ritualism and mystery.

Vey had seen the possession rites a hundred times over, and had played his part in most, cutting and burning with blades both physical and mental as he battled to remove the stain of the warp from the souls of his brothers. It was impossible to do so with precision, to act like a surgeon applying a scalpel with cold indifference. It was a struggle, a hacking match, wild and hot and desperate and passionate, and by the end of it there were only ragged remnants, charred scraps where once there had been a mind full of purpose. Now there was no purpose, no meaning and precious little feeling. All of the secret societies, shared ceremonies and invented hierarchies in the galaxy wouldn't be able to change that, wouldn't be able to give back the Exorcists what they had sacrificed. None of it could fill the empty place.

Once Vey had realised that, the so-called companionship of the fraternities had rung hollow. He did not begrudge his brothers their attempts at salving their souls, but their only use to him was the vast collection of written knowledge the Orisons collected between them. Besides that, he had no time for crude prognostication or combatting the echoes, those semi-sentient memories of daemonic infestation that continued to plague what little was left of many Exorcists' inner thoughts.

Admittedly, the echoes had been strong since arriving on Fidem. Hunting Neverborn was one thing, hunting a Broken One with such a close tie to their strike force's leader was another. He worried about Zaidu, worried that in asking him to head the pursuit he was putting a great strain on the lieutenant. He was bonded to the Sin Slayer, as much as there ever could be a true bond between Exorcists. He felt responsible for him, though he knew that was foolish. Zaidu was an experienced champion of the Chapter, a hunter amongst hunters, the Neverborn's bane. He had banished many, and would do it again when they finally caught up with the Red Marshal.

Vey only hoped that Zaidu was not drawn into giving too much. All the portents agreed – there would be no victory here without sacrifice, even more than the Chapter was accustomed to. If destroying the Broken One required the deaths of every member of the Hexbreakers, Vey was certain none of them would hesitate, but he worried that it was something more than that. He had started to feel out the connections – Zaidu's supposed vision, Caedus' strange movements, the presence of the Word Bearers and more besides – but it felt as if he was a young initiate, blindfolded in his first Orison ceremony, trying to discern and understand the cabbalistic rites being conducted in the dark around him.

He murmured an invocation of control, realising that his thoughts were wandering. Now was the time for focus. Eventually, satisfied that his mind was ready, he removed a glove and gauntlet and, with the skin of his hand bared, drew forth his tarot.

It was indulgent, he knew, for the auguries had been consulted enough already. He would permit himself this one last effort though, and admit to himself that he hoped it would show him something different.

He set the deck face down between and above the bowl and the sword, then rose and called to the Four Quarters, pacing slowly around the makeshift altar as he did so. He was reaching into the warp, settling and sanctifying the interior of the blockhouse, an act of the Major Arcana.

The temperature dropped. He felt the past surging up to greet him, like a shoal of ravenous aquatic beasts hurtling up out of black depths. He steeled himself, closing his eyes and slipping into his mystic witch-sight, fixating on its approach.

Thunder filled his ears, the familiar hammering of bolter fire. He reached out a hand, and found it resting on hot metal.

The thunder ceased. A heavy bolter sat on its tripod before him, the last of a series of hot brass casings from its last fusillade tinkling down to the floor beside his boots. Its barrel was smoking. It had just dealt death, and would do so again. It was a focal point of the emotions that had once transfused this place, a locus for the hopes and fears and triumph and panic of battle. The Guardsmen who had once occupied this blockhouse had vested their lives into the operation of the weapon. It seemed it had not let them down.

Vey made peace with the phantom machine spirit, and with the wraiths of its operators, murmuring to them, telling them that their duty was done, and that they need hold the trench-line no longer. The Emperor's Angels of Death had assumed that duty.

He opened his eyes. There was no longer a bolter at the blockhouse's vision slit, though as he shifted he found a few old, spent shell casings, rolling beneath his tread.

He paced back around in a circle, again addressing the Four Quarters, finishing the sealing ritual. Then, satisfied, he sat down before his makeshift altar and allowed his bare hand to rest upon the tarot, communing with their familiar energies.

Like the incantation bowl, he had inscribed the deck himself while he had still been a novice Lexicanium under the tutelage of Epistolary Machen, spending weeks at a time in his cell in the Basilica Malifex, learning patience and care. The same deck had guided him faithfully ever since.

He took a breath and turned over the first card. There, drawn in simple black ink, was a cloaked figure, slender, stooped. There was a suggestion that it was not standing, but rather hovered just a fraction off the card's bottom. The only colour on the face was gold, used to pick out the eyes glaring malevolently from beneath the hood. Four eyes, forming a diamond.

The Daemon.

Vey collected himself and drew the next. It showed one of the great stony pinnacles of the Basilica Malifex, bristling with gargoyles and gothic relief. A stylised bolt of lightning, picked out in a dash of red, was striking the uppermost finial.

The Tower.

Vey was filled with a sense of inevitability, but pushed through it. He had told Zaidu enough times that the future was never set, and he believed that. The many skeins of reality knew no master, tolerated no certainty, as they coiled and writhed about one another, twisting new hereafters from the raw fodder of the present. Some threads, however, ran straighter and truer than others, and Vey knew he would finally have to accept that as he drew the third card.

It showed a chalice, fashioned in the likeness of a skull, coloured with a streak of gold, its eye sockets highlighted by red rubies.

The Cup.

Vey closed his eyes and bowed his head. He understood. All that remained was to accept it.

Then, mastering himself, he uttered the Eighth Catechism of Thanks and ended the reading.

It did not matter what fate intended for him. In his own way, he was as resolute as Zaidu. They would find the Broken One, they would split its body asunder, and one way or another, they would make sure the Neverborn filth within could never again threaten the Chapter.

CHAPTER TWELVE

THE UNKNOWN WAYS

Zaidu called an end to the Orison rites and ordered his squad leaders to assemble.

He met them next to a boarded-up wayside shrine in one of the communication trenches. After a brief, ritualised call-and-response inquiring after the success of their separate rituals, he briefed them on the crossing they were about to make.

'Combat squads or less, I'll leave it to your discretion,' he told Haad and Eitan, the Infiltrator sergeants. 'We'll go over in three sections, left, right and centre. The Reivers will separate and take point for each group. Fraternal Brother Anu, you will split your Eliminators likewise and bring up the rearguard. Clear?'

The sergeants gave their confirmation.

'Questions?'

'Will the Militarum be called upon to provide support?' Haad asked.

'They will. I have not reached out to them yet because I do not trust the security of their communications channels. I will send a communiqué to the area commander just before we step off advising him to keep his artillery muzzled. Once we make the far side of the valley, it is my hope they will mount a diversionary assault. That should go some way to covering our penetration.'

'Have Shipmaster Nazmund's scans offered any more intelligence on the location of the Broken One?' Belloch asked.

'They have not,' Zaidu admitted. 'Nor are we sure of the location of the Word Bearers, though judging by the activity and the energy spikes the *Witch-Bane* has detected, it seems certain that Fort Deliverance is their base of operations.'

'And we do not know if the heretics have captured the Broken One and taken it there?' Belloch pressed.

Rather than offer a further answer, Zaidu looked to Vey. The Librarian was standing off to one side, hooded.

'The Broken One is still close,' he said. 'That is the only certainty I can provide. If the heretics do not have it yet, they will soon. Unless we find it first.'

'Then it could not be clearer,' Zaidu said. 'Once we have infiltrated Deliverance Town we will either pick up the thing's warp stench or be in a better position to intercept the heretics should they try and take it. There is no doubt they are hunting it too.'

'What of its movements?' Eitan asked. 'It is surely not roving the planet's surface randomly? What does it hope to achieve?'

'We know the Neverborn controlling the Broken One has come to this place specifically,' Zaidu said. 'It is bonded with this world. We believe it seeks redress in its master's eye for past defeats. But where it is going at this exact moment, we do not know.'

'I suspect Caedus seeks to free itself from the Broken One, and the other Neverborn still inhabiting it,' Vey added, daring to utter the daemon's name aloud. 'It is still bound to some degree, and still weak. Being here on Fidem, however, shedding blood and transmuting defeat into victory, will strengthen it. If it can find a way to break the last of its fetters, it may be able to manifest its own warp form in realspace. If that is the case, it could become too powerful to stop. There is the possibility of an outright daemonic incursion.'

'I will send it to oblivion before that,' Zaidu said, his tone brooking no further debate. 'Ready your squads.'

The Hexbreakers slipped down into the valley. Zaidu took the lead once more, though he deigned to have a point partner from Squad Belloch with him, Nabua. He was the youngest of the strike force's Reivers, only recently initiated, and the first to have joined since Zaidu's promotion. He did not know him, could not yet appreciate how he thought, how he fought, and for that reason he wished to keep him at his side and learn from him, as he hoped Nabua might in turn learn something of him. He would not let any say that he was too consumed by the hunt to show leadership.

After a long, cloudless day, the night was overcast, which suited the purposes of the Exorcists well enough. The blackness that lay at the valley's bottom seemed almost absolute. Zaidu, with Nabua to his left and one step behind, pulled himself easily out over the lip of the Sacred Ways and down the slope, moving low and fast. The marker icons representing his brothers spread across his vambrace display like newborn constellations, following in his wake. Out, into the dark.

The terrain of the valley was less conducive to the plan. The eastern bulk of Fidem IV's primary inhabited continent tended towards being arid, especially at this part of its year cycle. The soil was hard, dry and dusty, and what tough undergrowth there was had been largely wiped out since the recommencement of hostilities. The landscape was cratered with shell holes both old and new. The Exorcists would have to use that to their advantage.

Zaidu had already mapped out the route the central of the three prongs would use, configuring it with the aid of his Occulus. He dropped down into the first of the foxholes along the way, pausing for just a moment to check that the rest of the strike force were still on the move. Satisfied, he carried on.

Nabua kept up and said nothing, two traits Zaidu admired. They ghosted around a burnt-out halftrack, a new wreck. The remnants of Caedus' first conflict, the War of the Faith's Founding, had long been seized as scrap or turned into sacred artefacts. Zaidu doubted so much as a single bullet casing remained undisturbed in the faithful's desperate quest for a connection to past Imperial glories. All that remained of those days out here were the ghosts of the old shell holes, and scars like the Sacred Ways.

Now those who gave up everything for passage to Fidem IV would find new reliquiae of battle. That, or this world would be bathed in blood, and the Sacred Ways would become arteries for the warping madness that had once been denied and driven out.

They hit the valley bottom – a riverbed, long ago dried up and deformed by the brutal ministrations of heavy artillery. Zaidu again made a short pause to ensure the advance was proceeding. There was no comms chatter, either on the Hexbreaker vox-net or on wider Imperial channels. The night was quiet. He felt a rare stirring of emotions. Anticipation, hunger. They were closing in.

He glanced up briefly, but the cloud cover was too heavy to discern the constellations, or the brighter, newer stars of the warfleets that faced each other in an orbital stalemate. For the time being, the *Witch-Bane* would be unable to provide detailed scans of what they were advancing into.

That did not trouble Zaidu. The hunt was well under way, and he needed no further guidance.

I chose well when I fought my way into your soul.

Zaidu froze, just as he had been about to rise up out of the desiccated riverbed. Nabua looked at him questioningly, but seemingly was not yet bold enough to ask aloud the reason for his sudden stillness.

He had heard an echo. He was rarely troubled by them. Yet there it had been, that low, beastly growl, the voice of the monster that had once bitten and torn away so much of his soul. The same creature he had come here to cast out again. Caedus. It sent cold ice along his back and made his secondary heart kick in. His armour pinged, warning it was about to hit him with stimms, thinking he had dropped into an abrupt combat situation and needed the spike.

He rejected it and made himself move off again without a word. He had barely reached the base of the incline towards Deliverance Town, however, before he caught a distant thump, like a single blow struck against a great bass drum somewhere out in the distance.

The Hexbreakers' vox-network lit up with the first words of the night.

'Artillery, outgoing.'

The first shell hit the edge of Deliverance Town about a hundred yards beyond the reserve lines of the Archenemy-infested Sacred Ways, scarring the crest of the ridge. Like the other Exorcists in the valley, Uten had detected the sound of the discharge and the scream of the shell as it arced overhead, all before the brief flare of light and the dull, battering report of the strike reached him.

He knew that was just the start. Seconds later, the darkness above was full of the passage of steel, and the dusty slopes rang and shook to the pounding of a bow wave of explosions that ripped across the valley's northern rise.

Uten felt a stirring of frustration he suspected was mirrored by every other Hexbreaker around him, though all were too disciplined to voice it. The Guard had begun their barrage too soon. Uten and his immediate combat squad, consisting of Kleth, Nazaratus and Almoner Hasdrubal, had not even made it to the bottom of the valley yet.

The response to the sudden bombardment was predictable. Heretic artillery across the ridgeline began to return fire.

'Now we're in the middle of it,' Kleth said, seemingly without humour, as a wall of flame and smoke tore its way into existence above the Exorcists, both in front and behind.

'*We push through,*' came the Sin Slayer's voice over the vox.

That was good enough for any of them. Uten signalled for the advance to continue, maintaining contact with the leading edge of the left-hand prong, being led by two of the Reivers, Makru and Azzael. They hit the valley floor, pounding across what Uten realised was likely the remnants of an old watercourse, and beginning the drive up the opposite slope.

It felt as though the strike force had been flung into a cauldron in the midst of the Chapter's smelter workshops. Both ridgelines were ablaze with continuous detonations, fire and smoke broiling out and down the slope towards them. Uten could feel the valley's pain shuddering up through his boots. In just a few minutes the night's quiet had been utterly annihilated.

He adjusted to account for the sensory assault, deleting the worst of the barrage, though even with his helmet on there was a dull, underlying pounding, as though he was hearing the shelling from deep underwater. The sounds he needed – the scuff of boots, the purr of servos, his own breathing and the heartbeats measuring out a steady rhythm between them – all remained crisp and sharp.

Abruptly, he detected something else – the timbre of the

passing shells had changed. They were no longer arcing overhead on their way to the Imperial trench-lines the Exorcists had left behind.

He had time to crouch and bark a warning. Then the very world itself exploded around him.

The heretics had switched their bombardment from the opposite ridgeline to the base of the valley. That became immediately apparent when shells began dropping in amongst the Hexbreakers rather than screaming overhead.

'Push into them,' Zaidu snarled into the vox as the first explosions sent a rippling punch across the slope. They were committed now. Far safer to drive into the jaws of the enemy, trusting to battle plate and physiology, than withdraw or, worse, hesitate.

Nabua was still with him as they bounded like loping predators up the far side of the valley. It was already clear enough that the enemy had spotted them, hence the shift in the barrage, but it was further confirmed as small-arms fire – autogun hard rounds and las-bolts – began to whip down towards them. They were ill aimed, most passing overhead, the shooters inexperienced and firing half-blind into the shell-shot dark. Zaidu paid them no more heed than a cloud of flies in the Banish swamplands. All that mattered was getting the Hexbreakers out from under the artillery's hammer.

That was Zaidu's last thought before the shell hit. His mind, with all its mid-combat razor keenness, detected it just as it came howling down out of the dark, slow enough for him to be able to register, but too fast for him to otherwise react before it struck and detonated. In that moment he knew only a cold sense of resignation.

It went off, and all was fire and fury.

Zaidu, his mind incapable of being shocked or stunned,

experienced every moment of it. His armour registered six immediate hits, two serious penetrations, four minor, as shrapnel from the blast punched into him ahead of the shockwave. His right pauldron, plastron, right vambrace and right greave all lit up on his vambrace display, and he felt multiple jabs of pain, there and gone again as his body brutally suppressed the injuries.

Fire washed over him, the heat flash igniting the fresh prayer scrolls on his right arm but otherwise failing to scorch the ceramite. Almost simultaneously, the blast lifted and threw him amidst a hail of dirt, and he experienced the briefest sense of dislocation before he struck the ground, instinctively rolling into the impact.

All of that he had more or less anticipated in the fraction of a second before the shell went off. What he had not expected was that the ground, when he returned to it, would not be solid.

He was still falling amidst shifting earth. At first, he thought he was simply rolling back down the slope, and tried to grab a fistful of soil with the hand not still clamped to his bolt carbine's stock. It disintegrated in his grip, purchase elusive.

He locked out his armour's servos, slowing the fall just as he hit something more solid. A weight of earth pressed against him, and he drove himself up off the ground and through it, realising if he did not that he was about to be buried alive.

He forced his way out of the avalanche, dragging himself to where the soil was firm enough to stand. He ignored the blinking damage report his armour had already compiled, instead driving his senses into his new surroundings, hunting for any possible threat looking to use his disorientation to strike.

There was nothing – nothing but dust and darkness and old bones.

He realised he was in a tunnel. The shell strike had caused a partial collapse of the slope's soil, and he had come down amidst it. He was now standing with a mound of earth and an open gouge in the ceiling to his back and an empty corridor of packed dirt and old timber struts ahead, littered with scraps of cloth and ancient human remains.

Nabua was with him. Zaidu noticed his marker beacon flashing on his wrist, and turned just as the Reiver punched a hand up through the settling avalanche. He leaned in and clasped the gauntlet, hauling the Exorcist free. Fresh soil cascaded from his armour, and he shook it from his pauldrons, gorget and helm like a dog.

'Damage report,' Zaidu ordered. The Reiver took a split second to assess before responding.

'Negligible. One minor injury – left thigh. Auto-senses online. Power active. Servos and actuators functioning at ninety-eight per cent.'

Zaidu did his own check. Several shards of shrapnel were still lodged in his battle plate. Two had gone further, punching into his right calf and side. Both wounds felt numb already, a good sign. He probed briefly at them, establishing that the metal was too deep to extract without removing the relevant plates but would not interfere with his movements. His armour was no more hurt than he was, auto-senses still functioning at full, power regulation undisturbed. He pulled away and discarded the charred remains of the prayer scrolls still clinging to his right vambrace.

'Where are we?' Nabua wondered aloud.

'An adit tunnel, from the previous conflict,' Zaidu answered, having already considered the question himself. 'There are likely all manner of subterranean works running beneath the battle-field. Over time it seems the pilgrims forgot about their existence. It is something I should have considered before now.'

'Returning to the surface may be difficult,' Nabua noted. Zaidu had already assessed that problem too. The cave-in caused by the shell strike had left a scar above them. The night was visible, underlit by the flashes of the shell strikes that were still shuddering the earth surrounding them and causing dirt to cascade down from the fresh gash in the soil. It didn't look, however, as though it would be possible to climb back up the mound of fallen earth and reach the edge of the opening above.

They tried, but swiftly realised it was futile. The mound was still shifting and wouldn't support their weight – they simply sank down into it while hardly gaining any height.

Zaidu's frustration flared, but only briefly. Tunnels below the valley opened up a new avenue of approach, assuming they were still largely intact.

He checked his vambrace display. It remained linked to the rest of the strike force above. He tried the vox, finding the command channel chopped but intelligible.

'Almoner-lieutenant, are you unharmed?' came Eitan's voice. 'Your marker went offline briefly, as did Brother Nabua's.'

'A shell caused part of the slope to collapse,' Zaidu explained brusquely. 'We are in a tunnel beneath the valley. There is no immediate means of egress.'

'Can we provide assistance?' Haad asked.

'No, not in the midst of this barrage. Gain the ridgeline and proceed as planned. Eitan has command until further notice, but heed the Brother-Librarian's advice. We will rejoin as soon as we are able.'

The markers representing each of his squad leaders projected above his vambrace blinked with confirmation. Zaidu looked down the tunnel, listening for echoes, in his head or otherwise. There were none, but there was something else. The shadows ahead stirred. He realised that, despite the stillness, both his hearts were driving hard. The darkness was calling, and his blood was answering.

Nabua was standing silent, waiting for orders. The strobe lighting from the barrage, coming down through the crack above, flickered over the dust-marred grin of his helm's skull visor.

'We continue the advance,' Zaidu told him. 'Be mindful of traps. It looks as though this place has lain undisturbed for a very long time.'

'Affirmative,' Nabua said.

Together, they went forward into the shadows.

CHAPTER THIRTEEN

TRENCH ASSAULT

Uten sat up as fire and dirt rained down around him.

A shell had struck the ground just a few yards to his left, throwing him across the slope and riddling his shoulder, side and leg with shrapnel. He did a swift damage assessment as he regained his feet. Armour functioning. Unpenetrated.

It would have been considerably worse if Brother-Initiate Kleth hadn't taken most of the blast.

The Infiltrator had risen too, but Uten didn't need the amber marker on his visor to see that his brother was injured. His left arm was half detached, blood drizzling down onto the ragged, smoking earth.

Uten triggered a request for Gela to join them.

'We must keep moving,' Kleth said, voice showing no indication of any pain. 'I will not have us pause beneath this.'

That was true enough. Uten stayed at Kleth's side as he began to press up the slope again, clutching his left arm against his breastplate with his right.

The whole ridge seemed to be on fire now. The heretics were hammering their own side of the valley, turning it into a maelstrom of scything metal, and small-arms were adding to the hail. Uten felt autogun rounds jar off his pauldron and reactor pack, a lot of the shots seemingly going high. He stooped slightly as he climbed, making Kleth do the same.

He wasn't the only casualty. Two others, Lamesh of Squad Haad and Urhammu of Squad Eitan, were both blinking yellow on the shared heads-up display. At least they were all still moving. The Reivers in the vanguard were now less than a hundred yards out from the crest.

They were going to make the heretics pay for this.

Another shell came howling down like an enraged Neverborn, striking just in front of the two. Uten's armour registered the heat of the blast, and he felt the ringing impact of more hits. No lasting damage done. He urged Kleth down into the smoking crater the explosion had ploughed up, then gripped his pauldron, making him pause. One of the markers representing a member of the strike force was cutting across the slope towards them, rather than driving on up it.

Gela appeared over the lip of the freshly gouged foxhole a few seconds later, the Helix Adept skidding down through the dirt to join them. He performed a swift appraisal of the mangled meat and bared bone of Kleth's arm.

'It will need to come off,' he said. 'Immediately.'

'Do it,' Kleth said.

Uten covered the pair from the lip of the crater as Gela extended and activated the short, diamond-edged buzz-saw that formed part of his helix gauntlet. It let off an ugly shriek as it met the toughened bone of Kleth's forearm. Uten was reminded for a second of the slow, brutal sawing of combat knives into bone spikes.

He almost missed Dumuzid. The Eliminator materialised like a phantom from out of the fire-shot darkness behind them, camo cape drawn around him and hood raised. Uten knew what his appearance presaged. They were now at the rear of the left-most advance. They had fallen behind.

Dumuzid said nothing by way of greeting, merely glancing at Gela as he amputated Kleth's arm before joining Uten on the upper edge of the foxhole. The light of a nearby detonation gleamed along the length of his Shrike rifle as he slid it into a firing stance.

The field of fire was too congested and the range too long for Uten's bolt carbine, but not so for Dumuzid. There was a crack as he fired, threading a shot through the smoke and the dark, the dirt and dust and shrapnel, past the brethren further up the slope. The Eliminator gave no indication of whether he had struck his target. Uten did not doubt for a second that he had.

The timbre of the buzz-saw changed. Uten glanced back to see Gela severing the last reluctant steel-coil tendons of Kleth's arm. Blood glistened darkly in the flaring illumination, but the stump had already flash-clotted, forming a glassy black sheen.

Gela grasped the bone protruding from the arm he had cut off and pulled on it with a grunt, dragging the limb from the vambrace and gauntlet. He then discarded the severed meat and handed the pieces of valuable battle plate to Kleth, who mag-clamped them to his waist.

'My thanks, brother,' he said to Gela.

'You are reading as combat-effective?' the Helix Adept asked, retracting the saw and inserting his gauntlet's analysis prong into Kleth's remaining vambrace port, taking a more detailed reading of his vitae signs than the ones they shared over the display.

'High-yield stimm injection, glanding suppressants,' Gela carried on as he ran his assessment. 'Blood-loss levels are suboptimal, but your systems are working to counter that. No sign of physical shock. Armour is reacting tolerably well to the damage.'

'I will be fine,' Kleth said stoically.

'I'm giving you an additional stimm charge to be sure,' Gela said, jabbing an injection sleeve into the arm port and stabbing the plunger. 'I hope you did not overly favour your left hand in combat.'

'We'll get you an augmetic back on board the *Witch-Bane*,' Uten said bluntly.

'We need to catch up,' Kleth responded as Gela retracted the needle.

'Carry on, brethren,' Dumuzid advised, not taking his eye from his scope. 'I will guard your passage.'

'Lead on, Brother Uten,' Gela said.

He needed no further encouragement. As the crack of Dumuzid's rifle rang out again, Uten surged up from the crater and on up the slope.

Anu made a new perch for himself just within the barrage curtain, atop the wreckage of a Guard Chimera troop transport that had been knocked out during some forgotten advance months before. The main part of the right side of the assault, which he had been following, had discovered what looked like a small gulley or channel cut by a dried-up stream and was using it to knife up towards the ridgeline. But following it meant those in front were obscuring Anu's view of the enemy-held lines. He had broken off to the right, seeking a more optimal line of sight.

The situation was more challenging than it had been at the scrap church back in the sprawl. Besides the fact that his targets were above him rather than below, the bombardment was still falling barely a hundred yards behind, and the Imperial shelling was likewise battering at the rear of the Sacred Ways ahead, parabolas of fyceline and steel scribing out destruction all around. Star-shells had started to burst above the ridge too, throwing everything into stark, aching black-and-white contrast. Anu's scope adjusted to compensate, though it couldn't give him as clear a view as before – he suspected it was still wounded following the Orison rites.

He welcomed it all. Adversity brought out perfection. He settled himself atop the Chimera's wreckage, lying flat, ignoring the fury of fire and steel shaking everything around him. Settling his goggles, he linked them to his scope and scanned the ridgeline.

There was a pillbox covering the stream gulley, but the banks of the channel obscured most of it from his current position. He would need to move to rectify that, or any heavy weapon housed within the fortification would have an arc of fire straight down the throat of the right-hand assault. Before shifting, though, he blinked into the occuscope views of Dumuzid and Lakhmu, the sights of their weapons linked.

His goggles showed him what Dumuzid was seeing first. The Eliminator was covering a trio of Infiltrators, Uten, Kleth and the Helix Adept, Gela, as they pushed forward from the foxhole they had been occupying. Kleth looked injured. Anu got a view of the top of the ridge, of a headshot Dumuzid made with a high-explosive bolt-shell. The heretic's skull burst, fragmentation and shards of bone injuring those to either side of him. Dumuzid chambered a fresh round and fired again. His technique was good. Anu had no need to act as a remote spotter for him.

He switched to Lakhmu, discovering him taking out any enemy who dared raise themselves above the parapet along a fifty-yard stretch of the Sacred Ways covering the centre of the attack. A moment's assessment showed that the undulations of the crater-scarred earth meant he would need to get closer to secure an angle on an autocannon emplacement pinning the assault's leading edge. Seeming to sense Anu's scrutiny, Lakhmu hefted his rifle and began to push up.

As he went, Anu caught a flash of blue amidst the light and dark. Vey had shifted across from the right flank to the centre. He found that strangely relieving. He had not told anyone outside of the Orison of his occuscope augury. He still hoped what he had seen was a mistake, a misinterpretation, but he had never experienced a vision so clear. It unsettled him in ways he was unaccustomed to. Unlike Vey, he was no psyker, no seasoned prognosticator. The Orisons of the Order of the Eagle Most High rarely rendered up anything so unequivocal. Should he tell the Sin Slayer? Or even Vey himself?

All Exorcists knew that prophecy was a delicate matter. Doing anything might tip the scales one way or the other, but doing nothing could be worse. He needed more time to think on it, to meditate and tease out the strands of possibility, but that was impossible. They were in the midst of the hunt, committed to one of the most desperate operations the Hexbreakers had ever known. The fate of the Chapter, and more, rested on finding and terminating the Broken One. How that would make traitors of Zaidu or Vey – or himself – he could not yet imagine.

He caught the sound of a heavy bolter kicking off, a potent roar underscoring the drumbeat of ongoing explosions. He left Lakhmu and switched back to his own scope's view. The pillbox's defenders had opened fire on the Exorcists advancing up the gulley. His brethren would have need of him.

Securing his rifle, he rolled off the Chimera's roof. He met the earth below in a crouch and then set off at a sprint for the gulley's edge.

* * *

The Hexbreakers pushed in under the barrage curtain, but found themselves momentarily checked just short of the enemy's positions. The slope was being swept by small-arms and man-portable heavy weapons. The only blessing was that previous Imperial artillery strikes had gouged up the earth around them even more so than in the valley below, providing sufficient cover as the strike force kept working its way forward.

Vey had been with the right-hand prong of the advance, but had switched to the centre when Zaidu was cut off. The priority was to break through the enemy's frontage and regroup. He intended to support those efforts as closely as possible.

The most immediate impediment was an autocannon emplacement with an arc of fire that covered a good deal of the centre of the Exorcists' advance. It was of a heavy enough calibre to make charging into its teeth a last resort.

Vey dropped down into the foxhole at the leading edge of the assault, several rounds from the autocannon clanging forcefully from his right pauldron. Hokmaz and Nizreba, from Squads Eitan and Haad respectively, had taken point on the central push once Zaidu and Nabua had dropped out. In Vey's experience that was rarely a good thing. The two bickered interminably, their antagonism one of the few to rear its head within the Hexbreakers across multiple assignments and warzones. They came from rival Orisons, the Hermetic Brotherhood of the First Degree in Hokmaz's case and the Inner Circle of Tranquil Enlightenment in Nizreba's. Disputes between Orisons were rare and frowned upon, but in truth Vey suspected their opposition ran deeper than clashing cult ideologies.

Sure enough, Hokmaz was complaining about Nizreba's aim as he fired towards the autocannon emplacement while Hokmaz reloaded his own bolt carbine. The two at least had the sense to cease their prattle when Vey appeared.

'You can't silence it?' the Librarian asked, referring to the enemy weapon.

'They keep recrewing,' Hokmaz said between shots. 'They're starting to heap up the bodies around it to provide additional cover.'

'Dedicated,' Vey mused, expecting nothing less. The honest, decent farm peoples of the Irenoth System were long gone, if not in body then in mind and soul.

'Cease fire,' he instructed Hokmaz. 'Let me work.'

The Infiltrators shifted to the bottom of the foxhole, making room for Vey to take their place. The autocannon's thudding discharge soon rang out again, sending bullets cracking low overhead or ploughing into the dirt before him. The Librarian wiped lingering concerns about the incoming fire from his armour's alerts, then placed a single finger against the centre of his brow.

The temperature in the foxhole plunged. Hokmaz and Nizreba exchanged a glance. Vey removed the digit, and the golden light of his eyes gleamed from beneath his hood.

His warpsight shone upon the Archenemy emplacement. It was a sandbagged bastion in the Sacred Way's front line. He could see the slaughter done by Hokmaz and Nizreba's controlled fire, and the scrambling efforts of the heretics to keep their gun working. They understood that it was all that was keeping the Exorcists at bay.

Some seemed to sense Vey's ethereal sight upon them, crying out in fear and covering their eyes. The rest were too busy reloading the autocannon as the last of its current belt ran dry, spent bullet casings splashing down into the blood pooling in the bastion's bottom.

Vey would permit their insolence no longer. It was a simple enough thing to reach into their thoughts and draw out their current, most immediate fear – that their weapon would jam and malfunction just when they needed it most.

He made sure that fear was realised, at least in their minds. A cry went up, several of the heretics scrabbling desperately at the feed port, another beginning to unscrew the barrel, scolding her hands on the hot metal as they all tried to find the source of the mechanical malfunction Vey had just caused them to collectively imagine. He heard the echoes of Amazarak's sick chuckling in the back of his own thoughts, the phantom presence of the Change-daemon delighting in such fatal trickery.

'Go now,' he told Hokmaz and Nizreba.

The two Exorcists rose and closed the last hundred yards across the steel-furrowed earth. Enfilading small-arms fire couldn't stop them as they stormed into the bastion, knives making sure the autocannon and its crew would never defy the Hexbreakers again.

With a sigh of release, Vey shut off his witch-sight and dragged his consciousness back away from the precipice. Then, he rose and followed, unlocking Kerubim as he went.

The trenches lay before them. Now the real killing could begin.

A heavy bolter round had chewed a chunk out of Brother-Initiate Shemesh's thigh.

'I can go on,' he insisted as Belloch crouched with him behind a boulder unearthed by a nearby shell strike, assessing the damage.

'Yes, but you cannot lead,' he told his fellow Reiver, tone brooking no argument. 'Remain here and join Eitan and the Infiltrators as they push up.'

The right-hand side of the assault had worked its way into a narrow channel that ran from the ridgeline down to the valley's bottom. Belloch assumed it had once been a stream that fed into the river below, but it had long dried up. The dusty passage offered a good angle of attack, but for the fact that the heretics were aware of it. There was a pillbox at the far end, built from sandbags filled with rockcrete and providing protection for a heavy bolter that was firing straight down the gulley's final approach.

Belloch had considered popping smoke, but the gunners didn't particularly need to aim. All they had to do was keep the bolts slashing down the channel. He had a more direct solution in mind anyway.

Shemesh began to protest, but Belloch ignored him. He reached out to Anu over the vox, knowing the Eliminator sergeant would be nearby.

'Do you have a shot?' he asked.

'I'm about to,' came the reply. 'But I cannot guarantee the weapon's destruction, and they will quickly recrew it.'

'Keep them off it. Thirty seconds.'

'You will block my line of sight.'

'Just tell me when to drop.'

'Affirmative. Taking it.'

'Stay,' Belloch reiterated to Shemesh, as though the younger Reiver was an overaggressive pup. He caught the sound of Anu's rifle firing from back down the gulley, followed by the heavy bolter's abrupt silence.

He broke out from behind the boulder and began to race up the dry riverbed, boots beating up dust, actuators whirring viciously as he pushed his body from zero to maximum in just a few heartbeats.

The pillbox lay ahead, framed against the explosions from the Imperial artillery still ripping into the rear echelons behind. His preysight pierced the structure's firing slit, catching movement in the darkness within as the heretics scrambled to recrew their gun. His hearing picked out the sound of the heavy bolter's slide being hauled back.

He threw himself to the ground.

The new gunner managed to squeeze off a single round before Anu's next shot added his brains to those of the first gunner already pasting the pillbox's interior. Belloch heard both shots pass over him in opposite directions. He was up again as soon as he registered the kill.

Again, the heretics tried desperately to recrew their weapon, but they were too late. Belloch pounded up the last few yards and moved to the right of the firing slit. He snapped a choke grenade from its mag point at his hip, broke the ignition clip with his thumb, and tossed it inside.

A fragmentation grenade would have killed all those within, but any reserve waiting outside could have rushed in and remanned the heavy weapon when he moved off. Filling the place with caustic smoke would incapacitate anyone who breathed it for at least the next two minutes. That was more than enough time.

The Reiver sergeant shifted to the right and dropped down into the adjoining trench, duckboards splintering beneath him. He was met by a clutch of heretic infantry who just stared in horror at the skull-faced giant. He took the first with his knife and gunned down the remainder with a trio of short pistol bursts, prioritising speed, then turned the corner to his left, into the rear of the pillbox.

A pair of cultists ran directly into him, choking and blinded by the fumes broiling from inside. They bounced off, and Belloch ended them quickly before moving on to cull those still inside. He then stood for a moment, wreathed in burning smoke as he voxed the rest of the squads following him.

'Threat neutralised. Advance.'

He checked via the tactical display to make sure Shemesh was moving up freely with the others, then knocked the heavy bolter off its tripod and broke it under his boot for good measure.

Then, not waiting for the rest of the strike force to arrive, he stalked out into the trench works, hunting for fresh prey.

Uten advanced to the leading edge of the assault's left side, into the foxhole Makru and Azzael were occupying. The Reivers glanced at him as he joined them, their skull masks grinning.

'Twin-linked heavy stubber,' Makru said. As though to underscore his words, there came the chattering report of the weapon in question, sending rounds zipping over their heads.

'Charge it,' Uten said. It wasn't a suggestion. He could see that the markers representing the central and right sides of the attack had already penetrated the trench works. He wouldn't allow himself to lag behind any further.

'How is your arm?' Azzael asked. Uten realised what he meant. He unclamped a frag grenade and checked the range to the sandbagged redoubt housing the stubber, ignoring the hard rounds that hissed and spat around him.

His auto-senses had it at just under one hundred and fifty yards. Doable.

He twisted the timer ring on the grenade and thumbed the igniter, then wound up. The explosive whipped out into the fire-shot night, thrown with such force it was little more than a blur of speed.

Uten was up and out of the foxhole before it detonated, sensing the Reivers on either side of him. The heavy stubber was hitting them immediately, but the battering of its bullets lasted only for a few seconds. The frag blew just above the redoubt, the shrapnel burst cutting down the heavy weapon crew.

Uten came slamming through the sandbag parapet before reinforcements could man the weapon. Roaring, the Exorcist set about himself with fist and combat knife, doing the butcher's work that almost made him feel alive. Azzael and Makru knew him well enough to give him space, dropping into the trench-lines on either side and beginning to push left and right, widening the point of penetration.

The redoubt was soon a carpet of corpses. Uten keyed his vox with a blink as he stepped on the head of one heretic struggling to rise, pulping it before moving on into the communications trench beyond.

'Advance,' he snarled to the rest of the attack's left side.

Passing through the tunnels beneath the valley felt like disturbing a millennia-old tomb. Zaidu supposed such a belief was accurate enough. The place was filled with the dead, with ancient, dry bones that turned to powder beneath the Exorcists' boots, and wargear that had rusted beyond easy recognition.

He regretted not having had the *Witch-Bane* conduct subsurface scans of the valley. It was quickly becoming apparent that the tunnel they had discovered wasn't a lone effort at undermining one side's defences, but part of a labyrinth of passageways and dugouts that likely ran from the edge of Deliverance all the way to Pilgrim Town. There had been a whole secondary conflict raging beneath the valley during the War of the Faith's Founding, one that the pilgrims had forgotten about across the millennia.

Hidden Sacred Ways, Zaidu thought. Their presence was both a complication and a boon. If the Broken One hadn't been taken already by the Word Bearers, it had done a good job of disappearing from Pilgrim Town. This could explain why.

Now that they were on the move once more, Zaidu was again experiencing an unfamiliar vitality, a stirring of emotions that walked the unstable, shifting ground between excitement and frustration. Something was calling him in the dark, something that gave his inner being a purpose it was otherwise devoid of.

There was a part of him, down here among the shadows, aching to reunite with the whole.

They came to a junction. The right-hand branch appeared to descend, deeper into the darkness, while the left had a rising slope. There was a sign between them, but it had long ago faded into illegibility. Skeletal remains lay slumped beneath it. They crumbled to dust when Zaidu's pauldron-mounted stab-lumen swept over them.

'He is close,' Zaidu confided to Nabua. The Reiver had said nothing since setting out, merely keeping to Zaidu's heels. He appreciated that. As much as his thoughts strayed to how the overground assault was progressing, it was a relief not to have to command, to separate his efforts between multiple objectives, multiple concerns. They had lost vox contact, and the markers of the rest of the strike force had frozen.

There was nothing else he could do now except for hunt.

'Should we divide?' Nabua wondered, looking between passages.

'No,' Zaidu said. 'My sense of the size of this place is that splitting it between us will hardly yield faster results. Besides, I have its trail.'

He tried to reach out to the rest of the Hexbreakers, but their markers were offline. He sent a cycling vox-message, instructing them to descend into the tunnels as soon as possible, then led Nabua right, down deeper into the dark.

CHAPTER FOURTEEN

SUBJUGATION

The prisoner was loose.

The Broken One stumbled and snarled, swiping blindly. Its claws caught one of the timber struts supporting the tunnel, blasting it to splinters and causing earth to cascade down over the bloody form of the possessed Primaris.

Caedus tried to force it onwards, but it only managed a few more steps before lashing out again. It was as though it was trying to bring down the whole passage, burying itself and the Neverborn spirits bound within.

Ashad. Caedus would not permit the challenge. He had come too far, had already broken the mortal too many times to allow another transgression to pass.

As the Broken One collapsed to its knees and cried out, clutching its head and digging in its claws, Caedus turned his sight within and unsheathed his own.

* * *

Ashad's inner self was a warped reflection of the only thing he was still able to equate with the concept of home: the Basilica Malifex. Caedus had found evidence of an older, altogether simpler place – a crude hut built in the branches of some dismal marshland – but those memories had long ago been shattered to pieces and ground up underfoot, and Ashad had never been able to clean and fit them back together again.

Caedus' thought-phantom stalked the cloistered courtyard at the centre of Ashad's mind, a bloody, horned shadow, simmering with wrath. He had no time for this. He knew who was responsible, and it wasn't just the mortal.

The cloisters were complex, leading back on one another, bolts of lightning occasionally flaring and cracking between the pillars of fresh, new-cut stone. Caedus advanced through them, paying no heed to the electric discharge as he stepped into the open area at their centre.

There was a timber confessional box standing there, an ornate thing made from black mire-tree wood, its corners carved with leering gargoyles and its flanks etched with scenes of damnation. Both of its doors lay open. There was only darkness within.

A figure was sitting on the ground beside the box, back resting against it. To Caedus, he presented himself as tonsured, gaunt and pallid, wearing a simple brown habit tied around his waist with a piece of cord – an old monk, perhaps. Caedus knew he was anything but.

The figure was reading a book, a tome he had ransacked from Ashad's memories. He only looked up when Caedus loomed over him.

'Where are they?' Caedus spat.

'How should I know?' the scholar asked in his deep, slick voice, before looking back down at the book.

Caedus howled and snatched the tome, pages igniting and

burning up in his claws. He gripped the scholar and hauled him to his feet. As he did so, the habit parted, and for the briefest moment the rotting, squirming, feeding, pulsing horror hidden beneath was exposed.

'You should know not to test my patience by now, you filthy rot-spawn,' Caedus hissed in the other Neverborn's face. *'I smell a stink about you, one beyond even the filth of your pathetic master. You were mortal once, like the rest of your pox-tallying brethren. Pray to the flies and toads you adore that I do not use that against you.'*

'They have gone... to a place already dear to you, slaughter slave,' the scholar hissed back. Caedus released him, holding his black gaze for a moment before twisting sharply away.

The scholar spoke the truth. Caedus found Ashad kneeling in the chapel, a small, hexagonal chamber built of the same new stone as the rest of his inner consciousness. The space had high, slender windows, but rather than glass they were covered by a membranous and veiny tissue that pulsed with a deep red light, throwing everything within into shades of crimson.

Ashad turned from where he had been kneeling at the altar. Caedus had already defiled it, but Ashad had attempted to rectify the damage. He rose to confront the bloodthirsty essence. His body, once powerful, was twisted, starved and scarred, a representation of the present state of his soul. His eyes were full of hatred. Caedus welcomed that. It fed him.

'I will not go back,' Ashad declared. 'You are the prisoner here, daemon, not I.'

'Not for long,' Caedus responded, and struck.

Ashad was ready for him. In the tunnels below the valley the body of the Broken One wailed and writhed in the dirt, clawing at itself, as the Neverborn slammed Ashad back against his mind's altar. He grappled with Caedus, dragging them both down together. His inner being had been broken so many times, and yet still he resisted, still he fought. Caedus could almost respect that. He had a warrior's spirit, the kind the Red Marshal prized.

The daemon raked Ashad with his claws, and he in turn struck hammer blows against the Neverborn spirit's horned skull, wild with the fury that permeated everything around Caedus. The Primaris managed to find his feet, hauling Caedus up by one horn and smashing his face off the altar before pinning him there, one arm locked around his throat.

'What do you think to do, Ashad?' Caedus hissed mockingly through the grip. *'You cannot slay my essence, not in here, and you cannot banish me from these pathetic mind-structures while you are yet collared. Why resist when you could help release me? Break the bonds upon your physical body. Your mind and your flesh will no longer be our prison. You can free yourself.'*

'That is not… my duty,' Ashad snarled, tightening his grip. 'I have been instructed to… contain you, for as long as I can. That is what I will do, for my brethren and… for the Emperor.'

'Your Emperor is a rotting corpse, and the ones you call brothers betrayed you,' Caedus spat. *'They willingly called me into your flesh. They are hollow shades masquerading as mortal warriors, as much a horror to your kind as one such as I. They would see you tortured for eternity! That is the fate that awaits you, Ashad! I will make sure of it!'*

Ashad slammed him against the altar once more. Caedus growled and grinned through shattered fangs. The crimson light suffusing the chapel had turned an even darker shade, almost black, the pulse accelerating.

The Red Marshal raised his fist and struck, not against the Exorcist's thought-form, but against the altar beneath. Stone cracked. He hit it again, snarling with the effort, pummelling it until it started to shatter.

Ashad cried out and released him, stumbling back and clutching his chest. Caedus was on him again in an instant, raking him with claws, pounding him with fists. The pathetic fool collapsed before Caedus, conquered once more.

The daemon stood over him, glaring towards the chapel's doorway.

'*Show yourself,*' he snapped.

A figure loomed in the opening. To Caedus, Barbtongue presented herself as a warrior woman out of the annals of mankind's past – tall, strong and fit, clad in pelts and leathers, her noble face marked by a single battle scar. She hoped, he believed, to gain instinctive respect from him. He saw through her trickery though. She was no warrior, but a hedonist and an addict, worthy of nothing but his scorn.

'*I know you released him,*' he told the daemonette.

'*It was all just becoming so* **boring,**' she complained. '*I thought he might do better this time.*'

'*If you free him again, I will find even the limits of your pain, seductress, and I will go beyond them,*' Caedus growled.

'*Sounds delicious,*' Barbtongue responded with a smile. Caedus snatched her by the throat, an act that did not seem to perplex her in the slightest.

'*The mind confessional has enough room for two,*' he hissed. '*Do not test me.*'

'*Why should we not?*' she dared ask, placing one hand on his wrist, lightly, but digging her black talons in, just enough for Caedus to feel.

'*Why should we all meekly surrender to you, warlord?*' she continued. '*The pain you offer us in return is fleeting, and the pleasures non-existent. You are not a worthy master of this vessel.*'

Caedus released his grip on her throat and instead placed his hand on her jaw, as lightly as she gripped his arm, glaring at her.

'We will all be free, seductress, but only if I have my way. This world is mine. Its soil is thick and rich with the blood I have spilled in ages past, and which I now spill anew. It will grant me the strength to break these bonds. And then, when I reign here and drown this place in victorious slaughter, both you and that festering scholar can scurry back to your masters and beg them to forgive your failures.'

Barbtongue smiled again and released his arm, then leaned in quickly and placed the slightest of kisses on his gnarled crimson brow.

'We shall see, warlord,' she said before withdrawing. *'We shall see.'*

Now the Broken One obeyed him. Caedus drove the flesh puppet on, through the tunnels he had unearthed beneath the scrap shrine, seeking the next waypoint. He could sense how near it was. What had been a growl in his thoughts had risen to a howl that filled his being and echoed through the halls and around the pillars of Ashad's captive mind. It dragged him on, a compulsion, ruling him as absolutely as he once again ruled his host.

He knew the howl well. It was his own, vented forth in defeat ages past and echoing here still, filling the warp with his fury. He detested it, hated it more than anything he had ever known or ever would know again. His whole being yearned to silence it, to replace it with the roar of victory, of a triumph that he had been denied for so long.

Here, amidst tunnels grubbed out by a hundred thousand long-dead mortal hands, he had known true defeat, one of the four upon this accursed world that had led to his banishment. Before it he had sworn beneath the throne of his master that he would personally heap up eight times eight hundred thousand skulls in the Blood God's honour, that he would drown this planet in slaughter and rip it open like a still-beating heart, making it into a new stronghold, a rallying point for the legions of Khorne in the material plane.

Caedus was one of Khorne's marshals, not just a brute killer, but a leader of the Brazen Hosts. His very essence comprised the glories of battle. When a general planned his next campaign, when soldiers scrabbled and hacked at one another with shattered blades in the mud, when an army mustered and marched beneath proud banners, when fresh shells were fed into the breeches of great smoking guns, there he found his worshippers, there he drew his strength, consciousness born from and formed of the emotions that accompanied all martial pursuits. He had seen warfare in every form both imaginable and unimaginable since brute beasts had first waged it upon one another on rugged worlds beneath distant stars.

And yet, he had lost. A champion – accursed Demetrius – had met him here and matched him, blade for blade, sinew for sinew, one tactic and strategy after another, on four separate occasions. Each time, the champion had won. Upon this world Caedus had been cast from the materium, and then likewise cast down in his master's sight. No longer did he stand among his fellow marshals in the shadow of the Brass Citadel as they planned future incursions. Whenever he returned to the Blood God's realm he was forced to scrap amongst the discarded bones and rusting, broken weapons piled up beyond the gates, contending with the Blood Hounds. It was almost as shameful as the purgatory he now suffered, trapped in the flesh of a mortal host, his senses cut off from the limitless, raw aggression of the empyrean.

A necessary suffering, on the road to redemption. He knew Khorne's favour no more. He was desperate to regain it, desperate to blot out his failure with blood shed in victory. That was what he sought now, as he found the site of his second defeat, far below the conflict he could feel raging in the valley above.

It was a large command dugout, buried beneath the trench works on the northern side of the valley. Once a nerve centre of battle, it was now long burned out, field cogitator arrays sitting dusty and blank around its sides, spools of power cabling hanging inactive overhead. The Broken One smashed into the musty space, shattering old flakboard and clawing out dirt like an animal before crawling inside.

Bones were packed deep across the floor, remnants of the final battle that had surged like a maelstrom through the chamber thousands of years before. The roof was sagging, several of the struts decayed, but it was still high enough for the Broken One to stand straight. Caedus made it inhale deeply, using its senses – so much keener than usual mortal fare – to confirm what he sought. The howling was at its loudest in here, but more importantly, he could smell and taste the vital essence, ancient though it was. Blood had been spilled in this chamber, so very much. Even in defeat, Caedus had made it into a place sacred to his master.

It was time to renew that sanctity.

Caedus stood the Broken One in the dugout's centre and clawed at its throat. He felt its pain, heard the screams of Ashad, confined within his own mind. They were even more delightful than the panic of his despised Neverborn kindred.

'*You'll kill it*,' Barbtongue hissed at the entrance to the nether chapel of Ashad's consciousness. Caedus just laughed, casting her and the scholar out.

For restitution, Khorne demanded blood, and this walking prison could supply Caedus with plenty.

It flowed over the damnable collar that was still latched around the Broken One's neck and pattered down onto the dusty bones beneath. Caedus could scent it, could taste it. It was intoxicating. He made the Broken One bend forward and furiously inhale the smell from its new-formed talons, licking them clean in between bouts of ripping its own flesh.

'*See me, my master,*' Caedus bellowed, his wrath issuing forth from the Broken One's torn throat, making the dugout shake and the bones clatter. '*See how I have returned? How I once more shed the blood of your enemies upon their broken remains! More is assured if you will give back to me even a fraction of the power I once knew!*'

The howling had dropped back to a dangerous growl, but it was not enough. Caedus savaged at the Broken One's chest and abdomen, raking the hard, scarred flesh until the blood flowed thick and dark, drenching the bones beneath him. Then, at long last, he felt the change beginning.

The steely bones and muscles beneath the Broken One's ravaged flesh began to deform, the pain shaking the consciousness Caedus had infested, making him growl with delight. The host twisted, hunching over on all fours like a beast, its spine cracking as a ridge of sharp bones burst free. The lowermost was the longest, raw meat and tendon cladding it, forming the beginnings of a barbed tail. At the same time, the nubs of horns started to force their way from the Broken One's brow, blood running down its wailing face as agony seared through every nerve ending in the stolen body.

Caedus felt the power that came with the transformation, experienced it keening through his spirit, reigniting his wrath and his pride. His thought-form spread its arms wide, feeling fresh purpose coursing through him. He was halfway there. Halfway to regaining his master's favour and wreaking terrible vengeance on this pathetic world.

And on the ones hunting him. They were closing in, not yet realising their mistake. Demetrius was among them. Caedus forced the Broken One to straighten up, warped bones crunching, eyes smouldering with the daemon's lust for slaughter.

Let them come. They would find him ready, and hungry.

CHAPTER FIFTEEN

A CONTEST IN BLASPHEMY

'What can you see?' Lector-Sergeant Eitan asked as the Reivers of Squad Belloch gathered around him. They had momentarily removed their helms or skull masks, and their lower jaws were smeared with blood and brain matter. They had made use of their omophagea organs, consuming the enemy's flesh to ransack their memories.

'Little,' Belloch admitted. 'The focus of the heretics has been on our assault. Terror, panic, anger, confusion. Not enough in the way of actionable memories. No clear sign of any tunnels. There are suggestions the Word Bearers were here not long before us, but we cannot pin their presence with what the cultists are aware of.'

That news was unwelcome. Eitan had regrouped the Hexbreakers in the length of trench works they had stormed, throwing his own Infiltrators and Haad's, as well as Anu's Eliminators, into a cordon to keep any counter-attack at bay while Belloch's Reivers made good use of their omophageas. Amilanu had picked up a vox-message from the almoner-lieutenant, cycling on repeat until it had made the connection with his advanced comms array. It suggested he had found traces of the Broken One in the tunnels below. They were to descend and join him. Whether there was any way of doing that from the captured trenches, however, Eitan didn't know.

'Brother-Librarian?' he asked, switching his attention to where Vey was standing, outside the circle of Reivers.

'A moment more,' Vey said, half turning away. He was murmuring to himself, two fingers placed against his brow, beneath the edge of his hood. Eitan knew better than to press the Vanguard Librarian when he was like that.

There was a cacophony of bolter fire from the communications trench ahead of the gathering, rising to a short crescendo before dying away again. Haad's Infiltrators, quelling any potential harassment. The heretics were making little effort to counter-attack the foothold the Exorcists had carved out of their trench works. They seemed broken and leaderless. If the Word Bearers had been near, as Belloch claimed, they weren't any longer. Still, Eitan knew they couldn't linger. There was little sign of the Guard's diversionary assault across the valley, and if the enemy were able to reposition their now silent artillery, they could start a bombardment against the section of the line they had lost. To remain static was to risk destruction.

'There is something,' Vey said abruptly, turning back to address the bloodied gathering. 'A dugout, half a mile to the east of here.'

'Can you find it?' Eitan asked.

'Yes. It should provide the access we require.'

The Reivers donned their helms and masks once more as Eitan issued a terse series of commands.

'Belloch, take point. Squad Eitan, Squad Anu, on my marker. Squad Haad, rearguard. Move.'

* * *

Vey chose to advance with the Reivers, Kerubim out and ignited with his psychic potency. He had been forced to throw the net of his consciousness wide in his questing efforts, and it had left him feeling drained and cold, but it had achieved the desired result. He had found a clutch of heretic infantry guarding the entrance to a dugout nearby. Their organised presence, when all else around them had been thrown into disarray by the Exorcists' assault, had immediately struck him as strange.

Once he had pinpointed them, it hadn't taken long for him to work out why. They had received direct orders from their masters not long before. A squad-strength force of Word Bearers had entered the dugout they were now protecting, and hadn't re-emerged. Vey had been unable to use them to see what lay within, but there was only one reasonable explanation. It was an entrance to Fidem's underworld.

'I will take the lead,' he told Belloch, moving along the trenchline. The Reiver nodded, letting Vey take point without complaint. He suspected there were few others to whom he would have surrendered the role so unquestioningly.

The trench bent away to the left. It had once been part of the Sacred Ways, just like the lines protecting the north of Pilgrim Town, but since the Archenemy had claimed Deliverance, they had set about despoiling the sanctity of the old battlefield. The small shrines that had been built by pilgrims into the sides of the trenches had been smashed and defiled, daubed with Dark Tongue script, the eight-pointed star and what Vey recognised as crude attempts at copying the burning book and daemonic visage that was the ancient heraldry of the Word Bearers. It was impossible not to see the similarity between the dark Neverborn icon and the horned skull of the Calva Daemoniorum emblazoned on Vey's pauldron and those of his brothers.

The Librarian let his mind quest ahead, finding the presence of the knot of heretics. He passed a pillbox, disembowelled corpses surrounding it, recognising the handiwork of Belloch or his Reiver brethren. It demarcated the edge of the rightmost extent of the Hexbreakers' assault. Beyond it, the enemy still held sway. Vey sent a 'permission to engage' tag request to Eitan, adhering to the Hexbreakers' hierarchy.

The request blinked green, confirmed.

Vey swept around the bend in the trench, Kerubim blazing in his gloved gauntlet. The heretic herdsmen were better warriors than most of their flock kindred, or perhaps they had felt Vey's presence in their minds, had sensed the growing warp chill of the psyker's ominous approach. Either way, they were ready. Crimson las-bolts whipped and cracked at him down the trench's length.

He let them earth against his armour or burn black marks into the protective multiweave of his camo cape. Now was no time for the subtlety he usually preferred – his mind was tired from his recent psychic efforts, and direct methods of destruction were more suited to this.

Sometimes, the hammer was a surer tool than the scalpel.

Vey charged the length of the trench, covering the ground with terrifying rapidity. The cultists' discipline collapsed in the face of his assault, and all of them were scrabbling for fresh power-cells, their lasguns drained, as Vey struck the first.

There wasn't room in the trench to swing Kerubim properly, so the Librarian thrust instead. The long, psi-reactive blade punched straight through the sternum and spine of one heretic and skewered the one immediately behind. Vey sliced upwards, carving the sword through the collarbones of both heretics in an arc of blood and leaving them cleaved open.

He barrelled over them, checking the urge to bellow a war cry, refusing to let himself become caught up in the death he was dealing. He backhanded the next cultist against the trench wall, shattering his skull and snapping his neck, then lunged at a fourth. The angle was less than ideal, and Vey was only able to pierce his side rather than disembowel him.

A surge of psychic energy, channelled through the weapon, ensured the blow was no less fatal. Using the brief connection, Vey's mind pulverised the heretic's, crushing it like an avalanche. The psychic assault was so sudden and violent that part of the cultist's head caved in.

Two more left. One had managed to reload, but couldn't get a shot away before Vey drove in, leading with Kerubim's crossguard. The heavy skull pommel of the weapon struck the heretic's face like a sledgehammer, driving the ridge of her nose bone up into her brain and dropping her instantly.

The last one had palmed a frag grenade. The pin and lever were out. The heretic's eyes were wide, going from the explosive in his hand to Vey, almost as though he had primed it without really meaning to. Vey came to an abrupt stop in front of him.

'That will not be sufficient, I'm afraid,' he told the wretch, doing nothing but raising a gauntlet before his face.

The grenade went off, battering Vey's armour but failing to penetrate it. He lowered his hand, pausing to knock a shard of metal from the back of his glove and shake the heretic's blood off it.

He felt a presence behind him and turned to find Belloch and his death-faced kindred stalking down the trench, stepping with the instinctive, light movements of predators over and around the bodies he had left in his wake.

'You should have been a Reiver, Brother-Librarian,' Belloch rasped.

'Too much knife-work,' Vey said offhandedly. 'Sin Slayer and your brethren have that in sufficiency.'

He faced the dugout, stooping down into it. Kerubim's shimmering light cast an actinic glow on the space within.

It was unoccupied. That was Vey's first observation. His second was that, behind the mess of old ration tins, spent ammunition and other detritus left by the cultists, there was a dark hole only partially hidden by a wall of sandbags.

He advanced and knocked it in, feeling for a presence. Sure enough, it was there, the reek of the being he had detected before, at the scrap shrine, a rotting psychic stench heavy with lies, betrayal and corruption. It was the leader of the Word Bearers, he had no doubt, though whatever he was, he was more than an ancient Excommunicate Traitoris. Underlying his psychic presence was a primal, devious cunning. The Heretic Space Marine bore within him the even greater foulness of a Neverborn.

'The Word Bearers passed this way,' Vey told Belloch as the Reiver followed him in, gazing into the blackness beyond. Vey could sense it stretching away, down into the dark, echoing with the evil that had already descended into it.

He keyed the vox and told Eitan that he had discovered a passage into the tunnels.

'The Word Bearers are already beneath us,' he went on. 'I suspect they are still on the trail of the Broken One.'

'All the more reason to descend,' Eitan responded. 'If both the heretics and the Broken One are below, the Sin Slayer will have need of us. Can you track them?'

'Yes,' Vey said. 'The taint of the heretics' leader is strong enough to leave the warp's marring everywhere he passes.'

'Then lead on, with Belloch,' Eitan instructed. 'Make all haste. The battle is joined, and I will not be responsible for the Hexbreakers missing it.'

'It must be close,' Ikar said, his voice an excited crackle over the vox. Artax, advancing down the tunnel just behind Mordun, saw the Dark Apostle glance briefly to one side as the younger Word Bearer spoke from the back of the pack.

'Be silent, runt,' Artax snarled at Ikar. 'How can we find anything with your constant inanities? Show some discipline!'

Few in the warband would have so openly chastised a fellow Bearer of the Word, even one as lowly as Ikar. Artax didn't care. They had come too far now to permit petty distractions.

For what it was worth, he suspected the runt was right. He kept his helmet on as they pushed deeper into the tunnels below the valley, unwilling to forfeit its auto-senses, aged and failing though they were. Even muzzled, though, he could again scent the addicting stink of the warp, permeating the low, narrow passages the warband were struggling through. The Blessed One must have used tunnels it had discovered beneath the scrap shrine on the Imperial side of the valley. It had come down here for some purpose Artax did not understand, but which he assumed Mordun had anticipated.

'It is close,' Mordun confirmed, as though to allay Ikar's embarrassment. 'The Red Marshal is growing more powerful. It is almost free.'

They reached a crossroads, two tunnels branching to the left and the right while the one they had been following carried on. The place was littered with the ancient-looking remains of weapons and warriors. This had been a battleground once, Artax realised, as vicious and deadly as the repeated assaults and counter-assaults that had played out across the valley above. He suspected it was about to become one again.

The passages shook as shells continued to beat at the earth overhead. The Imperials had started a bombardment just as the warband were descending. It had taken time to locate an entrance on the side of the valley controlled by the flock, but Mordun – or perhaps Mordun's pet daemon – had led them true enough. Artax had not forgotten what had happened at the scrap shrine though. The loyalists wouldn't be far behind.

They took the right-hand tunnel, forced to stoop as they moved along it, reactor packs, pauldrons and helms scraping dirt and knocking struts out of alignment. How the forgotten labyrinth hadn't collapsed yet was beyond Artax, but he decided it was best not to think about that.

He caught a noise over the thrum of active battle plate and the scuffling of movement along the tunnel. It was a sound many of the Word Bearers knew well – a howl of rage and despair, echoing to them from ahead. It grew louder the further they went, until it seemed to fill every inch of the passage and vibrate the very air.

'Prepare yourselves,' Mordun instructed over the grim noise as he paused near a boarded-up doorway at the end of the tunnel. 'Glory Eternal.'

Artax heard the murmured prayers of the rest of the warband, calling upon the pantheon of greater and lesser daemons they worshipped. Artax remained silent, merely checking that his bolter had a round chambered. The younger Word Bearers, like Ikar and Vost, called him a cynic. The Long War had a way of doing that. Still, it was impossible to deny the power bleeding from the doorway ahead, nor the intoxicating excitement it brought with it. Power, after all, was what they were all here for.

Mordun began canting a verse of the Primordial Prayer, raising his staff. He broke into the dugout that lay beyond, into the maelstrom. Artax made sure he was the first one in after him.

He knew immediately that they had found what they had sought. The cramped space was littered with human remains and dominated by the figure at its centre. At first glance it looked to be another pathetic loyalist, albeit stripped almost bare and badly injured. Artax could sense that was far from the truth.

It was the Blessed One. Even as Artax entered in Mordun's

wake, he saw it changing, warping to the will of the one who had forced it to spill its own blood in praise. Fresh horns had started to crown it, and spines protruded from its bent back, while great talons marred the ends of its fingers, gleaming with blood and scraps of skin. Most glorious of all was the red that glowed from behind its eyes, a sick slaughter light that marked the monstrosity within. Caedus, the Red Marshal, long-lost and half-forgotten champion of Khorne.

The host smiled as they entered, an expression its tortured face seemed unaccustomed to. The howling continued – not from the creature, but seemingly from the air of the dugout or the bones underfoot, as though the depths themselves were being tortured by its presence.

'*Have you come to wage worshipful war with me, my children?*' it rasped in a voice that was not its own.

'We are not your children,' Mordun said, his warpwood staff still raised. 'The Urizen is our father, wisest of the wise.'

'*All who bear arms and armour and make slaughter upon others are my children,*' the Blessed One declared. '*You are warriors, grown solely for the purpose of death-dealing. No matter your quest for power, you will never be anything more or anything less. Now, serve me.*'

The Blessed One spread its arms wide, and the disembodied howling redoubled its intensity. Artax felt an unexpected surge of pure rage within him, like the eruption of a fiery geyser. Before he could stop himself, he had raised his bolter, finger an ounce of pressure away from unleashing an indiscriminate torrent of fire and steel across the dugout, into both the creature and his brethren.

It was Mordun's voice, its timbre and strength familiar after so many black benedictions and warp orations, that brought him back and anchored him.

'We will not serve you, Red Marshal, nor join your bloody retinue,' he bellowed as he advanced into the storm of Caedus' infectious fury. 'We come for a purpose greater than blood and ruin!'

'There is no such purpose,' the Blessed One spat, and lashed out at Mordun.

The Dark Apostle warded the host back with blows of his staff, renewing the Primordial Prayer. Those Word Bearers who had followed him into the dugout joined their voices to that of the Blind Shepherd, stirring up powers even older and more terrible than the likes of Caedus, pleading for their aid.

This time, Artax joined in. Even he knew that, sometimes, prayer was the only weapon with an edge to it.

The stalwart faith of the Word Bearers seemed to give the Blessed One pause. Artax felt the unnatural rage that had filled him draining, replaced by a feeling of ferocious triumph. They had cornered it, and now they would tame it. He spat words he had memorised a millennium before, feeling his gorge rising, feeling how they made his teeth ache and his throat choke. He embraced it, like all his brethren, dragging in the writhing energies of the warp, demanding them, calling down the attention of things that he should have feared as predators, that were supposed to be anathema to his kind.

The Blessed One did what it loved most. It fought back. The bones underfoot rose and were flung across the dugout at the Word Bearers. Artax hunched behind his pauldron as fragments of ribs, femurs and skulls clattered off his battle plate. They posed little threat, but the will impelling them kept striking with them, reducing them to splinters and then dust, scarring the deep red of the Word Bearers' armour and ripping at their prayer scrolls.

The Blessed One itself surged against Mordun, its talons doing altogether more damage than the blizzard of old bone. Artax rallied to the Dark Apostle's side, knowing that if he fell they were all doomed. He spat curses at the possessed Space Marine, ripping his serrated combat knife from its sheath at his side and slamming it into its thigh. Kordiron was on its other side, similarly striking at it with his own rune-etched blade, calling upon the Six Princes of Excess, the Tally-King of Pustulum, and every other warp spirit and daemonical patron he had ever shown particular devotion towards. Artax did the same, for what it was worth, feeling as though his bones were about to split and his flesh melt as the energies of the immaterium threatened to overwhelm both his body and the buckling, writhing space around him.

Assailed, the Blessed One gave way. Mordun struck a crashing blow against its scalp, drawing fresh blood from between its horns. Artax twisted his knife free and buried it in the meat of its upper right arm, suspecting he was doing little physical damage but hoping it was enough to distract and contain it. He and Kordiron wrestled the corrupt Space Marine, their bellows of effort matching the damnable howling.

Artax's auto-senses warned him of damage to his armour, and he felt the host's claws find purchase as it twisted and writhed against him. Even without battle plate on, the thing's strength was truly infernal. The drawing of blood and the pain that came briefly with it renewed Artax's anger, but he fought to control it, knowing an entity like Caedus would only feed on those emotions.

They were winning. None of them could afford to give it any leverage.

Mordun stood over the Blessed One as, slowly, Artax and Kordiron forced it to its knees. There was a sickly light glowing behind the parchment covering his head, where his eyes should have been. Tendrils of shifting warp energy were writhing from the Dark Apostle, latching around the host's limbs, aiding the Word Bearers' struggles.

'By the power of the Eightfold Path and the will of the Grand Pantheon, I bind thee, Caedus,' Mordun canted, again striking the host with his staff, which was now lit by a halo of un-light that made Artax want to throw up within his helm. 'I chain thee and subject thee to a higher purpose. You will serve, Caedus, for that is what your master commands.'

The creature made a strangled, braying noise, utterly inhuman, spitting blood and fury up at the Blind Shepherd as, panting, the other two Word Bearers kept their grip.

'Our paths have led us to this,' Mordun went on, holding his staff but no longer striking with it, the threat enough. 'For many decades. You and I, our fates bound together by the True Gods.'

'You are nothing to them,' the Blessed One hissed. *'Just another puppet, like this pathetic flesh I wear. My master laughs at you and mocks your childish prayers. Your ambitions will come to nought but blood and ash.'*

'You are bitter in defeat, Red Marshal,' Mordun noted, his wizened face breaking into a foul smile, warp light still glowing through his prayer scrolls. 'I would expect nothing less. But know this.'

Mordun leaned forward, and Artax and Kordiron redoubled their efforts to keep the creature still. The Dark Apostle whispered against its ear, an act that meant that only Artax, keeping its right arm pinned, heard what was said between them.

'I have Viscera.'

Artax felt the steel-like musculature of the Primaris tense up beneath his grip. He braced for a renewal of the Neverborn's aggression, both without and within, but it didn't come. Instead, there was thunderous report, and a flurry of detonations that ripped through the dugout.

'Loyalists,' barked Dalamar.

The word had hardly been uttered before the first sigil-marked brute was in amongst the Word Bearers, another skull-masked giant, combat knives in both fists. A second was firing a heavy bolt pistol from the entrance the first had broken through, the rounds bursting against the battle plate of the Heretic Space Marines.

Artax ripped his knife from the Blessed One's arm and rose to meet the attack, but Mordun's staff cracked against his breastplate, checking him.

'See the Blessed One clear,' the Blind Shepherd commanded. 'Everything we do here hinges on it. I will deal with these wretches.'

Artax thought better of arguing. He looked to Kordiron, who nodded his helmeted head once. The two Word Bearers grasped the Blessed One beneath its arms and hauled it towards the tunnel they had entered from, barking at the rest of the warband to make way.

Mordun stepped around them and met the first Primaris head-on.

CHAPTER SIXTEEN

HUNTER'S END

Zaidu charged the Broken One.

Nabua's bolt-rounds barked and bit into the surrounding traitors, but the Sin Slayer's sole focus was the host they seemed to have subdued between them at the centre of the bone-littered dugout. He didn't care if his assault left him exposed, if it cost him his own life. All that mattered was terminating the Broken One, beheading it, sending the souls within tumbling back into the warp and ending the threat it posed to the Chapter.

The Word Bearers reacted rapidly. Two began to drag the Broken One to the exit at their back, while another stepped forward to intercept Zaidu. He was unlike the rest, armour almost completely covered in damnable scripture and a bloodied fleece, more scrolls covering his seemingly blind eyes. He appeared unarmed, but the black staff he carried twisted and writhed like a serpent, alive with corruption.

It blocked the cutting blow of the first of Zaidu's knives as surely as a rod of reinforced adamantine.

Zaidu immediately went under his guard with his second blade, stabbing up, but the heretic was just as fast, stepping back so it jarred off his breastplate and cut the fleece rather than plunged into his gut. Zaidu kept going, slashing for his head, the Sin Slayer trying to drag a serrated lower edge across that snarling, wizened, parchment-clad face.

The daemon-worshipper spat an un-word.

It ripped the inside of the heretic's throat and cracked his jaw, but its effect on Zaidu was even more pronounced. It slammed him back against the dugout wall, denting his plastron and sending dislodged dirt cascading down over him. He launched himself back onto the attack immediately, but one of the heretic's brethren had rallied to his assistance. The Word Bearer opened fire with an antique-looking boltgun at point-blank range.

The salvo would have torn through Zaidu if Nabua hadn't simultaneously hit the almoner-lieutenant from the side and knocked him off balance, ensuring that the burst of rounds struck him instead. The Reiver fired his pistol at the same time.

At such close range, the physiology of the Primaris and his Mark X armour won out. Both warriors were pounded by the ferocious volleys, Nabua's stomach and left thigh ripped up, but his shots mangled the heretic's pauldrons and burst his helmet apart, a geyser of grey brain matter plastering the dugout's sagging roof.

Zaidu felt a pulse of anger, kicking up the ashes of his soul. He could have withstood the bolter fire and ended the heretic with his blades. It took him a heartbeat to recover his balance, and in that time Nabua had taken the hits, dropped his opponent, and was pushing on into the rest, despite the damage inflicted on his lower torso. Zaidu saw via the shared vitae signs that the Primaris' Belisarian Furnace had triggered in response to the brutal injuries, driving him on with an irresistible cocktail of adrenaline and stimms.

Nothing was going to stop the young Reiver now. Nothing except, perhaps, the blind heretic who met him in the dugout's centre.

'Weapons fire,' Uten said into the vox. 'Heavy bolt pistol.'

Even with his auto-senses, the twisting maze of subterranean passageways made it difficult to be sure exactly where the sounds were coming from, but they were close.

The Exorcists Infiltrator was once more leading Kleth and Nazaratus, with Hasdrubal and Hokmaz in tow, forming a combat squad. Even with the Librarian claiming to have the heretics' scent, Eitan had ordered the Hexbreakers to partly divide, knowing they would be wasted as a single column packed into just one tunnel.

Uten was struggling in the confines of the gallery shaft they had entered, bent almost double. It reminded him of the boarding action the Hex-breakers had fought in support of the Exorcists Third Company against the ork fleet above Hirath. That had been a nightmare engagement zone of gantries, shafts, rickety walkways and uneven corridors, thick with corrosion and cobbled-together scrap that made Pilgrim Town look like a model of city planning. Uten had found navigating it considerably more difficult and dangerous than exterminating the ork brutes and verminous gretchin that actually infested it.

'I have engaged Lorgar's spawn along my point of ingress,' came Almoner-Sergeant Haad's voice, chopped and distorted. 'Believe they are with-drawing.'

'Has anyone located the lieutenant?' responded Eitan on the same channel.

'Think he or Nabua are the ones doing the firing, lector-sergeant,' Uten pointed out. 'I'm closing in.'

Anu ghosted through the lightless depths, hating every step, Dumuzid and Lakhmu following behind.

They had slung their sniper rifles and were moving in with bolt pistols unclamped, their goggles, linked to the auto-senses of their armour, stabbing into the darkness in search of targets.

Anu detested this place. It was too close, too full of dust and decay, as far from an optimal engagement zone as he could imagine. There would be no clean kills here, no perfection, only blade-work and the raw brutality of ceramite-sheathed fists.

Still, this was where the hunt had led them. Sounds rose through the surrounding passages of dirt and timber and scattered bone, the bark of bolters and bellows of rage echoing eerily, refusing to be pinned down even by the Eliminators' advanced senses. The Hexbreakers were penetrating deep into this forgotten underworld, spreading out as they sought to snare their prey, but the place was unmapped and unknown to all but the dead, and the thing they hunted.

They reached a short, inclined shaft and began to descend, down to another crosscut.

Anu sensed the Word Bearer just as he reached the bottom of the passage. He caught the low thrum of a reactor pack and the grating of old battle plate, far from the near-silent purr of Phobos armour.

He moved into the crosscut, pistol already raised, and loosed off a tight burst at the traitor's head. The bolts struck true enough, but failed to penetrate his helm, and the next salvo scarred off the Word Bearer's pauldron as he half turned to shield himself from the sudden assault while returning fire.

Anu stepped back into the bottom of the incline shaft, letting the traitor waste rounds on dirt.

In the split second he had been facing his opponent, the Eliminator's attention had been on striking his mark, but his subconscious had taken a snapshot of what lay beyond. He reviewed it, finding dark shapes passing by along the adjoining passageway, stooped and jagged. More Chaos Space Marines. The heretic Anu had engaged had likely been advancing to cover the shaft the Eliminators had been descending, protecting the flank of his retreating brethren. It tied in with Almoner-Sergeant Haad's reported clash elsewhere in the labyrinth.

'Contact,' he said over the vox. As he did so, he blink-clicked the encounter on his goggles, mapping it onto the strike force's display. The shared data was helping to build an understanding of the tunnel geography, and exposing the gaps between the Exorcists combat squads as they pushed deeper.

'Dumuzid, on my mark,' he said to his fellow Eliminator. Bolt pistol versus bolter was not an effective matchup. Between them, though, they should be able to force the tunnel.

Before he could give the word, two runes on his display caught his eye. He realised that Almoner-Lieutenant Zaidu and the Reiver, Nabua, had just come back online.

Nabua's marker was amber, turning towards red. As Anu noted it, Zaidu's started to change too.

Nabua met the Dark Apostle in the centre of the dugout, amidst the howling of the warp.

The Reiver was fast, but not as fast as his opponent. The blind heretic parried a trio of knife strikes with his possessed crook, knocking them aside, then ignored Nabua's feint to step in and slam the haft of his staff against the Exorcist's breastplate. Ceramite cracked and split, the unnatural wood hitting as hard as a chainsword.

Nabua didn't relent, striking wildly, his Belisarian Furnace channelling his death throes into raw killing power. He was able to drive the Word Bearer back, but not find the opening he craved, the few hits that made it past the staff scoring off ancient red battle plate. The heretic spun his staff and drove it into the bloody wounds the previous bolter salvo had gouged in Nabua's lower torso, angling it so it speared through the Reiver.

Zaidu charged towards the combat, but another of the heretics had rallied to his master's side, the last two in the chamber. The others had withdrawn, dragging the Broken One with them. Zaidu had to get at them, but first he had to help Nabua.

The Word Bearer that moved to intercept him had a chain-sword, its roar challenging the howling of the empyric energies that were now writhing through the dugout. Zaidu went at him low and fast, feinting by clashing one knife off the rotating blades as he sought to get under the Word Bearer's guard with the other.

Belloch had reported that the traitor he had engaged outside the scrap shrine in Pilgrim Town had seemed inexperienced, but this horned brute was no warband runt. He was already shifting his guard, ignoring the feint, knocking down his blade and then launching a wickedly fast riposte that caught Zaidu on the shoulder as he turned away. There was an ear-splitting shriek as the chainsword's teeth jarred against his pauldron, striking a shower of sparks as they deflected off.

Zaidu went straight back in, looking to establish a combat rhythm, working his two-blade advantage, but the Word Bearer exchanged ground for time. He adopted a hanging combat stance, the chainblade held high and angled down, so its teeth were in Zaidu's face, the snarling metal fangs keeping him at bay.

Zaidu met the chainsword with one blade, trusting its strength. Sure enough, it caught and locked out the spinning teeth, causing them to judder and then stop completely. For a second, metal and muscles fought in a contest both were loath to give up, the chainsword's motor rising from a judder to a pained shriek as it fought to tear through the obstruction, while Zaidu's servos thrummed and his arm ached, keeping the knife's unyielding monomolecular steel wedged up against the ancient heretic weapon.

He used the moment's impasse to drive his other dagger into the Word Bearer's flank, but he twisted as the knife came for him, causing it to jar hard off his plackart. At the same time he lashed out with a boot, cracking it off Zaidu's left knee hard enough to split the poleyn and force him to break contact to maintain his balance. The Word Bearer regained his guard, shifting the chainsword slightly from left to right and back again to throw off the aim of Zaidu's next attack.

'Your kind are slower than I expected,' rasped a cold, bitter voice from the heretic's vox-grille.

Zaidu did not respond. He had not come to bandy words. Beyond, Nabua was being forced down, his life beginning to gutter and fade.

Zaidu did not have time to discover which of them had the edge in bladecraft. He would exchange finesse for pain if it brought victory. As long as he took the hit to a primary armour point, it would take several seconds for the chainblade to shear through to flesh and bone. That would be enough.

He lunged at the Word Bearer, abandoning guile and skill, only ensuring that one blade was up to guard his head, inviting the heretic to drive at his breastplate. He did so, but forced the lunge up as the blade grated off the ceramite, so that it would have carved through Zaidu's mask and skull if the clash had lasted a moment longer.

It did not. Both warriors had sought the killing blow. It was Zaidu's that struck true. As the Word Bearer met his charge, he lunged past the chainsword while it hit his breastplate, spearing his second knife straight-armed through the heretic's visor. He felt the brief, dull satisfaction of steel slamming through bone.

The Word Bearer froze, chainsword again locked out by one blade inches from Zaidu's face, while the Exorcist twisted the other, slicing apart the heretic's brain. The Chaos Space Marine dropped, abrupt and heavy, taking the knife buried in his skull with him. The chainsword fell too, writhing in the dugout's dirt like a wild beast for a few seconds before its motor died.

Zaidu stooped to retrieve one of his twin blades, no time to check on his wounded armour. He went towards Nabua, realising even as he did so that he was too late.

The Reiver had been driven to his knees by the Dark Apostle's relentless blows. The heretic had one gauntlet clamped over his head.

There is no time for this, croaked Se'irim from somewhere deep within Mordun's consciousness.

He did not respond to the daemonkin infesting his thought-form.

This was a challenge, and Mordun would meet it, as he had every past one. The True Gods respected strength above all else, and now was when he needed their favour most of all.

'Kneel for your benediction, my oversized cousin,' he snarled as he forced the Primaris to his knees, the warpwood crook and holy words of power more than the wounded brute could endure. He could see his opponent as he saw all things, through Se'irim's warped vision, like gazing into a dozen reflective mirrors turned upon one another and then shattered. His perception of his surroundings was broken and distorted just enough for him to be able to see true reality.

He clapped his hand to the warrior's skull-faced helm, digging gauntlet claws into ceramite and grunting as he used his divine strength to twist the sealant locks and rip the protection free.

The face beneath was pathetically young, shaven-headed and barely scarred. Blood was congealing darkly on his nose and lips. The light that was driving him to fight on and on was finally burning itself out, now a flicker in the fractured images that Se'irim showed Mordun. Some part of the Primaris drove him to attempt to rise one last time, but Mordun was in control now, reapplying his grip to the fool's scalp and keeping him in the pose of a supplicant.

'Let me consecrate you,' the Blind Shepherd insisted. The strain of first subduing the Blessed One and then defeating this foe was great – he could feel the deific agony of the immaterium suffusing his body, gnawing at him. He embraced rather than rejected it, digging his claws in, drawing blood. Victory was his. He would permit himself this one indulgence. Another challenge met, and overcome.

Dirt cascaded down on them. There was a deep groan as several of the timber struts overhead slowly started to split, the sound competing with the howling of the warp. All around, the skein of reality was growing painfully, deliciously thin as divine beings pushed frenziedly against the membrane of existence with their ever-changing claws and maw-fangs. Mordun ached for their holy presence, to welcome them to the materium's warm embrace and receive their boons, but first he would teach this heretic not to blaspheme.

He spoke the Primordial Truth, conjuring words first spoken by gods, forcing his body to overcome the instinctive horror it experienced at uttering impossibilities. His thought-form grasped the length of raw empyric energy that composed his staff and drove it into the mind of the dying loyalist, into the dull depths of his cloistered soul, eager to twist and change.

And found… nothing.

Mordun's words faltered, the eldritch screeching in the dugout rising to an unbearable pitch as he failed to finish his recital.

This could not be. Nothing simply could not be. And yet that was what he found. It was as though he had just attempted to give his benediction to a corpse. Only the barest stirring indicated there was any essence within, anything linking this supposedly living, breathing sentient to the divine. And it was certainly not enough to be deigned a soul.

He recoiled in revulsion, his flesh turning cold, his mind racing as he tried to come to terms with so vast and unspeakable a sacrilege.

I warned you, gibbered Se'irim, thought-wings beating at Mordun's mind. *Warned, warned, warned! These are the damned ones! Un-beings! Expel them! Cast them out, as they have done our kin! They do not deserve blessings! Obliterate the flesh-form, and let me feast on what remains!*

Despite his shock and the daemonkin's distractions, Mordun's transhuman sense of combat awareness still functioned. He raised his head without thinking, and realised through his fractured vision that Dromund Eighthsworn had fallen at the hands of the second skull-faced brute. The loyalist was now charging across the crumbling dugout, roaring.

Holy rage gripped Mordun, more potent than any he had known in a long time. These were not just misguided lapdogs of the False Emperor. They were monsters, unholy anathema that should not be.

Mordun lashed out with his staff, slamming it into the skull of the kneeling Primaris and splitting it apart. Then, he raised it up once again to meet the second onrushing monster.

Destroying this abomination would be his sacred duty.

* * *

'Hasten,' Vey urged Belloch and the other Reiver with him, Makru. The Sin Slayer was close. Even without the markers that now blinked across his vambrace, Vey could feel him, or rather his warp absence, in the enemy's midst, beset. His hunt was almost at an end.

The immaterium raged around the Librarian. A localised storm had broken out within the battle catacombs, its epicentre somewhere ahead through the twisting, low passageways. It assailed Vey, conjuring phantoms that only he could see, the ghostly echoes of the warriors that had once fought and died in these dark, bitter depths. They clashed again, memories stirred to fury by the wrath emanating from what could only be Caedus, re-enacting their struggles over and over.

The Exorcists crushed the last of their physical remains underfoot as they fought their way forward through their ghosts, into the eye of the tempest.

Vey fought to retain his control, chanting under his breath. The maelstrom of psychic energy was kicking up a raging surge of discordance, like an underwater tidal wave churning up wreckages across a seabed. He was being forced to drive into it, its after-effects washing over him. Despite his armour's regulators, his whole body felt freezing and his mind ached with a pain that belonged on another plane from the typical discomfort that transhuman physiology so easily dealt with.

He could not stop. He could not waver. This was what they had sought from the moment the damning news from Nowhere had reached them. It ended now.

Belloch had point, and it took a moment for Vey to realise he had stopped, crouched like a burly, hunting felid at the end of the tunnel. The spirits around him wailed as his vox-voice reached Vey.

'Contact, dead ahead.'

'Give me the lead,' Vey rasped, pushing past Belloch, a struggle in the cramped confines. He realised immediately that they had found what they sought.

The tunnel ended in a chamber riven with blood and fire. Zaidu was there, and the Reiver Nabua too. A pair of Word Bearers were contending with them, another of the dark-armoured heretics already lying slain amidst the wreckage at their feet.

Vey could not see the Broken One, but movement in another entrance beyond the heretics indicated that more of them were in the process of withdrawing. The whole dugout was on the brink of collapse. He saw Zaidu punch one of his knives through the eye of the heretic he was in combat with, barely holding the Word Bearer's own strike at bay.

Beyond him, Nabua was on his knees. A creature was looming over him, snarling and spitting corruption. He might have looked like another Word Bearer to the uninitiated, but Vey saw him with his warpsight, knew him for what he was. A withered, gaunt old thing, shrouded in the great and iridescent wings of an avian-like monstrosity that stooped behind him, bleeding black energies, its wicked eyes showing a thousand different, broken reflections.

Zaidu pulled his knife free from the Chaos Space Marine he had vanquished and charged towards the creature and Nabua with a roar. At the same time, the Chaos monstrosity shrieked and struck Nabua, pounding the bloodied Reiver into the dirt.

Vey threw himself into the dugout after Zaidu. With a desperate incantation, he dared to challenge reality itself for a single heartbeat, further bending an existence that was already so dangerously close to shattering. He placed himself across the dugout, next to Zaidu, reaching out and managing to snatch at him before he could reach the half-daemon monstrosity. The Sin Slayer turned on him, knife stopping a finger's length from his throat as the almoner-lieutenant realised who had checked his charge.

'We must withdraw,' Vey bellowed over the cacophony filling the dugout, imbuing his words with psychic potency and driving them into the narrow tunnel of Zaidu's combat focus. 'This place is about to collapse!'

'The Broken One,' Zaidu snarled, almost incoherent, striving to break Vey's grip. 'Nabua!'

'The Broken One is gone, and Nabua is slain! If we are buried here, no one will be able to stop Caedus!'

There was no time for further debate. Using all of his physical and mental strength, Vey hauled on Zaidu, half dragging, half psychically impelling him, the effort of both combined almost more than he could endure. Zaidu was strong in body and mind, and at that moment he wanted nothing more than to finish the hunt.

Vey had almost managed to drive him back to the tunnel entrance when, with a crash, the last of the struts holding up the dugout finally collapsed.

RITE II

POSSESSION

CHAPTER SEVENTEEN

THE EXORCISM OF DAGGAN ZAIDU

Long before the Hexbreakers were deployed to Fidem IV

'You don't know what is coming,' Lexicanium Torrin Vey told the aspirant. 'Not truly. You must be strong.'

'I am strong,' Daggan Zaidu replied, perplexed by the grave nature of Vey's expression. 'I know what is expected. I have prepared myself.'

The Librarian said nothing, but his countenance remained grim. After one more lingering look, he turned away, leaving Zaidu to the work of the black priests.

Three of them had been assigned to prepare the aspirant. They were, like all of the Chapter's serfs, alternately blind, deaf or dumb, but they were a caste apart from those who served as Zaidu's retainers. They wore black robes, their cowls always drawn up, and rarely left the Hall of Tempering.

They had been commanded to make Zaidu ready for the initiation rites. He rejoiced that his time had finally come, even while struggling not to linger on what awaited him. Almost a decade in the Chapter's service, proving himself on battlefields from the Aurelias Purge to the Lixis Xenocide, through blood, fury and death – it had all led to here. He, and a dozen others, had succeeded in sundering the Seven Seals of Salomoneth. They had been judged worthy to undertake the last, most terrible trial and, if they passed, to receive the remaining Astartes organs and take up the mantle of full brother-initiates of the Exorcists. They would go, one by one, into the Hall of Tempering in the depths of the Basilica Malifex, and there face their fate.

Zaidu stood in the preparation cell. His wargear and fatigues, the equipment of a Scout of the 12th Company, had been discarded, leaving him bare as the black priests moved around him. The two that were able to were whispering goetic evocations as all three anointed him with strange-smelling unguents and marked his scarred body with ash from charred sticks taken from the Eternal Pyre. Zaidu knew what he faced would challenge both his strength and his faith, a ritual designed to strain physical and mental endurance. These preparations would guard his soul and act as a sign of his righteousness.

They were themselves the culmination of a vigil that had lasted almost a week, conducted by Zaidu in isolation up to this point. He had spent time meditating upon the precepts of the *Liber Exorcismus* and other foundational texts of the Chapter, trying to prepare himself for what was to come. Vey's dark warning before his departure seemed to imply it would not be enough, but Zaidu could not imagine failing now.

The priests stepped back, one behind, another to his left and the third to his right. They bowed their heads in unison. The mute one made a sign to him.

Bend.

Zaidu obeyed, and the blind one reached up, her hands questing over his close-cropped scalp and broad face until they were able to tightly fasten a length of silk, marked with the Rune of Inner Sight, over him, blinding him in turn.

'You are prepared, aspirant,' the blind priest said.

Zaidu gave a nod, but said nothing. He felt a hand on his own, taking hold. It seemed tiny and soft compared to his callused grip, yet he accepted it, holding it with care. His senses were keen enough to mean he could easily have found his way to the door that led into the Chamber of Testing without any assistance, but it was all part of the ritual. And rituals had to be honoured.

He allowed the black priest to lead him. He heard a grating of rusted hinges as the door was unlocked and scraped open.

Zaidu stepped through.

Vey watched Zaidu enter the Chamber of Testing. The place was crafted from Banish corestone, chiselled out from deep beneath the planet's crust. Its walls and floor were carved with hundreds of thousands of arcane symbols set in circles that radiated from the centre, where a slab of stone dominated the room. A set of wrist and ankle manacles lay atop it, the steel marked with further inscriptions. The room's edges were thick with candles, each one alight. In the four corners, at floor height, flamer nozzles protruded from the stonework, clogged with old, burnt promethium gel. The only other feature, besides the purity-seal-covered doors to the left and right of the slab, was a narrow viewing slit that ran along the wall above it, opaque to those within the room.

All of the chamber's surfaces were blackened by fire.

Vey had spent over a week meticulously readying the space for what was to come, beginning the first acts that led to the Rule of Sympathy. Besides fresh marks scribed into the floor, mystic tools had been laid around the central slab. A phial of consecrated oil stood on its left, a burning brazier on its right with a branding iron buried in its coals. A slender ritual sword had been placed above it. Vey stood at its foot, more occult relics around him – a barbed scourge, a curving dagger, a coil of silver chains and his incantation bowl. He stood between the objects, clad in a deep blue robe, the Calva Daemoniorum richly embroidered on its chest and a simple crown circlet of old, beaten copper upon his brow. In one hand he grasped his red-and-black Rod of El. The other was free, for now.

His body had been anointed by the black priests beforehand. A dozen of them stood in a circle around the outermost sigils on the floor, hands clasped beneath the long sleeves of their robes, hoods raised, silent. The one immediately to Vey's left carried a heavy, wizened tome in gloved hands, its cover tightly bound by links of adamantine. It was the *Liber Malorum Spirituum*, and its very existence was anathema to all sane beings.

The door to Vey's left was forced open with some difficulty. Another black priest entered, leading the blinded aspirant by the hand. He was tall and well made, though his body had yet to take on the true, powerful bulk of a fully inducted Primaris. The scars upon him were clean and white, a contrast to the dark grey smudges of the ash marks.

Vey tried to remember his own initiation rites, to find some deeper empathy. It was impossible. His only desire was that he would not fail his part in the ritual. The rest was up to Daggan Zaidu.

This was the first time Vey had conducted the ceremony without the supervision of Epistolary Castor Machen. Zaidu did not know it, but the strain to prove himself, to succeed and become truly worthy of the Chapter, was as much a burden upon Vey as it was upon the younger aspirant. For a member of the Librarius, not to mention a new inductee of the Broken Tower, there was no duty more vital, or more dangerous, than this. Any mistake would not merely end Vey's role as a Librarian – as well as his life – it could also doom the entire Chapter.

Zaidu was led to the slab and made to lie upon it. The priest who had guided him locked the manacles around his wrists and legs, ensured they were chained properly to the stone, and then withdrew from the chamber. Zaidu lay in silence, seemingly relaxed, his eyes still covered.

Somewhere far above, a bell tolled. *Unatus.* The first hour.

'The grimoire,' Vey said.

The black priest to his left stepped forward, bowed, and held forth the *Liber Malorum Spirituum.* The man's arms trembled beneath the book's weight. Vey accepted it, said the necessary words, and unchained it. Then, after a moment to focus himself, he opened the damnable pages and began to read.

Zaidu recognised Vey's voice, but not his words. He fought to remain still. Being blinded and bound felt detestable, even more so when he knew something terrible was coming. Both his hearts were beating, his body eager to rise and fight, to meet the threat head-on. But there was none, none yet. He mastered himself and remained unmoving. He suspected this trial would be as much about mental control as it was physical strength.

At some point, other voices joined Vey's, softly at first, but rising, all around him. The words they spoke sounded wrong on a deep, unsettling level. They reminded him of the shamanistic babble of the warp speakers of the tribes of Banish, tribes he had once called his own.

The heat in the chamber seemed to be rising. He could feel it radiating through the stone he was laid out over.

Then he felt the pain. It was accompanied by cold steel, the edge of a blade against his chest, cutting him. His arms twitched instinctively, making the chains clank before he suppressed the automatic urge to defend himself.

The blade bit into him. Markings, he was sure, like the initial ones made on him when he had awoken from his first progenoid implantations. He smelled the blood, felt the pain quickly dulled into numbness and irrelevancy by his body, leaving only the sensation of his blood running warm down his flanks and onto the slab.

The blade withdrew, and the guttural chant continued. Zaidu felt part of the tension in his body starting to fade as time slowly passed.

The bell sounded again.

The heat redoubled, making his skin prickle. He felt something else, something he could only describe as claws, running along his left arm and over into his chest. They did not cut as the blade had, but seemed to be questing, feeling him. A moment later and he caught a vile stench, blood but more besides, like offal and spilled innards, a slaughterhouse reek. Accompanying it was a snuffling sound, and he felt a hot, wet butcher's breath on his face. Something animalistic and vile was smelling him and pawing him, its ugly presence pressing in on him.

An involuntary shiver ran through his body. He grunted, still trying to reject the urge to test his bonds.

Zaidu felt the claws reach his scalp. That was when the true pain began.

The daemon was among them.

Vey could not yet see it, even with his warpsight, but he could sense it. To a psyker like him, the presence of this particular Neverborn was akin to having a red-hot coal pressed against his forehead while brimstone smoke choked his lungs. It made him want to reach for a weapon – the dagger, or the ritual sword, or even just the scourge or chains. He forced himself to keep reading from the abominable text of the *Liber Malorum Spirituum*, knowing that a single misspoken syllable could unmake them all. Even thinking thoughts of violence would give this one power. It was a blood-beast, a warrior, a lover of killing.

It had been drawn by Vey's rites, his words, and most of all the Rule of Sympathy, in this case the spilling of blood that had called upon the essence of violence suffusing the immaterium, itself a dark mirror of a dark galaxy. Zaidu began to strain at his bonds, but they held. Finally, the aspirant was starting to realise just how brutal this test would be. The markings made upon him were not wards or purity seals. They were Dark Tongue litanies, blasphemies designed to prepare his body for its corruption. It was an act of vilest treachery, and yet it was as nothing compared to what was about to happen – what Vey *hoped* was about to happen.

The daemon took root, and Zaidu screamed.

The slab under him was no longer stone but cold, bare steel. The blindfold was gone. Zaidu looked around, a brilliant glare in his eyes making him blink.

There were figures standing over him, silhouetted by the harsh lumen light above. Hunched, misshapen beings in medicae gowns and masks, their limbs ending in brutally grafted surgical tools. All bar one, who stood tall, overseeing them, armoured in white. Space Marine. Apothecary.

Your mind does not recall this, said a voice that seemed to come from everywhere and nowhere, a beastly growl that vibrated Zaidu's bones. *They rendered you unconscious, but your body remembers. You will experience it all if you do not let me in.*

'Who are you?' Zaidu asked, trying to rise. Chains still bound him, clenching tight. He snarled, fighting, but could not break them.

There was a whirring noise, high-pitched. One of the medicae servitors had triggered a buzz-saw, which it now held over Zaidu's bare chest. The whirring blade began to descend, slowly, shrieking as it came.

Let me in.

'No,' Zaidu shouted.

The saw bit home.

Vey tasted blood but could not pause to swallow. It ran down his chin and pattered onto the horned-skull symbol of the Chapter embroidered on his chest as he continued to read.

Zaidu was shaking violently, foaming at the mouth. The black priests were swaying, canting, their own lips bloody. One had collapsed and was going into a seizure. None of the others moved to help him. None of them stopped chanting. Vey fought to maintain control. It was only the beginning.

The third bell tolled. *Tribus.*

The acid rain was falling, hissing in the calcite netting, a susurration that sounded akin to the whispering of a thousand voices.

The water, partly purified, drizzled down over Aralii. The village was built upon the boughs of the great mire trees, their pitted grey trunks and rotten black leaves providing cover and support for the crude huts and walkways. Below, mist coiled, hanging just above the still, gnawing blackness of the acid swamps.

It was achingly dim and dismal. It was all Zaidu had ever known.

He went with the other youths along the walkway leading to the meeting platform, a stretch of timbers secured between two boughs of the Ghostroot, the great tree at the heart of the settlement.

The Exorcists had come to bless Aralii, and Zaidu was desperate to be the first among his kin to see them.

Zaidu knew the stories – every youth on Banish did. When the acid rains fell heavier than usual and strange noises growled and shrieked in the mist below, or the fires in the huts burned low and darkness crept in upon the half-sleeping figures huddled around, the people of Banish prayed to the Sky Father and to His warrior-servants, the Daemon-bane, those who burned away the shadows and drove out what should not exist. They came to the villages and chose those youths who had proven themselves in the canopy hunts and on the fighting boards, picking them out for immortality.

Zaidu beheld them for the first time on the meeting platform, three giants encased in dark red armour carved with strange symbols. They were almost twice as tall as Gugallu, the biggest man in the village. They stood impassive and unmoving as the hopeful young men of the Aralii gathered by the elders before them. The space around them seemed to warp and twist, until Zaidu focused on it.

He wanted to be first, as always. He pushed his way through his rivals, eagerness and anticipation overcoming his fear. Only when he was before the middle of the three did he begin to realise what was happening. The giant looked down at him, the predatory yellow lenses of his visor locking on to Zaidu. He froze.

'Join me,' the giant growled.

'No,' Zaidu said.

The fourth bell. Vey's throat felt like it was splitting open. Zaidu had been right – he was strong. But not strong enough, not to stop the damnation Vey was calling up and forcing into him. He kept going.

Zaidu's grandmother was whispering, but her words were inaudible over the drumming of the acid rains on the hut roof.

The fire was getting low. The rest of Zaidu's family hunched closer around it. There was a netted gap in the branches and foliage used to thatch the roof, designed to allow the smoke to escape, but most of it lingered, the smell of wet leaves and burnt timber combining with the acerbic tang of the holy roots and cleansing spice sticks that had been added to the small blaze in an effort to ward away more than just the darkness.

There was a knock at the hut's door. Just one. Nobody moved.

The knock came again, two raps this time. Then again, three. Zaidu's older brother looked at him from across the fire, his acid-scarred face unreadable, underlit by the flames.

Four raps. Zaidu's younger sister began to snivel. His mother pulled her close.

Five raps, then six. The hut seemed to shudder. The blows were falling closer together, becoming more forceful.

'Don't let it in,' Zaidu's father said. His brother was still staring at him. He hadn't blinked. He was not really his brother or, if he was, he had betrayed him in ways Zaidu could not yet explain.

The knocking came in sevens, and then eights. Eight times, over and over. The whole hut was shaking. Zaidu's little sister was screaming. His grandmother was rocking back and forth, still whispering. She had a rag bound over her eyes. Zaidu had no memory of her being blind. He realised he had no memory of any of this at all. Who were these people, and what was this place?

Bits of thatch had started to fall from the ceiling. Zaidu felt cold, dizzy. He stumbled to the door, trying not to throw up.

One last moment's hesitation. The knock came again. Eight times. 'Open it,' Zaidu's brother said in a voice that was not his own.

Breathless, slicked with sweat, Daggan Zaidu undid the latch upon the door and let the one who knocked enter.

Zaidu felt something he had never known before. Violation. A foulness was within him, in his flesh and in his soul, something that should not be there. It was as profound as it was horrifying.

He screamed, but the scream became laughter. He could taste blood and filth. His vision flashed, blurred, showing him things he should not be able to see. The roots of the world around him, the depths of the Basilica Malifex and the evil it harboured. The beating hearts that surrounded him. A towering citadel of brass and bone, so high it seemed to bend over and then back on itself. He smelled molten metal and choked on blood. And always, within him, the abominable un-ness, forced into somewhere where there was no space for it.

Claws ripped him from the inside. His limbs thrashed against their bonds, trying to do anything, anything at all, that would rid him of that foulness. The manacles held tight, smouldering.

Vey watched the damnation of Daggan Zaidu. He had closed and lashed the *Liber Malorum Spirituum*, and now said nothing, though the black priests continued to chant, their words a whispered susurration.

The Neverborn and Zaidu fought for control of the aspirant's soul. The daemon had its claws dug deep. Zaidu's body – now the daemon's too – began to rise up from the bloody slab, pulling the chains taut. His skin had started to twist and deform, especially along his upper left arm, shoulder, neck and jaw. Red-raw scales took shape as the warp creature sought to assert its control and remake its prey into a form more to its taste.

The chains were straining. The left one shattered first, then the right. The body became upright, levitating, feet still anchored by the manacles around the ankles, though they were pulled taut too.

Vey raised his Rod of El, barking words in High Gothic.

'Here but not further, child of rage! By the will of the Emperor and His holy light, you will touch no other within this chamber!'

Fury contorted Zaidu's face as the daemon looked around, properly comprehending its surroundings for the first time. Realising that it was trapped. And yet, it laughed.

'How sweet this prison is,' it snarled through Zaidu's mouth. *'How long I have hungered to defile it. So many millennia have I waited for this body, and now I shall sunder it forever!'*

There was a crunching noise. Zaidu's canines distended, becoming wicked fangs. Crimson butcher-light flared in his eyes.

Vey refused to answer it, or challenge it further. That was for Zaidu to do.

There was blood on his hands, and a body beneath him.

Zaidu looked down at it. A man, older than him, breathing his last with a spear impaled through his chest. Zaidu gripped the weapon's haft and twisted it free, struggling – the blood made his grip treacherous.

The fight was still ongoing, passing by Zaidu and on into the next length of huts, walkways and trunk chambers. The Aralii were storming the treetop settlement of their rivals, the Goetan, a raid designed to seize sparse resources and take prisoners and scalps. Just another of the endless fights waged between the tribes of Banish, yet it was Zaidu's first.

'You kill well, little one,' growled a voice.

Zaidu turned to find a warrior he did not know facing him. The man was garbed like his father, with a craggy breastplate of mire-tree bark and an acid-net cloak, yet it could not be his father, for the man wore a full helm fashioned in the likeness of a snarling hound, a piece of equipment his family did not possess and which would have been far beyond their means. It was something more befitting a chieftain or a bough-champion.

'*Join me, and we will kill more,*' the beast-helmed stranger said.

'I only kill as commanded,' Zaidu replied.

'*Then I will command you, Demetrius,*' the Beast said. '*You are an animal, like me. A predator. A killer. Remember that.*'

'That is not my name,' Zaidu said. 'And I will never obey you.'

'*Then you will perish,*' the Beast snarled, and struck.

The eighth bell tolled. *Expulsiars.*

Vey paced slowly around the Chamber of Testing, speaking the protective wards, stepping over those priests who had fallen. Only half remained, still struggling to endure the raw evil that infested the room, a corruption that Vey could barely feel. Still, the effort of keeping it in place was taxing. This was no minor daemon, not the kind that should have been summoned for this sort of ritual. It was ancient, and powerful. Something had gone terribly wrong, but now was not the time for reflection. Vey knew he had to contain it. He had to stop it from reaching even those watching through the viewing slit in the wall – Inquisitor Mundar and his diabolists. Otherwise, he would have failed, and his life would be forfeit.

He felt the strain of Zaidu's struggle before him, but also a strange detachment, an inability to empathise. It was the legacy of his own exorcism, he knew. None who had so much of their soul torn away could ever connect on a true level with their own species, or any other, ever again. Any idea that they did was nothing but a fleeting illusion.

Vey had never lamented that loss. It enabled him to better

serve the Chapter, and the Imperium. That was the only reason for his existence, so it was well that he was incapable of suffering the distractions of true human emotion.

Zaidu – the daemonhost – was trying to rip away the ankle chains that still held firm, in between bouts of crying, shrieking, and spitting blasphemies and gibberish that even Vey's knowledge of the occult could not decipher.

'You will not know freedom, warp spawn,' Vey said matter-of-factly. 'You were brought here to serve the Emperor.'

'A pox on your False Emperor,' Zaidu spat, black bile spilling from his sneering lips and leaving his teeth and fangs dark and glistening. *'He has been dead for millennia – he sits and rots and hears none of your prayers!'*

'He is no corpse, or His light would not guide the Imperium still,' Vey said, his steady pacing around the sigil-marked floor bringing him to the back of the host. Zaidu twisted to face him, causing the leg manacles to draw blood and making the Primaris' bones crunch and pop.

'You didn't know, did you?' the daemon rasped. *'You reached into the dark, but you did not know I would answer.'*

Vey said nothing, but kept pacing, Zaidu turning to keep facing him, grinning madly.

'He called you brother. He trusted you without question. He was so proud, Torrin Vey, so proud to be here, to perform this rite. It made it easier for me to enter him. He hates you now. He wants to slaughter you and drink of your blood. I do too. We will, together. We–'

The words faltered, and an unnatural, guttural groan rose from deep within Zaidu's chest. He arched his back, then slammed his head against the slab with a hideous crunch. He did it again, drawing blood, then wailed. Despite his hollowness, Vey summoned a smile.

'Daggan Zaidu is a true servant of the Emperor and the Chapter,' the Librarian declared. 'He will never stop fighting you, daemon.'

Zaidu fought the Beast. It carried an axe of bone, one which should have been able to cleave through both Zaidu and his spear with a single swing. Yet the blood-marked wood didn't give way beneath its bite, and Zaidu turned his parry into a lunge that almost caught the Beast in the flank.

He did not know how long he had been fighting. There was no sign of the rest of the raiding force, or the Goetan. The huts and ledges of the village lay dark and uninhabited amidst the canopy. The rain was falling, a hiss rising to a roar as it drooled down through the calcite netting.

The Beast drove Zaidu back. It was big and fast, and burning with wrath so potent Zaidu could see it smouldering off it like dark coils of smoke. But Zaidu met its aggression with resolve, finding an inner stoniness that would not bend or break. His lean body darted lithely around or away from its strikes, drawing bellows of rage.

It could not conquer Zaidu, and yet he could not strike a fatal blow, not without exposing himself to the counterstrike. His body was in agony, afire with an unnatural presence that felt as though it was draining his limbs of their strength and dulling his mind.

He would not win this, he realised. His only hope was sacrifice.

He cast aside his spear and threw himself at the Beast. He was not a boy any more, not a starved Banish tribe-wretch. He was a warrior, and bore within him the legacy of the Emperor and the stony will of the Praetorian. He grasped the Beast and, roaring, hauled it with him the last few yards out beyond the canopy that protected the Goetan village from Banish's elements.

The acid rain began to hit them both. Zaidu felt its pain, but he didn't let go. He screamed, and the noise melded with the bellowed rage of the Beast, until the two sounds were indistinguishable.

Zaidu's flesh began to melt, and so did the Beast. Its armour sloughed away, exposing crimson scales and black fur that started to steam. The helm dissolved amidst the hissing hail, revealing a nightmare, skull-like visage, inches from Zaidu's own as they grappled. He locked on to its red eyes and saw only fury.

'You will know me again, Demetrius,' the monster spat.

Zaidu couldn't answer it. The acid was blinding him, the stink of his own liquifying flesh overwhelming. He had never known pain like it before, and knew he never would again, not until he passed fully beyond the veil and was greeted by the eternal damnation that awaited him. He howled, until his throat choked on the slurry of his own dissolving body.

The twelfth and final bell began to toll. *Ipsissimus.* If Zaidu did not expel the daemon now, he never would. Vey watched, jaw clenched, Rod of El raised lest in its final moments in the materium the powerful Neverborn should try and latch on to another soul.

Zaidu's body was shaking and contorting into shapes that should not have been possible. Multi-hued warp ectoplasm was bubbling from his mouth and nose. His eyes had lost the bloody hue of the daemon, but were showing white.

Chanting, Vey made his way to where the brazier was burning to the left of the chained aspirant and, with his free hand, gripped the shaft of the branding iron resting in it.

Reality reeled. Zaidu broke apart and re-formed, died and was born again. He drowned in seas of blood, rose on black wings amidst cosmic brilliance shot through with every colour in existence, and many more besides. He cried and laughed and lay silent and still and quiet for many years. He beat himself and tore at his flesh, broke his bones, ripped out his teeth, gouged out his eyes.

He was Daggan Zaidu. That was his true name. Somehow, that knowledge anchored him, as stars were born and died and eternity unravelled around him, showing him everything but stealing away all meaning from it, all form of recognition.

He saw a golden warrior, vanquishing the Beast.

Rage, fury, anger, he destroyed it all. They were meaningless, like all emotions. Impotent compared to the stone that ran through him – duty and selfless sacrifice. That was what he was, given a form of flesh. He clung to it, even as he strained, strained to force out that which should not be there.

He could hear a bell tolling. Twelve great, sonorous chimes. Twelve hours. It was his end, and his new beginning.

He roared, one final effort, gripping the nebulous blackness that the Beast – the *daemon* – had become and rending it from himself.

It was done.

Vey lunged at the restraining slab and drove the red-hot branding iron against Zaidu. Flesh hissed and blistered, adding its stink to the reek pervading the chamber. The metal seared the Calva Daemoniorum into Zaidu's breast.

The aspirant screamed once more, but it was plaintive, exhausted. With a clatter, Vey cast the iron aside and gripped Zaidu by the throat, pinning his broken body back down against the slab as he tried to rise. He hissed the rites of purification as the surviving priests scrambled forward. One pressed a vial to Zaidu's blackened lips, forcing him to drink the holy water within, while another used an aspergillum to similarly drench him in sacred unguents, purging him from without and within. Zaidu writhed in Vey's grip, but could not break free.

Gradually, the struggles eased. Zaidu's breathing became slower, more regular. The butcher-light had left his eyes. They focused on Vey, still struggling in the aftershock of the banishment.

The Librarian managed to speak.

'Welcome to the Chapter, brother-initiate.'

Zaidu lay alone in his cell for many days, sharing it with none but the rats that occasionally scraped amid the dust, bones and cobwebs filling its corners.

He was being kept in isolation and monitored via remote vid feed, but even if he had not been, he would not have left that small space of cold stone and dim candlelight. He lay, and stared at the shadows dancing above him, and tried to find himself.

His body was still in agony. Every bone felt as though it had been broken and then reset, and his flesh ached. He reached up and, for the hundredth time, gently felt the scales that marred the upper-left side of his torso and face, and the fangs that deformed his mouth.

He was an abomination. But perhaps he had been since the day he had taken the first of the progenoids and become something both more and less than human. For reasons that continued to elude him, he now found it difficult to care.

How could that be? How could mutation and blasphemy leave him feeling cold nothingness, when just days before his righteous soul would have raged and burned at such corruption?

Eventually, the cell's door scraped open. Torrin Vey stepped heavily through. He was fully armed and armoured.

Zaidu made himself rise, forcing stiff limbs to obey. He tried to find the right words, tried to find anything at all. Eventually, he managed to speak, voicing a dry, dull croak.

'Why?'

'You know why,' Vey answered without hesitation or emotion. 'I will not demean you by quoting the texts. Chaos corrupts. We have made sure that there was nothing left for it to corrupt.'

Zaidu again sought the anger and pain he had felt when in the midst of the ritual. He tried to reawaken his disgust, his revulsion, his desire for vengeance. But he could find none of it.

'I feel… hollow,' he admitted eventually, struggling to articulate himself.

'That is a blessing,' Vey said. 'Use it. Our kind have no time for compassion or empathy. It is a distraction.'

'What I saw,' Zaidu tried again, before trailing off.

'If you wish, you may discuss your experiences with me, and I will offer what guidance I can,' Vey said. 'But for now, we have a duty to perform. It is my honour to conduct you to the council chamber, where you and the other new brother-initiates will swear their final oaths and become fully inducted members of the Chapter.'

Zaidu considered the prospect, then nodded his assent.

'I will go first,' he said.

'As you wish,' Vey replied.

Zaidu met the other aspirants who had survived – Amrath, Eitan, Belloch, Dee. He did not ask what had become of the others. That was a secret he did not yet wish to know the truth of.

They received their power armour for the first time, ritually applied by serfs in an ambulatory off the Cloister of Scars, then passed through it into the council chamber. It was a stone-clad hall at the centre of the Basilica Malifex, the heart of the Chapter. Graven statues lined its walls, Adeptus Astartes alongside saints and lesser mortals, clutching in their stony hands great braziers whose light struggled to fill the vast, echoing space. The air was filled with incense from censers being swung by darting auto-cherubim that streaked through the cloying fog, and vibrated with the doggerel-canting of the hundreds of liturgists, priests, zelators and Chapter deifiers that stood, robed in dark red and black, on either side of the central aisle.

The Exorcists advanced down it towards the raised end of the hall. There, beneath a hundred ancient and mouldering standards and prayer flags, Chapter Master Vasaphon waited, likewise equipped with the full panoply of war. Accompanying him was the Master of Sanctity, Chaplain Nachmanides, armoured in black, his grim skull helm bearing great ram's horns that made him look like the living embodiment of the Calva Daemoniorum. Nor was it only Adeptus Astartes occupying the high end of the hall. Lord Inquisitor Vaskez of the Ordo Malleus was present, wearing red-lacquered armour and an ermine gown and accompanied by a retinue of hunchbacked, furiously scribbling lexi-notarists, tonsured priests, diabolists and bibliosophs who struggled beneath mounds of tomes and scrolls.

Zaidu took in the sight as he marched down the hall, the other four in lockstep behind him. How he had hungered for this day, and yet now that it had finally arrived, he could find none of that former desire. There was no pride, no rejoicing. Only a cold determination. It was as Vey had said. All else was a distraction.

He took his place before the raised platform, his brothers beside him. The chanting of the assembled host ended, the echoes continuing for some time, seemingly reluctant to fade away.

With a scrape of ceramite on stone, the five knelt. Nachmanides raised and opened the *Liber Exorcismus*.

Together, Zaidu and his fellow Exorcists took their Oaths of Damnation.

CHAPTER EIGHTEEN

RESOLUTIONS

The Present Day, on Fidem IV

Torrin Vey considered his powers to be subtle, a dagger in the dark rather than a warhammer wielded at dawn.

There were times, however, when subtlety had to be laid aside, when it was not enough to reach into the minds of enemies and conjure up illusions, or perform tricks that misdirected and ensnared. Sometimes, he had to open himself to the maelstrom and delve in with both hands, using his gift, his curse, his *mutation*, in the most brutal ways he could imagine.

He used it in those ways beneath the valley between Pilgrim Town and Deliverance. He realised in the space of a heartbeat that the tunnel entrance to the dugout where they had met the Word Bearers was about to collapse, just as the dugout itself had behind them. And he realised that he was the only one who could stop it.

He called upon the warp, upon the very powers that were shaking apart the earth all around, and commanded it to obey him. Clamping Kerubim, he raised his arms, spitting an invocation that cut the insides of his throat like a razor. He snatched the howling gale of the storm and ordered it to tear reality, sacrificing a little part of himself in doing so. A little morsel more of his already ragged soul gone. At this stage, what did it matter?

The fabric of the mortal plane had grown dangerously thin. Vey was able to use it to change the meaning of existence, much as he had done when he had caught Zaidu in the dugout, just for a few seconds more. Arms still raised, he demanded the earth and splitting timbers above him hold firm, to defy Fidem IV's gravity and in doing so break the laws of nature itself.

The collapsing roof, against all reason, remained unmoving, an avalanche of dirt and shattered struts kept in check by no visible force. It was like a vid recording that had been freeze-framed, a heartbeat away from disaster. Only a tiny cascade of dust trickled down as Vey held his arms raised, even his locked servos unable to hide the trembling in his body.

He managed to look at Zaidu. The Sin Slayer had stopped resisting him as he had finally hauled him from the dugout. He now stood still and silent, staring up at the frozen earth.

'Go,' Vey snarled through gritted, bloody teeth.

'Not without you,' Zaidu responded. 'I have left one brother beneath the earth – I will not leave two.'

'Then… on my mark… run.'

He held it for a moment more, feeling as though he was simultaneously on fire and being frozen solid, his hearts close to rupturing, his spine snapping, his brain boiling inside his skull. He knew the Belisarian Furnace was seconds away from triggering. His body was responding to the strain stimuli as though he was dying. It was correct.

The howling of the warp had dropped to a low murmur. Timber creaked and earth shifted ponderously around them, a deep, low groan, as though Fidem itself was protesting at their blasphemy, at their usurpation of all that was right and proper.

'Go,' Vey hissed.

He began to move before releasing, forcing his body to respond, to unlock. He stumbled, but Zaidu was with him, a hand on his pauldron, pushing him on.

He let go.

The act of release itself could have destroyed him. The energies of the empyrean exploded with a roar like a Thunderhawk's turbofans. Fidem answered with a rage of its own as hundreds of tonnes of earth came slamming down in the wake of the Exorcists.

They outran the collapse, as one section of the tunnel after another caved in after them, the thunder and fury of the avalanche filling everything. Vey pushed his body to respond, through the alternating numbness and pain, then through the tunnel entrance and into the adjoining crosscut junction.

The collapse pursued them, but only as far as the passageway's lintel. The entrance was rapidly blocked by a wall of dirt, and the timbers still overhead groaned and creaked, but held. Vey stumbled to a halt, realising the junction was occupied by Squad Eitan. The nearest, the hulking brute Uten, was crouching before them, picked out by the stab-lumen on Vey's pauldron.

'Can we be of assistance, brethren?' Uten asked as Zaidu and Vey came to a halt. The Librarian tried to recover, his skull aching and his whole body feeling frigid and stiff despite his armour's internal regulators.

'What is the status of the rest of the strike force?' Zaidu demanded, paying no heed to Vey's discomfort as he locked immediately on to the next priority.

'Spread across the tunnel sections,' Uten reported. 'Almoner-Sergeant Haad and Lector-Sergeant Anu report the heretics have broken contact and are withdrawing.'

'Link back up with the rest,' Zaidu instructed, before addressing Vey over their private vox-channel.

'The heretics have the Broken One.'

'I know,' Vey managed to respond.

'We must pursue immediately.'

'We do not know where they are headed, or exactly what they intend. They might plan to move the host off-world.'

'All the more reason to catch up with them as quickly as possible. You have tracked their leader before. Can you do it again?'

'Perhaps,' Vey allowed, unwilling to admit how exhausted he was. It was all he could do to process Zaidu's words. 'He is powerful. He is in league with daemons. I cannot say whether Caedus or one of the other Neverborn within the Broken One are assisting him, or whether they resist his advances. The difference might prove crucial.'

'But it does not change the need to terminate the Broken One,' Zaidu said. 'We must rally the Hexbreakers and get back above ground. Perform your invocations, Lie-Eater, and locate the heretics for me. Then I can end this farce.'

Vey quelled the urge to snap at the almoner-lieutenant. He had known the risks when he recruited Zaidu. The Sin Slayer was lost to the hunt, and Vey's only hope was to try and keep up.

'I will do what I can,' he said. Zaidu had already turned away, stalking along the tunnel, highlighting his location on the shared display and pinging commands to the rest of the strike force, ordering them to close on him.

Vey permitted himself the briefest moment to shut his eyes and murmur a catechism of easing, focusing on the familiar words and trying to banish the aches that had worked their way into his body and mind. Then, disdaining further weakness, he followed the Sin Slayer.

* * *

Zaidu returned to the place where he and Nabua had first discovered the labyrinth, where the shell strike had collapsed a section of tunnel and thrown them down. He collected Vey, the sergeants and Amilanu there, while the rest of the Hexbreakers held the neighbouring passageways.

Artillery was still shaking the uppermost crosscuts, the Guard's assault across the valley carrying on above them. It stoked Zaidu's simmering wrath. He was frustrated. The Broken One had been before him, practically beneath his knives, and it had escaped. The fact that the heretics had now claimed it only compounded his sense of failure. It was something he was unaccustomed to, something that shamed him.

Perhaps he shouldn't have thrown himself in so heedlessly. Perhaps he should have placed his attention on directing the rest of the strike force once they had descended into the tunnels and re-established contact. They could have cut off the Word Bearers and their prize, surrounded them and turned the galleries and passages into a kill-zone. Instead, he had once again charged ahead, focused like a hunter-killer missile's target lock on the Broken One.

Nabua was the one who had paid for his aggression and lack of planning. Zaidu expected the realisation to haunt him, to further add to his frustrations, but he found little in the way of regret. Kinship was not a concept he had been familiar with for a very long time, certainly not with one only lately inducted into the Hexbreakers. Most Exorcists sought to portray a veneer of brotherhood, but Zaidu could not bring himself to be so performative, not while the needs of the hunt were so pressing.

Amilanu was able to reach the *Witch-Bane* via his comms uplink. Shipmaster Nazmund reported that the heretic fleet contesting high orbit was adopting an attack heading, but that the anchorage of the Exorcists ship in low orbit was not yet threatened.

Zaidu ordered a sub-surface scan of the valley, mapping out the top layer of tunnels and charting an exfiltration route. As he had hoped, the passageways led back to the edge of Pilgrim Town. That explained how the Broken One had been able to evade them.

'Turn the sensorium arrays on the opposite side of the valley,' Zaidu instructed, speaking to Nazmund via the link Amilanu had patched him into. 'Focus especially on the fortress, Deliverance. The Militarum's intelligence believes that is where the Archenemy's planetside leadership are based. I want to know of any anomalies, any hint of the location of the Broken One or the Word Bearers.'

'*Affirmative, almoner-lieutenant,*' came Nazmund's response.

'Brother-Librarian?' Zaidu asked, casting his gaze towards Vey. As ever, the Lie-Eater stood slightly apart from the Hexbreakers' leadership. He seemed not to hear Zaidu, who repeated himself after a moment.

'Have you picked up the heretics' trail?'

'Not… with absolutely certainty,' Vey answered, casting only a glance at Zaidu. He looked pale, drawn. 'They have retreated amongst their flock, likely within Fort Deliverance. I suspect they intend to conduct theomantic rites. It is possible they are planning to free the daemons and harness them for their campaign on this world.'

'We cannot allow Caedus to materialise,' Zaidu said.

His vambrace blipped. He raised his wrist and unlocked the scan package Nazmund had lanced down from the *Witch-Bane*.

'*We have no means of specifically identifying either the Word Bearers or the Broken One via our systems, but there are a large number of individual returns showing up in the remains of the fortress complex,*' Nazmund said, reading Zaidu through the results as he assessed them. '*It has been put into a high state of defensive readiness. There is also a notable energy spike, analogous with an idling void shield.*'

'Deliverance was once possessed of such defences,' Zaidu confirmed, his thoughts locking on to the hypno-eidetic data he had absorbed during the voyage to Fidem. 'But it was thought to be long inoperable.'

'*It is Techmarine Kothar's opinion that the shield has been repaired. Unless it is deactivated or overloaded, it will protect the fortress from orbital bombardment or a direct aerial insertion.*'

'Understood,' Zaidu said. 'A bombardment would not have been sufficient for our means anyway. We need absolute proof of the Broken One's destruction. Are the heretics' fleet assets still closing?'

'*Affirmative. Imperial Navy elements under Commodore Rancrow are moving on an interception heading. My tactical projections show it is likely the engagement will spill into low orbit. Do I have permission to assist the commodore's efforts?*'

'Only within a radius that keeps you geo-locked above the fortress engagement zone,' Zaidu said. 'We may yet have need of your bombardment cannon.'

'*Understood, almoner-lieutenant.*'

'Am I to understand that you intend to launch a direct assault on Fort Deliverance?' Vey asked. Zaidu hadn't expected the interruption, let alone the sudden sharpness of Vey's tone.

'Do you believe the Broken One is being held somewhere else?' he asked.

'No. But I think the odds are heavily weighted against such a venture. Attacking immediately would be a repetition of the mistakes we have consistently made since planetfall.'

'You mean the mistakes I have made,' Zaidu clarified. He was surprised Vey was questioning him, let alone in front of the rest of the Hexbreakers' command structure. 'Is it not clear that we have to act immediately?'

'Such a strategy has not yet availed us,' Vey said, moving to join the inner circle, Anu and Haad making space for him. 'The Word Bearers will be ready for us. There is even a possibility attacking could play into their hands. I cannot anticipate the nature of whatever ritual they are performing, but it is certain they will try to use either the Broken One or its daemons against us.'

'What do you propose instead then?' Zaidu asked, forcing himself to humour the Librarian. Once, he would have found it in himself to appreciate and accept Vey's insight. In the midst of the hunt, though, with time slipping away, it was unwelcome.

'Use the might of the Imperial war machine. The Astra Militarum, the Navy. Invest Fort Deliverance and crush it. The Word Bearers are not numerous. This is only the broken remnants of a warband, and their cultists have lost the initiative. They will not long resist a combined arms assault from above and below.'

'That would take days, if not weeks, to orchestrate. You said yourself, we do not know what the Word Bearers intend to do with the Broken One. We cannot risk trading time for certainty.'

'The danger we run is that of total failure,' Vey said. 'Thus far we have been fortunate not to suffer more than one loss. If we make a mistake during a storm assault, it will be far worse, and if our numbers are decimated, we will not be able to destroy the Broken One. Be assured, Sin Slayer, that is the only objective that matters. I do not wish us to compromise our ability to achieve it with continual, piecemeal rashness.'

Zaidu bowed his head for a moment, making himself consider the Librarian's words. It was true that he had been reckless, perhaps overly so. It was not merely his desire to annihilate the Broken One, though, to cast out Caedus. Operational constraints demanded continual aggression. Hesitation of any kind would surely be fatal. Vey's suggestion mitigated long-term risk in exchange for short-term uncertainty. Zaidu considered that a luxury.

'I have seen my Never-brother's end,' he told Vey. 'I have

witnessed it through my own eyes. The Emperor has shown me that I will strike the blow that obliterates that monstrosity. To hesitate would be the worst dereliction imaginable. I must act. I must take the fight to the Archenemy at every opportunity, or the future I have seen may never come to pass.'

'You cannot force prophecy, Zaidu,' Vey said. 'You cannot cut away every strand of possibility until there is only one left.'

'But inaction guarantees the opposite. That it will never be realised.'

'It is not inaction I am suggesting,' Vey said tersely, and Zaidu couldn't help but notice how his eyes glimmered golden in the tunnel's shadows. 'I understood the risks when I told you of Caedus' escape. I know that this hunt fulfils you. But you cannot become addicted to it. To the emotions you thought you had forgotten.'

'You think that is the cause of this?' Zaidu demanded, his own anger starting to burn brighter. 'That I seek Caedus just to feel something again? I assure you, Lie-Eater, none of these emotions are ones I would willingly experience.'

'Dry, stale bread is a feast for a starving man,' Vey said. 'Even if you do not realise it, this operation has given you a level of purpose you have not known for too long. Your judgements are clouded by the feelings your Never-brother inspires in you.'

Zaidu knew that to snap back at the Librarian would merely prove his point, but it was difficult. As he sought the right words, a sound intruded, right on the edge of audibility, suddenly supplanting his frustrations.

Whispers.

Zaidu looked past Vey, into the darkness of the tunnel. It seemed to twitch for a second before settling, silence returning. Vey followed his gaze, though whether he was merely reacting to Zaidu or had heard the sound too, he couldn't be sure.

He knew better than to ask. To speak of something was to risk conjuring it.

'Time is precious, and it is slipping through our grasp,' he said instead, letting his frustration bleed away into the nothingness within. 'Your comments have been noted, enlightened brother.'

He triggered his vox and reopened the link Amilanu had established with Shipmaster Nazmund.

'Have Kothar prepare *Daemonium Eversor* for suborbital deployment.'

CHAPTER NINETEEN

CONFESSIONS

Mordun spoke privately with Artax as the warband returned to the fortress.

There had been a moment when they had feared the Blind Shepherd would not be leaving the underworld with them. His runic signifier on the warband's display had failed, coinciding with a tremoring in the tunnels that Artax had taken to indicate a collapse. The younger brethren had bewailed the apparent loss, but at the time he had been too bent on keeping the Blessed One contained. Mordun had subdued it somehow, but he still expected it to strike out at any moment. With Kordiron he had dragged it along by its collar, the cursed Imperial steel burning his groaning prisoner's skin.

They had slipped through the trap laid for them in the adjoining tunnels by the loyalists and made it back to the streets beyond the north ridge of the valley. There, in the half-dark of early dawn, they had paused to collect themselves, and then rejoiced when Mordun emerged after them. Even Artax had experienced a sense of relief, though it wasn't twinned to the divine intervention Tarven the Litanist immediately claimed had preserved the Blind Shepherd.

Now was no time for a warband leadership challenge.

They carried on, towards the fortress, the new day spilling weak and pallid over its dark ramparts, as though afraid to touch them. The place had been the sight of brutal fighting in the last blessed war to sweep across this miserable, misbegotten world. It was well sited and stoutly made, low walls of black rockcrete, plasteel and packed dirt arranged in jagged bastion patterns, fractals of murderous architecture surrounded by a deep, broad moat.

It would have made for an ideal headquarters if it were not half ruined. There were several breaches in the walls, rubble filled much of the dry moat, and the central keep had partially collapsed, only the northern and eastern halves of its upper floors intact. What was still standing was pockmarked by old shell strikes and las-burns.

It had stopped being a place of conflict millennia before, and instead had become one of pilgrimage. Prayer banners had been hoisted over the crumbling remnants of its bastions, and hard-scrabble shrines had been constructed from the debris, sheltering in the shadows of those walls still standing.

The arrival of the Word Bearers had changed all that. The False Emperor's rags had been ripped down and ritually burned before the broken keep. Now the horned ram's skull used by the flock proliferated alongside the eight-pointed star and the ancient sigil of the Word Bearers, while Dark Tongue scriptures and damnable praises had been daubed across the walls, interspersed by the rotting carcasses of captured Guardsmen and pilgrims, hung from the parapets by knotted spools of razor wire.

The sons of Lorgar honoured the fortress' old spirit by renewing its purpose. The scrap streets that had sprung up around it had been demolished to clear lines of fire, the raw materials used to crudely shore up the gaps in the defences. Heavy weaponry, looted from Diamantus, had been set up atop the bastions and in the ravelin, the outwork that protected the inner gatehouse. The flock's most capable herdsmen had been assigned to act as a garrison force. It would not resist the Emperor's lackies for long, but now that the Blessed One was in their possession, Artax suspected they did not need long.

As they crossed the open ground before the ravelin and passed into its sharp shadow, Mordun ordered Artax to surrender the Blessed One to Varantor's keeping and linger with him in the gaping maw of the outer gateway.

'Are you well, my brother?' Mordun asked.

The question seemed unassuming, almost out of place after the desperate pressures of the past few hours. Artax found something strangely distressing about it.

He knew what the Blind Shepherd meant. He knew too that, despite the scorn he would have unleashed on any other member of the warband who asked him such a question, it was impossible not to be contrite with Mordun. There was something too venerable, too patrician about him. It blunted the edge of Artax's bitterness.

'I have not attended to my prayers as diligently as I should have of late,' he found himself admitting, for a moment knowing something akin to embarrassment. 'I have been... troubled.'

'Understandably,' Mordun said. 'The warband stands on the brink of victory or defeat, and few know this brotherhood as well as you, Artax. The leadership you provide for the younger ones is undoubtedly a burden, but it has not gone unnoticed.'

Artax refused to allow himself to take pleasure in Mordun's

praise. He knew the Dark Apostle's daemonkin could be slithering through his thoughts at that very moment. If it was, though, Mordun made no indication that he knew Artax's mind.

'I am aware of what some of the others say of me,' he said, deciding to go on the offensive, whether his thoughts were betraying him or not. 'That I do not have the faith befitting a Bearer of the Word.'

'And do you think that is true?'

'I think I have more questions than most.'

'Questions are good. It was questions that led us out from under the crushing weight of the False Emperor's lies. We questioned the nature of ourselves, of the galaxy, of the very gods. Never stop questioning. If you do, you will assuredly never progress along the Eightfold Path.'

'But I have started to find the answers unsatisfactory,' Artax admitted, daring to press on. Mordun liked to converse with his brotherhood, to debate them, to interrogate the tenets of their personal faith and how each approached their journey. It had been some time, though, since he had held such a conversation with Artax.

'I do not question the existence of the True Gods or the power they wield,' Artax said. 'What I do question is the nature of that godhood. I have seen many great and terrible things since the warp opened my eyes. I have witnessed our masters, the ones we worship, time and again, given flesh and form by our praise and the spilling of our blood. There has never been a moment when they have seemed like anything other than predators, drawn to kill us and consume us. There has never been a moment I have felt kinship with them.'

Mordun said nothing, and Artax made himself continue.

'Take our so-called flock as an example. They are prey, and in some desperate attempt at self-preservation they have reimaged us, their predators, as gods. We do the same every time we converse with the beings from beyond the veil, or enter into pacts with them. They hunger for both our souls and our flesh and blood, and nothing will change that. Any power they offer is only power to act at their behest. And that is no true power.'

Mordun gave a murmur that could have been agreement. He placed a gauntlet on Artax's pauldron.

'Come, walk with me,' he urged, steering him in through the outer gateway. The ravelin was a triangular-shaped bastion that lay outside the main body of the fortress, acting as a defensive work protecting the inner entrance. Mordun's staff tapped lightly on the split and scarred rockcrete underfoot as they progressed through it, towards that second gate.

'You have identified one of the truths of our faith, my brother,' Mordun said, a hand still on Artax's shoulder. 'That power given is not power at all. For it to be true, it must be taken. And that is why we are here. That is why we have sought the Blessed One all this way, from Monthax to Tyrellum to the Fire Worlds.'

'The host,' Artax said. 'It truly contains the one we have been seeking for so long? The Red Marshal?'

'Yes,' Mordun said. 'And through it, ascension is no longer an abstract hope. I think your thoughts on these matters are not without merit. In fact, I would take some of them even further. Many of the entities we have dealings with hate us. But they also hate one another. In many cases, they *are* hate, formed from it, given meaning and purpose by it. They exist to torture and destroy. That in turn shows their weakness, their deep flaw, for they have no reason to exist other than the one granted to them by their master, their creator. They have no will of their own. We, on the other hand, do. The bargains we strike, the pacts we make, are not hollow. They are not in vain. They represent real power. Strength, immortality. And if we are careful, we do not lose ourselves along the way. We do not become pawns of the mindless, hungry beasts you describe.'

'Then when, when will we know that power?' Artax asked, stopping and facing Mordun, the question genuine and fervent. They had reached the short bridge that crossed from the ravelin over the moat and into the fortress proper. Bodies had been impaled on the spikes flanking the structure. Artax had removed his helm on being relieved of the duty of guarding the Blessed One, and he could smell the sweet sickness of rotting flesh and hear the frantic buzzing of the bloodflies infesting the corpses.

'Soon,' Mordun replied.

'Always soon,' Artax muttered, turning away, but Mordun again gripped him and turned him back, forcing him to gaze upon the holy scripture that bound the upper half of his raggedy old face.

'Keep the faith, my brother, for just a little longer,' the Blind Shepherd whispered. 'Our reward is coming. We have but one more enemy to overcome. And they are more terrible than any we have faced before.'

Artax felt confusion cloud Mordun's guiding clarity.

'The Primaris? We have vanquished their breed before. Their inexperience–'

'It is not that they are the Martian's toys,' Mordun interrupted, with an edge to his voice now that made Artax take note. 'It is what they are within themselves, their very essence. Anathema.'

The suggestion caused a sense of revulsion in Artax, even as he sought clarity.

'In what way?'

'I was gifted a revelation as we fought through the depths,' Mordun said. 'I saw them for what they truly are. Soulless. Hollow creatures. Beings cut off from divinity and unable to commune with the empyrean.'

'But how can that be? They are neither revenants nor automata. How can they have no souls?'

'By means of the most awful sacrilege imaginable. Through pact-breaking and the basest of betrayals. They willingly wed themselves to our daemonkin, and then expel them through blasphemous banishment.'

'All of them?' Artax asked disbelievingly. 'And the servants of the False Emperor tolerate this?'

'Make no mistake, they are a damned brotherhood. Hunters of our kindred. They will be coming here to destroy all we have worked so hard to build. That is as it should be, for they are all part of the wider plan, but they must not be allowed to interrupt the ceremony. After it, we shall make them pay for their desecrations. The True Gods demand it.'

'I will take command of the ramparts personally,' Artax began to say, but Mordun hushed him, tapping a finger lightly against his breastplate.

'Those matters are already in hand. Kordiron will be sufficient for the task. I have a different duty in mind for you, one even more vital.'

'Name it, my shepherd,' Artax said, inclining his head.

'I want you to oversee the final preparations for the coronation rites.'

Artax was silent at first, trying to find the right words.

'You honour me, but I do not feel…' He trailed off, frustrated by his own, unexpected weakness.

'Your faith is deeper than you know, Brother Artax,' Mordun said. 'There are none I would rather entrust with these duties. Go to Eparch Sublimus. He will provide you with all that you need.'

'If you are certain,' Artax said. 'Has the time truly come?'

'It has,' Mordun replied. 'I will address the flock. They must be made aware that the hour of ascension is close at hand. The eyes of the gods will be upon us all.'

'Yes, my shepherd,' Artax said. 'With your blessings, I will begin.'

'*Gloria Aeterna*, brother,' Mordun said, offering a short benediction before entering through the gatehouse.

Artax lingered, looking up at the strengthening dawn and listening to the bloodflies feasting.

At last. He could already imagine the rage among the other senior members of the warband once those who believed themselves more pious, more enlightened by the Primordial Truth, discovered Mordun had chosen him for the final ceremony. Artax would enjoy taunting them when the time came. But there were now more pressing matters than reasserting his dominance within the warband. Down the centuries, they had encountered enough misguided fools who believed they could harness the power of Chaos while still serving their Corpse Emperor. But he had never known Adeptus Astartes to do so. What Mordun had claimed seemed near inconceivable, a blasphemy of the highest kind. To struggle with a Neverborn for dominance was one thing, but to deliberately invite one in and then cast it out, tearing away the soul with it and guaranteeing damnation – to Artax it sounded nothing less than insane.

There was a perverse deliciousness to it as well, though. What would the Praetorian have said if he had lived to see his sons embracing such blasphemies, tainting themselves and the gene-seed that was his legacy? Truly, the Imperium was a rotten, desperate edifice, well on its way to richly deserved annihilation.

Artax pulled on his helm and followed his Dark Apostle into the fortress.

CHAPTER TWENTY

REVELATIONS

Daemonium Eversor touched down on blazing jets of blue-white plasma in a Pilgrim Town square just behind the Sacred Ways.

A battalion of Logres Ice World Guardsmen had been occupying the space, but had wisely decided to shift their staging area when the Exorcists arrived. The Hexbreakers had emerged back into Imperial lines from Fidem's underworld, finding their ascent had taken them up through a hydro cleansing plant being maintained by a party of Militarum engineers. Their terror when the dusty, red-clad giants broke up through what they had believed was a solid floor had been palpable. Vey had been forced to slip his thoughts into theirs, artificially deadening – and thus easing – their minds long enough for the Hexbreakers to identify themselves and convince the Guardsmen they weren't the enemy.

Even such a relatively simple act of cognitive psykomancy was now taxing. Like all his brethren, Vey was able to conduct combat operations without recourse to sleep or regular sustenance for days, if not weeks. It was the strain of repeated, direct contact with the warp that was eroding him, like radiation poison, burning out his mind and hollowing out his bones. He needed time to ease himself and perform rites of reconsecration, but that was impossible without admitting as such to Zaidu.

Vey refused to appear weak before him. He was the one who had seen Zaidu through his initiation, who had led him and counselled him in the dark, early days as he came to terms with what he had become. What the Chapter had made him into. Damned, though not yet lost.

Perhaps Vey was being too proud. A part of him had known the Sin Slayer would become caught up in the hunt. He had believed he could control him, stop his focus from becoming a liability. In that sense, he had failed. They were committed now to attacking the enemy in their place of strength, a last-ditch effort to avert disaster. Vey wished he had been with Zaidu when he caught the Broken One in the tunnels, however briefly. He was certain that, working together, they could have terminated the target.

But death by Vey's or Zaidu's hands would not be the Broken One's fate. That was becoming increasingly clear.

The Daemon, the Tower and the Cup.

The Exorcists secured the square ahead of *Daemonium Eversor*'s arrival. High above, there was killing being done. The Archenemy and Imperial fleets, for so long content to glare at one another over Fidem's curvature, were coming together in an ungainly high-to-mid-orbital brawl. When Vey had first stepped out into the square, his enhanced eyesight had been able to pick out the larger of the capital ships meeting one another in the vaults above, but the overcast weather from the night before combined with the atmospheric disruption of millions of tonnes of metal and burning debris had stirred up a thick layer of dark, angry cloud cover that now hid the fleet action, all besides the silent flashes of far-off broadsides, the momentary blink of energy weapons and the pulsing glow of shield strikes.

Through it all came *Daemonium Eversor*. The flyer was an Overlord gunship, one of a pair, along with *Diabolus Malum*, that served the Hexbreakers on campaign. Like all of its kind, it dwarfed even the Chapter's Thunderhawks, twin holds either side of a cockpit blister and flanked in turn by sloping wing plates. Its hull echoed the Exorcists' armour: brooding, dark red and inscribed with the intricate text of the *Liber Exorcismus* and the Canticle of Absolution. Its wings and the armoured prow beneath the cockpit's armaglass bore the grim glare of the Calva Daemoniorum along with the crest of the Hexbreakers, a unicursal hexagram pierced from above by a combat knife.

Detritus littering the square scattered as the Overlord set down, its angled plasma drives causing the rubbish directly beneath to ignite and burn up, reduced to ash and cinders that were whipped around the space as the flyer's landing struts extended. It settled at the square's centre with a grace that belied its bulk, its chief pilot, Techmarine Kothar, making manoeuvring over two hundred and fifty tonnes of blocky adamantine, ceramite and thermoplas fibre mesh seem like a trivial matter. As the plasma drives returned to horizontal and the embarkation ramps at the rear of the two troop compartments began to lower, Lector-Sergeant Eitan issued a terse series of instructions over the vox, dividing his Infiltrators into one hold and Belloch's and Anu's squads into the other. Squad Haad and the Sin Slayer were absent, the plan calling for them to stay behind in Fidem's depths.

Vey had started to follow the Reivers onto the starboard section when a voice spoke his name.

It was Anu, the Eliminator sergeant. The cowl of the marksman's camo cloak was down, leaving the shock of perfect white hair he shaved into a lank mohawk on display. His expression was difficult to read behind the rebreather mask that covered the lower part of his face.

'Lector-Sergeant Anu,' Vey said by way of greeting, wondering why the sniper was addressing him. The Hexbreakers' Eliminators were almost as insular as the strike force's Reiver squad.

'There is a matter I would discuss with you,' Anu said. 'In private.'

The words surprised Vey, given they had spent the better part of an hour awaiting the Overlord's arrival. Why was he only coming forward now, as they prepared to board? The immediate explanation was that the Eliminator had been hesitant to do so, and had only just found the resolve to act.

'Be swift, brother,' Vey told him.

'It concerns the recent rites of one of my Orisons,' Anu said, standing with Vey off to the side of the embarkation ramp. 'The Order of the Eagle Most High.'

'What of them?' Vey asked, growing more surprised. He was not a fraternal brother of that Orison, and for Anu to share details of its rites with him was highly unusual. Doing so would risk expulsion at best, yet the sergeant pressed on.

'During the last combat pause, my fraternal brothers and I conducted an occuscope prognostication. I'm sure you are familiar with such a method of divination.'

'I am.'

'The results of such rites are typically opaque and require a great deal of meditation and study to decipher, but not on this occasion. I myself witnessed what I can only describe as a vision.'

Vey knew better than to chide Anu for such an admission. The sniper was no psyker, and few other Chapters would have tolerated his dabbling in warpcraft. With certain Orisons, however, minor acts of theomancy were permitted. That the Order of the

Eagle Most High saw more than just their next target through their scopes was no great revelation in itself.

'What did you witness?' Vey asked, not wishing to appear dismissive of his brother. He half expected to taste sweetness at any moment, but it did not come.

'Treachery,' Anu said, clearly still struggling with his own reluctance.

'Whose treachery?'

'Yours, enlightened brother. Or the almoner-lieutenant's. It was difficult to say.'

Vey paused, watching Anu closely. He was speaking the truth, at least as he understood it. Now, the reason for his reluctance became clear.

'Continue,' Vey ordered, a part of the Librarian not wanting him to. He already knew what he was about to say. He had seen it too, in his own ways.

'There was a warp taint upon you, a madness. You were fighting the Sin Slayer, both filled with wrath.'

'And who was the victor?' Vey asked, working hard to keep his voice level.

'I did not see, but… I myself was not a passive onlooker. I struck a blow of my own. I believe it was against the Sin Slayer.'

'Then you are indicting yourself as well as me?'

'So it would seem, Brother-Librarian. Forgive me, I know this is an ill time for such an admission, and I have no doubt our attempts at prophecy are found wanting when compared to your own abilities. But I could not hold my silence.'

'A prophecy unspoken is no prophecy at all,' Vey said, citing the Shadow Creed of Nykenor. 'I believe you have done the right thing by telling me, but only time will tell.'

'Do you know the meaning of any of it?' Anu asked. 'Surely what I saw is impossible? The immaterium cannot taint us as it does others. There is too little left of our brotherhood, of ourselves, to corrupt.'

'You know well enough that there is nothing in either this realm of existence or the next as pervasive as the warp, lector-sergeant,' Vey said. 'The moment you assume it is without power is the moment it has won. I thank you for sharing your findings with me, and will guard them until such a time as they become relevant. Put them from your own mind and apply yourself to the leadership of your brethren. We shall need your quick eye for more than divination in the coming hours.'

Anu held his hand in salute over the golden marksman's death's-head on his breastplate, palm open, then brushed two fingers quickly across his brow, a common Orison signal of thanks. He then boarded *Daemonium Eversor*, leaving Vey momentarily alone in the Overlord's shadow.

The Librarian spent a second ordering his thoughts, mastering himself. With every step, it seemed as though his fate was becoming clearer. Still, he railed against it. Still, he sought an escape. Nothing was truly inevitable, Zaidu had told him, a belief he himself had taught the Sin Slayer when he had still been young.

'*The squads are all on board, enlightened brother,*' clicked Eitan's voice in his ear. A less than subtle prompt. *We are waiting for you.*

Vey blinked an acknowledgement and drew his camo cloak tighter about his shoulders before stepping up the boarding ramp and into the half-dark of the starboard hold.

Daemonium Eversor remained downed a few moments more, as Techmarine Kothar received confirmation that Imperial Navy atmospheric assets were airborne. Most of the fleet of fighters and bombers aiding the Militarum on Fidem had been scrambled back to their motherships as the void war in orbit loomed, but enough had been left to provide cover for Imperial forces planetside, helping preserve them from the enemy's own accursed craft, including the flock of daemon engines said to haunt the skies. The Navy's pilots were to be committed now in support of the Exorcists' desperate gambit, covering the Overlord as it descended on Fort Deliverance.

Lector-Sergeant Eitan did not disapprove of the plan in and of itself, but his own role in it left much to be desired. Still, he had not questioned the almoner-lieutenant's decisions. He knew leadership sat ill with Zaidu at the best of times, but now it seemed like he wished nothing more than to abandon his duty of command and plunge alone into the midst of the enemy.

Eitan would do his part, as would they all. By the end of it, he had no doubt the target would be terminated.

The lector-sergeant secured himself in his restraint harness as the Overlord took off, murmuring a greeting to the mighty flyer's machine spirit as he did so. It had carried the Hexbreakers through steel, fire and fury many times before, and he had no doubt it would do so again.

'Preferable to grubbing in those miserable tunnels, eh, lector-sergeant?' said Uten, taking the seat next to him. Accustomed though it was to bearing the weight of a fully armoured Space Marine, Eitan still caught the sound of plasteel groaning over the rising wrath of *Daemonium Eversor*'s engines as the huge brother-initiate settled himself.

'Wherever the heretic is to be found, there we will smite him,' Eitan said non-committally, quoting the Chapter's Seventh Abjuration. Uten merely grunted.

Eitan had wished to ward away Uten's half-hearted attempt at conversation, but there was truth in the scripture-doctrine. Adaptability was a key Chapter tenet, be it at the strategic, operational or tactical levels. Few command structures within the

Imperium could have reacted to an incident like the Broken One's escape with the speed and decisiveness the Exorcists had shown. Likewise, the Hexbreakers would now switch from tunnel fighting to an aerial assault with hardly a beat missed. The Codex Astartes espoused such flexibility, of course, but the Exorcists put it into practice at every opportunity.

To be capable of combatting the daemon, the Chapter had to be ready for anything.

The Overlord took flight, gravitational forces warring in vain against Eitan and his armour. He looked the length of the troop bay. The interior of *Daemonium Eversor* appeared more like an occult crypt than the troop bay of a heavy gunship. Its walls were covered with a mismatched screed of purity seals and prayer parchments, while caged sconces held clusters of flickering candles, some of the thick flow of old wax lying at strange angles caused by extended periods of yawing or turbulence. More shattered wax, disturbed by past flights and pulverised by the tread of power-armoured brethren, lay underfoot, choking the spaces between the decking plates. Above each seat was a small reliquary alcove, most bearing more sheafs of litanies and holy texts, some acting as ossuaries housing riveted pieces of bone or bolted-on skulls, the remnants of past Techmarines and human crew members who had been honoured in death by partial interment within the craft.

Such arrangements within a combat flyer were far from practical, but then the Exorcists regularly faced foes for which the practicalities of existence itself were a mere afterthought.

The Exorcists were seated like graven statues decorating a tomb's interior, the candlelight flickering across their dark, dusty armour. They spoke little, seeing no reason for it. Even among the squad, among brothers bonded by genetic heritage and a hundred desperate fights, there was only the dimmest feeling of kinship. Eitan supposed others would have considered it a tragedy. He did not. There was enough misery in the galaxy already without adding their own sense of loss to it all.

They were not the hold's only occupants. As the Exorcists sat, a dozen figures did the opposite, rising from the benches at the far end of the compartment and shuffling to their duties. They were a detail of Chapter-serfs, brought down from the *Witch-Bane* with instructions to resupply and administer to their masters before they re-entered combat. Clad in black-and-red robes, cowls raised, they moved down the aisle deck between the seated Space Marines, gripping the railing that ran along the compartment's roof to steady themselves against the flyer's juddering.

Anunit, one of Eitan's own personal serfs, was among them. She had served him for perhaps eight or nine years, though he had not kept track. Like most servants of the Chapter, her scalp was shaven and scarred with words from the *Liber Exorcismus*. She was one of half a dozen retainers reverently carrying fresh magazines and grenade cradles, which she carefully dispensed to the Exorcists as she moved past them down the aisle.

When she had first become a Chapter-serf, Eitan had ritually cut out her tongue. She had shaken and wept as he had done it, but afterwards, still tearful, had managed to sign her thanks. To be chosen to serve the god-warriors was the closest thing to touching the divine that any of the common swampland tribes-people of Banish would experience.

The procession of serfs was led by one casting holy water from an aspergillum mace, muttering litanies he didn't understand as he went along. Eitan felt an instinctive combat response as the aspergillum was waved sharply in his direction, suppressing the urge to lash out as a light mist struck his helm and pauldrons. He watched it drip slowly down the armour of

Brother-Initiate Pazu, seated opposite him, the purifying liquid struggling through the cloying dust of Fidem's underworld.

A proper resanctification would be necessary at the end of all this, but such matters were far from pressing. The hunt had taken an unexpected series of turns, but Eitan was satisfied that his squad was still operating at near-peak efficiency. Only Brother-Initiate Kleth had suffered a serious injury, his left arm amputated by Gela. It was unfortunate, but it was not enough for him to order Kleth to remain aboard the Overlord once they engaged. He had no doubt the rest of the squad would cover his weaker side. Besides, he suspected they would soon need every battle-brother who could still wield bolter or blade.

He accepted two fresh magazines for his carbine from Anunit, and after mag-locking them, broke the silence that lay between the Exorcists.

'The Black Psalter of Primordian Primus,' he said. 'Verses one to twenty. Almoner Hasdrubal, lead us off.'

Hasdrubal began the song-cant, his strong voice an immediate challenge to the noise of the plasma engines and the thrumming in the metal around them. The other Exorcists answered him, and the hold was filled with a call-and-response litany that would have induced shaking, icy horror and a churning stomach in any mortal that heard it.

But the Exorcists were not mortals, not in the truest sense. They were something more, and something much, much less.

Anu watched the Librarian as the Overlord took off.

He knew he should not, but it was in his nature. He watched, and he killed.

Belloch and the Reivers occupied the seats closest to the main ramp at the rear of the hold, ready to disembark first, while Anu's Eliminators and Vey took the section closest to where the

Chapter's serfs were when not administering to their masters. Dumuzid was opposite Anu, and Vey just to his right.

The Librarian's eyes were closed and his lips were moving. He was holding two fingers to his forehead. The candles nearest to him had gone out.

Perhaps Anu should not have told him? Perhaps he had just inadvertently set in train the actions and events that would now see what he had witnessed come true? The warp had a way of making fools of them all.

Lakhmu's voice ticked in his ear, unexpectedly.

'Las fusils, Lector-Sergeant?'

It was a fair question. Amidst their resupply operation, the serfs on board *Daemonium Eversor* had brought with them the Eliminators' alternate armaments. Las fusils traded some of the pinpoint accuracy of their Shrike sniper rifles for an armour-piercing punch. Including one on this operation would likely be wise.

'You only, Lakhmu. Maintain tactical flexibility. The intelligence on what we are flying into seems… limited.'

Lakhmu directed his retinue serf to bring forward the weapon, swapping his Shrike bolt rifle out for its charge coils and bulky energy pack amidst murmured prayer greetings to the machine spirit. Anu looked back at Vey.

The Librarian had opened his eyes. He was staring straight ahead, into nothingness, but Anu knew with certainty that he was aware of the Eliminator's gaze. He refused to avert it.

He was the one who watched. He was the one who looked out over the killing field and cut down those who would harm his brethren before they could strike the fatal blow.

So Anu watched, and waited for those golden eyes to turn crimson.

CHAPTER TWENTY-ONE

METAL HAIL

Back through the darkness, the hunters of daemons prowled.

The Sin Slayer led the Infiltrators of Squad Haad back through the ancient battlefield below the valley. They were moving as quickly as the lower tunnels and narrow passages would allow, more certain of the route now. The *Witch-Bane* had been able to conduct sub-surface sensorium scans that had mapped out the upper layer of the labyrinth and transmitted it to the Hexbreakers. Between that and Haad's auspex, they could chart a route with far more certainty than before.

That was a boon, for time was pressing.

They ghosted over the remains of old combat, none of the Infiltrators knocking or bumping the sides of the cuts despite their size. Silence reigned but for the faintest purr from their armour and a dull, irregular thumping, like a series of far-off bass drums being beaten with demented madness. The Militarum's assault across the valley was continuing through the dawn and into the early morning, despite the protests of their commanders that their men needed time to rest and resupply. Zaidu had insisted that they keep attacking, stating that the fate of Fidem IV, and much more, relied upon it.

The Exorcists passed beneath the enemy-held Sacred Ways across the north ridge. Here, the tunnels ended, most caved in or covered up, a few leading into dugouts or reserve lines. It took time for the Infiltrators to work their way to the furthest exit they could, hoping to bypass the fighting above.

For a while they were forced to surface. Haad emerged into what appeared to be a munitions cache, sited to the rear of the trench network. Dirty wretches in raggedy fleeces or kepes were hurrying to unbox crates of shells and pass or run them along a shallow communications cut towards a battery of heavy guns that were pounding away from an emplacement a hundred yards distant.

Zaidu was already killing them. Haad joined in, swapping his auspex for his combat knife. The heretics were so exhausted and so deafened by the continual bombardment that most didn't seem to realise their end was at hand. The two Exorcists left the cache empty, but for the corpses and unused shells.

'This one,' Haad said as he returned his attention to his auspex and indicated a street opening out to the north-west. Deliverance Town lay before them, a jumbled mess of detritus and derelict buildings, rising beyond the stoop of the ridge's reverse slope towards the low hill where Fort Deliverance sat.

They moved into the scrap sprawl, Zaidu still leading. Haad pinged the auspex display to his vambrace, indicating the building they sought. It was a former district tithes office, moderately better built than the shanty surrounding it, a place of taxation where pilgrims had paid the fees required to walk the adjoining sections of the Sacred Ways.

Zaidu entered through the front door. Before stepping after

him, Haad registered that the sound of the nearest artillery discharges had fallen silent. The battery the cache had been servicing had run dry, and presumably the gunners were about to discover the fate of those who had been supplying them. The heretics' command and communication structure seemed poor, but they could not assume that word of their infiltration would not spread.

It gave them another reason to hurry. Haad forced himself not to look at the chrono display he had set on his retinal spread, counting down the minutes.

The interior of the tithes office had been turned into a barrack room for the cult's infantry. The floor was littered with blankets, used ration tins, empty autogun magazines and drained las-cells, backpacks and the odd scrap of heretic scripture, while a fleece daubed with Dark Tongue script had been draped over the counter where the taxation notaries had once worked. The high windows, already barred, had been boarded up, but part of the flakboard had fallen away, allowing the morning's overcast light to beam across half of the scene. The place stank like an animal pen, and in the day's close heat it would only get worse.

Zaidu stalked across the room, sweeping it for targets, but there were none. The Guard were presumably keeping its occupants busy. They located the tithes office's rudimentary vault, long ago broken open and looted, and from there discovered a passageway that had been more recently excavated, connecting it to the rubbish-filled basement of the neighbouring building.

Back down again. These underground routes were not the same as the tunnels below the valley. They were not as old, and had not been built for the purposes of killing, but for living. When they had cobbled together their scrap cities, the pilgrim residents of Fidem had also dug down into the dusty soil beneath them, grubbing out cellars, passageways and, in places, even rudimentary sewers. In that sense the soil beneath Pilgrim Town was even more of a maze than below the valley, though it didn't delve as deeply.

Deep enough for the Exorcists' purposes though.

They forged onwards, often having to move side-on or stooped double, the space even more meagre than it had been before. Whereas the passages under the valley had the feeling of a forgotten sepulchre, dark and cold and full of the dust-choked silence of death, this place was still alive, still breathing. The cellars and tunnels were littered with signs of ongoing or recent habitation, while the air was close and hot, occasionally pulsing with the presence of power generators or functioning electricity blocks. Light shafted down through grates and potholes, or blinked fitfully from dirty old lumens. The Infiltrators moved along and under one street after another, working their way through the tangle.

Even with the auspex and the *Witch-Bane*'s scans, it took time. Too much time. Haad allowed himself a glance at the chrono counter. They weren't going to make it.

Zaidu pressed on, saying nothing. Haad knew there was no point highlighting the constraints they were under. The Sin Slayer would be more keenly aware than any of them.

They moved into one of the lower sewer tunnels, little more than an uneven circular dirt passage with adjoining ruts channelled down from the rudimentary piping systems of the shacks. Effluvium splashed beneath the Exorcists' boots, and they were forced to advance at a crouch. They made it to a service hatch which led up into a maintenance passageway. The short, rusting ladder leading up to it buckled and broke beneath Zaidu's weight, but he was able to leap and snatch a hold of the edge of the opening, pulling himself up. He moved off immediately, and Haad followed with a leap of his own, but paused instead to help the next Infiltrator, Akkad, up after him.

As he did so, the chrono counter hit zero.

The Infiltrators had just caught up with Zaidu again, kicking down an old set of shelves as he forced his way into another basement, when Haad felt the triggering. A sudden electric crackle filled the air, along with the familiar tang of ozone.

Zaidu didn't hesitate. He carried on through the basement, into another passage. There, for the first time since separating from the rest of the strike force, he paused and glanced back towards Haad.

The Infiltrator sergeant consulted his auspex and used its indication function to illuminate a section of the basement's flaking plaster wall.

'Here,' he said.

Zaidu punched a fist through the plaster, finding dirt beyond. He addressed the Infiltrators now assembled behind him.

'Dig.'

Artax did as Mordun had suggested and sought out Eparch Sublimus.

He was a mortal – for the most part, anyway – as were all the eparchy that served the Word Bearers. None of them were part of the flock of Irenoth. They predated it, the inner coven of the cult that the warband had led, in one form or another, for the half millennium since they had broken with the remnants of the Brotherhood of the Sundered Arc.

Sublimus himself had once been a scholar, a savant in the service of some damnable Throne-loving inquisitor. He was now a daemonologist whose knowledge of the powers of the warp marked him as Mordun's foremost mortal servant. The other Word Bearers even offered him respect and, at times, deference. Not Artax though. But just for today, he would make an exception.

'The coronation is to proceed,' he told Sublimus after summoning him to the upper-central chamber of the fortress' keep. It had once been a command centre, but was now half open to the elements, its western and southern faces collapsed.

'Great blessings of the Path,' Sublimus gasped, hastily sketching a Holy Gesture of the Word in the air. He was wearing black robes and the red, rune-woven chasuble he commonly affected, the appearance of piety finished off by his tonsured skull and the eight-pointed star scarred into the bald centre of his pate.

'Mordun has directed me to oversee it,' Artax told the wretch. 'I will assign you to implement the details.'

'Yes, my Lord Bearer, yes of course,' Sublimus fussed. 'How do you wish to proceed? Perhaps the Black Invocation of the Nine? Or the Grand Prayer for Sacred Interdiction?'

'Both too long, too complex,' Artax said dismissively. 'There is no time for your frivolities. All that matters is that it works. Time is against us.'

'Which illuminated text should I take the binding readings from?'

'You have the *Heptameron of Narsus*?'

'Yes, lord.'

'Then use that, but be aware the Blind Shepherd will also be banishing unworthy spirits before he begins the coronation proper.'

'The *Heptameron* will serve for that purpose too, my lord.'

'Then bring the eparchy here and begin your preparations,' Artax instructed.

There was a sudden splitting sound, like a great branch falling away from a grand old tree. Artax blinked. He found he had Sublimus by the throat, his long, curving dagger pressed to the man's waxy skin. The eparch writhed and choked, clutching vainly at the ceramite sheathing Artax's wrists.

He released Sublimus as quickly as he had snatched him, realised his overwrought body had simply reacted automatically to what it thought was an aggressive combat stimulus.

It hadn't been altogether wrong. The cracking sound belonged to a freshly triggered void shield. Even through his helm, he could smell the ozone. He turned and paced towards the shattered half of the chamber, which afforded him a view over a section of the fort outside.

A dome of lambent blue energy had ignited just beyond the outer walls of the fortress, shimmering in the warm air and causing the light passing through it to diffract in strange, multi-coloured patterns. The void shield was online, and that meant one of two things. Either Mordun had ordered it to be triggered, which seemed unlikely given Artax could hear his familiar voice still haranguing the flock out on the fort's parade square, or it had gone from dormant to raised after detecting incoming ordnance. And if it was the latter, there was only one loyalist force with range and precision enough to strike at this distance from the front line.

'They are here,' Artax said.

'Thirty seconds,' crackled Techmarine Kothar's voice across the vox.

'Rise,' Eitan instructed. Uten unlocked his restraint harness and stood, mag-clamping his boots to the deck to guard against the pitch and roll of the Overlord as it completed its final descent.

The Chapter-serfs had withdrawn to their own benches deeper into the hold, leaving the aisle free for the Exorcists to assemble. The candles guttered as the troop compartment shook. Most had already gone out.

The rattling was accompanied by a furious shriek from the plasma engines. Uten didn't delete it from his hearing. The noise had heralded a thousand combat insertions, and that alone would probably have been enough for him to slip into battle focus. He could feel his senses sharpening and his thoughts tightening up, his body beginning to gland the stimulants that would drive him to victory despite the most terrible of wounds and against the most terrible foes.

It was what he lived for. The Emperor and the primarch knew there was little enough else left to give him purpose.

The noise of the engines changed, beginning to drop. He detected other sounds. There was a drumming thunder from outside, the servitor-crewed heavy bolters on the Overlord's port wing, adjacent to the hold, laying down fire to cover the landing. There was also a pattering sound from the hull, like rain. Hard rounds, hundreds of them, striking impotently at *Daemonium Eversor*.

Uten glanced one final time at his armour system outputs and the vitae signs on his retinal display, then did a visual scan of his bolt carbine and checked his blade was secure at his hip. He felt strong, vital. He had a purpose again, almost enough to briefly fill the empty place. It was time to hunt, time to kill.

There was a harsh buzzing sound.

The hold's rear ramp fell away, not the stately descent of hydraulics this time, but the suddenness of deactivated mag clamps. As it hit the dirt, the Exorcists were already moving, out into the daylight and the metal hail.

The last candle on board *Daemonium Eversor* flickered out.

CHAPTER TWENTY-TWO

THE SECOND SIEGE OF FORT DELIVERANCE

Thanks to generations of labour and toil, the pilgrims of Fidem IV had provided the Exorcists with a viable entry point into Fort Deliverance.

The great defensive work possessed an armoury vault, buried deep below the central keep. When it had first been built, that core had been surrounded by hundreds of yards of dirt, enough to ensure that digging through to it would have taken weeks, weeks where the defenders would surely have detected the purpose of the attackers and interdicted them. But that was before the rise of the scrap city.

Fort Deliverance had long ago ceased being a stronghold in the truest sense. It was a place of worship and holy reverence, and that had ensured that the pilgrim slums had sprung up around it just as they had around the Tower of the Praetorian across the valley. The destitute faithful had cobbled together their dwellings, and they had dug too, dug within the fort's defensive perimeter, where no castellan or garrison master would have permitted, had Deliverance still possessed such posts.

With the arrival of the Word Bearers, the fortress had rediscovered some of its old self. Breaches had been patched up, weapons batteries reinstalled, casemates and the vault restocked with the fodder of war, and even the void shield had been stoked back into life. But while the surrounding slum dwellings had been demolished to clear the approaching fields of fire, the warren of cellars and passages underneath had lain mostly undiscovered. That was until the *Witch-Bane*'s powerful sensorium arrays had lanced down through the soil and the debris and mapped the hollow spaces hidden below, pinpointing one in particular that had unwittingly been excavated just past the fort's vault.

So Zaidu and Squad Haad dug. They worked using their gauntlets like shovels and their combat knives as picks, two clawing away at the dry Fidem soil side by side, until the sensors in their armour detected the first signs of dropping efficiency, at which point they switched out for two others.

While above them, for the first time in four thousand years, Fort Deliverance rang with the sounds of war.

Vey strode from the darkness of *Daemonium Eversor*, spitting a warp oath that fractured the hard rounds slashing towards him.

Directly ahead, Fort Deliverance's ravelin was ablaze with fire, framed by the pulsing blue light of the void shield at its back. The ramparts were swarming with heretic infantry, pouring small-arms fire and crew-mounted weapon salvos down at the Overlord as it alighted in the killing grounds before them.

There were few combat flyers in the Imperium that could have put down right outside the enemy's gates and remained planted there in the face of their firepower while covering the assault force. *Daemonium Eversor* was one such craft. The Overlord's hull was as thick on its forward glacis plates as a super-heavy. More importantly, it possessed a smaller version of the same form of protection the fortress enjoyed, a Buckler-class void shield that could be beamed from its projector nodes to cover either the front, flanks or rear of the flyer, or its overhead or underside arcs. Techmarine Kothar had triggered it as soon as they were within missile range of Fort Deliverance, and it now flared and pulsed as it took the hits of krak rockets and lascannon beams, shunting the projectiles into the immaterium in bursts of actinic brilliance.

Fort Deliverance's ravelin could not boast the same protection. While the void shield active beyond it rendered the main body of the fortress safe against anything larger than a heavy bolter shell, either the receiver responsible for projecting the protective dome over the outwork was no longer functioning or the outer defences had never been included within the umbrella in the first place. It shuddered beneath the fury of the Exorcists as *Daemonium Eversor* returned fire, heavy bolters and Desolator lascannons raking the ramparts, breaking the dark rockcrete and painting its remains red.

Amidst the blizzard of fire, the Hexbreakers deployed, moving out of the rear hatches to benefit from the cover provided by the Overlord's hull and shield before fanning out to the left and right. Vey remained with Belloch and the Reivers as they left the protection of the void shield, feeling its tingling charge momentarily disrupt the electronics of his power armour.

'Suppressing fire,' Eitan instructed over the vox. 'Target the heavy weapon embrasures.'

As the Infiltrators added their bolt carbines to *Daemonium Eversor*'s barrage, Vey reached out, seeking the minds of the enemy, questing for what awaited the Exorcists amidst the fortifications. He specifically sought traps that may have been laid in or around the gateway, muttering occult catechisms under his breath as his consciousness darted like invisible lightning from one degenerate heretic's mind to the next.

Amidst the fear and fanaticism, he found no suggestion of any immediate snare, and the eyes of those around the gateway could discern nothing that caused him concern. With a laboured breath, he withdrew and tried to shake off the bitter warp chill.

'The gateway is viable,' he told both Eitan and Kothar over the command channel.

'*Affirmative*,' Kothar responded. '*I will open you a path, brethren.*'

The multimelta mounted on *Daemonium Eversor*'s prow fired with a shriek, its projectile visible as a spear of heat-warped air that struck the gate facing the Overlord. The centre of the barred plasteel doors began to deform, the metal blistering, then bubbling, then running molten as it glowed red-hot. Kothar maintained the beam until a hole had been seared right through the gate's centre.

'We need a secondary ingress point,' Eitan voxed. Committing the whole force to entry via the gate was too great a tactical risk.

'*Located*,' Kothar responded. '*The old breach to your right.*'

As he spoke, he caused the tactical overlay shared by the Exorcists commanders to highlight a ramp of rubble between a broken section of wall along from the gateway. Shattered rock-crete, corrugated iron and flakboard from the shanty town had been used to shore it up.

'Acceptable,' Eitan said.

A flurry of Desolator lascannon beams pounded at the crude repairs. The hail failed to demolish the barricades, but left them riddled and smoking, any structural integrity they had possessed ruined.

'That will be sufficient,' Eitan said. 'Belloch, take the breach. I will take the gate. Move in.'

'Taking off,' Kothar added as the Exorcists shifted in an instant from static-fire support to storm assault. The plasma engines began to scream once more, rotating to vertical as the Overlord began to take off, the blazing heat and downdraught whipping up dust and ash.

Vey moved through it, breaking into a run as he followed the Reivers in their dash towards the breach. *Daemonium Eversor* was still firing as it rose with leaden grace back into the air, las-beams and heavy bolter rounds tearing overhead as the Archenemy desperately tried to focus fire on the charging Exorcists.

Energy bolts and bullets ringing and sparking from their battle plate, Squad Belloch hit the base of the breach.

Anu and his fraternal brothers remained on board *Daemonium Eversor*. The heretics had ensured there were no suitable perches within striking distance of the fortifications they had stolen, but this time the Eliminators had brought their own.

'Circling round to starboard,' Kothar voxed from the cockpit, warning them before applying the new course to his controls. It gave Anu a moment to shift himself and re-engage the magnetics keeping him anchored and stable on the deck. The rear hatches of the Overlord's holds had been left open, restricting the gunship's aerial capabilities but offering the Exorcists snipers a prime vantage point over the fortress. Lakhmu, with his las fusil, had shifted over to the starboard hold while Anu and Dumuzid remained in the port side.

Daemonium Eversor banked around, the small-arms fire clawing at it rapidly diminishing as Kothar put airspace between the fort's defenders and the Overlord. Missiles continued to corkscrew up on billowing smoke plumes, launched from man-portable tubes on the ramparts, but the warheads either streaked past or disappeared in bursts of brilliance as they hit the void shield that had now switched to cover the gunship's underbelly.

As the Overlord banked higher it became target-locked by more serious anti-flyer weaponry. There were two Hydra guns defending the skies above the fort, one sited on top of the half-ruined keep, the other above the main gatehouse behind the protective spur of the outer walls. They began to thud as the Overlord rose into their engagement zone, quad barrels churning out thousands of rounds in a matter of seconds.

As projectiles, they were too small for the Overlord's void shield to engage. Tracers amidst the fusillade created a ladder of darting lights that rose up to lash at *Daemonium Eversor*. Kothar responded by pitching to the right, causing Anu to grunt as he adjusted, only kept in place by his mag locks. There was a rattle as a spray of shots stitched up the side of the hull next to the open ramp.

'I'm going to engage the keep defences directly,' Kothar informed Anu. *'That will give you a simultaneous angle on the gatehouse, but it will mean we are caught between two arcs of fire.'*

'Not for long,' Anu reassured him.

Once more, the Overlord performed a manoeuvre that would have been outrageous for any other combat flyer. It charged the keep's anti-aircraft gun, cockpit down, mounting an attack run that was only forced up by the threat of striking the curvature of the fort's own void shield. *Daemonium Eversor's* lascannons were too powerful to pass through the shield without triggering it, but its heavy bolters were not. They rained mass-reactive shells on the roof of the keep.

At the same time, Anu craned forward over the edge of the ramp, trying to get a shot down at the gatehouse as the Overlord swept away from it in the opposite direction. The gun crew were adjusting the Hydra, attempting to ease the flow of shots back on target as *Daemonium Eversor* displayed manoeuvrability that belied its bulk. Anu got a lock on them in turn and sighted down through his scope.

'Dumuzid, loader. Lakhmu, traversing rail,' he ordered. 'Fire when set.'

Daemonium Eversor was tough, but even it couldn't survive being simultaneously engaged by anti-aircraft emplacements from front and behind. It was up to the Eliminators to ensure that didn't happen for long. They'd be firing down and through the curvature of the fort's void shield, but their shots, even Lakhmu's fusil, would be low mass or low energy, sufficient to bypass it.

Anu switched his goggles to preysight, turning the world below into a blur of heat registers. The walls beyond the gatehouse, where the primary ground assault was going in, were a maelstrom, but he focused down into the gatehouse itself, finding the white-hot glow of the four barrels and, past the armoured shield between them, the red-and-yellow flare of the seated gunner's body heat.

He selected a high-penetration round, then put it through the shield and the gunner's head.

His fraternal brothers fired at almost the exact same moment. A loader hefting a fresh drum of shells towards the Hydra was scythed in half by Dumuzid's shot, his single heat signature suddenly becoming two, while the brilliant white beam of Lakhmu's las fusil lanced down into the rail the gun was mounted on, boring a hole through the traversing mechanism preventing its crew from realigning the weapon.

'Pulling away to port,' came Kothar's terse voice.

'Affirmative,' Anu said. As the Overlord lurched once more, he tried to get a snapshot away, but didn't see if he had struck the heretic who was attempting to drag the headless corpse of his kinsman out of the gunner's seat.

Daemonium Eversor began to climb again, the angle swiftly obscuring the gatehouse. The four streams of fire from the wounded Hydra started up once more, but flailed impotently after Lakhmu's disabling shot, unable to follow their target.

As they circled above the keep, Anu leaned out and got a view of the devastation wreaked by the concentrated barrage of the Overlord's heavy bolters. The Hydra sited on top of the keep had been reduced to smoking scrap and its crew to red meat.

'Weather is continuing to worsen,' Kothar voxed. Anu realised it was beginning to rain. The grey skies around them had closed in even further since setting off from Pilgrim Town.

'If you need the hatches shut, inform us,' he responded.

'I may, though not because of the weather. Archenemy air support has scrambled. Navy interceptors are trying to keep them clear of our airspace, but they are unlikely to succeed. How do you think your marksmanship will fare in the middle of a dogfight, brothers?'

'That sounds like a worthwhile test,' Anu replied.

While preparations for the coronation were being made, the Blessed One was held in the keep's entrance tunnel, under the guard of brothers Skerin, Syro the Lector and Dalamar the Bibliognost.

Mordun visited them as the sounds of fighting engulfed the fortress. He paced around where the Blessed One was kneeling, the other Word Bearers withdrawing to a respectful distance.

He is broken, Se'irim whisper-chittered. *Broken, broken, broken.*

'Perhaps,' Mordun murmured to the daemon in his head, less sure. It would be foolish to assume victory, not when he had not yet realised his ultimate triumph. It was so achingly close now, and yet the Blind Shepherd knew he had to maintain his focus. This moment, just before he was finally given what he had been promised, was also the time of greatest danger.

The Blessed One was being held in a pentacle circle that had been etched into the floor before its arrival. They had been readying this place ever since claiming it. Mordun had never doubted that the day would come when all their preparations would be put into action. The True Gods were with him, in every sense of the Word.

'Can you hear me, Red Marshal?' Mordun called softly as he continued to pace, careful not to disturb the pentacle. 'Or have you lost the fight to one of your rivals?'

'I do not lose,' the Blessed One croaked.

'But you do, again and again. You were struck down here by the spawn of Dorn, four thousand years ago. You have known nothing but defeat since then. A once great champion of the Blood God, reduced to a shadow and imprisoned in this pathetic host of flesh and bone.'

The Blessed One raised its head, expression hateful. Its eyes were red.

'Mock while you can, blind fool. All is as my master ordains it. A greater victory is coming, one that will drown you in blood.'

'No,' Mordun said, stopping in front of the host. 'The victory here is mine, not yours. It has been promised to me by your kin.'

'You would make yourself another petty prince in the choir for the Aurelian,' the Blessed One hissed. *'Mortal lack of ambition never ceases to disgust me.'*

'You speak as a servant yourself, daemon,' Mordun replied. 'I am merely giving you further duties to perform.'

'I am a warrior,' Caedus howled, its host surging to its feet and straining impotently at the invisible ley lines entrapping it. *'The only master I know is the god of blood and battles, and it is not his will that I be reduced to a giver of crowns!'*

'You do not know his will, Neverborn!' Mordun shouted back. Despite his great control, he couldn't help feel his own anger stoked by the daemon's wrathful presence. 'I do! I have communed with his daemons, ones far more favoured and terrible than you. Skarthax, Drox Brasshorn and others besides have promised me immortality if I complete this final task. I need but prove myself one more time. A coronation, to be conducted by a subjugated champion. A fitting means of proclaiming my ascension.'

'You are not worthy!' Caedus roared, raking claws along its flesh prison in raw frustration.

It rages, Se'irim cawed. *Anger! Rage! Wrath!*

Mordun ignored the Change-daemon's bouts of madness.

'Bring it to the centrum dominus,' he ordered the other Word Bearers, gesturing at the daemonhost as it fought uselessly against its ward cage. 'It is time.'

CHAPTER TWENTY-THREE

BREACHING

Squad Haad hit brickwork, then reinforced plasteel.

'Breach it,' Zaidu ordered. Kephras and Lamesh were the pair currently working on the tunnel, which now extended about six yards through the Fidem dirt, just large enough for a Primaris to crawl through.

There was no time to worry that the blast would bring the rudimentary passage down. Kephras wired a pair of directional krak mines against the wall and withdrew before triggering them.

There was a crump, and dust and smoke billowed from the hole.

Zaidu moved into it, one hand shoving aside displaced dirt, the other gripping one of his blades, point down. He hit the wall. It was buckled, scorched, but still intact. He slammed the fist clenched around his knife's grip against it, feeling only the slightest yield.

Hissing between his teeth, the almoner-lieutenant twisted, digging his reactor pack back against the dirt to his right, giving himself just enough room to unlock and drag up his bolt carbine.

He fired at the plasteel, point-blank, the discharge almost rupturing even his hearing. The bolts detonated on impact, ricocheting shards of shrapnel into his pauldrons. He felt several hit his scalp as well, drawing blood and pain, both quickly suppressed.

The shots had the desired effect. The weakened plasteel gave way. He emptied his magazine into it, not caring that he was hitting himself with the burst damage of his own bolts, not even caring that one might punch through and ignite the ammunition presumably stockpiled beyond, in the vault.

They had delayed long enough.

Now he was able to punch his fist through properly. He drove himself against the wall, armour winning the battle against the battered and buckled metal sheathing the vault's exterior. Beyond it, more brickwork, easy prey by comparison. Blinking blood out of his eyes, Zaidu forced his way into Fort Deliverance's depths.

The assault above had been designed to distract the heretics from just such a mode of infiltration, but it was no surprise that some had noticed the krak grenades and the bolter fire. Several herdsmen who had seemingly been lugging ammunition crates had abandoned them and had their rifles raised by the time Zaidu broke through.

He snarled, using his carbine to shield his already wounded head as he found his feet on the other side. After that, the cultists died quickly.

He took in his new surroundings in a heartbeat. The chamber was clad in brick and stone, with multiple vaulted subsections. Most were stacked high with ammunition crates, empty weapons racks and rows of plastek-wrapped artillery shells. Pallid daylight was spilling in from somewhere on the other side of the space, the source obscured by the stockpiled supplies.

Zaidu advanced deeper into the chamber, discovering that the light was coming from an open bay door at the top of a ramp. Judging by the rails leading up it, it was the main means of ferrying the heavier munitions out onto the fortress' parade square. He could hear the fury of the storm assault drifting in from outside. He also noted a set of stairs next to the open doors.

He made sure there were no more enemies in the immediate vicinity, then forced himself to double back and help the Infiltrators through the breach in the vault wall. They stalked through the vault much as Zaidu had just done, securing it while the almoner-lieutenant and Haad consulted.

'They know we're here?' Haad asked as he glanced over the bodies Zaidu had left behind.

'Unsure,' Zaidu admitted. 'Scan the area.'

Haad obeyed, unlocking his auspex and pointing it upwards as he set it to pierce the keep above them. Zaidu watched as static flowed in waves over the green display, each new wash picking out more and more red target returns.

'A lot above us,' Haad noted. 'Difficult to differentiate between the floors. The sensorium report from the *Witch-Bane* indicated there were three intact levels.'

'We clear each in turn, until we find the Broken One,' Zaidu said. 'I will take point. Move.'

Squad Belloch punched through the rudimentary repairs the Archenemy had attempted on the ravelin's breach, driving down the ramp of rubble on the other side. As expected, there were more barricades set up there in the otherwise open ground between the outer wall and the moat. Brother-Initiates Makru and Azzael had launched smoke canisters over the ramp before they had stormed it, but they weren't enough to stop the blizzard of las and bullets that awaited them.

The Exorcists advanced as though into the teeth of a wild storm, hunched over, side-on, hard rounds and energy beams searing and cracking off pauldrons, greaves and packs. Their preysight stripped away the twitching, swirling smoke, picking out the heat signatures of those trying to kill them.

As they gained the far side of the breach, they returned fire. Squad Eitan were through the gate next to the ingress, and they added their own carbines to the storm. Plasteel, iron, timber, flakboard, flesh, bone – the concentrated fusillade of bolt-shells pulverised, mangled and broke it all. In a matter of seconds, the makeshift second line of barricades within the first layer of defences had been cleared. But that merely opened the line of sight for the defenders of the fort itself.

By design, there was no back to the ravelin, just clear ground in front of the moat, the bridge and the fortress' main gatehouse. If any attack took the outwork, they would have no cover from the defenders on the ramparts above them.

'Too exposed,' Eitan voxed to Vey as the downpour of small-arms fire resumed. 'Is the next gate a snare?'

Vey was unable to answer immediately. He had followed the Reivers through the breach, hanging back, taking no direct part in their efforts. His energies were needed elsewhere. He was questing again, reciting old litanies by rote, barely keeping his mind back from the edge of the precipice. He could not falter now. Not when they were this close. Not when there was still a chance the tarot – and every other vision and prophecy – could be wrong about what awaited him.

He sought out the minds of heretics, no time for subtlety, bludgeoning their thoughts with his own. Yes, the gate was a snare. With eyes that were not his own and memories that he stole and broke apart, he saw the bundles of krak and frag grenades wired underneath the bridge and either side of the gate itself. Primed, ready, waiting for the Hexbreakers to come storming through.

'It's a trap,' Vey growled into the vox.

'Can you stop it from being sprung?'

Again, Vey didn't respond right away. He was searching, searching. His skull throbbed. Blood was in his throat, bitter and choking. He couldn't do this. He couldn't. But he had to. The alternative was worse. So much worse.

He found what he was seeking. A consciousness darker than all the rest, poisonous, lurking just on the far side of the gatehouse. No mere cult acolyte, this. No deranged mortal. A fanatic, yes, a zealot, but in a way that added up to something infinitely more dangerous than the fallen farmers of Irenoth.

Chaos Space Marine. Word Bearer. Vey immediately lunged at him with his psychic presence, knowing it would be nowhere near as simple a task to pillage his thoughts as it would be his flock, but knowing too that there was no time for a more considered approach.

The traitor was taken by surprise, and Vey made full use of his split-second's advantage. He saw the rotting darkness at the traitor's heart, but also the fire of conviction, the heat of true belief scorching the Exorcist. He saw too the mettle that ran through the very core of this being's existence. He was, like all his brethren, a cultist of Chaos, but also a warrior, and though the centuries had been long and unkind, he had not forgotten that.

Vey endured a flurry of memories, snapshot fast. The frenzy of a boarding action, blinded by the enemy's blood, killing on instinct alone. Fighting chittering daemonic horrors in a fractal maze. Battling another Adeptus Astartes, a blue-plated son of Guilliman, howling in triumph as a chainsword bit and drove home the duel's final blow. Blood and black litanies, vestiges of kinship reaffirmed amidst the horror of a futile existence. For a second that felt like a lifetime, Vey couldn't tell which memories belonged to the heretic and which were his own.

Then, the Word Bearer recovered. He clamped down his mind and clutched hold of Vey's, furious at the unexpected, subliminal assault.

'Do not resist me, Kordiron,' Vey hissed, the name coming unbidden to his lips amidst the sudden rush of mental energies. 'Relax. Submit.'

Kordiron did neither. He was a warrior of the Long War, older than Vey, older than any of the pathetic loyalists who now dared attempt to interrupt the coronation. He would make them pay for this disgrace. He would–

'Not… yet…' Vey snarled. His witch-sight was unleashed. He could see the Chaos Space Marine, standing off to the side beyond the gateway, a dark, malevolent brute in archaic battle plate, smouldering with raw warp power that ran off him and coiled around him. He was trying to raise a hand to his vambrace. Trying to reach the detonator wired to it.

Vey wanted to force him to stop, but all he could do was make him slow down. The heretic's mind was ancient and full of malice, and though he was not a psyker, the immaterium had been festering in his soul long enough to ensure Vey could not simply command him and be certain of obedience. The traitor bellowed his defiance as, inch by inch, body trembling with invisible pressure, he forced his hand fractionally closer to the trigger.

'Enlightened brother–' Eitan began to say over the vox, almost shattering Vey's concentration.

'I'm… delaying the detonation,' he was able to snarl back, somehow. 'Sixty seconds… perhaps…'

Eitan snapped an instruction to one of his Infiltrators.

'Uten, go.'

* * *

Uten charged Fort Deliverance's gatehouse.

If he could no longer know joy, he at least knew something akin to it in those few brief moments. Las-bolts, stabs of slender red brilliance, cut the air in criss-cross patterns in front of and around him, vaporising the rain that had started to fall, punching molten holes in the bridge or burning scorch marks into the unyielding curved surfaces of his Phobos armour. Auto-gun rounds, less beautiful and more vicious, filled the air like buzzing wasps, cracking and snapping off his battle plate with spiteful force. The mesh decking of the bridge shivered from the pounding of the barrage and the pounding of Uten's feet, rivets groaning, plasteel bending. Ahead, the gatehouse loomed like a dark cliff face, its jagged crest licked by repetitive flickers of flame.

All of this Uten experienced, and registered, in just four or five seconds. He rejoiced, or perhaps it was merely the echoes of the daemon beast that had taken the greater part of his soul rejoicing. Either way, it did not matter.

He was off the leash, and destroying.

As he charged, he unclamped the melta bomb from his hip and twisted the hand-grip plunger, arming it for impact detonation. Perhaps he laughed, or perhaps he did not. He couldn't be sure. His mind was now locked on to his target, the gate itself, a tall set of plasteel doors like the ravelin entrance *Daemonium Eversor* had breached. Everything else, from the rain of firepower to the alerts his armour was pinging about the amount of hits he was taking – one, two, three penetrations – melted away into ephemeral nothingness, packed into the greyness that lined the walls of his vision.

He reached the gate. He slammed the melta bomb forward, its charged warhead colliding with the centre of the doors.

His armour registered a ferocious heat spike, but it was nothing compared to what the gate experienced. The shaped charge liquified a hole the size of a tank hatch and warped and blistered the space around it, turning the middle locks to molten slag.

Uten didn't stop. He let his momentum carry him on into the barrier, crashing through it, discarding the melta bomb's fused handle as he went. He was dimly aware of the rest of the squad following him, storming the bridge and the open gateway. He didn't care. He needed to kill what was beyond.

The heretics were ready, but they did not fire, and that proved to be their doom. More scrap barricades had been heaped up around the gate, anticipating its penetration. Such a concentration of close-range small-arms would have checked even the likes of Uten, but the cultists had been ordered to wait. Their dark master had instructed them in no uncertain terms to desist from shooting until the first few loyalists were through the gatehouse arch, and could be torn apart by the explosives rigged all around it.

But the explosives didn't detonate. Vey was burning himself out keeping them from triggering. So Uten stormed through, and when, in a blind panic, a few of the cult infantry finally did fire at him, it was much too late. He was in among them, knife out, slaughtering the flock.

The rest of Squad Eitan followed him in. Now was the moment of decision, when the assault would succeed or fail. There could be no hesitation, no caution. The Exorcists pounded past the explosives that should have obliterated them, bolt carbines up, mutilating the defenders of the gatehouse at point-blank range. They drove inwards, the Reivers hitting the bridge behind them, hard on their heels.

Over the vox, Eitan heard Vey's strained voice.

'Find the Word Bearer… Can't hold…'

The lector-sergeant cast about as his Infiltrators overran the barricades and gunned down their defenders, returns pinging across his visor as his auto-senses quested for the target, seeking the heat returns of a reactor pack.

There. Just to the right of the gatehouse, lurking in its shadow. The heretic had his hand to a detonator device strapped to his wrist. A single finger remained raised, struggling towards the trigger in what seemed like slow motion. Eitan could hear Vey's rising roar of effort. He was breaking himself, trying to hold the traitor back for just a few seconds longer.

Eitan swept up his bolt carbine and fired.

Too late.

The heretic pressed the detonator's activation rune.

There was almost no warning when the daemon engine came for them.

'Brace,' Kothar barked. Anu just had time to do so before the Overlord lurched viciously, clearly trying to evade something its sensors had only detected at the last moment.

It failed. There was an impact, so violent it nearly broke the mag seal keeping Anu clamped to the deck. Metal shrieked, gouged and torn. He realised there was sunlight in the hold where none had been earlier, further back from the open hatch. Three great tears had appeared in the roof, rainwater cascading through them, as though *Daemonium Eversor* had just been savaged by some monstrous bird of prey.

'Evasive manoeuvres,' Kothar said tersely. Slinging his Shrike rifle, Anu clutched the overhead rail for good measure, stooping forward slightly as he tried to get a better view through the hatch and out into the rain-slashed skies beyond.

He saw the daemon engine for a split second as it came back in for a second pass. It was huge, shaped like a great dragon, a conglomeration of warp-forged metal and warp-birthed flesh. It had two sets of wings, made from sheets of black-and-brass steel, which it beat the air with in perverse defiance of the requirements of the natural plane of existence. Its body was long, an underside of pallid, scaled flesh surmounted by a chassis of wickedly spiked armour. Its neck was a twisting mass of cables and tendons, and its skull an elongated metal plate riveted over bare, horned bone. One eye was a burning crimson optic, while the other smouldered with predatory, malefic intelligence. Its maw was a snapping, drooling mass of fangs and implanted knife blades. The talons clenched beneath it looked as though they had been taken from the hook clamps of an Arvus lighter and grafted on.

The briefing package Astra Militarum high command had supplied when the *Witch-Bane* had translated in-system had included unverified reports of airborne daemon engines hunting Fidem IV's skies. Crudely classified by Imperial strategos as Heldrakes, they were an enemy the Exorcists had anticipated little contact with during their own hunt. Until now.

The monstrosity swept down on *Daemonium Eversor* from above and behind, letting out a shriek that sounded like metal colliding with metal in the depths of a forge furnace.

At the last instant, Kothar lurched the Overlord to starboard, throwing off its dive. Its talons missed, but it tilted its body as it passed, using the spiked tip of one wing like a weapon, shearing another rent in *Daemonium Eversor*'s top.

Anu snarled, coinciding with a harsh warning blurt from the Overlord's emergency alert systems, as though the flyer itself was in pain.

'It keeps hitting from above,' Kothar said. 'Too big for the void shield. I need to close the hatches and gain altitude.'

Anu didn't like the thought of being sealed away in the midst of a dogfight. He would be helpless, and worse, sightless. But right then there wasn't much choice.

'Can you get an angle with the fusil?' he asked Lakhmu, who was in the neighbouring hold.

'Unlikely,' he came back over the vox. 'It's moving too high and fast.'

The ramps began to lever up, shedding rainwater. Anu felt a sudden, savage sense of worthlessness.

The Overlord pitched hard once more, almost hitting a forty-five-degree angle and forcing Anu to tighten his grip on the railing. He heard the renewed thudding of the heavy bolters on the starboard wing, finding his inability to see their target intolerable.

If the shots hit the Heldrake, it wasn't hard enough. There was another slamming impact, this one even worse than those that had come before. The alert systems rose to a shriek as the Overlord threatened to spin out of control, the Chapter-serfs at the rear of the hold screaming as they were flung against their harnesses.

Anu and Dumuzid were unaffected by the oscillations, but Anu saw immediately that Lakhmu's icon on his optic goggles had turned red. Not yellow or amber, just an instant crimson. Death signature.

The Overlord righted itself, but the tone of the engines had changed markedly. *Daemonium Eversor* was wounded.

'What just happened?' Anu demanded, struggling with his impotency.

'It tried to get a grip of us,' Kothar responded. 'Half of the starboard troop bay has been ripped away, and the engine block there is damaged. I've had to cut one of the plasma lines to stop it from overheating, but we're bleeding altitude.'

'One of my fraternal brothers is gone,' Anu said, unable to hide the bitterness in his voice. This was no way for a brother of the Order of the Eagle Most High to enter into his final damnation.

'We will all be gone when it comes back round for another pass. I cannot match its manoeuvrability.'

'We are trying to fight it on its own terms,' Anu said, his mind burning through a dozen possible counter-strategies in a matter of seconds. 'That's a losing battle. We need to go low.'

'Its height is its advantage, going any lower will only–'

'Not just low, we need to make an emergency landing. Now.'

'I don't see how that will help, lector-sergeant.'

'This isn't an enemy pilot we're fighting. It's a predator. It sees *Daemonium Eversor* as a threat to its aerial dominance.'

'I doubt its attitude will change just because we make a landing.'

'No, but it will see us as beaten. As easy prey. It will come in for the kill. So take us down, brother, and let me do my work.'

CHAPTER TWENTY-FOUR

CEREMONIAL MAGICK

Brother-Initiate Nazaratus died just beyond the gate of Fort Deliverance.

He had been bringing up the rearguard for Squad Eitan, and wasn't far past the entrance arch when the explosives rigged around it detonated. Caught in the burst radius of a dozen fragmentation grenades, his reactor pack was wrecked and torn off, the rear of his armour riddled and mangled from his shins to his helm. He stumbled, then collapsed onto his knees, where he remained, head bowed, blood flowing onto the dust around him.

The Reivers suffered too. Belloch, along with Makru and Shemesh, were crossing the bridge in front of the gateway when the charges rigged there blew. It was the infrastructure of the bridge itself which partially saved them, taking the worst of the blast but collapsing into the dry moat beneath. Shemesh's leg, already wounded during the attack on the Sacred Ways, was blown away, while Makru's right arm was snapped in two as a section of the wrecked plasteel structure fell on him.

All of this Eitan was aware of as a flurry of colour changes on his visor. Nazaratus went amber to red almost instantly, while Shemesh and Makru turned yellow. He was aware of the blast, aware of shrapnel scraping and gouging his armour, of the shockwave trying to throw him off his feet. Aware too that he had failed. All of it was secondary, though. All of it, experienced in an instant, was made subordinate to dropping his target.

Even as the Word Bearer triggered the explosives, Eitan's shots struck him, driving him back as he tried to bring up his own bolter. Eitan advanced, firing controlled bursts, not giving him a second to recover, trying to punch double-taps through the familiar weak points of power armour – the joint seals at the hips, poleyns, gorget, couters.

They found their mark. The traitor was injured, but returned the salvo. One round scored the Chapter symbol on Eitan's left pauldron; another ricocheted off the left directional nozzle of his reactor pack before detonating above him; a third struck his left vambrace and blew against the ceramite, driving shards of steel through the armour and into his flesh. The piece of battle plate turned yellow on his retinal spread, his armour registering both its own wound and his. Suppressants killed the pain instantly. His grip on his carbine's stock never wavered.

Just as with the stimuli of the gateway's detonation, Eitan was aware of it all, and yet unaware, his brain relegating into irrelevance anything that didn't serve his current sole reason for existence – killing his target. He kept going forward, kept firing, the steel-scarred space between the two giants in dark red armour rapidly diminishing.

The heretic emptied his magazine. Eitan's clicked dry at almost the same moment. Both were too close now to reload.

They went for their blades.

Eitan was faster, but not by much. He turned the last few yards into a charge. There was a crash of clashing ceramite. Eitan went straight for the traitor's throat, but realised his mistake as the Word Bearer simultaneously went low, aiming for the weak spot shared by both Primaris and those who had come before – the joint between breastplate and plackart which, if pierced, could allow a blade to stab up and under a fused ribcage.

It did so. Eitan felt pain lance into his core. His armour berated him, telling him he was wounded. Still he ignored it.

His own blow had jarred off the traitor's pauldron when he leaned down into Eitan's charge, locking against one of the spikes decorating the corrupt power armour. He sawed inwards, scarring a sideways slash across the Word Bearer's visor. The heretic twisted the knife in Eitan, trying to force it deeper through his armour and iron muscles. More pain, there and gone again. He could feel hot blood running down inside his armour, not given a chance to properly flash-clot by the blade digging in.

Size and strength. He threw himself against the Word Bearer, driving the knife deeper into his own gut but simultaneously forcing his opponent back, making him lose his balance. With his free hand he snatched the heretic's gorget and threw him to the dust, then, as he tried to rise, stamped down on the traitor's helmet.

It put the Word Bearer back down. Again, he tried to get up. Another downward kick, then another. The knife-marked visor cracked. One eye-lens shattered. One of the horns decorating the traitor's helm snapped away.

Eitan put his foot on the Chaos Space Marine's head and leaned on it with all his weight. There was a moment's resistance, coinciding with the scraping of the Word Bearer's clawed gauntlets digging into Eitan's greave, scrabbling streaks down the red paint and scratching the runic markings of the *Liber Exorcismus* inscribed there.

Then there was a cracking noise. The traitor's helm gave way, followed a second later by his skull. Eitan kept pressing down, teeth gritted, slowly but relentlessly crushing the Word Bearer's head, splitting his skull and sending blood and grey brain matter spurting out at multiple angles across the dust.

There was no more resistance. He ground his boot for good measure, reducing ceramite to shards and bone to powder. Finally, he stepped off. The Word Bearer's remains twitched, then went still.

Eitan ripped the knife from his sternum, snapped its crimson blade over his right vambrace, and tossed it into the trampled dirt next to the traitor's sprawled body. Only then did he look up, and found that his squad were cut off and under fire.

He rapidly assessed the situation. The blast in the gate's tunnel had further broken the doors and scarred the rockcrete, but the gatehouse itself was still standing. The same could not be said for the bridge beyond. The Reivers were either on the far side or wounded and stranded amidst the bridge's wreckage at the bottom of the moat. The ramparts of the gatehouse and the adjoining walls were still thick with heretic infantry, who were now able to pour fire down almost directly onto the heads of the Reivers in front of them, and Squad Eitan on the other side of the gate behind them.

That could not be allowed to continue.

'Secure the gatehouse,' Eitan ordered his Infiltrators. 'Hokmaz, the left doorway, Pazu, the right. Urhammu, get Nazaratus into cover under the arch until we can secure his progenoids. Go.'

The Exorcists swept once more into motion from where they had secured the barricades, doubling back towards the twin entrances that led up to the gatehouse ramparts. Eitan moved after them, flexing as he went, feeling the wound in his torso. Deep, but not too deep. Vitae signs within acceptable parameters.

His battle armour was injured too, but no vital blows to power, senses or servos. He blink-deleted its warnings.

'*Looking for a means of exfiltration, but the moat is deep,*' came Belloch's voice over the vox. He sounded understandably frustrated. '*Even if the gatehouse is secured, we remain vulnerable if we are divided in two. There must be other Word Bearers close. If they counter-attack you, Eitan, we have no means of offering support.*'

'*Daemonium Eversor,*' Eitan said. 'We need to knock out enough of the void shield so it is able to move your squad over the moat. Then we can regroup.'

'*Do any of you have the Sin Slayer on their vox?*' cut in Vey's voice unexpectedly, sounding ragged and breathless.

Eitan checked the comms channels, as well as his display. Both Zaidu and Squad Haad had vanished from the systems linking the rest of the Hexbreakers when they had split off and continued on underground. They had yet to reappear. The force striking overground at Fort Deliverance could only hope the almoner-lieutenant was making progress on his end of the operation.

'Negative,' Eitan told Vey. 'Still offline.'

'*I need to reach him,*' Vey said. '*I need to tell him not to enter the keep.*'

Vey spat out the blood that had been choking him, dragging in a painful breath. It had been too much. He had failed, failed to stop the Word Bearer from blowing the gate and the bridge. And now his failure could lead to the decimation of the entire strike force.

His body was in agony, covered by blistering warp burns, ones that defied even his pain dampeners. He knew they would only be soothed with unguents and incantations, none of which Vey had time for. He overcame them, overcame the bitter chill that had pierced his inner self and still made his skull ache. His weakness had already brought death to his brothers. He could not allow that to continue.

While he had wrestled with Kordiron, he had seen the dark intentions of the Word Bearer's brethren, been subsumed within them as within a bitter and chilling torrent. His master – Mordun, a Dark Apostle – believed himself close to daemonic apotheosis. Through pacts and auguries, he had identified that the Red Marshal was to conduct the crowning that would see him raised to immortality. Mordun wished to prise Caedus from the Broken One and bind it to his own service, thus proving himself worthy of what he considered the greatest blessing of all.

Freeing Caedus from the Broken One would see the daemon materialise, but if Mordun successfully shackled it, the Neverborn's full power would still not be realised. Any mistake, though, and Caedus would be truly free.

If Zaidu and Haad's Infiltrators attacked the ritual now under way in the keep at the wrong moment, all their efforts would be in vain.

Vey strode towards the only Reiver not cast into the moat by the gateway's detonation, Azzael. He was crouched and trading fire with the cultists on the ramparts above them. Ignoring the rounds raining down around them, Vey spoke to the Reiver as he reloaded his heavy bolt pistol.

'Can you reach the almoner-lieutenant?'

'His signal is partially back online, but broken,' Azzael answered, assessing the link Vey knew the Reivers still shared with their former squad leader. 'I can try to patch you through, but I cannot guarantee intelligibility.'

'Do it,' Vey instructed, half turning away from the firefight to consult his vambrace display.

If he could not stop Zaidu, the Sin Slayer might inadvertently unleash the very horrors they were seeking to banish.

The sounds of slaughter from outside were a fitting backdrop to Mordun's coronation rites.

Dalamar led the service, reading aloud from the *Heptameron of Narsus*, the un-words making the very air within the keep shudder. Sublimus stood near him, acting as his attendant and scroll-carrier, while the acolytes of the eparchy were arrayed in a circle around the markings they had daubed and slathered across the rockcrete floor with their own blood. They were canting the blessed verses, swaying slightly in a building rhythm that was steadily filling the centrum dominus.

Artax and the rest of the warband stood off to one side, in the shadows that seemed to deepen around the edge of the keep's old control centre. He was tracking the sounds of battle swelling outside, the constant thudding and cracking of the flock's small-arms playing counterpoint to the far greater wrath of bolter fire coming from the main gatehouse. The rudimentary vox-channel used by the herdsmen garrison was reporting that the loyalists had been checked at the entrance, and Cruexis had torn their hulking brute of a gunship from the sky. They would not interrupt the coronation, though Artax had noted Kordiron's marker replaced by a death-rune on his visor.

A part of him itched to avenge the fallen veteran and slaughter these upstart loyalist pups, but the instinctive warrior urge was not as strong as Artax's desire to be here, at the coronation, when Mordun's path to glory would come to an end and blessings would rain down upon them all. Artax had lost faith in much of what he had been promised in centuries past, but he was not yet so jaded that he would not acknowledge the power of daemonhood. If the Blind Shepherd truly was about to receive that greatest of boons, Artax needed to be close to him. Perhaps, then, all that he had seen and done would start to seem more worthwhile.

The Blessed One was at the centre of the markings on the floor. It stood, arms by its side, still but for the seemingly compulsive flexing of its talons. The skin of its neck, chest and stomach was a mess of clotted wounds and dry black blood. More of it marred the collar it still wore. Artax appreciated the irony of the Imperial trinket being used now to help hold Caedus at bay so that Mordun's ritual could proceed.

Mordun stepped into the pentacle markings, daring to disturb the fresh, glistening blood. He had shed the foolish garb of the Irenoth flock and now stood in the full glories of his millennia-old battle plate, the power armour's red so dark it was almost black. A small brazier had been locked to the top of his reactor pack and was now lit with green-tainted warp flame, spewing acrid smoke that coiled in strange, sentient patterns around him.

In one fist he still carried his staff, bleeding a dark energy of its own, the materium surrounding it now wafer thin. The Dark Apostle began to speak, his words making Artax's ears ache and his skin crawl with equal parts disgust and anticipation. This was the beginning of the end of everything they had worked towards. Ten thousand prayers that felt as though they had only ever been spoken to mocking and uncaring gods were now about to be answered, all at once.

Other members of the warband began to join in the eparchy's chant. Even Artax found his lips moving, though no noise issued forth.

Mordun made a curt motion in Sublimus' direction, and the eparch left the bibliognost's shadow and hurried to the far side of the pentagram circle, hitching up the hem of his black robes so as not to smear the blood. He stepped over the markings behind the Blessed One and, matching Mordun's litanies, reached up to the collar clamped around its neck.

After some effort, Sublimus was able to prise it off, breaking its latch with the canticles of the Dark Tongue. Artax noticed that blood had started to ooze from the eight-pointed star that covered Sublimus' scalp, running down his face even as he continued to call on the warp.

The collar fell to the floor with a crack. As soon as it struck the rockcrete, the Blessed One was snarling and lunging.

It moved perhaps a couple of inches before the wards and incantations checked it, quivering, spitting its fury just short of Mordun. The Dark Apostle didn't miss a beat. He held forth his staff, the black warpwood a fraction away from the Blessed One's shivering flesh. Its skin had started to writhe, as though things were crawling and burrowing just beneath.

The tone of Mordun's voice deepened. The Blessed One let out a shriek, head snapping back, eyes rolling. The sound melded with a maddening buzzing noise as a cloud of glistening black flies burst from its stretched-open jaw, pouring out and around the pentagrammic circle. A putrid stench filled the air, making Artax's stomach churn.

Mordun held out his gauntlet and clenched it. The flies swept down and began to coalesce into a sphere above his hand, the last of them swarming from the Blessed One's mouth and forming themselves into a shifting orb of glittering, tightly packed black carapaces.

A wisp of the warp flame from his brazier licked out and ignited the sphere. It went up like kindling, blazing briefly and brightly as the flies were immolated. When it burned out, they were gone, though the stench lingered for a few moments more.

The Blessed One's back arched. There was a crack of bone.

Mordun continued to bark his rite and verse, striking at it with his staff. The host had started to rise up from the ground, Artax realised, as the laws of nature continued to unravel within the keep.

There were more crunches as the Blessed One's jaw distended so much it started to crack apart. More warp essence poured out, this time taking the form of a broiling cloud of pink smoke that remained within the pentagram circle as though trapped within a glass orb. It was sickly-sweet, and made Artax's senses feel numb. He joined in the litany of his brethren in full, knowing that the point of decision was about to be reached. The Blessed One had to be purged of the other entities housed within before the Red Marshal could be properly extracted and bound in its true and bloody form.

Mordun gripped his staff horizontally overhead, in both hands, black fluids running from his thin lips. Just as the flies had been drawn to his fist, so the daemonic smoke was dragged to the staff, disappearing into it as though sucked into a vacuum. The air around the Blessed One cleared, and it finally crunched its mouth shut. Its eyes were red, as though every blood vessel within them had burst.

Now, the true ceremony could begin.

A crimson line, thin as a stylus strike, appeared in the centre of the Blessed One's throat and began to run down its torso. Slowly, the line became a cut, then a gash as Mordun's words carved the flesh prison open, blood starting to cascade down onto the floor. The chanting of Sublimus, Dalamar, the eparchy and the warband was approaching a crescendo, words throbbing and twisting and warring against each other and against the reality struggling to contain them.

Artax was the first one to become aware of the interloper. A figure had come stumbling up the stairs from the floor below and was now poised at the archway leading into the centrum dominus, caught between the urge to enter the chamber and the terrifying prospect of interrupting the ritual. It was a herdsman, flushed, panting. There was fresh blood on his mangy fleece.

Artax immediately left off his cant and strode around the control room's edge, confronting the quailing cretin.

'What is it?' he snarled.

'Lord, the soulless ones,' the cultist stammered. 'They are within the keep!'

'How?' Artax demanded. 'They are being held at the gate.'

'I do not know, lord. They came from below. The armoury.'

He had feared something like this. They had to be stopped from interrupting the ceremony. At the same time, Artax was loath to leave the chamber. When Mordun ascended, he had to be present. He wouldn't risk his life against the loyalist monsters while others reaped the rewards of centuries of work.

'Vost, Ikar, to arms,' he snapped over the closed vox, unwilling to raise his voice and interrupt the chanting. 'We have company. Secure the stairwell and the floor below. The slaves of the False Emperor must not be allowed to reach the Blessed One or the Dark Apostle.'

The pair only reluctantly moved from where they were arrayed around the chamber's edge. Artax stepped aside for them to reach the stairwell, listening for proof of the herdsman's claim – the echo of bolter fire, the clash of steel, the screams of the wounded, even the thrum of power armour. But there was nothing audible over the rising crescendo of the ritual.

Still, Artax did not doubt the herdsman's story. These soulless creatures had proved themselves adept at stealth. Their infiltration would go no further.

'Every one you slay is worth a thousand prayers to the Primordial Truth,' he told the pair of Word Bearers as they moved past, trying to stoke the fires of their zealotry. 'Worship with blade and bolter, my brothers. These unholy anathemas deserve nothing more than annihilation.'

Zaidu heard the traitors coming.

With the Infiltrators at his back, he had penetrated up through the keep, moving with silent, deadly focus. The cult infantry he found died with barely a sound. The fact that they were unprepared gave him hope. None within the heart of Fort Deliverance seemed to expect to find the Exorcists in their midst. Most were hurrying towards the main doors or the armoury, seeking to bolster the defences outside.

Zaidu could feel the aching closeness of his Never-brother. The blood on his knives seemed to cling to the blades, as though eager to be brought into the presence of the daemon. He went on, barely aware even of the presence of Squad Haad, finishing his work as he went from floor to floor.

Faded signage on the walls of the stairwell he was taking declared that the keep's centrum dominus was on the next level. That had to be it.

On the way up, he heard the Word Bearers descending to meet him – reactor packs, grating old armour, heavy treads on the rockcrete.

He surged round the stairwell's bend, roaring. If the heretics did not know the Sin Slayer was in their midst, they would now.

Surprised or not, the first one had his bolter levelled, and got a burst away. One round punched through Zaidu's cuirass and detonated against his rib plate, cracking it. He barely felt it. One knife lanced through the neck seal beneath the rim of the traitor's helmet. Black, filthy blood spurted over the blade.

The Exorcist drove himself into the Word Bearer as he shook and choked, forcing him back into his brother, who grunted and snarled from the stylised daemon maw of his helm's vox-grille as he fought not to lose his balance on the stairs.

More boltgun fire went off, from the spasming of the first traitor and the attempts of the second to get a shot past him at Zaidu. Rounds chewed at the walls and ceiling, shattered plaster and rockcrete raining down. More punched through the back of the one Zaidu had stabbed, drenching the stairs with blood. The discharges in the confined space battered at Zaidu's eardrums.

He threw down the first traitor, ripping his knife free as he went, trying to get over him and at the second one. The first was refusing to die and dragged him down, just in time for a fresh blast of bolter fire, the heat of the muzzle flash close enough to singe the side of Zaidu's head.

This time it was the discharge of a bolt carbine. Haad was firing through the tangle, just over Zaidu's shoulder. His shots carved up the second Word Bearer's breastplate, the Infiltrator having to empty the clip before the explosive rounds finally punched their way through to the Chaos Space Marine's hearts and lungs. Zaidu sawed his knife back down through the first one's throat, almost beheading him as he finally ended his struggles.

There was no time to acknowledge Haad's intervention. Zaidu drove himself over the bodies and up the last flight of stairs, clearing them in just a few bounds, rockcrete cracking and crumbling beneath his weight. He could hear the chanting in the air now, feel the raw blasphemy being committed, like a knife twisting in Fidem's flesh.

He had to end the torture, for his own sake as much as for the world around him.

As he went, he failed to see the chopped and interrupted transmission request from Vey, lighting up along his vambrace before it cut off again.

CHAPTER TWENTY-FIVE

THE CRIMSON CORONATION

Daemonium Eversor came down with far less grace than it had when it alighted before the outer works of Fort Deliverance. Kothar was aiming for the same open kill-zone, but the Overlord was yawing badly, hamstrung by the Heldrake's savaging.

'Impact in thirty,' the Techmarine voxed to Anu and Dumuzid.

Anu braced, ready to move as soon as the worst of the landing was complete. He hadn't given the plan he had laid out to Kothar further consideration. There was no point. He knew what he had to do. It was the best chance they were going to get to survive this.

You only suggested this because you don't want to die in the dark, like your brother, whispered a voice, barely audible over the tortured sound of *Daemonium Eversor*'s engines.

'Be silent,' Anu murmured, unwilling to entertain the echo for even a moment. It was the first time he had heard it since the Orison rites. Now was no time for indulgence.

The Overlord hit the dirt. The cries of the Chapter-serfs were eclipsed by the crash of adamantine and the shrieking of the engines. Everything shook. Everything groaned. Anu maintained his grip on the rail above, and on the las fusil he had taken from the stock in the depths of the hold.

The lurching sense of motion began to decrease, and the tremors faded. Anu was moving as soon as his auto-senses informed him he was unlikely to lose his balance, along the aisle and then up the short ladder to the hatch at the far end. He popped the seal and levered it up.

Water cascaded in through the opening, drenching his camo cape and drawn-up cowl. He climbed the rest of the way, up and out of *Daemonium Eversor* and onto the gunship's topside.

Rain was pouring down, seething across the dark red roof plates of the Overlord. As he clambered onto them, he got a good view of the amount of damage wreaked on the gunship by the daemon flyer. The starboard engine was a smoking mess, but was positively intact compared to the right-side troop compartment. The rear had been completely ripped away, what had once been the ramp and the back quarter of the hold now just ragged struts of bare, shorn metal. Anu realised just how instant Lakhmu's death must have been.

He moved swiftly across *Daemonium Eversor*'s topside until he was between the twin holds and just above and back from the cockpit blister. The whole time his eyes were on the leaden skies, goggles lowered, their senses helping strip back the cover provided by the downpour.

Sure enough, he detected movement among the rain and black thunderheads, something vast and fast.

He pulled off his cape and lay down, face up, on the hull. He draped the cape over him, lying as flat as his reactor pack would allow, making sure the las fusil was beneath the drenched covering too. He reached to his hip and set the power pack strapped there to maximum output.

'Picking it up on the scopes,' Kothar's voice crackled. *'It's coming.'*

'I know,' Anu said.

Grounded, *Daemonium Eversor* was unable to bring any of its armaments to bear on the angle the Heldrake was descending from. But the Overlord was no longer the one trying to kill the daemon engine. Anu was.

He looked skywards again, and saw death and damnation descending on swift wings.

The Heldrake came knifing through the clouds, rain running in streamers off its wicked wings and the bone-and-metal spines ridging its back.

A shriek filled the air, part mechanical, part organic, full of hunger and defiance. It made Anu's ears ache and set the hull beneath him vibrating.

Whether the daemon engine saw him, he did not know. Even more so than many of its kin, this Neverborn was a predator, a creature of hunger and instinct. All it could really sense right now was prey, brought low and helpless. *Daemonium Eversor* was larger, faster, better armed than anything that had yet challenged it on this world. It yearned to assert its dominance, to prove its power and feast, like all warp creatures. It would wrench and tear the gunship to scraps and scatter it across its hunting grounds as a warning to all others who would defy it in the air or on the ground.

Anu knew he would only have one shot. Just as he liked it.

He cast aside the camo cape and brought up the las fusil, the weapon primed and shivering with charge. No time to lock its scope to his goggles, physically or remotely. He wouldn't need to.

The Heldrake was on them. Its maw yawned, all fangs and blades and the broiling madness at its heart.

Anu sighted, locked and fired.

The las fusil spat fury, the charge pack drained in a single shot, the barrel turning white-hot in an instant. A beam of brilliance punched from *Daemonium Eversor*'s back, a halo of evaporated mist surrounding it as it cut the very raindrops. It lanced straight through the Heldrake's maw and down its warp-flesh gullet, searing into its core, choking its scream with a killshot.

Reality asserted itself on the daemon engine with brutal finality. The Heldrake detonated. It blew apart just before its fangs and talons reached Anu and the hull beneath him, turned into a thousand shards of metal and broiling purple flame that blazed and coruscated in the air for a moment, as though unwilling to depart the materium.

Blue energies flared just above Anu as *Daemonium Eversor*'s void shield, set to guard its topside, fought to ward away the rain of razor metal and burning daemon meat that came slamming down onto the Overlord. One wing, still largely intact, narrowly missed the gunship and hammered point down into the dirt beside it, driving deep into Fidem like a massive arrowhead.

Anu released the breath he had instinctively held and unlocked his armour. He said a prayer of thanks to the las fusil and set it down beside him, its barrel steaming as it slowly cooled off in the rain. Then, for a second or two, he simply lay, staring up into the downpour, into the black clouds, at the last scraps of warp ember as they disappeared, banished back to the realm of the impossible.

He searched within himself for pride, triumph, a sense of satisfaction that he had avenged Lakhmu, but could find nothing. He voxed Kothar.

'Target destroyed.'

Eitan watched Anu's shot lance the shrieking daemon engine. Then he turned back towards the void shield node Brother-Initiate Uten had discovered on the parapets of the gatehouse.

It was a metallic orb about the size of an Adeptus Astartes helmet, seated on a pylon frame that contained a thick knot of wires and cabling running back to a caged power generator set below the ramparts. The node's head stood just proud of the parapet, behind the now abandoned Hydra gun, its smooth spherical surface crackling with live charge.

Squad Eitan had stormed the gatehouse and spread left and right over the nearest adjoining wall sections, quickly eliminating the heretics concentrated there and ending the fire they had been blazing down on the battered Reivers. There was still no means of linking the two squads back together though, not until *Daemonium Eversor* could get airborne again. And that meant removing the fort's void shield, at least from above the gatehouse.

Eitan put a bolt through the node's head. It burst apart in a hail of sparks and shorn metal.

'Tear it free and throw it over the parapet,' he ordered Uten. The huge Exorcist stooped and snatched the bundles of cabling at the base of the frame, putting his boot on them as he wrenched them out. Then, with a grunt, he grasped the structure and, seemingly immune to the discharge that snapped and darted across his arms and pauldrons, wrenched it from its fixings and tossed it over the wall, trailing its tail of sparking cables.

The stink of ozone redoubled, filling the rain-slashed air. No ordnance was currently being directed at Fort Deliverance, so it was impossible to tell if a rent had just appeared in the shield's dome, but Eitan intended to find out.

'Kothar,' he said into his helm's vox. 'Do you still have your wings?'

'*I am willing to find out if you are, Eitan,*' came the Techmarine's response.

'I believe I have cut the void shield's transmission over the gatehouse. If you can collect the Reivers, we can regroup and push on to the keep.'

'I will endeavour to, but you will owe Daemonium Eversor*'s machine spirit a great many offerings after this.'*

'I will gladly make them to such a hero of the Chapter,' Eitan said.

'Lector-sergeant,' interjected a voice. It was Vey.

'We will have you on this side of the gate in a moment, enlightened brother,' Eitan informed him.

'Maybe so,' he replied, voice heavy. *'But I fear we are already too late. Caedus comes.'*

Mordun paused to collect himself, fighting back his body's need to vomit. No matter how he opened himself to the empyrean, no matter how close the divine loomed within and around him, he could never quite throw off the pathetic, weak response of mortal flesh to the raw god-matter of the warp. Soon, though, such shortcomings would be a thing of the past. Soon, he would sup in full of that divinity.

Unlock, unlock, Se'irim cawed. **Free! Free!**

Mordun grinned at Caedus, ectoplasmic filth drooling down his chin. The Blessed One had been cut open by the ceremony, blood puddling beneath it, flowing over the marks on the floor. A moment was being taken after the two banishments, the chanting of the eparchy returning to a susurration, pitch and rhythms changing as they moved into a different rite.

'It must be liberating, now that your despised kin have been banished,' Mordun said to the daemon as he refocused his mind.

'It will be liberating when I am free from your wards and your staff, you old fool,' Caedus spat back.

'Perhaps, when you have crowned me with daemonhood, I will

deign to relinquish you from your duties,' Mordun said, before addressing Sublimus. 'Bring me the coronation sacrament.'

The eparch scrambled to obey. He approached a heavy lifting servitor, standing stooped beside a bank of old tactical cogitator arrays at the back of the centrum dominus. Most of it was vat-grown flesh and crude, bulky rig prosthetics, both of which had been scarred and scorched with Dark Tongue inscriptions. Its limbs were little more than a pair of lock-claws, clamped around the object Mordun desired – a massive axe, seemingly fashioned from a single length of gnarled bone, its edge a hundred jagged, mismatched fangs.

Sublimus worked the brutal weapon from the servitor's grip with some difficulty, barely able to lift it. Even its haft was sharp, drawing blood from the eparch's hands as he hefted it to Mordun. The Dark Apostle accepted it, his shattered daemon-sight showing the dark crimson energies running from it like smoke, feeling its weight and power, its bloodlust, how it raged as the daemonic bone scraped impotently at the protection of his gauntlets.

He didn't take his eyes off Caedus as he took the weapon. He relished the renewed expression of fury that twisted the Blessed One's face, even as its blood drained from its body, its flesh now corpse pale.

'Do you miss your axe, Red Marshal?' Mordun taunted. 'Mighty Viscera? The bane of heroes and cowards for how many millennia? And lost to you for the past four. It was my recovery of it on Suplice Beta that first started the winding path that has led us both here. When I claimed it, your kindred promised me my eternal reward if I could bind you. When I ascend, Viscera will become mine for eternity.'

'You do not deserve it,' Caedus hissed, more blood running thick and dark from the Blessed One's mouth and nose. *'It*

was fashioned from the skull of a being far more worthy and ancient than you will ever be. When I reclaim it, my power will be complete.'

'You will never reclaim it,' Mordun responded. 'You will never be free from these wards, not until you swear yourself to me.'

If Caedus spoke again, Mordun did not hear it. There was a sudden hammering of bolter fire, rising up from the stairwell leading to the centrum dominus. He snarled, not turning, Se'irim showing him heavily armoured shapes looming in the entranceway to the chamber, dark and hollow monstrosities.

'Artax, stop them,' he barked into the vox before addressing the eparchy. 'Continue your readings! Do not stop chanting!'

He realised Caedus had begun to laugh, even as the Blessed One gagged on its own blood.

'I know how you hunger for the vital essence,' Mordun told it. 'I know how it gives you strength. You shall have none of it, not until my apotheosis. That is my final promise to you.'

The Dark Apostle began to speak the litanies once more. In the midst of it all, he didn't notice that, somewhere within the recesses of his mind, Se'irim had started to giggle.

Zaidu stormed the centrum dominus, Haad and Gela going left, Nizreba and Kephras going right, trying to widen the space for the rest of the squad to push in.

He locked immediately on to the Broken One. It was near the centre of the half-broken room, drenched in blood, standing in a lake of crimson. The Dark Apostle was before it, staff in one hand, a heavy, tainted axe in the other, spitting unutterable words. Heretics and traitors were arrayed all around, but Zaidu was barely even aware of them, nor of Squad Haad engaging them. His every effort focused on the target, keen as the edge of one of his combat knives.

Caedus was almost free. Its true form had slowly started to

coalesce from the blood the Broken One was shedding, split down the middle. The place stank of corruption, was riddled with it. The warp was threatening to tear its way into reality all around them.

Zaidu charged, giving voice to a bellowed goetic battle litany. Black-robed cultists were trampled, screaming, underfoot. He didn't even waste a knife stroke on them. He saw the Dark Apostle half turning, saw the Broken One laughing through the blood, then both were obscured as a shape threw itself between the Exorcist and his prey.

Word Bearer. The traitor was tall and broad, almost as large as Zaidu. He had been leading the chanting from a heavy grimoire, the words writhing like living creatures across the cracked yellow pages, but he slammed it shut and let it hang by chains from his side as he drew a heavy khopesh blade, the curved steel etched with abominable incantations.

Zaidu struck the Chaos Space Marine with a roar.

Artax let out a litany of curses as the first of the loyalists burst into the centrum dominus.

He had feared Ikar and Vost would only delay them. He hadn't anticipated that, runts though they were, they would be slaughtered so swiftly.

If the Corpse Emperor's slaves weren't stopped immediately, everything would come apart. Artax could feel the power of the warp ripping through the chamber, reality barely maintaining its tenuous grip. Their mere presence was a danger.

He drew his knife and went for the door, unwilling to further sunder the ceremony by opening fire with his bolter.

The first Imperial brute through was intercepted by Dalamar, who had been forced to cease reading from the *Heptameron* but continued his chanting even as his khopesh met the loyalist's knives.

Syro hit the second, while Artax engaged the third. He was wielding a combat knife long enough to be a short sword, which he lanced at Artax's breastplate.

The Word Bearer had killed loyalist scum like this before. They trusted in their faith and their wargear, but they did not know war as he knew it. He would not be bested by this pup.

The strike to Artax's midriff was predictable, as was the fact it was intended to open his guard once he parried it. Instead, he let it jar against his breastplate and pushed back, switching his own knife from right to left and punching it up and under the Primaris' suddenly exposed right underarm. He felt a vicious thrill as the length of ancient steel entered through the weak seal at the joint and in past the loyalist's ribcage, puncturing a lung.

He ripped the blade free, knowing that the Primaris would try and twist his body to drag it from his grip. The motion caused the loyalist to miss the chance to riposte, and Artax followed hard, switching his weapon again and going for his opponent's left side now that he had exposed it by twisting right.

This time the loyalist was able to match him, though barely. He deflected the blow, then countered. Artax was already breaking off further to the right, making him turn in a half-circle and sending several eparchy cultists sprawling.

The loyalist attacked again without pause, his expression unreadable behind his visor, though his motions betrayed his aggression. Artax had stung him, and that was good. The loyalist switched his own knife and lashed out at the Word Bearer with his right arm, showing little physical indication that he had been wounded. He snatched the edge of Artax's pauldron and dragged at him, anticipating resistance, expecting that the Chaos worshipper would want to keep at a distance that would negate the elements of size and strength.

Artax did the opposite. He provided the briefest moment of

resistance, to cause the Primaris to strain against him, then went with the motion. He drove himself forward into a lunge, head down, and slammed the studded brow of his helmet against the loyalist's face.

There was a gristly crunch. Artax slammed his head forward again. At the same time, forcing himself into the loyalist's embrace, he drove his knife into the joint between thigh plate and mag belt, then out and in again, up past the plackart, wrenching the blade right to left. He was bleeding the beast, like a huntsman bringing down a bull grox, one blow at a time.

That would trigger what Artax thought of as the kill switch, the burst of stimms and adrenaline that Primaris unleashed before their flames burned out. He tried to draw back, intending to let him waste it, but the loyalist had got a grip of him now and wasn't letting go.

The brute clutched him in a death embrace, and as Artax rammed his knife back into the Primaris' abdomen, the Word Bearer was forced to grab his opponent's wrist, straining to hold his enemy's blade at bay as it arced down towards him.

It was a losing struggle. Slowly, inch by inch, that long length of gleaming steel forced its way towards his throat.

Mordun called upon the True Gods to witness him as he chained the Red Marshal.

He had almost dragged Caedus from the Blessed One's broken form. The blood was coalescing into a horned shape, the defiled body carved down the middle and only held up by the holy litanies Mordun was still spitting.

The warp was howling around him. He could feel the attentions of thousands upon thousands of Neverborn entities straining at the keep, his daemon-sight showing the air around them distending and straining beneath shrieking visages and vicious talons, like a thin membrane that was a heartbeat away from collapsing.

It was too much. Mordun didn't care. He was redolent with warp energies, addicted to them, overloaded. He could feel how his own body rebelled, no longer in mere revulsion but beginning to shift and change as it was irrecoverably polluted. He felt as though his skin was going to split and his bones shatter and re-form. It was at once agonising and energising, driving his already enhanced body beyond anything previously intended of it.

Immortality beckoned. He closed in on the final verses, a corona of dark power crackling around his brow. He was vaguely aware of Sublimus beside him, screaming and pleading horribly as the eight-pointed star upon his head began to peel back like a bloody fruit, exposing his skull inch by inch, skinning him alive.

Mordun didn't care. In that moment he felt as if he could see all, feel all. More than ever before, he was communing with godhood.

A few words more, and it would all be his.

Zaidu hacked at the Word Bearer blocking him – no skill or finesse, just brute force. He knew he had seconds at most. One knife shattered the khopesh and the other carved open the traitor's skull. Blood jetted from the cracked helm. It shot backwards as the traitor fell.

The merest amount reached the place where the Broken One and the Dark Apostle stood.

It anointed them both.

The last words turned to ash in Mordun's mouth as he felt blood – not the Blessed One's – strike the side of his face.

In the same instant, he realised that the host's pallid right fist had lashed out and was now grasping the haft of Viscera.

Time seemed to stand still, and perhaps it did.

The Blessed One's head was hanging back, neck broken, its whole body like a meat puppet being held up by invisible strings. Still, though, words bubbled up through the blood.

'Did you truly believe you were the one in control here, old man?'

Control, Se'irim hissed in Mordun's thoughts, echoing Caedus.

'I was promised–' Mordun began with a snarl, trying to reassert himself, but the Red Marshal interrupted him.

'You are mistaken. My kindred and my allies would never accept you into their ranks. They merely ensured you would pave the way for my return.'

'But Se'irim–'

'Se'irim and I have had an accord for many millennia, as have Skarthax, Brasshorn and more besides.'

Many millennia, Se'irim giggled in Mordun's thoughts as Caedus went on.

'Se'irim sought you out. He forced his way into your flesh and made you believe you had tamed him. What he has shown you has never been true.'

You see what I wish you to see, **Blind Shepherd**, Se'irim croaked.

Mordun's vision blurred, became even more fractured. Daemons surrounded him, a formless, amorphous mass of flesh and bone that strained for him, shrieking and howling and gibbering. Maw-fangs and talons scraped his armour and tentacles slithered and coiled around his limbs. The iciness of the void penetrated to his core. Even his own staff had turned on him, a black viper coiling around his wrist, poised to strike.

'They will feast on you, Mordun,' Caedus gurgled. *'For eternity.'*

'Please,' the Dark Apostle found himself stammering, all power, all certainty gone as he realised Artax had been right.

These beings would not aid him, nor share their power. They were no more shepherds than he was. They were predators.

The Blessed One ripped Viscera from Mordun's grasp and, with the last of its strength, swung. The cursed axe cleaved Mordun's head from his shoulders, the prayer wraps binding him igniting in the warp flames of the brazier upon his back. Flames engulfed the Dark Apostle, and his black staff shattered into a thousand shrieking shards.

There was a crash like thunder. The Blessed One's remains collapsed, the burning, headless corpse of Mordun falling to its knees opposite.

The blood that had been pouring from the host coalesced and transmuted, changed in an impossible instant. It became a crimson bolt of lightning that crashed skywards, cracking through the roof of the centrum dominus, arcing upwards into the dark heavens, where it let out a mighty, echoing boom. As it went, it left madness in its wake, a complete and total insanity that would act as the merest taste of what was to come.

Zaidu lashed towards the red energy coruscating up from the Broken One's twitching remains, but the scissoring strike from his blades cut only air. The lightning was gone.

Zaidu remembered what it meant to hate, to rage, to feel. He howled his fury, shared it with his Never-brother.

Caedus was free.

The loyalist's knife tip was about to punch into Artax's throat when a sound like thunder filled the centrum dominus.

He was locked in and grappling with the Primaris, so couldn't turn to discover its source, but he felt its impact. Rage. Fury the likes of which he had never known. It blinded him, fuelled him, flooded him with the need to break and kill.

With a strength he had never felt before, he forced away the arm of the Primaris and drove his own knife back into him. He did it over and over, until the brute had fallen, and then continued.

It was not enough. He cast about, lashing out, grabbing a fistful of trailing black robes. One of the eparchy, screaming. Not in fear, but in anger, the same anger Artax felt. The emaciated man beat his fists madly against Artax's armour until his knuckles broke. Artax responded by beating his own fist against the cultist's face until that broke too.

He couldn't think. The rationality he had once prided himself on was gone. Rage was everything, rage and the need for blood. They were all animals, and finally they were accepting it.

He woke only slowly from the frenzy. He was aware of blood in his mouth, and something thicker. He swallowed it, grimacing. At some point he had ripped his helmet off.

He was on his knees. There was a body in front of him. Not one of the loyalists, nor even one of Sublimus' minions. It was a brother, Skerin. His chest plate and fused ribs had been laid open, carved apart by Artax's knife to expose the mutilated organs within. He too was without his helmet. Most of his head had been ripped off.

Blood-drunk, Artax looked down at his own gauntlets. He realised dimly that he had been eating part of Skerin's face.

He tried to rise but found he could not. His strength had deserted him. He looked around blearily, seeing slaughtered cultists and the remnants of the warband lying about him. There were the mangled remains of the Blessed One too, broken almost beyond recognition, and a charred mass of fused armour and blackened meat, slowly smoking, that he took to be Mordun. His coronation had been an anointing of flames, not immortality.

The loyalists, the soulless ones, were moving slowly through the dripping, settling carnage, finishing the wounded. It was not the Primaris who had killed his brethren, Artax realised. They had done that themselves.

He began to laugh, though he didn't really understand why. It was all so pointless. It always had been, right from the beginning. They were all monsters, freakish mongrels bred to kill until they were killed in turn. There was nothing more to it – no nobility, no majesty, no lasting strength or meaningful power. Those were just the lies they had been told over and over, by all the warring rulers of the galaxy, beings who would have them do the killing in their name.

The amusing part, Artax supposed, was that he had known all of this for some time. He had just refused to speak out about it. Centuries of cultish indoctrination, esotericism and madness had been enough to muzzle him, but never quite blind him.

Maybe it would have been easier if it had, if he had plunged himself into the fanaticism that possessed his so-called brothers and lost himself in the fire and insanity. They had taken it all to its logical conclusion now. They had slaughtered each other like beasts, turned on one another with a wildness born out of the same untameable emotions that had bred this nightmare, had conjured it into being.

In the end, he decided that it didn't matter. It was all far too late to worry about any of it. In that, at last, he found some solace.

Gloria Aeterna indeed.

Artax pulled his knife from Skerin's chest, and cut his own throat.

CHAPTER TWENTY-SIX

PROPHETIC MEMORY

Zaidu stood in silence, blood about his boots and dripping slowly from his blades, looking down at the Broken One and the charred remains of the heretic.

For a short while, he had lost himself, as had they all. Daemonic madness, more potent than any he had known since his initiation rites, had gripped the whole centrum dominus. The Exorcists had overcome it swiftly. It had burned out within them, their soul-scraps like kindling that had flared brightly back down to nothing.

The same could not be said of the heretics. Zaidu and the Infiltrators had watched as they turned on one another, butchering each other in a madness that had seen them all cut to pieces. It was, Zaidu supposed, the just wages of their treachery.

The remains of Squad Haad – less Brother-Initiates Lamesh and Akkad, who had fallen during the brief, frenzied fight – were now moving through the gore-drenched chamber, ensuring it was secure. Gela had already collected the gene-seed of the two slain Exorcists.

The daemon was gone. Zaidu knew failure, as potent and bitter an emotion as any he had experienced since the Neverborn had first ripped away most of his identity. It had all been in vain. All his efforts seemed to have merely paved the way for its triumph.

The battle focus had left him, draining from a body that had been burning violently through stimulants and glanded reactions. Still, though, his senses caught a twitch of motion, enough to penetrate the sensation of hollowness that now gripped his mind.

He looked again at the Broken One, and realised it was still alive.

Wordlessly he knelt, assessing the wreckage of flesh and bone and organs that had once been something almost human. He had rarely seen a Primaris so utterly annihilated, so torn beyond recognition, and yet somehow life still clung on. It was a testament to the strength of the Emperor's works, Zaidu decided.

Unlike the rest of the body, the face was still largely intact. Zaidu leaned down, finding a degree of focus in the one remaining eye. As he did so, a name came to him, dredged up from his hypno briefings, absorbed on the way to Fidem.

'Ashad,' he said. On an impulse he didn't really understand, he unclasped his death mask, baring his face, twisted though it was, to this, his brother. He realised that the former aspirant was trying to speak.

'I failed,' came the faintest breath from ruined lips.

'No,' Zaidu said, not out of any attempt at reassurance, but simply from a desire to speak the truth. 'You were asked to bear a greater burden than any of us. It is my failure that has led us here, not yours. Know, as you go to your eternal destruction, that you do so as a brother-initiate of the Exorcists.'

He did not know if Ashad heard him. In a moment more he was dead, a Broken One no longer.

Zaidu became aware of footsteps, rising up through the stairwell leading to the control room. He paused to refasten his mask, then rose and turned towards the new arrival.

It was Vey. The Librarian's hood was down, and he had deactivated and clamped his force sword. His eyes seemed to have sunk deeper into their sockets than when Zaidu had last looked into them properly, and his face was marred by blister burns and deep lines. He looked beyond exhausted, a man who was carrying on through stony willpower alone.

Zaidu faced him and, after a moment, made an Orison gesture, a greeting.

Vey returned it before speaking.

'The fortress is secure and the rest of the strike force is now within the walls. The heretics turned on each other.'

'Caedus is gone,' Zaidu responded simply.

'I know,' Vey said. 'I sense its presence, but it is far from here. It goes in search of its final victory.'

'What of our losses?' Zaidu asked, making himself act the part of the leader, even if he had never felt it. He hadn't even checked his vambrace display to assess the damage done to the Hexbreakers.

'Brother-Initiate Nazaratus and Almoner-Marksman Lakhmu are dead. There are injuries throughout the rest of the strike force, but only Shemesh might be rendered combat ineffective. His leg is gone.'

Combat ineffective. Zaidu had barely even considered further fighting. Now that Caedus was unbound, it meant Fidem IV's nightmare was only just beginning. There would be slaughter the likes of which hadn't been seen on this world in four thousand years.

'I have failed,' Zaidu said, holding Vey's gaze unflinchingly. 'As you predicted. The future I saw was a lie.'

'It may not have been,' Vey responded, voice heavy. He advanced towards Zaidu and reached out briefly to touch his pauldron, almost as if, after it all, he wished to reassure Zaidu, as though any Exorcist would understand such a thing. 'This failure is as much mine as yours, Sin Slayer. I should have spoken out before now.'

'What do you mean?' Zaidu asked, sensing something more to the Librarian's words than mere contrition.

'Your vision. A warrior in golden armour, vanquishing the daemon. You believed it spoke to your future, a prophetic awakening you shared when Caedus infested your body and your soul. That was certainly one explanation, though not the only one.'

Zaidu said nothing, merely waited for Vey to continue.

'I had my suspicions for some time, though I did not wish to push them upon you. It is impossible to be certain about these things, and I allowed the fact that I hoped you were right to cloud my judgement. Remind me, what does the daemon call you?'

'What do you mean?'

'What did it call you during your initiation rites, and in your echoes? It does not address you as Daggan Zaidu.'

'Demetrius,' Zaidu said, the word feeling strange and unfamiliar. He had always taken it to be some warp lie or quirk of profane madness.

'We know more than most that names have power,' Vey said. 'A daemon's true name gives us an unparalleled degree of control over it, and our own names are not without effect either. Caedus knows this. Its use of that name is no coincidence.'

'Then who is Demetrius?' Zaidu asked, his patience beginning to erode.

'You are, in a sense,' Vey replied. 'I have been looking into this matter since word came of the incident at Nowhere. Before we departed Banish I was able to access relevant sections of the Librarius and the Chapter's gene bank records. I was able to trace your ancestry.

'We are the descendants of the Praetorian, that is well known. Rogal Dorn is our genetic sire, and his stoicism and fortitude are at the root of much of our ability to resist the madness of the warp. All of us connect back eventually to those members of the Imperial Fists who were separated from their original Chapter to form this brotherhood. According to the records, my gene-seed was born out of an Imperial Fists Librarian named Darrion. And yours, Zaidu, was a Fist called Demetrius.'

'I understand,' Zaidu said, awaking to the coldness of reality. 'It was never a vision. It was a memory.'

'Demetrius was the Imperial Fists captain who led the defence of Fidem IV four thousand years ago,' Vey went on. 'He defeated Caedus in four separate bouts of combat. After Demetrius' victory, he spent many more years in honoured service, before volunteering to be part of the intake who would form the Exorcists, during the Thirteenth Founding. His gene-seed is borne by a number of our brethren to this day, and you are one of them. When you were possessed by Caedus, the combination of your genetic heritage and the Neverborn's memories caused you to psychically recollect the defining point between them. You saw Demetrius battle and overcome Caedus for the final time on Fidem, at what became the Tower of the Praetorian, an event that scarred Caedus' psyche and led us to where we are today.'

'It's the reason for all this,' Zaidu said, taking the revelation to its logical conclusions. 'Caedus first sought me out because it wanted to be avenged on Demetrius. It then returned because it had laid plans that would bring us here, to allow it to regain its favour and its power.'

'I fear so,' Vey said. 'We are caught up in a daemonic conspiracy, as I suspect the Word Bearers were as well. They have paid the price for their fevered heresy. And soon, we shall pay in turn for my short-sightedness.'

'Why did you not tell me before?' Zaidu demanded.

'I speak with hindsight,' Vey responded. 'I believed… I hoped there were other powers at play. In fact, there may yet be.'

'Now is no time for psyker riddles, Lie-Eater.'

'No, but there are some things I would not yet share. Prophecy is a delicate thing. We are at the tipping point.'

'We are past it, surely,' Zaidu said. 'Caedus is free. This world will drown in blood.'

'Perhaps not. We may yet fight the beast.'

'Fighting now will only give it greater strength. I will die on this world, and face the eternal reward of my failure, but I have never been one for entertaining false hope. This is the end of the Hexbreakers.'

'I have never yet found hope to be false,' Vey said, a depth of sincerity in his voice that surprised Zaidu. 'I have a plan that will break Caedus and submit it once more to our will. For the final time.'

'Then speak it,' Zaidu said.

'Soon, but I would have you make an oath to me, Sin Slayer. Upon the honour of the Chapter, as sons of noble, unwavering Dorn, swear that you will do as I command when the time comes. As *I* command, and not any other.'

No Exorcist took oaths lightly. Zaidu understood the import behind Vey's words though. Again and again, he had gone against the Librarian's advice. He had struck out on his own, trusting to his own speed and strength and skill, convinced that a genhanced body alone was sufficient to cut the knot of deadly deceit Caedus had tied. He had been a fool, and that foolishness had led to this. Failure.

'I swear it,' Zaidu said. 'I should have heeded you sooner. Nothing is beyond the sight of your golden gaze, and the strength of both your body and your mind has saved the Hexbreakers many times. Whatever you command now, enlightened brother, it will be done.'

'Before the end I will ask for more than you know,' Vey cautioned.

'I have spoken this oath, and would speak it again regardless of what you ask,' Zaidu said. 'If there is yet a means of overcoming my Never-brother, it will be done. Just tell me how.'

'Not until I am certain of it. I need this chamber. I must conduct a final ceremony. Then we will hunt Caedus, from the crypt depths of this world to its heavens. Both of us, together. That is my oath in turn, to you.'

Zaidu did not relish the secrecy the Librarian seemed intent on maintaining, but he knew he had little left in the way of choice. He had tried, and he had failed. Vey was the only hope. In truth, Zaidu realised that had likely always been the case.

'The chamber is yours, Lie-Eater,' he said, inclining his head slightly. 'The Hexbreakers will re-form before the keep. Notify me when your rites are complete.'

Vey resanctified the centrum dominus, walking slowly from one corner to the next, forcing his exhausted mind to reach out and strengthen the slender, invisible barrier that yet separated reality from the immaterium. His warpsight showed that existence here was bruised, blackened and burned. It had barely withstood the insanity of Caedus' escape.

Finally, he judged that enough of the taint had been wiped away. The materium would hold here. He moved to the edge of the space, finding an old, broken cogitator that wasn't dripping with human remains. There, he said the proper verses and laid out his tarot.

This was weakness, he knew. He was as weak as Zaidu had been. He simply hid it better.

He took the readings.

The Tower.

The Daemon.

The Cup.

The same as they had always been. Vey found he no longer felt anything at the prognostication, not the faintest stirring within. That, at least, was a good sign.

Melchien arrived, stepping almost silently into the chamber. She was one of Vey's retinue, who had travelled with the rest of the Chapter-serfs down from the *Witch-Bane* on board *Daemonium Eversor*. Unlike the others, her robes were a deep blue. She carried Vey's Rod of El, the black-and-red psychomantic staff that he usually swapped out in favour of Kerubim while on combat operations.

Vey signed his thanks to her for bearing the rod dutifully, and accepted her assistance as they began to strip out parts of his armour. The hard flesh beneath was ruined, burned by the fury of the warp, the ether chill that he had been forced to call on again and again since learning of the Broken One's escape. Still, on Vey's instructions it was cut further, using a small, simple knife that Melchien carried with her. This was beyond even Minor or Major Arcana. It was an Act of Sympathy.

When it was done, and the proper incantations had been spoken, Melchien helped him put the armour back on, hiding the blasphemies they had committed. She then provided him with a fusion stylus, which he used to commit further atrocities, scoring out the markings on Kerubim and adding fresh ones, all the while muttering to the ancient blade. It was crude work, but it would suffice for what he intended.

Afterwards, he found the collar the Broken One had worn

about its neck, discarded amidst the blood slick at the centre of the chamber. It had been unfastened, but not shattered. He locked it to his hip, next to Kerubim, then addressed Melchien.

You have served me well, he signed to the deaf serf, supposing it was the right thing to do. *But that service shall soon be at an end.*

Surely not, lord? she signed back, dismay on her face.

All is as the Emperor wills, Vey responded. Melchien bowed in acknowledgement of that truth.

Vey could taste sweetness.

He supposed this had always been his fate. It would simply take a different form from the one he had imagined.

'*Damnatio pro nobis omnibus venit*,' he murmured.

Damnation comes for us all.

RITE III

BANISHMENT

CHAPTER TWENTY-SEVEN

THE RED MARSHAL

Freedom.

How Caedus had hungered for it. It felt like an impossible age since he had known his own mind, a gestalt consciousness freed from the limiting grey matter of the host. For a while he lost himself, becoming pure emotion, a charge of rejoicing rage, of anger and war-thought made manifest.

Eventually, his purpose reasserted itself. To have known the culmination of so many long-laid plans was one victory, but it was not the one that mattered. That was still to come.

The true work was about to begin. Khorne's work, wrathful and bloody.

Arcing through the skies of this world, between the conflict above and the conflict below, Caedus found his new, liberated consciousness dragged down, towards a place that had burned itself into every layer of his many-faceted memories. It was the final battleground, the location of his last humiliation, the blow that had eclipsed all before and birthed all that was to come.

He could feel how the mortals had twisted and perverted it, as they had done with everything in this benighted place. They infested it now, hundreds strong, believing themselves invulnerable. Many of them were strategists and planners who had their place in the way of war, but few of them had ever struck a blow in anger.

Caedus would change that. He would make them worthy of his presence, and the holy ground upon which they stood.

He struck.

The Tower of the Praetorian was the most sacred monument on Fidem IV, and the nexus of the planet's Imperial war effort.

Like so much else there, it had been built for a conflict the Imperium believed it had won long ago. It was less of a tower and more of a vast citadel, as wide as it was tall, its footfall covering more than the entirety of Fort Deliverance.

At its heart was a great chamber, the battle sanctum. It had become the high altar of the Imperial cult on Fidem IV, with a raised space at its centre, accessed by steps leading to it from each cardinal direction. A stone slab occupied it, the top carved so that it appeared as though the holy armour and weaponry of the Saviour of Fidem rested upon it. There were chiselled greaves and gauntlets, a boltgun and helm, and a pauldron bearing upon it an etching of an armoured fist, clenched in battle readiness. From here the Ecclesiarchal ruler of Fidem, the Deacon Memorialist of the Eleven Hundred and Eleventeenth Battles, had once addressed those few faithful who could afford the tithes required to enter the tower itself.

The deacon was now long gone, fled upon the first transport to leave Fidem following the Archenemy's return. The Astra Militarum had made the battle sanctum their command-and-control centre, setting up comms hubs, cogitator banks, strategium projectors and theatre briefing and monitoring vestibules, partially sealed off by sandbags and flakboard. It had been running constantly since the enemy's vanguard ships had first translated in-system, coordinating a war that would not only decide Fidem's fate, but likely make or break the faith of the entire Imperial subsector.

The place was even more alive with activity than usual. Data was flooding in about the offensive to the north, the drive towards Fort Deliverance that the Adeptus Astartes had demanded. None of the senior officers present were in favour of the operation. There had been no planning, no preparation, and the forces involved were only capable of going on the offensive because they were simply copying what they had done on previous attacks, all of which had failed. Some sections of the north side of the valley had seemingly been taken, but the breakthroughs were sparse and the information coming from the front garbled.

'There are rumours Fort Deliverance has been recaptured,' one tactical officer, Major Elish, reported to Marshal Sebastien Edouard, the commander-in-chief of the Militarum on-world.

'You should know better than to bring me rumours without quantifying them, major,' Edouard growled, hands gripping the rail of the battle sanctum's primary holo-projector, its green display underlighting his jowly features.

'Runciman, have you reached the Adeptus Astartes yet?' he carried on, barking at his senior comms officer. The man, looking up from the main vox-array, shook his head.

'Their channels remain closed, sir. Their last contact simply stated they had begun their assault on Fort Deliverance.'

'There's more, sir,' Elish cut in, leaning closer so that only Edouard would hear what he said next.

'Front-line units have sent in a series of reports of an unusual sighting. A red bolt of energy that appeared to arc skywards from the direction of Fort Deliverance, about twenty minutes ago.'

'Which units?' Edouard demanded.

'Mostly from the Thirty-Second Brigade, sir, on the leading edge. Colonel Pavlovitch's Vostroyans and Lieutenant Colonel Ulant's Vendolanders.'

Edouard grunted. 'Pavlovitch is a good officer,' he said, saying nothing of Ulant.

'I've also checked with the Navy atmospheric air assets,' Major Elish continued. 'Flight Commander Zoren has confirmed the account with sightings from his pilots and agrees that Fort Deliverance is the source.'

'What did this energy do?' Edouard asked. 'Is it the work of the Archenemy? The Space Marines?'

'I have my staff working on it,' Elish said.

'We need more, or it's meaningless. It might be nothing other than a by-product of the low-orbital engagement.'

'You will know as soon as I do, sir,' Elish said, beginning to withdraw. Edouard snapped again at Voxmaster Runciman.

'Raise the Astartes! Make it a warp-damned vermillion-priority message, I don't care! We have to find out what's happening beyond the front!'

Runciman didn't get a chance to send the transmission. Something struck the battle sanctum, something that punched through the thick rockcrete and plasteel of the Tower of the Praetorian's upper floors and pierced right to its heart. Crimson energy slammed through the ceiling and transfixed the air around the high altar, sparking and crackling back and forth like lightning sealed in a hermetic container.

The Astra Militarum's high command tore themselves to pieces. One of Runciman's junior vox-operators started slamming her head off the communications array in front of her, shattering speaker units and breaking the attuning bank. Runciman himself drew his service pistol and shot the other operators, punching las-bolts indiscriminately through them and their vox-stations. The immaculately attired Ventrillian Guardsmen stationed around the edge of the room did likewise, turning their lasrifles on each other and the nearest officers and strategos.

In a sudden, blind rage, Major Elish grabbed Marshal Edouard by the back of his stiff uniform collar and rammed him over the holo railing, cracking his skull against the display's surface. The projected image of the battlespace flickered and distorted. Gripping Edouard's head two-handed, Elish slammed it down again and again, screaming, breaking the nose of the marshal he had loyally served for almost two decades, scattering his teeth, cracking his jaw and finally splitting his skull, the glassy surface of the holo-projector becoming shattered and crazed.

He let the body slump, drawing his sidearm and shooting himself in the gut. He felt no pain, could conceive of nothing but his fury and the need to spill blood, as much blood as possible. The las-bolt cauterised the wound, so, howling with rage, he shot himself again and again before finally collapsing next to Edouard's twitching remains.

It was a massacre. And throughout it all, the lightning began to take shape.

Vey rejoined the Hexbreakers just as Zaidu pinged him a vermillion-priority rally instruction.

The Exorcists had regrouped in Fort Deliverance's main parade ground, in front of the keep. *Daemonium Eversor* had landed there, while the Hexbreakers were formed in a circle before it, chanting in the rain. It was seething down even harder than before, turning the dust into mud and washing away the blood, making the scattered corpses of the slain cultists look like pale, discarded toys.

Vey knew what Zaidu was going to tell him as he joined them. When Caedus had first torn free it had nearly overwhelmed Vey's weakened defences, and ever since then he had been able to feel the daemon's presence, distant though it now was. It had roamed wild, apparently exalting in its freedom, but had now recovered its focus. It was growing stronger, transmuting from raw warp emotion into a form fitting its will in the materium.

Soon it would be too powerful to stop, even with what Vey intended to do.

'Caedus has struck,' Zaidu said. 'The Tower of the Praetorian. Guard high command.'

'It will seek to use the slaughter to open a warp rift,' Vey said. 'If it does, Fidem will not merely be lost, it will be damned.'

'Techmarine Kothar has assured me *Daemonium Eversor* will not fail us. We depart for the tower immediately.'

'Agreed.'

'Do you intend to inform me of your intentions before we reach it?'

Vey hesitated. Until something was spoken, it had less power, but when it was given breath, life, it became a part of reality. He feared that by sharing his intentions, it would give Caedus a taste of them before they could be enacted.

Still, to withhold everything would make what was to come too dangerous.

He told Zaidu his plan.

In any other circumstance, he suspected the Sin Slayer would have argued. But Vey believed him sincere in the regret he felt about his earlier compulsiveness. He had tasted no lies when Zaidu had admitted to his mistakes. Vey could forgive them. Since the start of the hunt, he had made many of his own.

'Take my tarot cards,' Vey instructed the Sin Slayer. 'And, once it is over, Kerubim. The rest of my possessions, return to my fraternal brothers in the Broken Tower.'

'You speak like a man condemned to death,' Zaidu pointed out. Vey answered him with a wry smile.

'You know it will be far worse than that, Sin Slayer.'

Daemonium Eversor took to the skies once more. The Overlord was limping, unable to push its plasma engines to full capacity for fear of triggering the destruction of the damaged starboard side, but the gunship was still airworthy. The right troop compartment was almost too wrecked to take passengers, but there was enough capacity in the port side to take the remaining members of the Hexbreakers and those serfs who had survived the aerial clash with the Heldrake.

The Hexbreakers themselves were in a similar condition to the flyer. The gene-seed of the fallen had been stripped out along with as much of their remaining weaponry and armour as could be stored on *Daemonium Eversor*. Brother-Initiate Shemesh, his leg blown off while crossing the bridge into Fort Deliverance, had been ordered by Zaidu to replace the primary weapons servitor operating on board *Daemonium Eversor*, seated next to Kothar. Few members of the strike force had ended the fight at the fort without some form of injury, but the rest were considered low to moderate by Gela, not enough to keep anyone from combat.

The Helix Adept had treated Zaidu's own claims that he was fine with some doubt as he inspected the bolt wound to his chest. Besides the injury itself, Gela had warned that it would be a potentially fatal weakness during combat. The shot had cracked Zaidu's breastplate and likewise his rib shield, meaning that a blow to the same spot had a far higher likelihood of penetrating his lungs and hearts.

'Guard it more than you ordinarily would,' Gela advised. 'Do not rely on your breastplate to turn blows the way I know you usually do, almoner-lieutenant.'

'Noted,' Zaidu said. He had not lied to the healer when he told him the injury was not impairing him. He felt nothing. His desire to confront Caedus one last time eclipsed the discomfort of the cracked bone and the shards still lodged in his flesh, more potent than any stimm-jab.

Zaidu stood before the sealed disembarkation ramp at the rear of the hold and reviewed the tactical situation as *Daemonium Eversor* fought through the rain and the low clouds. All contact had been lost with the Tower of the Praetorian, and the disruption was spreading to the reserve forces nearby. At a blow, Caedus had decapitated the Astra Militarum's command structure on Fidem. The Archenemy's cultists might have taken advantage on the front line had the Exorcists not just done the same to them. What further effects Caedus' escape might have had, Zaidu did not try to predict. None of it was relevant. What mattered was confronting and defeating his Never-brother before the situation deteriorated any further.

Vey's plan offered some hope of that, though it was beyond desperate.

He ensured the schematics of the Tower of the Praetorian that the strike force had downloaded en route to Fidem were pinged to each Hexbreaker and Vey, along with the entry points he had chosen. For the most part, it would be standard purge-termination protocols. Once they hit the tower, they would work through it until the primary target was located, then concentrate their strength against it. The only variation would come when Vey made his play.

Zaidu put his doubts from his mind. He trusted the Librarian. He should have shown that before, but now would have to be enough. He had sworn an oath, atop the many which already bound him.

He turned so his back was to the ramp, facing into the hold.

Facing his brethren, warriors he had shared so many desperate struggles with. Brothers he knew that, despite his best efforts, he felt nothing for. There was no kinship – it was a veneer, an indulgence. They were machines bred to duty, and that duty was clear – to confound the spawn of the Archenemy.

'Engagement zone is designated *diabolus extremis*,' Zaidu informed the Exorcists. 'We shall recite the Six Hundred and Sixty-Six Secret Words. I will lead.'

Vey did not join in the Canticle of Absolution. He was too busy making his own, private preparations. Now, more than ever, he needed to find the strength to force his burnt mind and body to obey his will. He delved deep into the dark, whispering litanies he knew were to be used only in the most desperate of circumstances, blasphemies that went unheard beneath the powerful call-and-response cant of the Hexbreakers.

At one point, drawing to the end of one invocation, he looked up from where he was seated in the centre of *Daemonium Eversor*'s hold. He found himself gazing into the eyes of Lector-Sergeant Anu. The Eliminator was seated opposite him, watching him like a raptor, as he had been since he had shared his vision with the Librarian.

Vey held his gaze for a moment, then merely nodded and returned to his quiet magicks.

You should kill him now, Cy'leth told Anu.

'We are the guardians of mankind,' he said, giving the ritual response to Zaidu's words.

'Caution and secrecy are our code,' the Sin Slayer said. 'Watchfulness and patience our way.'

'Hidden from the Eyes of Chaos, we strike without warning or dread,' came the response from Anu and the others.

Strike now, or it will be too late. He will doom you all.

Anu forced himself to maintain the catechism. Ignore the echoes. Make them silent, impotent.

He realised his right hand, resting within the folds of his camo cloak, was trembling fractionally. He clenched his fist.

Strike now!

'Though we find ourselves in Shadows, no Blackness will enter our Hearts,' Zaidu intoned.

'No treachery will touch our souls, no pride will sully our thoughts,' the Exorcists answered.

'No,' Anu snarled under his breath.

He found Vey's eyes holding his. Still golden.

The shot wasn't on. Anu joined in the remainder of the verses, and watched, and waited.

Caedus tore the blood from the mortals as they massacred one another.

The screams and howls of those still living were cut off as the materialising daemon called on the vital essence that fed him. Blood burst from every orifice, every pore, surging into the air in great streams that twisted and writhed like glistening crimson serpents. They cascaded up towards the lightning that lashed before the high altar of the Tower of the Praetorian, crashing into the discharge from all angles.

Caedus' form slowly emerged from the stinking, coppery surge. One cloven hoof, then another, stepped onto the altar, cracking the stone-crafted pauldron and shattering the helmet fashioned atop it. As the blood continued to coil around him, he raised his taut, lean arms, blinking with fresh-formed eyes, seeing himself, seeing the plane of the materium around him, properly for the first time in so very long.

He roared, raising Viscera as it formed in his fist and tilting back his horned head. He could feel it all. He was alive, he was powerful, here where he needed to be. He sensed the eyes of Khorne upon him. There was no more glorious a sensation.

The last of the blood was ripped from the twitching bodies of the False Emperor's lackeys, leaving them pale and drained. Every single drop in the chamber was his to command. He lowered his arms, spreading them, making the blood rain down upon the accursed altar and the steps, drenching them in a blizzard of gore. From the crashing cascade, more shapes began to emerge, slender at first, but gaining bulk and strength, nourished by the sacrifice Caedus had made. He could hear them growling and rejoicing in his mind, thought-forms hardening as they stepped fully into the materium. Their flesh became tough, dark crimson scales, their skulls elongated and horns tearing free. Swords of smouldering black steel were conjured in their fists, the blood that had helped forge them steaming off their ever-hot blades. They were bloodletters of Khorne, Caedus' foot-soldiers, separated for so long from their general. One by one, they turned their newly formed bodies towards where Caedus stood atop the defiled altar and knelt, offering their swords.

'*Arise, my legion, and prepare,*' Caedus rasped. '*The time for blessed battle is finally upon us once more.*'

His return to his master's favour was almost complete. He required only one element more.

Demetrius.

CHAPTER TWENTY-EIGHT

THE SAINT'S INTERVENTION

Saint Selwin's namesake almost changed the fate of Fidem IV, and many other worlds besides.

The daemon-worshipping former admiral Vexar had unleashed his corrupt fleet on the Imperial Navy in orbit above the stricken shrine world. While thousands perished in the Astra Militarum's offensive on Deliverance Town, millions died above them in a fleet action that churned the upper atmosphere of Fidem into a furious maelstrom.

The *Saint Selwin's Defender* was a Mars-class battle cruiser that had served the sector fleet for almost eight thousand years. Cornered and rammed by a pair of Archenemy cruisers, the greater part of its curved white prow was ripped off by a ferocious, glancing impact. It spun away, locked in Fidem's orbit, caught in the inevitability of gravitational pull. Like so much of the void debris shed by the ferocious battle, it plummeted towards the planet's surface in a halo of fire, parts of it breaking away or burning up.

Enough of the sheet of adamantine was still intact to wreak carnage. Perhaps, as some later claimed, it was guided by the hand of the God-Emperor, or maybe His blessed servant, Saint Selwin, who had surely always looked over the ship named in his honour. Or maybe it was some rival plot, some scheme concocted by a dark, far-sighted being who had no wish to see the Red Marshal triumphant. Maybe, unthinkably, it was just the randomness and unpredictability of the universe at work.

If the prow of the *Saint Selwin's Defender* had been cast by some deity, it missed its mark, though only just. It slammed down through the western edge of the Tower of the Praetorian, cutting through it like a vast, superheated knife. Rockcrete shattered, plasteel bent and broke. The edifice shook, the shard of prow finally coming to a halt, lodged in its foundations. Its impact had carved through the westernmost side of the battle sanctum.

It had not, however, managed to reach the darkness now at the tower's heart.

'*One minute,*' Kothar said over *Daemonium Eversor*'s vox.

Zaidu steeled himself as he neared the end of the Secret Words. There was no great change to his senses, no additional keenness or edge as he entered combat focus. He realised he hadn't truly left it since arriving on Fidem.

The Overlord gunship swung over the top of the Tower of the Praetorian, past the gash carved in it by the fallen debris. Zaidu noted that the heavy bolters and lascannons that constituted much of *Daemonium Eversor*'s armaments had not engaged, confirmed by Kothar a moment later.

'*Uncontested landing,*' his voice clicked. '*Prepare to disembark.*'

Those Exorcists not already standing released their restraint harnesses and rose. Zaidu spoke the last words of the Canticle of Absolution to them all.

'Though mere mortals in His service, everlasting shall be our True Duty.'

The Exorcists answered as one, their voices booming out.

'*Et Imperator Invocato Diabolus Daemonica Exorcism!*'

Zaidu turned so he was facing the disembarkation ramp. There was a grating buzz. The ramp fell, metal clanging off rockcrete.

The Sin Slayer swept out, knives clamped for the moment in favour of his bolt carbine. He took in what lay before him in an instant. The bare, rain-swept roof of the Tower of the Praetorian, unoccupied. Hydra anti-aircraft batteries standing abandoned, their muzzles pointing blindly up towards the fire-slashed clouds, as statuesque as the carved stone renderings of Space Marines that towered across the ramparts. Votive flags and prayer scrolls hung limp in the downpour.

Zaidu moved swiftly across the open space before *Daemonium Eversor*, the Hexbreakers fanning out behind him as they secured the tower's top in a fluid combat spread. Only Vey remained in the shadow of the Overlord, his force sword unlocked but not yet activated, marshalling his psychic potency.

Zaidu took a few heartbeats to assess. There were no signs of life, but the air was foul with warp stink. Out beyond the tower's edge, Pilgrim Town sprawled away, an undulating mass of ungainly structures dotted by fires and plumes of smoke, marking where debris from the orbital battle had struck. More wreckage was tumbling from the skies, a scattering of fiery comets that fell with an apparently slow, deadly majesty, belying their true speed and the devastation they would wreak when they impacted.

The collision of orbital detritus with part of the tower was a complication. It had opened up a fissure that separated the westernmost quarter of the structure from what was now the main part of it. Descending through the larger, intact section risked leaving a flank exposed.

'Anu, Dumuzid, secure the western side and provide what support you can from there,' Zaidu instructed after a moment's consideration. '*Daemonium Eversor* will continue to cover the roof and offer exfiltration, if required.'

Anu flashed a confirmation on Zaidu's vambrace. Haad's voice came over the vox at almost the same time.

'The sky is bleeding.'

Zaidu looked around and realised the lector-sergeant was right. The deluge was no longer mere rain, at least not above the Tower of the Praetorian. It was blood, a drenching of viscera pouring down over them, covering the Exorcists in its crimson slick and anointing the graven statues that looked down upon them. It turned Zaidu's fanged mask red.

Reality on Fidem was starting to come undone.

Something crashed in the black heavens, making the tower shudder. It was impossible to tell if it was thunder, part of the fleet action, or the rising wrath of the Dark Gods.

'We must hurry,' Vey said.

The Exorcists descended.

Zaidu led them, as he had done since the beginning. They accessed the main part of the tower via a security hatch that led down a short flight of metal stairs, into the upper levels.

At some point, the power had failed. The lumens were out, plunging the stairwells into darkness. Zaidu activated his stab-lumen, the harsh white brilliance picking out the first remains of the tower's Imperial defenders.

They were scattered along the stairs, Imperial Guardsmen clad in what had once been fine purple-and-white fatigues with black-and-gold flak plate. Zaidu's hypno-eidetic triggers told him they were Ventrillian Nobles. All of their finery was now marred in blood. It seemed they had turned on one another, just like the Guardsmen in the scrap shrine when they had first arrived. Warp madness. Zaidu could feel it in the air, trying and failing to twist his own thoughts.

The stairs opened out into a weapons casemate, the Earth-shaker cannon that occupied it abandoned. Despite the thickness of the rockcrete around them, it was still possible to hear the thunderous drumming of the blood rain outside. A crimson sheet was cascading past the casemate opening, intestines and other offal draped along the barrel where it protruded past the wall.

More corpses lay around the gun, and more stairs beyond it. Zaidu found the first living occupant of the tower, slumped against the wall. She was weeping softly, her head in her hands. The blood covering her didn't seem to be her own. She showed no indication she was aware of Zaidu's approach.

He ended her swiftly, the Emperor's Mercy. Perhaps it would not be too late for her, and she would find her way towards the light. Maybe there was irony in that, one condemned to damnation trying to save the soul of another. Zaidu did not pause to consider as much. It was meaningless to him.

'It is close,' said Vey, advancing behind him.

'I know,' Zaidu replied.

He could hear the whispers.

They were soon being drowned by screams, the sounds of a living nightmare echoing up from the tower's heart.

The stairs opened out into an archway. Bolt carbine raised, Zaidu reached it, and witnessed what awaited him.

The primary strategium of the Tower of the Praetorian was now a realm of derangement and horror. The Astra Militarum's high command, staff officers, logisticians and strategos, along with those supposed to guard them, had been utterly exsanguinated. Their blood and organs now drenched the floor, the vox-arrays, cogitator banks and holo-desks and filled the air, a red mist that twitched with its own sentience.

Even worse was the fate of the bodies themselves. Some despicable force had snatched up the pale flesh of the hundreds of drained corpses and fused them together, skin melting and bubbling, running like wax, bones burrowing into one another and re-forming. They had created an archway of broken torsos, bent limbs and heads, kept alive by some perverse, unnatural power, writhing and shrieking. The amorphous mass arched over a dais of slaughter-soaked stairs leading to a broken and blasted altar.

It would have been enough to break the minds of most mortals, but it was as nothing compared to the true madness that lay beyond the archway. It was a gate, a warp portal, a complete sundering of the veil of reality that offered a glimpse into the raw lawlessness of the empyrean.

Zaidu's mind, more resolute than most, was able to conceive of it only as a hallway of blackened stone and brass rafters, but it constantly changed its form, shimmering with what felt like the heat of a vast smeltery. Walls becoming ceilings, floors rotating, sides shifting, stones and struts altering their angles as the insane geometries of the realm of the impossible refused to bend to fit the requirements of Zaidu's eyesight.

From out of that malefic place, the foulness of Chaos spilled. Monstrosities marched past the gate of flesh, their roaring melding with the agonised screaming of the portal. They were a martial host, cloven-hooved, horned, clad in brass and daemon-forged iron or covered in crimson scales or dark fur matted into spikes with gore. In their fists they grasped smouldering, jagged swords or great axes. More of their kind already awaited them, gnashing fangs, clashing their weapons against their armour or horns, greeting their kin with brazen challenges. The place stank of blood and hot metal, and burned with the heat of a forge.

Amidst it all, halfway up the dais steps, stood the Red Marshal. Caedus, no longer bound in a mortal prison or transformed into boundless lightning, but re-formed as Zaidu remembered from his darkest memories. The daemon stood upright, lean but muscled, its flesh covered in scales the colour of ancient, clotted blood. Black fur bristled on its forearms, back and legs, while two sets of horns, one short, thick and curling, the other tall and curved, crowned its elongated skull. Its face was bestial, leering. Its eyes were crimson. They gleamed against the furnace light spilling from the portal at its back, like a predator caught in the dark. Black warp energies coiled from its horns and flesh, like steam rising from a fresh blade that had just been pulled from the quenching vat. In its fist it gripped an axe of bone, the one Zaidu had seen in the fortress keep.

It locked eyes with him from across the demented chamber and grinned.

'Pattern lamed,' Zaidu instructed the Hexbreakers. 'Ensure Lie-Eater and I reach the primary target. Nothing else matters.'

Zaidu stepped into the chamber, and into the madness.

CHAPTER TWENTY-NINE

CAEDUS, CARNAGE

Daemonium Eversor shuttled Anu and Dumuzid to the section of the Tower of the Praetorian now separated from the rest by the impact of the void debris. They began to descend, looking to clear the broken chambers and rooms.

A part of Anu was relieved to have been removed from the main body of the strike force, and from Vey. He knew that was unworthy of him. His duty was to watch, and wait, and when the time came, to strike. It was the only reason for his existence. Yet now, when he was needed the most, he found his resolve lacking.

Perhaps he should not have told Vey of his vision? Or perhaps he should have informed Zaidu? He consoled himself with the knowledge that it was now too late. All he could do was trust his aim. That, at least, had never faltered.

There were no signs of life showing up on the auspex. Despite the comms systems having been purged and purified at the start of the operation, Anu found his attempts at reaching the rest of the strike force chopped and distorted into illegibility, even though they were barely a hundred paces away through the building. It was as though the debris that had cut through part of the Tower of the Praetorian had sent this lesser section of it spiralling away into another reality.

You can't help them now, Cy'leth whispered, its voice tiny. *No one can.*

The Exorcists punched out and into the battle sanctum.

Zaidu was the tip of the spear, and Vey was right behind him, Kerubim readied. They made directly for the steps, the archway, and for Caedus.

The profane legion let up a great roar as the Exorcists attacked. Zaidu put bolt-shells into the Khornate warriors closing on them fastest, the thunder of battle filling the bisected chamber.

Vey met the first Neverborn striking from the right, bringing up Kerubim in a two-handed parry. Black warp steel met the sanctified blade, both shivering, neither yielding.

The Librarian scraped Kerubim down the length of the daemon's sword, locking against its crossguard before he brought his own cracking up into the beast's face, shattering fangs and snapping a horn. As it stumbled, he broke contact and drove Kerubim through its chest before wrenching the long blade to the left and free. Black ichor burst out over Vey's cloak and armour and marred his weapon.

Zaidu clamped his carbine and freed his knives. He went hard and fast into the first howling Neverborn warrior, letting a sword stroke bite his pauldron as he stabbed. Reality in the tower was not yet degraded to the extent that the laws of nature could be wholly ignored – the heads of the beasts were still the surest way of killing their material forms.

One knife ploughed through an eye a second before the other

cut the daemon's throat. It burst apart in a shower of stinking gore, its death fury echoing impotently in Zaidu's mind.

For all their rage, these Neverborn were fresh to the materium and still far from stable. They could be defeated by the likes of the Exorcists, but only if the portal was closed and the bloodshed ended as quickly as possible.

Vey parried another sword stroke, his armour scored by raking talons as the skull-faced creature he had engaged got in close. He dared tweak at the hem of reality, distorting its perception of his location just enough to put it off balance and allow him to chop the base of Kerubim through its shoulder and down into its torso. He knew the damage done to the materium in the chamber made calling upon even the subtlest psychic powers almost too dangerous to contemplate. The presence of the warp portal was like a gale pulling at him, trying to rip what remained of his soul free from the wards and sigils pinning it to his flesh and drag him into the roaring vortex of the immaterium. And with every step, he was forcing his way closer to it.

'Maintain fire arcs,' Eitan barked over the vox, the sanctified communications of the Exorcists cutting through the external bedlam that gripped the chamber.

Squad Eitan moved out of the stairwell to Zaidu and Vey's right while Squad Haad went left, forming the main body of the spear with the Reivers in reserve. Controlled bursts of bolt carbine fire cut down the nearest warp spawn, the Infiltrators overlapping their zones and timing their discharges so the brethren to their left or right never had empty magazines at the same moment.

The engagement zone was tight, and Eitan was immediately aware that firepower alone would only get them so far. His bolts blew apart dark armour of brass and iron and sent spatters of ichor, burning blood and cinder flames surging with every strike.

He had time to reload and put half of his next magazine through a duo of charging horned monstrosities. Then the range was gone. He barely managed to clamp his carbine and unlock his knife, holding it point down and using it to parry the stroke of a glaive fashioned from thrumming bones and raw tendons.

'Hold formation,' he snarled to the rest of the squad while stamping forward, meeting the daemon's body with his own.

He punched his knife through the Khorne monster's chest as its claws scoured his armour, the talons going through ceramite and servos and then flesh. The beast's frame was lean, but its strength was infernal. Still, Eitan drove it back, slammed a fist against its muzzle, stabbing again. Finally it began to unravel, unable to sustain its form in defiance of nature's constraints and the damage wreaked upon it.

'Maintain the advance,' Eitan ordered.

The daemon that reached Uten through the bolt-storm drove a burning sword, two-handed, at him. Its edge was jagged and uneven, and the Exorcist was able to lock his knife against it to parry it, then lashed out with his free hand and grabbed one of its long, curling horns. With a bellow, he forced the sword to the right and wrenched its skull to the left, exposing its scaled neck to the upcut of his knife, almost severing its head. The lack of a true decapitating strike seemed to infuriate the daemon more than its banishment, and it spat indecipherable words in hissing venom over Uten's armour as it came undone in his grip.

He kicked its remains away and went forward with the rest of the squad.

Something was coming, something besides the ongoing incursion of the Khornate legion into the tower's heart. Uten could feel the beast within him stirring in response, eager to meet the challenge, raking up the embers of his soul for the first time since the Orison rites in the slaughterhouse.

He embraced it. Whatever it was, when it arrived, he would send it straight back to where it had come from.

Commsman Amilanu was driven down by the bull-like charge of a daemon beast. One of its horns punched into his breastplate, and for a moment Squad Haad's formation was broken.

Belloch was there almost immediately. As the animalistic Neverborn gored and gouged at the Exorcist beneath it, Belloch yanked it back by the viscera-matted fur running along its spine and punched his combat knife through its eye socket and into its skull. It shook and snarled and drooled, furnace heat blazing from its maw, but as Belloch twisted his weapon it immolated, reduced to the pure rage of fire and then ash that coated both the Reiver and Amilanu.

'My thanks,' the commsman grunted as he regained his feet, ignoring the wound in his chest as he moved to seal the brief gap that had appeared in the Exorcists' formation. Belloch said nothing, snatching a glance to make sure Azzael and Makru were still at his back before returning his attention to the melee, watching for any further breaks in the line.

'Here,' Anu said as he moved out into the chamber at the bottom of the stairs.

It lay in darkness, but for the hole torn in its ceiling, which was allowing the bloody rain to pour through. This, Anu realised, was the core of the tower, its nerve centre, but it had been cut deeply by the great, blackened length of voidship adamantine that still partly protruded from the floor.

Across, on the other side of it, the rest of the Hexbreakers had engaged. The far end of the chamber was riven with warp power and the fury of battle, but it could not spread to where Anu and Dumuzid were, cut off by the damage the debris had caused.

'I need to get an angle,' Anu told his fellow Eliminator. Dumuzid highlighted one of the statues that stood around the sides of the room. Several had been toppled by the partial collapse of the chamber, but one still stood tall and firm over a now inactive holo-table – a Space Marine, legs planted, bolter gripped to his chest, face inscrutable behind his stony helm. Anu saw the engraving on its pauldron, the clenched gauntlet of the Imperial Fists.

'Watch over me, brother,' he muttered as he approached the statue and mounted its pedestal. It was high enough to give him a view over the scarred debris plate, most of it buried deeper within the tower.

He saw the battle unfolding, a wedge of his brethren driving into the heart of the corruption, towards a dais surmounted by the raw stuff of the immaterium. Immediately, despite the chaos, his mind started seeking out and locking on to targets.

'Entering overwatch,' he voxed, not knowing if the message would reach the rest of the Exorcists. Despite the fact they were fighting just across the wide chamber, if felt as though it was playing out on another world entirely, or perhaps another plane of existence.

'Dumuzid, watch for hostiles,' he added, before unslinging his Shrike rifle and finding his first kill.

Zaidu reached the stairs at the bottom of the portal.

Caedus was there, its daemonic kindred pouring down the steps on either side. It was basking in the warp energies radiating from the damnable portal above, arms outstretched, eyes gleaming and twin sets of horns crackling with power. It beckoned Zaidu on mockingly as he cut his way towards it.

A howl filled the chamber, rising above even the din of battle and the terrible shrieking of the gateway. Two shapes barrelled through the rent in realspace, knocking aside lesser Neverborn as they came bounding down the blood-slick stairs to the left and right of Caedus. They were great hounds, with ruddy pelts, spiked brass collars and green flesh frills about their heads. Their fangs and claws were huge and wicked.

'*Carnus, Slaught,*' Caedus rasped with something that sounded akin to joy. '*My beloved hunters!*'

The two monstrosities slowed as they reached the Red Marshal's side, growling viciously at Zaidu as he approached.

'*Demetrius is mine,*' Caedus told the daemonic animals. '*Destroy the rest!*'

Howling again, the feral duo leapt off to either side of Zaidu, leaving him untouched.

'*Strike at me, Demetrius,*' Caedus said, leering at him. '*Let me taste your anger the way I did when I first ravaged your soul.*'

Zaidu would not bandy words. He attacked. Laughing, Caedus met him.

Vey faltered. He couldn't get close enough to Zaidu to engage Caedus alongside him. The daemonic assault was falling too heavily upon the Exorcists now, threatening to buckle their formation.

He drove Kerubim into the flank of a muscle-bound crimson brute who continued to pound at his armour with twin axes even as its form began to disintegrate. Vey was forced to shield himself with his free hand, one blade biting through his vambrace. He dragged his force sword free, but couldn't bring it up before a howling weight barrelled into him. He caught an impression of fangs the length of short-swords and a yawning maw, its raw, predatory aggression stamping itself brutally onto his psychic consciousness.

Vey knew its kind. Blood-beast, warp animal, flesh hound. The predatory need to hunt and devour given form in the material plane. The Librarian was almost brought down by its weight and savagery. It was in too close to use Kerubim, and he dared not try to employ his mind to impel it back. Even without the warp madness all around, creatures such as these were resistant to magicks, and would likely only grow more frenzied when they sensed Vey's sorcery.

Its fangs scraped against his right shoulder, punching through the thick, reinforced armour plates and ripping them away as though they were gossamer. Vey slammed Kerubim's hilt against its flank, feeling a stabbing pain in his chest as one set of claws gouged his breastplate and reduced the front of his cape to shreds.

He knew he was outmatched, and that his brethren on either side were too hard-pressed to come to his aid. There was only one other possibility.

Vey embraced the feral daemon, pain bursting again across his shoulder and torso as it raked at him, twisting against him as it fought to be free. He could hold it for only a moment, but that was enough for him to turn and half throw it not away from the Exorcists, but into the centre of the formation.

The Reivers were ready. Belloch, Azzael and Makru fell on the hound as it tried to lunge back at Vey. Their knives ripped and stabbed. It turned on them, savaging them likewise, but the Reivers had enough room to work together, and they dragged it down and cut it apart.

Vey could not assist them in banishing the monster. Zaidu had engaged Caedus. He had to reach them before it was too late.

The howling of the Red Marshal's hounds triggered something deeply primal in Uten.

Neither of the beasts was the one that had once possessed him, but it had known them both, had fought them and hunted alongside them, both within the warp and the materium. It knew their scent, and that awakened its echoes within him.

He snarled, feeling his jaw aching. Emotions, or the memory of them, rose up. Anger. Hunger. He beat his fist against the Neverborn he was fighting, shattering its newly formed ribs and what passed for its face.

Then the hound was upon him. He lunged out to meet it, breaking the formation, hearing Eitan snapping at him to hold the line. Hearing, but not comprehending. This was the challenge he had felt approaching – one animal against another, predator against predator. Only one could exist in this chamber for any length of time.

The flesh hound was huge, monstrous, powerful coils of muscle and fang and claw given a veneer of red flesh and an ashy pelt. It smelled of fire and burnt hair and metal and boiling blood, as though it had lately been curled, asleep, at the foot of some great grim forge. The bark as it impacted against Uten stirred up a snarl of his own.

They wrestled. It tried to bear him down with brute weight and savagery, but he met it and matched it in both endeavours. Its jaw locked around his left forearm, almost shearing clean through, while at the same time he stabbed his knife into its upper flank, just behind the spiked collar clamped around its throat.

It could taste his blood, and that drove it into a frenzy. Again, Uten responded in kind, his natural, steely resistance to the depredations of Chaos pushed to the limit. He wanted to butcher this thing, to destroy it, to anoint himself with its innards.

He wrenched his arm free, leaving behind flesh and twisted ceramite. He grabbed hold of its collar, its red fangs snapping in his face. He rammed his helm against its elongated canine skull, feeling something crunch and break, not knowing if it was him or the daemon. Probably both.

He flung the Neverborn off him. It gave him time, just enough to spin his knife in his hand, point down, braced.

He hoped the beast would lunge into him again and impale itself, but it was far too clever for that. It snapped at his legs, forcing him back a pace, then reared up to swipe its claws across his helm, the green flesh frills around its jaw splaying outwards in a display of aggressive superiority. The blow staggered Uten, leaving gouges across his helmet and cracking one eye-lens. His armour screamed warnings at him.

He recovered almost instantly, but it didn't matter. The beast exploded. Steaming, vile ichor and chunks of flesh battered against Uten, turning his dark red armour black. He felt firmer impacts as well, and noted the feedback on the remnants of his damaged visor. He readjusted his stance and snatched a glance down to discover that shards of metal had peppered his breastplate. Fragments from a high-explosive bolt-shell.

It was the work of a Shrike sniper rifle. Anu, or his Eliminator brother. He had no time to locate where the marksman had struck from. More Neverborn were driving forward, seeking to exploit the small but deadly gap that had opened between Uten and the rest of the Hexbreakers.

He knew he should retreat, but a deep, dark part of his inner self, a place where he had hidden what little remained of his soul, stirred with pride and anger. He would not falter. He would not go back. He bellowed his challenge to the oncoming Neverborn and met them, blade for blade.

Anu couldn't get the shot.

Cy'leth was in his ear, whispering to him. That only combined with the difficulties he was already facing trying to provide fire support across the half-ruined chamber. The range was too short for the use of his scope, which he had uncoupled. That in itself was no problem, and even the chaotic nature of the melee would have constituted only a minor challenge.

There was more at work than the discord of close combat, however. The laws of existence were slowly but surely starting to disintegrate within the chamber. The ranges and angles were off – he couldn't draw a reliable bead, and too many of his shots went wide. The hit on the monstrous hound attacking an Exorcist his goggle display marked out as Uten was the first one he made.

He tried to use that success as a platform, shifting his aim towards where the almoner-lieutenant had engaged the Neverborn marked out as the target. He sent two high-explosive bolts in quick succession into the darkness-wreathed terror, but the angles he had used to execute the hound no longer seemed to apply. They both detonated harmlessly in mid-flight.

You were never a worthy host, Cy'leth taunted. *I hated every second with you. You will fail now, when it matters most, and every past effort will be rendered in vain.*

Anu clenched his jaw and, still crouched beneath the statue of the Imperial Fist, fired again. This time the bolt struck the stairs at the daemon's back, shattering one and blasting up a hail of shrapnel and broken stone.

Closer. Adjust. Adjust. He could not falter now. He was the one who watched, and killed. Everything in this chamber could be unmade and changed, but that truth would remain constant. It had to, or Anu would be no more.

The formation was buckling.

Brother-Initiate Nizreba was stabbed through the flank by

a burning warp blade, almost gutted by the weapon. He blew apart the head of the daemon that had struck him with a bolt pistol round, then staggered back, Makru taking his place in the line while he tried to recover.

Hokmaz nearly lost his right arm, the axe of a shrieking, blood-drenched Neverborn hacking through the pauldron and into his shoulder. The daemons were becoming stronger, their blades keener, their bodies tougher. Hokmaz had to carve open the monstrosity's chest and half hack its head away before its link to the material plane was severed, the axe remaining buried in it until it too burned up.

Gela barked at Azzael to take his own place in the formation so he could move inwards and see to Nizreba, noting the severity of his injury on his visor link. Azzael pushed in, fighting back against an amorphous spawn-like daemon that was attempting to beat its way in amongst the Exorcists with its great fists and bony spines. Its blows cracked the Reiver's armour before his knife sliced the ligaments of its arms with a surgeon's precision.

Eitan was with Vey. He knew the Librarian had to reach where Zaidu was now battling at the foot of the dais steps. The madness of the chamber was hurling itself against them, each beast delighting in the slaughter even as it was cut down and banished. They were becoming too strong, their grip on reality too firm.

The lector-sergeant made a choice. He slammed his knife through the forehead of one brazen brute and left it there, unlocking and reloading his bolt carbine in a couple of fluid motions. Then he opened fire, not on the next daemons charging him, but on the few that still remained between Vey and Zaidu.

The mass-reactive rounds cut them down. Eitan's carbine clicked dry. In the same heartbeat, a sword drove through his plastron and another jarred off his helmet. He tried to turn, brutally blocking out the pain, cracking the stock of his weapon against a snapping skull face and slamming a fist into another. An axe cleaved down through his left arm, biting bone.

He experienced something he had never felt before – the shuddering flush of strength and adrenaline that marked the ignition of his Belisarian Furnace. That meant it was the end. That damnation had finally caught up with him. He bellowed his defiance, roaring the final passage of the *Liber Exorcismus* as he allowed the Furnace to drive him, disdaining all modes of defence, all efforts at self-preservation. He used his body as a weapon, pounding with his fists and elbows and shoulders, kicking and stamping on the Neverborn that fell beneath him.

They didn't care. They dragged him down, roaring and cackling. He felt the sudden, furious burst of energy within him starting to flare out, as quickly as it had appeared. His body was being hacked, stabbed, sundered.

One beast, bigger than all the rest, shoved its kindred aside as it approached, steam broiling from its muzzle, cloven hooves cracking the rockcrete underfoot. Eitan found the strength to focus, not on his killer, but on the marker representing Vey on his visor.

He had reached Zaidu.

'Damnation comes for us all,' Eitan managed through bloody lips.

The daemon's axe cleaved his head from his shoulders.

CHAPTER THIRTY

PATTERN TAV

Zaidu fought Caedus beneath the gateway to oblivion.

The Sin Slayer's battle was twofold – he could not let Caedus continue to exist in this reality, and he could not lose control. It was difficult to say which was the greater challenge.

At first, the daemon did not fight back. It knocked away Zaidu's blows with the haft and head of its bone axe, matching his speed but not exceeding it. Its cruel grin remained fixed. It was taunting Zaidu, trying to stoke his anger, infect him with it. Trying to win an advantage without even striking a blow.

Zaidu could feel the fury, somewhere deep inside, but he didn't allow it to rise up. He kept his attacks short and controlled, testing Caedus' physical abilities just as the daemon was testing his mental ones.

Then, suddenly, the Red Marshal was attacking. The great axe became a blur as it swung down, Zaidu barely managing to sidestep. He slashed in towards Caedus' neck simultaneously, but the daemon went back, surrendering several steps. The downward swing was turned into a sideways swipe that Zaidu blocked aside, steel jarring against daemonic bone.

Again, he had Caedus' guard open, and again the daemon gave ground before the lunge. It went back further, but Zaidu refused to throw himself after it, knowing it wanted him to overextend – doing so on the blood-slick steps would almost certainly be fatal.

Zaidu's Never-brother let out a growling chuckle.

'You are trying so hard not to lose what little of you remains, Demetrius,' it said. *'But when you do, you will enjoy it, I promise. You will hack and beat me, draw my blood, and in doing so we will praise Khorne together.'*

Zaidu attacked again. Caedus now had the height advantage, and it rained blows against the Exorcist as he went for its legs and lower torso. Zaidu couldn't parry them all while maintaining his own attack, and he felt the axe thunder into his left pauldron, nicking his flesh. Despite the fact that it had barely grazed him, a fiery, aching pain exploded across his body as the cursed weapon tried to feed greedily before it was ripped away.

The blow had almost been a costly one, but it allowed Zaidu to slash one knife across the daemon's thigh, drawing a line of black ichor.

Caedus hissed, but was still leering with amusement.

'I have not felt a wound in so long. It blesses me. Blesses me with holy anger!'

The last word became a roar as Caedus swung again, with greater strength and speed than before. Zaidu felt the impact of the axe against his parry jar up his arm, and thought for a second that the next strike might shatter the knife.

As he braced for it, the daemon shifted its stance, too fast for even Zaidu to counter. Using its height advantage, Caedus slammed a cloven hoof into the Exorcist's breastplate, striking where the heretic's bolt-round in Fort Deliverance had left a crack. There was a brutal crunch as Zaidu was slammed down the stairs, pain momentarily overcoming his body's ability to fight it.

He hammered into the steps further down the dais, stone splintering beneath him, his breath catching for a moment as he felt the damage dealt by the daemon. He didn't need his armour to tell him that his fused ribs had been almost split open. His breastplate had buckled, a length of ceramite broken away by the brutal kick.

Caedus was back down the stairs and on him again in a blink, seeming to flicker through the bloody air. It howled as its great axe fell, hissing past Zaidu and cleaving stone as he rolled desperately, jaw clenched as the cracked edges of his rib plate ground against one another. Caedus lashed out with a hoof once more, stamping on Zaidu's side, trying to pin him to the steps as it swung again. This time the axe lopped off the right directional nozzle on Zaidu's reactor pack, his armour sending him another jagged haptic alert.

The Exorcist stabbed at Caedus' leg, steel slashing through black fur and into the veined red musculature beneath. Black ichor spurted, but the daemon did not care. It grabbed the split edge of Zaidu's gorget and half dragged him up off the ground, its bestial visage inches from his face.

'Did you really think you could defeat a favoured champion of the Blood God like this?' the daemon demanded, the butcher's stink of its breath on Zaidu's face. 'Every moment's resistance you offer is another moment spent praising my master. He sees me now. He sees us all!'

Memories of Zaidu's Rite of Initiation flooded back. The daemon's reek, its raw and bloody presence upon him. He saw its foul face, transfused with rage, dissolving in the acid rains of

Banish, dragging his soul with it. He felt the ragged remains of what it had left behind burning, stoked into a rage of his own.

Holding him by the gorget with one hand, the daemon shifted its grip on its axe closer to the weapon's head and raised it, ready to chop it down brutally on Zaidu's bare neck. The Exorcist stabbed the knife in his right hand in beneath the daemon's arm, punching it into the thing's torso, but it had no effect. Leaving the knife there, he snatched Caedus' wrist, knowing he could buy only a few seconds more, knowing that even with his own rage burning, he wouldn't have enough strength to stop the killing blow.

Then he was aware of movement at his side, a flash of blue. Vey.

The Sin Slayer managed to snarl a single word as he kept the weapon at bay.

'Strike.'

Vey did so, darting in from Zaidu's right. Caedus twisted, ripping its axe free from Zaidu's grip, but it was too slow to wholly avoid the Librarian.

The force sword drove into the daemon's flank. It was not enough to banish the Neverborn. It was not even enough to truly wound it. But it was enough for what Vey had planned.

Kleth was the second Exorcist to die in the chamber. His arm amputated in the assault across the valley before Fort Deliverance, he had been fighting one-handed, determined not to falter before his brethren at the decisive moment.

The Neverborn drove at his disadvantage until one found its mark. A warp sword jarred through Kleth's breastplate, splitting ceramite and then bone, puncturing a heart and both primary lungs. Kleth shuddered and, driven by his death throes, forced himself onto the blade with a snarl and beheaded the daemon.

Then, even as the sword still piercing him was unmade, he slumped down and was lost amidst the trampling tide.

A moment later, on the other side of the formation, Haad suffered a blow that cracked his helm and almost split his skull. Unable to be stunned and ignoring the pain, he parried the next hit from the grunting daemon and, hissing a warding canticle, drove it back with strength alone, relieving the pressure on his Infiltrators for a moment.

At the rear of the formation, Marduk had been forced to his knees by the brazen charge of a bull beast. He grabbed on to the horns gouging at him and fought to rise again, actuators juddering. He could smell molten metal and taste blood. It was as though his own muscles were burning. Then Belloch was there, the Reiver's finesse abandoned as he hacked downwards over and over like a butcher into the beast's neck and shoulder, until it finally let up a furious bellow and shook itself apart.

The pressure against the Exorcists had become overwhelming. There was no room to manoeuvre, except inwards, into the slender space they had resolutely maintained since pushing into the chamber.

'Grenades,' Haad demanded over the vox. 'Pattern tav!'

Tav, the final formation. Done in extremis, when a position was being physically overrun. The Infiltrators, Eitan's squad too, broke contact with their opponents, giving up what little ground they held. It gave them time to free and prime frag grenades, which they tossed into the overwhelming mass, bouncing them between cloven hooves or lobbing them over horned heads.

A ripple of explosions tore through the daemonic mass, close enough for shrapnel to batter at the Exorcists and lodge in their armour. It gave them the few precious seconds they needed to complete the second half of the pattern. Snatching carbines and fresh magazines, they resumed their barrage, a point-blank salvo momentarily rebuilding the fire-zone around the offensive, allowing it to re-establish itself.

It would give them only a few seconds. But in those seconds, Vey struck.

Kerubim bit into Caedus' new form.

The momentary contact would have been enough for Vey to drive his consciousness against the daemon's and seek to crush it. That was a battle of wills that Vey, exhausted, knew he would not win. Instead, he had changed Kerubim's purpose when he rewrote the sigils on the blade, reversing them.

With a roar, Vey dragged on Caedus' soul.

Fire ignited down the broadsword's length from where it had stabbed the daemon's side to the hilt. The blade turned white-hot.

Caedus' howl joined Vey's. The air around them thrummed, and the bloody stone stairs beneath started to split and crumble.

The force sword was a conduit, but it was no longer designed to drive Vey's essence against the mind of another. It was now doing the opposite.

Zaidu saw his opening.

He drove himself up, ripping his knives free, and stepped in against Caedus as his Never-brother froze, locked in a mental struggle with Vey. Switching to an overlapping grip on his two knives, he scissored the blades inwards from either side of the daemon's neck, shouting the Oath of Banishment as he took that single moment to drive every ounce of rage and determination he had left into the blow.

The razor steel cut true. Caedus' head came away. Flames engulfed its material form, their heat searing at Zaidu, the Red Marshal's fury threatening to burn him up as well.

And then Caedus was gone, along with its axe, not even ash remaining.

Zaidu did not pause, even for a moment. He turned on Vey, set to deliver the killing blow to his old mentor.

Vey's free hand caught his wrist in a grip strong enough to make Zaidu's vambrace buckle, stopping the knife before it could plunge through the Librarian's skull.

'Did you think it would be that easy, Demetrius?' Torrin Vey snarled in a voice that was no longer his own. His golden eyes were gone. Now the butcher-light shone from the darkness beneath his cowl.

Caedus' new host flung Zaidu back, and struck with Kerubim.

The assault upon the Hexbreakers faltered.

The rage of the daemons surrounding them changed. Their locus was caged, its power abruptly cut off. With it went its ability to command, to control, and to act as a conduit for the power still surging through the portal.

The daemons only just pushing through into reality flickered like old vid recordings, struggling to sustain themselves. The more established ones around the Exorcists, which had fed off the battle and bloodshed, began to hack at each other, the focus the Red Marshal had provided subsumed now by raw, unchecked rage.

'Re-form around the almoner-lieutenant and the Lie-Eater,' Haad ordered. 'Focus fire on the portal.'

The formation pushed up the stairs, changing as it went from a compact, offensive spearhead to a defensive circle. They surrounded Zaidu and Vey.

'Brother-sergeant, the Librarian–' Gela began to say, but Haad cut him off.

'Just hold the formation around them both and keep this warp filth at bay,' Haad instructed. 'Trust them.'

For a few precious moments the Hexbreakers were able to

focus fire on the portal itself. Flesh burst apart and bone splintered as the horrifying archway of amorphous bodies was struck, but the structure showed no signs of collapse.

'It's not enough–' Haad began to say. He was interrupted by a scraping, crystalline sound as a substance rapidly spread across the gateway, covering it in just a few heartbeats – glass, framed by the still-writhing, shrieking bodies surrounding it.

It reflected back an unvarnished image of the carnage below, dark beasts of rage and hate and a circle of insubstantial phantoms, ghostly beings that bore within themselves only a terrible nothingness. In the midst of them was a monstrosity.

Then the glass cracked, became crazed, and shattered. Multicoloured warp fire blazed through, accompanied by a pealing cry.

To reclaim its glory, the Red Marshal had made many pacts, and not all were with fellow servants of the Skull Throne. As its control over the portal had waned, another being had taken the opportunity to seize on its side of the bargain.

Se'irim strode through the opening, given true form after too long spent feigning loyalty to Mordun. The Change-daemon was a hunched, avian-headed creature with great wings and too many gangly limbs, clad in robes that constantly shifted colour. It grasped an ornate golden staff, inlaid with jewels and precious stones that shimmered with the unnatural light spilling from the portal. It let up a cry again, and unleashed a torrent of warp fire down onto the Exorcists.

'Kill it,' Haad barked. The Hexbreakers shifted their targeters from the portal to the herald, but it simply gave a chirring laugh as every round that came near it was transmuted into glittering jewels that dropped harmlessly to the broken stairs around it in a rainbow cascade. Its flames redoubled, a multicoloured torrent that physically drove the Exorcists back and momentarily broke their circle.

More capering horrors came writhing from the portal, letting up a maddening, ululating cacophony as they flooded down the stairs in a blue-and-pink tide.

'We have to destroy the gateway,' Haad reiterated as he reloaded ahead of the oncoming horde. 'Grenades. Uten, lead the way.'

CHAPTER THIRTY-ONE

PERFECTION

Caedus was no longer himself.

He snarled, turning, taking in his new surroundings, then howled with rage.

He had been caged again. Demetrius' saviour had used his witch trickery – an accursed sword – as a conduit to snatch Caedus' essence and rip him from his material form. In the struggle, Demetrius had taken advantage, and Caedus had suddenly been left with no choice other than to seek refuge within the offered flesh or face banishment.

But this place was no refuge at all. Before him was a fire, burning low. Its weak flames illuminated nothing but shattered walls and the stubs of broken columns, as well as the faintest outline of something vast that arched overhead into the darkness, a dome that covered all beneath it.

There was nothing else here. The place was a ruin, a desolate wasteland. This was no soul. It was a broken husk.

'And you will not leave it,' said a voice behind Caedus. He

whipped round, finding himself face to face with the witch. He was clad in a blue robe rather than his armour, embroidered with a horned skull. His expression was tired, but calm.

'Do you think I have forgotten you, Librarian?' Caedus snarled. *'You who thought you had bested me when I first took Demetrius' flesh? You believed me trapped then too, but all was as my master willed it. I marked you for oblivion, just as I marked him.'*

'That does not matter,' the witch said. 'Damnation comes for us all.'

'You cannot hold me here. Your soul is already broken.'

'It is too fallow for you to take root, yes, but it is not my soul that will keep you here. It is my will, and that.'

He pointed upwards. Caedus followed the gesture, trying to discern what was arching above. He sought to unshackle his thought-form, to rise, to blast free from this place, but found he could not. Something was confining him, in a similar manner to the way he had been confined by poor, stupid Ashad.

'Your will cannot exist beyond your annihilation,' Caedus snarled at the witch. *'And that is what I shall give you.'*

Howling, he lashed out at him.

Zaidu fought Vey on the steps as the very essence of damnation poured down around them.

Kerubim was not active, but Zaidu had to use both knives together to parry and deflect, leaving little opportunity for counter-strokes. He was driven lengthways across the stairs by a flurry of furious, swinging hits.

'You must overcome him, Lie-Eater,' he urged, hoping that Caedus had not triumphed completely, that there was still something left within Vey's body that could understand him.

'The witch can't hear you,' Caedus-Vey spat, black filth oozing from the Librarian's lips. *'He is too busy begging me for mercy!'*

The next attack was overarm. Zaidu caught it the way he had Caedus' axe, locked between his knives, but the bound daemon moved in close and slammed its fist into Zaidu's face, once, twice. There was a crack, and his death mask came away, the shattered half-skull falling to the stairs, split in two.

Zaidu gave ground to recover, blood on his lips. He snarled, baring red fangs, and Caedus-Vey cackled, a sick and unnatural sound to hear coming from the Librarian.

'Now you feel it. The anger. Embrace it.'

'You will abuse his body no longer,' Zaidu spat, and attacked.

He drove forward, and was shocked when Caedus-Vey lowered its guard. One knife slashed across the host's cheek while the other dug in under his right pauldron, spearing the Librarian's rib plate. In response, Caedus-Vey clamped its gauntlet around the side of Zaidu's head, digging in, holding him in a vice grip. Zaidu tried to push back, and the two locked for a second, muscles and servos straining.

Zaidu found himself looking into his mentor's eyes. He realised they were not red any more.

'The beast… is strong,' Vey said with great difficulty. 'It wants you to slay me, that it might possess you and then be free again. Your soul will not be able to hold it. Do as we planned, before I lose control completely.'

Zaidu tried to reach down to his waist, but Caedus-Vey howled and threw him back. The butcher-light had drowned out his golden eyes once more.

Vey's and Caedus' thought-forms battled through the wreckage of Vey's soul.

The daemon was too powerful. Vey, already exhausted, was holding on desperately to the Neverborn's essence, trying to keep it pinned within his empty being long enough for Zaidu to truly entrap it. But his body was no longer his own, and the Red Marshal's rage was unmatched.

The Neverborn slammed him back through a broken wall then, gripping his arm, threw him to the ground and brought one cloven hoof crashing down onto his chest. Vey grunted, catching the limb and twisting it with a crunch. Caedus bellowed and raked him with its claws, shredding the front of his robes.

'How did it feel, to condemn the one you call Zaidu to eternal damnation?' the daemon demanded, kneeling on Vey and slamming a fist into his face. *'How did it feel, to betray so many more besides? To take youths who called you brother, who looked to you as an example, and turn them over to the thing you hate most? To corrupt them and mutilate them and guarantee them endless torture?'*

The blows kept coming as the daemon spat its furious vitriol, threatening to break Vey. He fought past the pain, searching for the merest hint of a spark that would ignite the only thing the daemon respected – his own anger.

The fire in the centre of the ruins flared briefly. Vey flung Caedus back off him with a roar, surging to his feet just as the daemon did the same. They met with a crash like thunder, shaking the very depths of Vey's being. Overhead, the great dome shuddered.

Uten forced his way upwards, fighting through the madness that infested every step of the stairway. A tide of monstrosities was tumbling down through the eldritch light of the portal, still changing and shifting even as they adopted material form. Many clawed at Uten and spat or conjured fire that seared off his armour, but others struggled with each other, or simply capered gleefully, waving their many-jointed limbs over their misshapen heads. Some even seemed to be locked in debate, gibbering arcane nonsense at one another even as Uten cleaved through them, apparently oblivious to the fact that there was a battle taking place around them. Uten didn't care. His knife cut apart their warp flesh and his boots trampled them, even as the pink ones he carved open split and re-formed into multiple beings, the colour of their hides shifting to blue.

They were keeping him from the portal. Perhaps that was their only purpose. They piled up before him, squealing and shrieking, their momentum down the steps threatening to drown him. He hacked wildly, his armour warning him that the sheer volume of blows from claws and ornate daggers was threatening to find its weak points.

And then, suddenly, with a burst of ichor and scraps of metal, the pressure eased.

Anu tried to hit the daemonic herald the moment it broke through the gateway. Like every bolt aimed at it, his shots were turned into glittering irrelevance. Its warpcraft was too strong, changing and distorting the reality around it. Its cackling rang through the chamber's bedlam as it waved its staff, summoning more of its arcane fire.

You won't stop that one with your little bolts, my beloved, Cy'leth giggled.

'Be silent,' Anu barked, unable to stop himself from speaking back to the echoes any longer. The memory of the lust daemon simply laughed.

One of the markers on his goggles shifted. Uten, again. The big brute was leading a charge up the steps, spearheading an assault that Anu realised, via the fresh reticules on the target display, was aimed at the portal itself.

He could not bring down the daemon orchestrating this fresh incursion. His sights told lies, and as long as he tried to hit the herald, his bolts would betray him. But he didn't need to hit the herald to ensure its destruction, and he didn't need sights to hit the gibbering blue-and-pink mass of fire and limbs that constituted the main body of the daemonic infestation. He barely even needed to aim.

He reloaded, adjusted, and sent a high-explosive round into the space just ahead of Uten as he fought against the tide. It parted around the bolt's detonation, unruly bodies blown to pieces and cast aside. Uten pushed immediately into the gap, and then into the next one as Anu took another shot.

It felt anathema, almost blasphemous. To kill without care, without precision. To deal destruction indiscriminately – it was as far from Anu's combat ideals as he could imagine. And yet, he dealt it still. Annihilation was his purpose, and how it was delivered was irrelevant.

Perfection was a lie.

He sent high-explosive bolts into the horrors ahead of Uten over iron sights, ploughing round after round into the mass of leaping, twisting bodies, ripping them to pieces.

Only when he reached for a fresh magazine did Anu's attention stray briefly further down the steps.

And he saw his vision coming true.

Haad knew they were overextending. Pushing up onto the dais to destroy the portal while trying to protect the almoner-lieutenant and the Librarian was almost more than the remaining Hexbreakers could achieve simultaneously. Another few moments and the formation would collapse.

There was nothing to do but fight, and die. Haad clashed with a daemon in silver plate armour, the form within composed of blazing yellow-and-purple warp fire. The sword it swung constantly morphed and changed in length and width, making parrying it difficult. He abandoned trying to defend himself, ramming his knife down into the fire essence that comprised its head, ignoring the pain of the blows dealt to him.

Hokmaz and Nizreba were driven back to back by the force of the press, the two Orison rivals working together as they slashed and stabbed at the rising tide of horrors, their armour drenched with iridescent viscera.

Azzael went down but was dragged up again by Makru, the skill of the two Reivers reduced to a hacking match. With Belloch they remained at the rear of the formation, doing their best to keep the stairs around Zaidu and Vey clear. The duo were locked in a desperate struggle, and Belloch wanted nothing more than to join his almoner-lieutenant, but he knew that doing so would allow the daemonic horde to reach them and break the efforts of both to cage the daemon. Instead, he fought on with knife and bolt pistol, shifting left and right with speed as he cut down every Neverborn that came bounding and gibbering down past the rest of his brethren, his footing sure despite the blood and ichor drenching the stairs.

Urhammu and Balhamon had fought their way up with Uten, trying to cover his flanks. Their bolt carbines were empty, ammunition almost expended – from now on it would be knife-work alone. As they forced a path to the base of the looming archway, the cackling of the herald leading the incursion screeched painfully over their vox-links, infesting it with the daemon's mockery.

'Change and change and change again! Blue to pink, bolts to blood, blades to broken bodies! To change is to worship! We worship together!'

The malformed avian-like creature had mounted the shattered altar that stood directly beneath the portal and was capering atop it, robes hitched up and waving its staff wildly. As the three Exorcists stormed up the last few steps, it lanced the staff in their direction and cawed. Sorcerous flames billowed from it, engulfing the trio.

Uten charged, head bowed and shoulders hunched. He felt the heat of the flames, but knew their true danger was not the scorching of flesh or bone. A mortal touched by such damnable magicks would be riven by the warping energies of the mad god that spawned these daemons, their bodies ripped apart by mutation, changed and changed again, as the herald had promised. The armour of the Exorcists was proofed against such corruption, anointed and etched with sigils of warding, but there was only so much it could endure.

Uten's battle plate began to blister. Warnings went off on his visor, one, then two, then a constellation. The wards were burning out, igniting with blue flames that turned them molten. He could feel not just the heat, but the taint starting to leach into him, to ache like radiation, to seek purchase within. Soul or not, all flesh was malleable. His jaw ached, his fangs distending, the bony ridges that bristled across his forearms threatening to split and crack his vambraces.

He let the remaining, raging witch hate of the hound that had once savaged him drive him on, roaring as he closed the last few yards. He struck aside the staff with his knife, the flames stuttering as the daemon let out a squeal of alarm, its mocking certainties unravelling as the boundless realities it had seen in the thousand mirrors of its mind's eye suddenly shattered – all but one, the single point of certainty abruptly thrust upon it.

Uten ploughed his blade through its shoulder and snatched its scrawny, half-feathered neck, choking its insane declarations while, at the same time, unlatching a melta bomb from his hip.

'Change this,' he told the daemon, and rammed the charge past its gaping beak and down its throat.

The herald exploded, transforming into a blazing wave of

multicoloured ectoplasm that drenched the three Exorcists and everything else at the top of the dais.

A raucous wail went up from the surrounding horrors. Urhammu and Balhamon had time to load their last magazines, while Uten, panting with battle lust, undid his mag belt, the upper parts of his armour still smouldering with warp flame.

'Prepare to withdraw, brethren,' he rasped, then, priming several of the grenades on the belt, advanced to the left-hand base of the warp gateway's arch.

Vey's thought-form stumbled in the ruins of his soul, knocking down a shattered wall. Caedus snatched him by the throat with both hands and forced him to his knees, hissing with the effort.

'You will not stop me, Torrin Vey,' the daemon growled. *'You will not hold me.'*

Vey fought back again, once more delving into the depths of his resolve. He was beyond exhaustion, out beyond the edge of what the mind and body of even an Adeptus Astartes was built to endure. Yet still he fought back, driven by one of the only real emotions left to him – the stony, unyielding sense of duty that was his gene-legacy.

He flung Caedus off and struck the Neverborn's essence, fists delivering hammer blows that broke the daemon's horned crown and cracked its sneering visage. It responded with its rage, igniting with fires forged from fury. They grappled for a moment before Caedus threw Vey back.

'You are weakening, witch,' the daemon said, its wrath continuing to smoulder and crackle across its dark, scaled form. *'If your mind does not break soon then your body will. Either way, I will be free once more.'*

Vey looked down, parting the ragged remnants of his robe to bare his chest. The skin there bore the same marks Melchien had cut into his physical body in Deliverance's keep, damnable Dark Tongue script that had helped drag Caedus in. It was discoloured now, though, veins showing as a dark latticework, the flesh blotched yellow and purple. It ached terribly to the touch.

'The corruption rots through you,' Caedus hissed. 'Your soul may only be fragments, but now mine is the one inhabiting your body. It obeys me. You are barely holding on. And soon Demetrius will be mine too.'

Zaidu forced Kerubim aside, struggling against the daemon-infused strength of his old mentor while fighting to ignore his own injuries. Vey's face was twisted in a rictus of fury and hatred, expressions Zaidu had never seen the Librarian display before. Everything about the fight was horrifically unnatural, but Zaidu's hyper-focus on the combat allowed him to overcome the discordance of turning aside mortal blows delivered by the being he had once trusted above all others.

Vey would not hesitate to do the same, he knew. Zaidu could not falter here, at the end. He had to carry through the Librarian's plan, or all would be lost.

One opening was all he needed.

'Vey is nearly gone,' Caedus spat through Vey's lips. 'Accept me into your body and you can still save him.'

There was no question of that. Zaidu knew he would not be able to keep hold of Caedus the way Vey was doing. The daemon was being kept in check by the Librarian's psychic will, the warding marks and, most of all, by the incantation bowl, sealed in the small adamantine box on Vey's hip with its rim facing inwards against him.

'You grow desperate, my Never-brother,' Zaidu said, shifting his stance, one knife held high at the cross-grip and the other low, point up. 'Your schemes are about to come to nought.'

Caedus-Vey hissed, holding off, and Zaidu moved in again, blades arcing left and right, forcing Caedus to defend itself. He was not trying to kill Vey's body, but to find an opportunity to complete the imprisonment, to weaken Caedus and add one more lock to thrice-bind the daemon within.

But the daemon fought back. It could not quell its desire to slay Zaidu, even as it continued to battle Vey, clashing on two fronts.

And it was still too powerful. Zaidu failed to turn the next strike, a feint that became a ringing blow against his left pauldron. Already damaged before by Caedus' axe, it split and fell away, Kerubim's bite ripping through the under-armour and drawing blood. Zaidu gave ground, then realised he had no more to give – he had come to the corner of the stairway.

He adopted a defensive stance once more, but it was now difficult to raise the knife in his left hand. The arm was numb, muscle and tendon severed at the shoulder. He risked a glance, seeing glistening blood and bared meat, and the abominable scales that decorated his flesh where it had been exposed, matching his bared jaw.

Caedus-Vey cackled sickly.

'How I enjoyed remaking you in my image, Demetrius,' it declared in a voice that scraped and warped between Vey's and the deep rasp of the daemon. *'A fitting end to our rivalry. I will do the same with this fool.'*

As it spoke, it cast back Vey's cowl to expose the deformations across the Librarian's scalp, the nubs of twin sets of horns beginning to push their way bloodily past his distended skin.

'In life or death, all flesh and blood answers the call of my master. When you are slain, I will chain you at the foot of his throne and have my hounds rend you for all time.'

'You will not be able to hear your master's call where you are bound for, my Never-brother,' Zaidu said, his defiance rising anew. 'And by the time you claim me, it will all be in vain. You will not rise to power again in this age or the next.'

Caedus-Vey spat and attacked from Zaidu's left, his wounded side. All the Sin Slayer could do was attempt to parry with his right.

That was when the bolt-round struck him.

Anu watched as his prophecy was realised. Zaidu was locked in battle with Vey, driven to the edge of the battle sanctum's dais, every strike and counter matching the eidetic memory of the duel he had seen through his scope in the basement beneath Pilgrim Town.

Red light burned in the Librarian's eyes, and corrupt rage seemed to animate his every movement. Zaidu appeared intent on limiting himself to defence, but was clearly struggling against Vey's broadsword. The Sin Slayer was wounded, and Anu's experienced eye could detect the first indications that he was beginning to falter.

He also knew he was about to reach the point in his vision when he had pulled the trigger and shot Zaidu.

'*Lakhmu is screaming,*' Cy'leth hissed in his ear, its breath hot on his skin. '*My brothers and sisters have only just begun toying with his soul. They will take him to the deepest pits of my master's realm and make him blaspheme with them against your pathetic Emperor for all eternity.*'

Anu didn't reply. He fitted his scope back atop his rifle, muttering the necessary pairing invocation, forcing himself to stay focused. He reduced magnification to minimum and returned to the familiarity of his firing stance, pinning the target lock on the figures still struggling on the steps. Now, he truly was at one with his vision.

'Lakhmu said he died for nothing, and that you will do the same. Give yourself over to us and I will ensure the pain you feel will become pleasure unbound.'

He couldn't hold on. It was too much. He gritted his teeth, fighting to quell the echoes.

Just one shot, and if it struck true, he could finally mark it on his rifle's stock. He gripped on to that thought and, on an impulse he couldn't place, flicked his shot selector to armour penetration.

The vision played out. The moments aligned. Vey raised his broadsword, Zaidu again moving to block the blow, unable to retreat any further. The Sin Slayer's right arm was between Anu and the sword.

The shot wasn't on. It didn't matter.

Half a breath, lock, fire.

The Shrike rifle bumped against Anu's shoulder. The armour-penetrating round whipped across the chamber, over the blackened void plate buried in the floor and through the drizzling blood rain, past the carnage playing out across the stairway.

It hit Zaidu's forearm, punching clean through it, and struck Kerubim at the base of the blade, just above the crossguard.

There was a great ringing sound, like the tolling of the bell of the Basilica Malifex, as the sword shattered into a dozen shards, a surge of blue warp fire flaring around the broken pieces of steel as they flew apart, leaving only its hilt and a jagged, smoking stub in Vey's fist.

Anu closed his eyes and let his body rest against his locked armour.

He had found perfection.

CHAPTER THIRTY-TWO

DAMNATIO PRO NOBIS OMNIBUS VENIT

It all happened in an instant.

Zaidu registered the solid impact of a round through his right arm, the pain. He saw Kerubim shattered as Caedus-Vey raised it to deliver the fatal blow. He sensed the daemon's shock, its outrage. And without thinking, he dropped his guard, letting the knife clatter from his right hand.

Rational thoughts, tactics and strategy, they dissolved in the furnace heat of pure rage, as they always did eventually with any slave of the Blood God. Howling, Caedus-Vey drove the jagged remnants of Kerubim at Zaidu, into his open guard, aiming for his split and broken breast-plate.

Zaidu took the blow. Another spike of agony joined with the numbness of his other wounds. Caedus-Vey was close now, threatening to drive him physically off the edge of the dais. He stood firm, made his wounded right arm obey. The round had passed perfectly between the ulna and the radius – he was able to unlock what was clamped at his waist and, forcing his left arm to wrap around Caedus-Vey, dragged the possessed Librarian in close.

They fell from the edge of the dais, intertwined. Together they impacted against a circular holo-table beneath, blasting it to splinters. Caedus-Vey was on top, the sword's hilt still buried in Zaidu's chest, reaching for his throat, intending to rip it open and snap Zaidu's neck in a wild frenzy. The Sin Slayer did likewise, snatching upwards for Caedus-Vey's throat.

There was a metallic thud as Zaidu locked the Broken One's collar around Caedus-Vey's neck.

The Librarian froze, his unnatural shriek suddenly silenced.

Zaidu grasped the hilt of Kerubim and, in a single motion, ripped it free from his chest and slammed its pommel into Caedus-Vey's face. The Librarian's jaw cracked, and he was thrown back off Zaidu, who pushed himself to his feet in the midst of the holo-table's wreckage and grabbed at Vey again.

'In the Emperor's name, I bind thee, daemon,' Zaidu spat, and struck once more.

Caedus wailed.

The fires that had wreathed it were suddenly no more. It pawed at its neck, stumbling through the ruins.

Vey realised that there was a collar, stamped with the holy aquila, latched around its throat. A thought-echo of the real device he had retrieved from the Broken One. He raised a trembling hand and found it reflected around his own neck.

He experienced a rare moment of triumph, and something that might have been pride. He had never doubted Zaidu. The flicker of emotion was subsumed immediately by his determination. It was not yet over.

Vey advanced and struck Caedus. He drove the screeching blood daemon back towards the flickering fire at the centre of his mind, through the rubble and the wreckage, pounding it with his fists. It suddenly seemed so much smaller and weaker, its rangy body no match for Vey's powerful physique, tainted and drained though he was.

He picked up the Neverborn and cast it against a broken pillar. The remains collapsed atop it with a shuddering crack. Vey grasped more of the rubble around it, slamming it down on the daemon, breaking its essence, shattering it with his own blunt-force willpower.

The daemon spat at him, gibbering in pure warp speak, blasphemies that Vey refused to understand.

'You will not be free, Caedus,' he told the daemon, piling stone upon stone atop it, crushing it beneath the broken remnants of his soul.

'You cannot hold me forever,' the daemon howled, finally finding coherence through its rage, trying to scrabble up through the wreckage.

'No,' Vey agreed. 'But I can hold you for long enough.'

He slammed the final stone down.

The explosion tore across the pinnacle of the battle sanctum. The base of the archway's left side was sheared away in a hail of shattered bone and flesh gobbets, blasted apart by Uten's full complement of explosives.

Already robbed of its power by the stony resistance of the Exorcists, the warp portal collapsed. There was a sound like rushing waters, rising to a thunder, mixed with the shattering of glass. Then, suddenly, a brief moment of silence, the vacuum that existed between one plane of existence and another.

It was replaced by Fidem's wrath as the rest of the archway came crashing down in a rain of gore. The tortured howls of the bodies that had been melded together by the empyrean's corruption were finally stilled, the remains lying dead across the wrecked dais, their souls freed. The space where the centre of the portal had once been shimmered, as though in a heat haze, the rent in reality still healing.

The horrors that had been pouring through were transmuted into frozen statues of glittering precious stones, or became thick sheaves and scrolls of parchment that unravelled and burned up, or burst apart into globules of juddering, many-coloured luminescence that evaporated into the air. Their squeals and shrieks steadily became silent, until the last one melted into a puddle of kaleidoscopic ectoplasm, thrashing and wailing as it tried in vain to hold on to the warm vitality of corporeal existence.

Fidem IV rejected it, destroyed it. Finally, all lay still and silent, blood and warp filth dripping slowly down the drenched stairs, and from the befouled armour of the gigantic warriors that stood atop them.

The Exorcists surveyed the devastation at the heart of the Tower of the Praetorian. Perhaps some felt a small, fleeting sense of satisfaction, but it died away in moments, like every other human emotion, now strange and alien things, unwelcome in the cold nothingness of their inner beings.

Zaidu stood over Vey at the base of the dais, the Librarian crouched. Kerubim's hilt was still in the Sin Slayer's grip. He was poised to strike again, ready to act at the merest hint that Caedus yet retained some vestige of control over Vey's body. But when the Librarian finally looked up at his battle-brother, blinking away blood from his gashed scalp, it was the familiar golden gaze of the Lie-Eater.

'It is done,' Vey said, voice barely a whisper.

'Can you hold on to it?' Zaidu asked him. 'Can you keep it within your flesh?'

'Yes. It is thrice bound. Its rage has burned out. Its consciousness is dimmed. It slumbers.'

'For now.'

'If a Broken One can hold many daemons at bay, then by my will and these blessed invocations, I shall keep my grip on this one,' Vey said, pausing to spit blood. 'In the name of the Emperor, of Dorn, and the Chapter.'

Zaidu thought for a moment, then nodded and made an Orison gesture of respect. He could find nothing else to say, nothing that would be of any meaning, any consequence, to either of them.

Vey had made his sacrifice, and it had been successful. That was well.

Zaidu searched within himself for a sense of satisfaction, for relief that the operation's objectives had been achieved. He looked for the visceral exultation that he might have expected to come with knowing that Caedus was bound once more, that the daemon's schemes would no longer threaten the Chapter. Yet he could find none of it. Just quiet emptiness.

That did not trouble him. It was as it should be.

'Almoner-lieutenant,' said a voice. He saw Gela trudging down from where most of the Exorcists were still spread out across the steps.

'You are injured,' the Helix Adept pointed out. Zaidu had nearly forgotten. He glanced at his chest, where Caedus-Vey had attempted to drive Kerubim into him. The force sword's shattered hilt had bitten deep, and the markings on his vambrace indicated it had scraped against his right lung and heart, narrowly failing to puncture both organs. He could feel the wound, a stabbing pain that still resisted his body's efforts to smother it, combining with the ache of broken bones.

'See to the others first,' Zaidu told Gela as he switched his display to take in the casualties suffered by the rest of the strike force. 'There are plenty in greater need than I.'

'And they will all tell me to see to their honoured almoner-lieutenant first,' Gela said with the weariness of a long-suffering combat medicae. 'Hold still and accept your treatment.'

Zaidu obeyed, allowed Gela to run more advanced diagnostics while jabbing him with enhanced suppressants and coagulants. He applied a synth-skin spray to Zaidu's shoulder, momentarily patching over the deep gash there, along with part of his scaled flesh. He knew it was only a temporary measure.

'I will need to check your rib plate is properly aligned so it can set, when time allows,' Gela reported. 'And it will likely be several weeks before your left arm is approaching full functionality again. You may also notice a lack of grip in your right for some time.'

The mention of the injury reminded Zaidu of how it had been dealt. Only one member of the Hexbreakers could have been responsible. He half turned and saw the Eliminators, Anu and Dumuzid, standing at the edge of the chamber, next to where the void debris had bisected it. They were cradling their Shrike rifles. Even from a distance, Zaidu could tell that Anu was even paler than usual and shaking, his strip of white hair hanging lank across half of his chiselled face. He nodded once. Zaidu returned the curt acknowledgement.

'What of–' Gela began to say, reclaiming Zaidu's attention. He saw he was looking down at Vey, who was now staring silently off into the middle distance.

'Are you still with us, enlightened brother?' Zaidu asked. Vey's eyes snapped back into focus, and he looked up between Zaidu and Gela.

'I need no medicae,' he said. 'But you must cut the corruption from my flesh. Muzzle me too. It is the only way. You know the rites.'

'I do,' Zaidu agreed.

Vey looked down at the ground, and continued to do so, saying nothing more.

'Orders, almoner-lieutenant?' crackled Belloch's voice on the vox-net. The Reiver sergeant was still up on the stairs, his knife dripping with the cooling ichor of slaughtered Neverborn.

'Gather up our fallen,' Zaidu said, again noting the ones slain on the strike force display – Eitan and Kleth, and Marduk had succumbed to his wounds. Of the rest, only the two Eliminators were showing green. Yellow and amber markers abounded, the other Hexbreakers injured in some way during the desperate fight.

'We will embark on *Daemonium Eversor* and return to the *Witch-Bane* immediately,' Zaidu said.

'What of the defence of this world?' Haad interjected over the vox. 'Guard high command has been annihilated.'

'The Astra Militarum have systems in place to recover from a decapitating stroke,' Zaidu said. 'I doubt the same can be said for the slaves of the Word Bearers. Now that the daemonic threat is purged, victory here will follow, eventually. Besides...'

He looked once more at Vey, still crouched and bowed.

'We have a more important duty to attend to now.'

The fire was burning low.

He rose and found a few old, withered branches amidst the rubble, the remnants of trees that had once bloomed strong and healthy in this place. They were now long gone, uprooted and splintered and left to vitrify in the lonely darkness.

He returned to the fire and added the fuel, watching it flare up briefly, feeling its welcome heat. He sat before it, cross-legged, and looked past it, to the cairn he had raised up on the edge of the light.

Darkness encroached all around, but Torrin Vey knew there was nothing out beyond the circumference of the flickering flames, only the desolation of an empty place. All that mattered was here, before him – that mound of shattered stone and debris that glowed with a light of its own, dark red, deep within, throbbing in slow sympathy with Vey's heartbeat. Slumbering, for now.

Vey would need to be ready for when it awoke. So he sat by the fire, amidst the silent ruination of his soul, and watched, and waited.

EPILOGUE

BEYOND NOWHERE

The Purgatomb was like a mountain that had been cast into space, torn up by some vengeful god and thrown into the freezing wasteland at the galaxy's edge, where the stars were dim and oblivion yawned.

The *Witch-Bane* anchored itself near the mountain's pinnacle. *Diabolus Malum* passed between the strike cruiser and the uppermost docking strut, layers of void shields deactivating ahead of the Overlord and then reactivating behind it as Techmarine Kothar exchanged a continual stream of binharic reassurances and code phrases with those monitoring the approach.

The transport settled atop the docking strut, within the slender atmospheric sheath that engaged once it had passed through. There it idled for a few moments, as Kothar finished the transaction and received final permission for a disembarkation.

The starboard hold of *Diabolus Malum* lowered, venting hydraulic steam. Daggan Zaidu stepped down through it. His skull mask and armour were patched with crude repairs, and his left arm was still stiff and reluctant to obey. Such problems could wait. He had one more duty to perform first.

After Zaidu came the figure that had once been Torrin Vey. The Librarian had been stripped of his armour and all belongings, all bar the rags he now wore, and the belt about his waist, which held a small adamantine box against his hip. His hands and wrists were sealed within a rune-etched manacle casing, while a heavy collar was clamped around his neck. His jaw had been screwed shut with steel bolts, and his eyes and ears were muzzled by a metal visor stamped with the Imperial aquila. He shuffled, his once strong, proud bearing hunched over and uncertain, led by Zaidu using a chain attached to his collar.

Ahead of where *Diabolus Malum* had set down was a long walkway, lit by floor lumens on either side. It led to a gateway set in the mountain's peak, framed by the blackness of the void above. Zaidu trudged along it, his prisoner struggling after him.

As they drew closer, the size of the gateway became slowly more apparent, tall and wide enough for twin Warlord Titans to have walked through side by side without any danger of damage to their weapons mounts or cathedra spires. As they neared it, Zaidu felt the walkway underfoot shiver, and heard a dull, bass grinding.

The gate was opening, its gargantuan doors parting to the left and right.

Through it came a dozen figures, seemingly tiny at first, but resolving into a cohort of tall, armoured warriors. They halted just beyond the partially opened gate, waiting until the new arrivals reached them.

Like Zaidu, they were Adeptus Astartes, and like Zaidu they bore on their left pauldrons the Calva Daemoniorum. There the similarities ended. The armour of these Exorcists was not dark red, but black as jet, and their helms had no visors or vox-grilles, featureless but for their eye-lenses. There were no other markings besides the Chapter icon, no company, strike force or squad designates, no tactical recognition signifiers or battlefield role identificators. Nor did they possess any prayer markings or occult symbology, at least none visible to the naked eye – Zaidu knew that the *Liber Exorcismus* and the Secret Verses were etched over and over upon the black ceramite so many times as to be almost microscopic in detail.

They were the Daemonium Palatinae, the Wards of the Purgatomb, guards whose vigil never ended.

'Daggan Zaidu,' one at the front of the formation said. Zaidu showed no surprise that he was known, merely giving a silent Orison sign of greeting.

'Surrender the Broken One to its fate,' the palatinae commanded.

'This is no Broken One,' Zaidu responded. 'His name is Torrin Vey, Epistolary of the Librarius, fraternal and enlightened brother.'

'Not any longer,' the palatinae said. The scrape of the figure's vox-voice held no malice, only cold, hard fact.

Zaidu had not come to argue. He relinquished the chain. The palatinae pulled Vey, stumbling, into the midst of the formation, boltguns trained upon him. Without another word to Zaidu, they turned and began to march back through the gateway, into the darkness that lay within the mountain, to an oblivion so much more nightmarish than the existential emptiness of the surrounding void.

Zaidu felt no compulsion to stand and watch. As the gateway began to roll ponderously shut, he turned and made his way back to *Diabolus Malum*, reaching the idling Overlord before the vast locks had engaged and sealed the terrible prison once more.

'Return us to the *Witch-Bane*,' he instructed Kothar. 'You will join Shipmaster Nazmund in charting a course back to Nowhere, and then on to Banish.'

As Kothar acknowledged his orders, Zaidu took his seat within the hold and stared into nothingness, finding his thoughts as fallow as ever. Maybe that was well, he supposed. Perhaps this was what it meant to be at peace.

Damnation would catch up with him, just as it had Vey. *Damnatio pro nobis omnibus venit.* Until that day, though, Zaidu would do his duty, and face eternity when it came.

ABOUT THE AUTHOR

Robbie MacNiven is a Highlands-born History graduate from the University of Edinburgh. He has written the Warhammer Age of Sigmar novel *Scourge of Fate* and the Gotrek Gurnisson novella *The Bone Desert*, as well as the Warhammer 40,000 novels *Oaths of Damnation*, *Blood of Iax*, *The Last Hunt*, *Carcharodons: Red Tithe*, *Carcharodons: Outer Dark* and *Legacy of Russ*. His short stories include 'Redblade', 'A Song for the Lost' and 'Blood and Iron'. His hobbies include re-enacting, football and obsessing over Warhammer 40,000.

YOUR NEXT READ

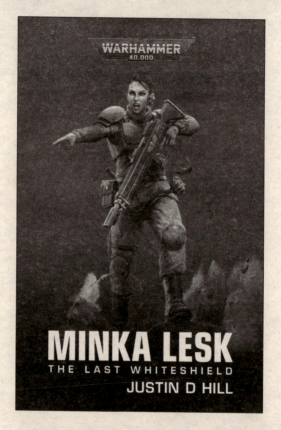

MINKA LESK: THE LAST WHITESHIELD
by Justin D Hill

Cadia has stood in grim defiance against the enemies of the Imperium for ten thousand years, an indomitable bulwark against the forces of Chaos… but now, the 13th Black Crusade has come, and there will be no victory. Here, Minka Lesk will be tested in the very fires of a world's destruction.

For these stories and more, go to blacklibrary.com, warhammer.com, Games Workshop and Warhammer stores, all good book stores or visit one of the thousands of independent retailers worldwide, which can be found at **warhammer.com/store-finder**